THE BORZOI SERIES OF STORIES AND TALES

FRENCH STORIES AND TALES *edited by Stanley Geist*

GERMAN STORIES AND TALES *edited by Robert Pick*

SPANISH STORIES AND TALES *edited by Harriet de Onís*

These are Borzoi Books
published by Alfred A. Knopf in New York

FRENCH STORIES AND TALES

FRENCH STORIES AND TALES

Edited by Stanley Geist

New York

Alfred A. Knopf

1954

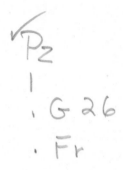

THIS IS A BORZOI BOOK
PUBLISHED BY ALFRED·A·KNOPF, INC.

FIRST EDITION

EDITOR'S NOTE

These sixteen stories, ranging from the anecdote to the short novel, were chosen for their merit as works of the imagination, with no object but to make a fresh and lively volume of more than routine interest. There are neither Specimens nor Period Pieces. Almost all were translated for this book. They speak well for themselves; the editor does not have to speak for them.

One kind of story—the kind that periodically threatens in America to swallow up all others, and that might be called "suburban"—is missing. For the French have never learned to write stories that are "comfortable" (or safely uncomfortable) in the American sense, just as they have never learned to build houses in which an American can take his ease. The plain fact of the matter is that the French middle class has never really, like the American, come into its own. Though it has been in power for some time, it remains a middle between extremes. It inhabits the abandoned shells of the aristocracy, still haunted by regal ghosts, and has at its elbows a peasantry who are something different from farmers. It offers by turns harsh or brutal surfaces and edges that are razor-fine; it holds to rituals of thought and sentiment and social conduct whose formal intricacy might be Chinese, but it lives on terms with the barbarous and the monstrous that are too close for comfort—too close, that is, for the idea of the comfortable to get ahead very fast.

Bourgeois as they may be, therefore, literature and life in France are about equally arts of form which go about equally for their substance beyond the suburban pale. And the stories in this volume might be called "representative" in that they play, so to speak (and they do *play*), on notes higher and lower than those of any suburban keyboard: as high and low, even when they seem to be trifling, as the notes one hears in the stories of Hawthorne, Poe, Melville, and James (for we too have some non-suburban writers). The situations and states of mind dealt with are now and then extreme to the point where, in order to be dealt with at all, they must have recourse to methods that violate common sense; and one turns a page to discover that forms so "childish" as melodrama or so "artificial" as comic opera have their uses.

The French notion that literature is first of all an art—more precisely an artifice—has always struck foreigners as unreasonable. More unreasonable still is the notion that creating artifices, whether of language or of love or of women's fashions, is one of mankind's essential activities. The internal landscape of the nation is littered with Eiffel Towers, which are obviously absurd except as created artifices rising from a marsh into a void. They have no other bona-fide business being where they are; and it is incidental that they sometimes turn out to be handy for attracting tourists or designing skyscrapers or transmitting messages through thin air.

The notion that artifice is essential leads into troubled waters. It leads even unliterary Frenchmen, for example, to regard our famous American "sincerity" less as a virtue than as an incomprehensible bad joke; and one might populate a big city with the Frenchmen who have come back from an encounter with sincerity sporting bruised heads. It leads a writer so "realistic" (the schoolbooks say) as Balzac to celebrate the heroine of "The Other Diane" for her magnificence at lying. It leads to the conclusion that cunning, which we like to flatter ourselves by thinking an alien vice, is an important virtue—intellectual and literary as well as social. There is no author in this volume whose worth does not depend in some measure on the practice of that virtue; and in the "Theseus" of Gide, who was one of its eminent modern practitioners and a puritan in the bargain, one finds cunning vindicated on thoroughly humanistic grounds.

It leads, finally, to a concern with a particular mode of artifice that has almost the status of a national religion: the theater. The dividing line between stage and society is not very clear in France, where the baker's wife, as a large American public has learned, cannot sell a loaf of bread without at the same time "putting on an act." Every little Frenchman is born with histrionic talents or must pick them up in order to survive. Three of the stories that follow have to do with personages of the stage and with various meanings that the stage has for the imagination; several others are "theatrical" in a more general sense. None of them was chosen on that account.

All this is unreasonable enough, coming from a nation that prides itself on being the Temple of Reason, and that has hypnotized other nations into believing it is. (All nations, not even excluding the United States, live by some such established and untouchable myth about themselves, though not all manage to get it believed.) It took a cosmopolitan Jew, Bergson, to demonstrate to his countrymen how unreasonable, when set against the actual "feel" of human experience, in France or anywhere, was rationality itself, and his countrymen have not forgiven him for it. Any observant tourist might have told them as much after six months. But he would have missed the point: that Reason is in France *the* essential artifice, *the* Eiffel Tower: the one in Paris.

Among these stories there are no examples of artifice in its pure state—as in Descartes, for example, or in Marivaux. But the uses of artifice are here sufficiently made known. One, already suggested, is that it enables a writer to deal with the monstrous and the barbarous, and to make something of the everyday, without fidgeting in embarrassment, without thrashing, stammering, huffing and puffing, or turning all colors. Another is that it makes room, perhaps at its middle, for a prodigious simplicity of heart: prodigious because it is of the sort that includes and thrives on knowledge, so that it does not have to deny anything that might call simplicity of heart into doubt.

—Stanley Geist

ACKNOWLEDGMENTS

For help and advice of various sorts the editor owes thanks to André Du Bouchet, F. W. Dupee, Eileen Geist, Stuart Gilbert, Jean Hélion, Maria Jolas, Ralph Manheim, Francis Ponge, Carol Sands, Nathalie Sarraute, and Pierre Schneider.

Thanks are due as well to the following for permission to use the material indicated:

Éditions Albin Michel: for "A Romance" and "The Spoiled Cake," by Jules Renard, from *La Lanterne Sourde*.

M. Georges Duthuit and *Transition* magazine: for the English translation (here somewhat revised) by J. G. Weightman of Marcel Schwob's "Paolo Uccello."

M. Charles Fasquelle and Fasquelle Éditeurs: for "Julien" (*"Pour une nuit d'amour"*) by Émile Zola, from *Le Capitaine Burle;* and for "Paolo Uccello" and "Crates," by Marcel Schwob, from *Vies Imaginaires*.

Alfred A. Knopf, Inc.: for "Theseus," by André Gide, translated (and here slightly revised) by John Russell.

M. Henri Martineau: for the text and manuscript notes of "Mina de Vanghel" as published by him in the Divan edition of Stendhal's *Romans et Contes*.

Librairie Plon: for "Monsieur Folantin" (*A Vau-l'Eau*), by J.-K. Huysmans.

CONTENTS

FRENCH STORIES AND TALES

MINA DE VANGHEL

by Stendhal (1783–1842)

Mina de Vanghel was born in the land of philosophy and imagination, at Königsberg. In 1814, at the end of the campaign in France, the Prussian general, Count de Vanghel, abruptly abandoned the court and the army. One evening at Craonne in Champagne, after a bloody battle from which the troops under his command came off victorious, a doubt had suddenly assailed him: has a nation the right to change the internal and rational ways by which another nation chooses to regulate its material and moral existence? Preoccupied by this great question, the general determined never to draw his sword again until he had succeeded in resolving it. He retired to his estate in Königsberg.

Kept under close surveillance by the Berlin police, Count de Vanghel gave himself up entirely to his philosophic meditations and to the education of his only daughter. Still a young man, he died a few years later, leaving his daughter an enormous for-

---

Stendhal learned young—from books, from the grandfather who gave him Don Quixote *along with Voltaire, from an old aunt who had "Spanish" notions of chivalric adventure and honor, later from the theaters of Paris and Milan and from service with Napoleon's armies—a large repertoire of attitudes, at once histrionic and of the spirit, behind which greenness of spirit and freshness of heart might save themselves from being violated by the universe while seeming to do battle with it.*

"Worldly sophistication" was one—though he was never at his ease among sophisticates, and preferred Italian manners to French. His famous "candor" was another. A third was a soldier-like attentiveness to this or that private code of "Duty"— which might be a self-imposed obligation to sleep with an actress, or a duty to some such "mad" ideal of conduct as is represented in "Mina de Vanghel."

tune, an indulgent mother, and disgrace at court—no small
thing in a proud country like Germany. It is true that as a
lightning rod against this misfortune Mina de Vanghel possessed one of the noblest names in East Germany. She was only
sixteen; but already the sentiment she aroused in the young
military men of her father's circle amounted to veneration and
awe; they loved the romantic, mysterious nature that her eyes
sometimes betrayed.

A year passed; the period of mourning came to an end, but
the grief she had felt at the death of her father was in no way
diminished. Mme de Vanghel's friends began to voice that terrible word: *consumption*. However, the period of mourning was
scarcely over when Mina was obliged to appear at the court of
a reigning prince to whom she had the honor of being distantly
related. Leaving for C——, the capital of the Grand Duke's
domain, Mme de Vanghel, alarmed by her daughter's romantic
ideas and by her deep grief, was counting on a suitable marriage
and perhaps a little love to turn her daughter toward thoughts
in keeping with her age.

"How happy I should be to see you married in this country!"
her mother said.

"In this ungrateful country!" moodily the young girl rejoined. "In a country in which the only return my father ever
received for his wounds and twenty years of devotion was to be

---

*Like his innumerable aliases (he was born Henri Beyle),
and the equally innumerable, most often transparent mystifica-
tions that he liked to perpetrate, his attitudes were in effect so
many toy pistols or shields. He never wearied of trying to dupe
with them the dense, dull, stuffy, stiff-necked Universe that was
forever plumping itself in his path like the provincial middle-
class interior of his father; and the uneasy contempt he felt for
this Adversary sharpened the delight he took in tweaking the
Adversary's tail.*

*What is odd about the poses he struck for himself is that he
lived up to them, like his heroes and heroines, with the good
faith of a child; though he knew, much of the time, what he was
about. Odder still, his toy shields did keep him fresh, green, intact ("Well, I'll be damned," one catches him saying with elated
surprise, "here I am in bed with an actress!"); and toy pistols*

spied on by the vilest police that ever existed! No, I'd rather change my religion and die a nun in the depth of some Catholic convent!"

All that Mina knew about court life she had learned from the novels of her compatriot, August Lafontaine. These Albani-like paintings often depicted the loves of a rich heiress exposed by chance to the seductions of a young colonel, the king's aide-de-camp, hotheaded and goodhearted. To Mina this love born of money was detestable.

"What could be more vulgar and more insipid," she said to her mother, "than the life of such a couple a year after their marriage, when the husband, thanks to his marriage, has become a major general and the wife a lady-in-waiting to the crown princess! What becomes of their love if they lose their money?"

The Grand Duke of C——, never dreaming of the obstacles August Lafontaine was preparing for him, was anxious to keep Mina's vast fortune in his court. Still more unhappily, one of the Duke's aides-de-camp began to woo Mina, possibly with *authorization from above*. Nothing more was needed to make her decide to fly from Germany. The enterprise was far from easy.

"Mother," she said one day, "I want to leave this country, I want to exile myself."

---

became in his hands real weapons of power and knowledge.

But the disconcerting means by which he arrived at knowledge—not only through his poses, but also by way of comic-opera librettos, and by way of philosophical systems that are sometimes hard to distinguish from comic-opera librettos—give to knowledge itself, on his pages, an air of screwiness. And one's impression of screwiness is not wholly false; for Stendhal was, among other things, a great clown and comedian of the mind, a master of psychological improvisations held together only by Stendhalian logic, a virtuoso playing on the abrupt twists and turns of his own bizarre mind, a high-wire artist whose double somersaults in mid-air on a one-wheeled cycle happened to depend on a Rube Goldberg contraption hooked to tent poles.

He was also, of course, a writer; his pretense of disdaining

"When you talk like that," Mme de Vanghel replied, "you frighten me: your eyes remind me of your poor father. Very well! I shall remain neutral, I shall not exercise my authority; but don't expect me to solicit the Grand Duke's ministers for the permission we must have if we wish to travel in foreign countries."

Mina was miserable. All the successes her beautiful big blue eyes and distinguished air had won her rapidly dwindled when it was learned that she had ideas that ran counter to those of His Most Serene Highness. More than a year went by in this way. Mina despaired of ever obtaining the indispensable permission. She conceived the idea of disguising herself as a man and of going to England, where she counted on selling her diamonds and living on the proceeds. Her mother noticed, with a kind of terror, that Mina was secretly busy with all sorts of experiments in an endeavor to change the color of her skin. A little later Mme de Vanghel learned that the girl had had a suit of man's clothes made for her. Mina soon began to notice that whenever she went horseback-riding she would always run into one or another of the Grand Duke's police officers; but with her German imagination, which she inherited from her father, the difficulties in her way, far from deterring her, only made her enterprise seem the more attractive.

Quite unwittingly, Mina had won the favor of Countess

---

literary style became a notable literary style.

Stendhal was born and grew up in Grenoble, went to Paris as a young man, crossed the Alps—then Europe, as far as Moscow —with Napoleon, and died in Italy after having spent in this beloved land of "energy and passion" as much as possible of his life. "Mina de Vanghel" was written when he was in his late forties, during the winter of 1829–30, between sessions of work on his first long novel, Le Rouge et le noir—*about five years before* Lucien Leuwen *and eight years before* La Chartreuse de Parme. *It was not published until after his death, in 1853.*

Other Works: *Novels:* Armance (*1827*), Lamiel (*1889*). *Stories:* L'Abbesse de Castro (*1839*). *"Treatise":* De l'Amour (*1822*). *Travel books:* Rome, Naples, et Florence (*1817*), Mémoires d'un touriste (*1838*). *Personal writings:* Vie d'Henri Brulard (*1890*), Souvenirs d'égotisme (*1892*).

D——, who was the Grand Duke's rather eccentric mistress and as romantic a woman as you could find. One day while Mina was out riding, a police officer began following her at a distance. Losing all patience, Mina confided in the Countess, telling her of her plan for flight. A few hours later Mme de Vanghel received a note, written by the Grand Duke himself, permitting her an absence of six months to go to take the waters at Bagnères. That was at nine o'clock in the evening; at ten o'clock the ladies were on their way; and most fortunately the next morning, before the Grand Duke's ministers were yet awake, they had crossed the frontier.

It was at the beginning of the winter of 182— that Mme de Vanghel and her daughter arrived in Paris. Mina was a great success at the embassy balls. It was said that those diplomatic gentlemen had orders unobtrusively to prevent this fortune of several millions from becoming the prey of some seductive Frenchman. In Germany, people still believe that the young men of Paris are interested in women.

In spite of the exuberance of her German imagination, Mina, who was now eighteen, began to have flashes of common sense; she noticed that she was unable to become friendly with any Frenchwoman. From all of them she met with an extreme politeness, and after knowing them for six weeks she was farther from their friendship than on the first day. In her distress, Mina supposed that there was something in her own manners, something uncouth and disagreeable, which paralyzed French urbanity. Never had so much modesty been seen coupled with such real superiority. By a piquant contrast, the energy and the unexpectedness of her decisions were hidden by an expression that still showed all the naïveté and all the charm of childhood, and this cast of countenance was never spoiled by a graver air of reason. Reason, to be sure, was never a pronounced trait of her character.

Notwithstanding the polished barbarity of its inhabitants, Paris delighted Mina. In her own country she loathed being bowed to on the street and having her carriage recognized; at C—— she had seen a spy in every badly dressed man who took off his hat to her; the incognito in the republic called Paris captivated this singular nature. Although Mina's rather too German heart still hankered after social intimacy and warmth,

she found that in Paris, by way of compensation, there was always a ball to attend or some amusing play to see. She bought
the house where her father had lived in 1814, and which he had
told her about so often. Once she had moved in (getting the
tenants out was a problem), Paris was no longer a strange city
for her. Mlle de Vanghel recognized all the nooks and corners
of her new abode.

Although his chest had been covered with medals and decora-
tions, Count de Vanghel had been at heart only a philosophic
dreamer, like Spinoza and Descartes. Mina loved German philosophy's obscure search for the truth and Fichte's noble
stoicism in the same way that a tender heart loves the recollection of a beautiful landscape. The most unintelligible words of
Kant only recalled to Mina the sound of her father's voice reading them. With such a recommendation, how could philosophy
fail to be touching and even intelligible! She persuaded several
distinguished savants to come to her house to lecture, with no
one to listen to them but her mother and herself.

In the midst of this life, spent with philosophers in the morning and at embassy balls at night, love never so much as grazed
the heart of the wealthy heiress. Frenchmen amused her, but
they did not touch her.

"Undoubtedly," she would say to her mother, who was always
singing their praises, "they are the most agreeable men one
could meet. I admire their brilliant wit, and am constantly
amazed and amused by their subtle irony; but don't you find
that the moment they try to show any feeling they become stiff
and ridiculous? Do they ever for a moment forget themselves in
their emotion?"

"Why all this criticism?" replied the wise Mme de Vanghel.
"If France doesn't please you, let us return to Königsberg. But
don't forget that you are eighteen and that I might be taken
from you; you should think of choosing a protector. If you
should lose me," she added, smiling with a touch of melancholy, "the Grand Duke of C—— would marry you to his aide-
de-camp."

One fine summer day Mme de Vanghel and her daughter had
gone to Compiègne to watch a royal hunt. The ruins of Pierrefonds, which Mina suddenly spied in the midst of the forest,
made a deep impression on her. Because she was still a slave to

German prejudices, all the great monuments in Paris, that *modern Babylon,* seemed to her to have something *cold, ironical,* and *evil* about them.

The ruins of Pierrefonds she found touching, like the ruins of those old castles that crown the summits of the Brocken.[1] Mina begged her mother to stay for a few days in the little inn in the village of Pierrefonds, where they were thoroughly uncomfortable. One rainy day Mina, who was still as impetuous as when she had been twelve, came out and stood under the porte-cochere of the inn to watch the falling rain. A poster announcing an estate for sale in the neighborhood caught her eye. A half-hour later she arrived at the notary's, conducted by one of the maids from the inn holding an umbrella over her head. The notary was quite astonished to hear this young girl, who was dressed so simply, discussing the price of an estate worth several hundred thousand francs, then to find himself asking her to sign an agreement and accepting a deposit of a number of thousand-franc notes on the Bank of France.

By good luck, which I shall carefully refrain from calling strange, Mina was cheated by only a very small amount. This estate was called Le Petit-Verberie. Its previous owner was a Count de Ruppert, famous in all the chateaux of Picardy. He was a tall, very handsome young man. Everyone admired him at first sight, but the next moment felt repelled by something hard and vulgar about him. Soon Count de Ruppert looked upon himself as a friend of Mlle de Vanghel; he amused her. He was perhaps, of all the young men of that day, the only one who recalled the amiable rakes whose story, much embellished, is related in the memoirs of both Lauzun and Tilly. M. de Ruppert was just going through the last of a large fortune; he aped the failings of the noblemen of the age of Louis XIV, and was unable to understand how Paris could fail to take an exclusive interest in him. Disappointed in his dreams of glory, he had fallen madly in love with money. A reply received from Berlin raised his passion for Mlle de Vanghel to the highest pitch. Six months later Mina said to her mother:

"We must really buy an estate so that we can receive our friends. We might lose a few thousand francs if we ever wanted

[1] The Brocken: mountain in Germany and the central point of the Hartz range, elevation 1,095 metres. (Stendhal)

to sell the Petit-Verberie, but that would be little enough to pay for the pleasure of knowing all the agreeable women we now count among our intimate acquaintances."

Yet Mina did not adopt the manners of a young French girl. While admiring their seductive charms, she kept the naturalness and freedom of her German ways. Mme de Cély, the most intimate of her new friends, said of Mina that she was *different* but not queer; her charm excused everything; her millions did not show in her eyes; although she had not the *simplicity* of the best society, she was a captivating young woman.

This tranquil life was suddenly interrupted by a bolt out of the blue. Mina's mother died. As soon as her grief gave her time to think of her situation, she realized how awkward it was. Mme de Cély had taken her to her chateau. This friend, a young woman of thirty, said to her:

"The wisest thing for you to do would be to return to Prussia, or else, as soon as your mourning is over, marry someone here in France and in the meantime send at once to Königsberg for a companion, preferably a lady related to you."

To this there was one great objection: German girls, even wealthy girls, believe that they can only marry a man they adore. Mme de Cély suggested ten suitable matches. All these young men seemed to Mina vulgar, cynical, almost wicked. Mina spent the most miserable year of her life. Her health was affected, and her beauty almost completely disappeared. One day when she had come to stay with Mme de Cély she was told that she would meet the celebrated Mme de Larçay at dinner. Mme de Larçay was the wealthiest and the most attractive woman of that region. People often talked of the elegance of her parties and the wholly dignified and delightful way, never in the least ridiculous, in which she was managing to get rid of a considerable fortune. Mina was amazed to discover so much that was common and prosaic in Mme de Larçay's character.

"So that's what you have to become in order to be liked here!"

Sorrowfully—for to German hearts it is a sorrow to be disappointed in the *beautiful*—Mina stopped looking at Mme de Larçay, and out of politeness turned to talk to her husband. He was a man of great simplicity whose only recommendation was that he had been a page to Napoleon at the time of the Emperor's retreat from Russia and had distinguished himself in that campaign and in the ones that followed by displaying a courage beyond his years. He told Mina very simply and very well about Greece, where he had spent one or two years fighting for the Greeks. His conversation delighted Mina; he seemed to her like an intimate friend whom she might have been meeting after a long separation.

After dinner they all went to see some of the famous spots in the Forest of Compiègne. Mina more than once was on the point of consulting M. de Larçay on the awkwardness of her situation. The fashionable airs of Count de Ruppert, who that day was following the carriages on horseback, brought out all the more strikingly M. de Larçay's natural and even naïve manners. The great event in which he had played a part at the beginning of his career, giving him the opportunity of observing the human heart as it really is, had contributed to the formation of an inflexible, cool, and positive character, convivial enough but devoid of imagination. Such characters have an astounding effect on natures that are all imagination. Mina was amazed that a Frenchman could be so simple.

That evening, after he had left, Mina felt as though she had parted from a friend who for years had known all her secrets. Everything now seemed to her vapid and irksome, even Mme de Cély's tender friendship. Mina had not tried to hide any of her thoughts from M. de Larçay. With him, fear of the petty French sarcasms had not forced her continually to mask her German mind, which bristled with frankness. M. de Larçay had mostly rid himself of all those little words and mannerisms decreed by fashion. This made him seem eight or ten years older than he was; but it was also the reason he filled Mina's thoughts for the whole hour after his departure.

The next day she had to make an effort to keep her mind on what Mme de Cély was saying. It all sounded so coldhearted and malicious. She no longer regarded as a fantastic ideal to be forgotten the hope of finding a frank, sincere mind that would not always be looking for the chance of a witticism in the simplest remark; she was thoughtful all day. That evening Mme de Cély happened to mention M. de Larçay. Mina gave a start and got up as if someone had called her; she grew very

red, and was hard put to explain her strange action. In her
agitated state she could no longer hide from herself what it was
essential to hide from others. She fled to her own room.

"I am mad," she said to herself. It was then that her troubles
began; they made rapid progress; in a few seconds she had got
to the point of reproaching herself.

"I am in love, and the man I love is married!"

That was the thought that troubled her conscience all night.

M. de Larçay, about to leave with his wife for the watering-
place of Aix-en-Savoie, had forgotten at Mme de Cély's a map
on which he had traced for the ladies the little detour he intended to make on his way to Aix. One of Mme de Cély's
children found this map; Mina got hold of it and slipped off
into the garden. She spent an hour following the journey M. de
Larçay had planned. The names of the little towns he would
pass through seemed to her noble and strange. She imagined
them in the most picturesque settings; she envied the inhabitants
their good fortune. This gentle madness was so strong that it put
a stop to her remorse. A few days later someone at Mme de
Cély's remarked that the de Larçays had left for Savoie. The
announcement threw Mina's mind into an uproar; she discovered that she had a keen urge to travel.

Two weeks later a middle-aged German lady arrived at Aix-
en-Savoie in a carriage hired at Geneva. This lady was accompanied by a maid whom she treated so badly that Mme
Toinod, the proprietress of the little inn where the travelers had
stopped, was scandalized. Mme Cramer (that was the German
lady's name) summoned Mme Toinod.

"I wish to engage a maid," she said, "one of your local girls
who knows *who's who* in this town and the surrounding country. I'm wasting my time with this pretty young miss whom I
was stupid enough to bring with me, and who knows nothing
at all about this place."

"Heavens, but your mistress does seem to be put out with
you!" Mme Toinod said to the young servant as soon as they
were alone.

"Don't speak of her," cried the girl, who called herself
Aniken, with tears in her eyes. "What was the use of making me
leave Frankfurt, where my parents have a good business? My

mother employs the best tailors in the city and is just as good
as the Paris dressmakers."

"Your mistress told me that she would give you three hundred
francs to return to Frankfurt whenever you wished."

"I'd receive a very poor welcome. My mother would never
believe that Madame Cramer had not discharged me for a very
good reason."

"Then stay in Aix. I could find you a situation. I run an employment agency and furnish servants for the visitors who come
here for the waters. It will cost you sixty francs for my pains,
but you will still have ten good gold louis left out of Madame
Cramer's three hundred francs."

"There will be a hundred francs for you instead of sixty,"
replied Aniken, "if you get me placed in a French family. I want
to perfect my French and then go into service in Paris. I know
how to sew very well, and as a pledge of my trustworthiness I
will deposit with my masters the twenty gold louis I brought
with me from Frankfurt."

Chance now favored the romance that had already cost Mlle
de Vanghel two or three hundred louis. M. and Mme de Larçay
arrived at the Croix de Savoie, the fashionable hotel of Aix.
Mme de Larçay found it too noisy and took an apartment in a
charming house on the edge of the lake. Aix was very gay that
season; there was a great assemblage of wealthy people, there
were many magnificent balls where everyone was dressed in
Paris styles, and every evening the fashionable world congre-
gated at the Redoute. Dissatisfied with the girls of Aix, who
were neither very handy nor very reliable, Mme de Larçay let
it be known that she was looking for someone capable. She was
referred to Mme Toinod, who made a point of bringing her
obviously unsuitable girls. Then Aniken came along; her hundred francs had done wonders for Mme Toinod's native talents.
Mme de Larçay was pleased with the German girl's serious air;
she engaged her on the spot and sent for her trunk.

The same evening, after her masters had left for the Redoute,
Aniken strolled dreamily through the garden bordering the
lake. "Well," she thought, "so my mad scheme has succeeded!
What will become of me if I'm recognized? What would Mme
de Cély say! She thinks I'm at Königsberg!"

The courage that had sustained Mina so long as there was a

necessity for action was beginning to fail her. Her mind was in a turmoil, her breath came rapidly. Repentance and fear of disgrace were making her very unhappy. But now the moon rose behind Haute-Combe; its bright disk was reflected in the waters of the lake, ruffled by a wind from the north; great white clouds in curious shapes kept passing swiftly over the face of the moon, seeming to Mina like enormous giants.

"They have come from my country," she said to herself. "They are looking for me to give me courage to persevere in this strange role I have assumed."

Her rapt and ardent gaze followed their rapid movement.

"Shades of my ancestors," she cried, "acknowledge your own blood; like you, I have courage. Do not be terrified by the strange costume you see me wearing; I shall always be true to honor. This secret passion for honor and heroism you have transmitted to me finds nothing worthy of it in the prosaic age in which I am fated to live. Can you blame me for creating a destiny in harmony with the passion that inspires me?"

Mina was no longer unhappy.

A song rose softly in the distance; the voice seemed to be coming from the other side of the lake. Mina listened attentively, but the dying sounds scarcely reached her ears. Her thoughts took another turn, she began to feel sorry for herself.

"What do all my efforts amount to? All I can hope for is to discover that the heavenly pure soul I've always dreamed of really exists in this world! That soul will remain hidden from me. Have *I* ever talked in front of my maid? The only result of this unhappy disguise will be to force me to associate with Alfred's servants. Never will he condescend to speak to me." She wept copiously.

"But at least I shall see him every day," she suddenly thought as her courage returned. "A greater happiness was not meant for me. . . . My poor mother was right when she said: 'What follies you will commit one day, if you ever fall in love!' "

The voice from the lake began singing again, but this time much nearer. Mina now realized that it was coming from a boat on the lake, and noticed the wake of moonlit ripples flowing across the water. She could distinguish a tender melody worthy of Mozart. After fifteen minutes she forgot all her

qualms of conscience and thought only of the joy of seeing
Alfred every day.

"After all," she finally decided, "doesn't every human being
have to accomplish his destiny? In spite of the happy chance of
birth and wealth, it seems that my destiny is not to shine at court
or in ballrooms. I attracted all eyes, I felt myself admired—and
in the midst of those brilliant throngs I was bored to the point
of melancholy! Everybody flocked around me, eager to talk to
me, and I was bored. Since my parents died, the only happy
moments I've known have been when listening to Mozart without any boring people around. Is it my fault if the search for
happiness, natural to all men, should have led me to take this
strange step? It will probably end in disgrace. What of it! The
convents of Europe will offer me a refuge."

Midnight rang out from the church tower of the village on the
other side of the lake. The solemnity of the hour made Mina
shudder; the moon had disappeared; she returned to the house.
Leaning on the balustrade of the balcony that overlooked the
lake and the little garden, Mina, hiding behind the vulgar name
of Aniken, waited for her *masters*. The music had restored all
her fearlessness.

"My ancestors," she said to herself, "left their magnificent
castle at Königsberg to go to the Holy Land; a few years later,
braving a thousand dangers, they returned alone, disguised as
I am. The same courage that inspired them has thrown me
among the only dangers that, in this childish, dull, and vulgar
age, are not beyond the reach of my sex. If only I come out of
it with honor, generous hearts may very well be amazed at my
folly, but in secret they will forgive me."

The days passed quickly and soon found Mina reconciled
to her fate. She was obliged to sew a great deal; she took the
duties of her new estate lightheartedly. Often she felt that she
was acting in a play, and laughed at herself when she would
make some inadvertent gesture that was not in character.
One day after dinner when the carriage was brought around
for the afternoon drive and the footman opened the carriage
door and unfolded the steps, she caught herself breezily starting
to get in.

"The girl is mad," said Mme de Larçay. Alfred looked at
her curiously and thought: "How graceful she is!" Mina was

not in the least disturbed by any idea of *duty* or by fear of ridicule.[2] All such *prudent* considerations were beneath her. Her only misgivings came from the fear of rousing Mme de Larçay's suspicions. Hardly six weeks earlier Mina had spent a whole day with her at Mme de Cély's in a very different role.

Every day Mina would get up very early so that for two hours she could devote herself to the task of making herself ugly. A few snips of the scissors had made short work of her wonderful blond hair, which, as she had been told over and over again, was so hard to forget; thanks to a chemical preparation, it had taken on a queer mixed color, a sort of dark, mousy brown. A light decoction of holly leaves applied to her delicate hands every morning made the skin look rough. Every morning, too, her lovely fresh complexion took on the unpleasant shade that white people with a drop of colored blood in their veins bring back from the colonies. Satisfied with her disguise, which made her look rather too ugly, Mina was careful not to betray any ideas that would seem at all out of place. Completely absorbed by her happiness, she had no desire to talk. Sitting by the window in Mme de Larçay's room, busy arranging dresses for the evening, a dozen times she could listen to Alfred talking and have fresh occasion to admire his character. Dare we say it? . . . Why not, since we are describing a German heart? She had moments of joy and exaltation when she went so far as to imagine that he was a supernatural being. The sincere zeal and unmitigated enthusiasm with which Mina acquitted herself of her new duties prompted the reaction that might have been expected from Mme de Larçay, who had a vulgar nature: she treated Mina with arrogance as though she were a poor girl who should be only too thankful to be given work. "Anything genuine and spontaneous will always be out of place with these people," Mina said to herself. She let it be guessed that she wanted to make up her quarrel with Mme Cramer. Almost every evening she asked permission to visit her.

Mina had been worried for fear her manners would give Mme de Larçay some strange ideas; but she realized with

[2] For me: Kingpin: the opposite of German craziness. At this point the courage or steadfastness of a Frenchman would break down. (Manuscript note by Stendhal)

pleasure that her new mistress saw in her only a lady's maid, and a maid less clever with her needle than the one she had left in Paris. M. Dubois, Alfred's valet, was harder to deal with. He was a Parisian of forty, who dressed with great care and believed it his duty to make love to the new maid. Aniken got him to talk and found out to her relief that all he cared about was piling up enough money to open a café in Paris. So without more ado she proceeded to give him money. Soon Dubois was waiting upon her with as much respect as though she were Mme de Larçay herself.

Alfred noticed that this young German girl, at times so awkward and timid, displayed very different manners at others, besides having intelligent and clever ideas quite worth listening to. When Mina saw by his expression that he was listening, she would allow herself certain judicious and subtle remarks, especially when she thought there was a good chance Mme de Larçay would not hear or would not understand.

If, during these first two months that Mlle de Vanghel spent at Aix, a philosopher had asked her what her aim was, the childishness of her answer would have amazed him and he would have suspected her of hypocrisy. To see and to listen to the man she was mad about, at all hours of the day, was the sole aim of her life; she desired nothing else, she was much too happy to think of the future. If the philosopher had suggested that this love might well cease to be so pure, she would have been even more annoyed than astonished. Blissfully, Mina studied the character of the man she adored. What made it stand out particularly was its uniqueness in the fashionable society to which he belonged because of the fortune and rank of his father, who was a member of the upper chamber. If he had lived among middle-class people, the simplicity of his manners, his horror of affectation and imposing airs, would have stamped him in their eyes as an utter mediocrity. Alfred never tried to say clever things. This trait was what had largely contributed to attracting Mina's attention on the very first day. Viewing Frenchmen through the prejudices of her own country, she always thought their conversation like the refrain of a satirical song. Alfred had known enough people of fashion to be witty with the sole aid of his memory; but he would have thought it beneath him to embellish his talk with witticisms that he had not invented himself on the spot and which might be as familiar to one of his listeners as to himself.

Every evening Alfred took his wife to the Redoute and then came home to indulge his newly acquired passion for botany, inspired by the proximity of Jean-Jacques Rousseau's boyhood haunts. Alfred kept his boxes and his plants in the little salon where Aniken always worked. So every evening, for hours on end, they were alone together without a word being spoken on either side. Neither of them knew what to say, but they were happy. The only attention Mina showed Alfred was to dissolve some gum arabic in water beforehand so that he could glue his dried specimens in his herbarium, and she allowed herself this pleasure only because it could be passed off as part of her duties. When Alfred was not there, Mina would admire the pretty plants he had brought back from his excursions in the picturesque mountains surrounding Lake Bourget. She began to take a real interest in botany. Alfred found this merely useful at first, then strange.

"He loves me," thought Mina. "But I have just seen how my zeal in the performance of my menial duties has succeeded with Madame de Larçay!"

Mme Cramer pretended to be ill. Mina asked and obtained permission to spend her evenings with her former mistress. Alfred was astonished to find his interest in botany waning, almost gone; he took to staying late at the Redoute, and his wife teased him about his being bored at home alone. Alfred admitted to himself that he had taken a liking to the girl. Annoyed with himself for his shyness when with her, he had a moment of fatuity: "Why shouldn't I behave like any of my friends?" he thought. "After all, she's only a chambermaid."

One rainy evening when Mina had stayed at home, Alfred made only a brief appearance at the Redoute. On returning, he acted surprised to see Mina in the little salon. Mina noticed this bit of duplicity and it spoiled all the pleasure she had anticipated from the evening. It was probably because of this state of mind that she could repulse Alfred's advances with unfeigned indignation. She retired to her room.

"I've been mistaken," she said, weeping. "Frenchmen are all alike." She was again and again, in the course of the night, on the point of leaving for Paris.

Next day the scorn with which she looked at Alfred was not assumed. Alfred was piqued; he paid no more attention to Mina and spent all his evenings at the Redoute. Without knowing it, he had taken the wisest course. His coolness made her forget her intention of going to Paris.

"I'm really not in any danger from this man," Mina said to herself, and not a week had gone by before she felt she might forgive him his momentary reversion to type. As for Alfred, from the boredom he suffered with the great ladies at the Redoute, he realized that he was more in love than he had supposed. But he held out. His eyes, indeed, would rest on her with pleasure, and he would talk to her occasionally, but he no longer returned to the house every evening. Mina was unhappy; almost unconsciously she began taking less pains to make herself ugly.

"Am I dreaming?" thought Alfred. "Aniken is turning into one of the loveliest women I've ever seen."

One evening, happening to come home early, his love betrayed him into asking Aniken's forgiveness for having treated her with disrespect.

"I saw," he said, "that you excited in me an interest I had never felt for anyone before; I was frightened, I wanted to cure myself or make you hate me, and since then I have been the most miserable man in the world."

"Ah! how happy you have made me, Alfred!" cried Mina in a transport of delight.

They spent that evening and the following evening confessing that they were madly in love with each other and promising to remain virtuous.

Alfred's reasonable nature was little inclined to illusions. He knew that lovers discover extraordinary perfections in the women they love. The wealth of intelligence and delicacy he discovered in Mina convinced him that he was really in love.

"Can it possibly be pure illusion?" he would ask himself every evening and compare what Mina had said to him the night before with the conversation of the fashionable women he met at the Redoute. As for Mina, she felt that she had been on the point of losing Alfred. What would have become of her if he had continued to spend all his evenings at the Redoute? No longer trying to play the part of a common working girl, she now took pains, as never before in her life, to make herself attractive.

"Should I confess to Alfred who I am?" Mina kept asking herself. "The soul of discretion himself, wouldn't he condemn my mad behavior even though what I have done was for him? Anyway," Mina thought, "my fate must be decided here. If I say I'm Mademoiselle de Vanghel, whose estate is only a few miles away from his, he will know that he is sure of seeing me again in Paris. No, it must be, instead, the prospect of never seeing me again that decides him to take the extraordinary steps that are unfortunately necessary to the happiness of both of us. But how can a man as levelheaded as he is bring himself to change his religion, divorce his wife, and go to live with me on my lovely estates in East Prussia?" That mighty word *unlawful* never even entered her head to disturb her plans; it did not occur to her that she was straying from the path of virtue, since for Alfred's sake she was ready to sacrifice her life a thousand times over.

Little by little, Mme de Larçay became decidedly jealous of Aniken. The curious change in the girl's appearance had not escaped her; she attributed it to extreme coquetry. Mme de Larçay could have taken her to task and dismissed her. But her friends pointed out that it would be foolish for her to give importance to a passing whim: the main thing was to keep M. de Larçay from having Aniken come to Paris. "Be prudent," they said, "and your worries will end with the end of the season."

Mme de Larçay kept an eye on Mme Cramer and tried to make her husband believe that Aniken was nothing but an adventuress who, having got herself into some trouble with the police in Vienna or Berlin, had come to hide at this resort town of Aix, and was probably waiting for the arrival of some rascally accomplice of hers. This idea, presented as if it were a casual conjecture—probable enough, but too unimportant to be worth clearing up—threw Alfred's singularly well-poised mind off balance. It was perfectly clear to him that Aniken was not a chambermaid; but what grave consideration could have led her to assume so disagreeable a role? Nothing accounted for it but fear. It was not hard for Mina to guess why Alfred looked troubled. One evening she had the imprudence to question him; he confessed. Mina was dumfounded. Alfred was so near the truth that it was difficult at first for her to defend herself. The false Mme Cramer, ignoring the role she was supposed to play, had hinted that money was of little importance to Mina. In despair, seeing the effect these words had produced on Alfred, she was on the point of telling him the truth. Naturally the man who loved Aniken to distraction would also love Mlle de Vanghel; but as Alfred would be sure of seeing her again in Paris she could never hope to persuade him to make the sacrifices their love demanded.

Mina spent the whole day filled with these mortal anxieties. It was the evening that was going to be difficult. Finding herself alone with Alfred, would she have the courage to resist the sadness in his eyes, to allow an all too natural suspicion to cool or even kill his love? When the evening arrived, Alfred escorted his wife to the Redoute and did not return. There was a masked ball that night and a lot of noise and excitement. The streets were encumbered by all the carriages belonging to people who had come from Chambéry and even Geneva out of curiosity.

This burst of public gaiety redoubled Mina's gloom. It was impossible for her to remain any longer in the little salon where for several hours she had been uselessly awaiting the arrival of the fatally attractive man who failed to come. She sought refuge with Mme Cramer, her paid companion. Here she ran into more trouble. The woman asked coldly to be allowed to leave, adding that, though very poor, she could not bring herself to continue any longer in the far from honorable role she had been asked to play. It was not in Mina's nature to act circumspectly; at critical moments a mere word was enough to make her see everything in a new light.

"It's true," she thought, struck by her companion's observation, "my disguise is no longer a disguise for anyone. I have lost my honor! I dare say everyone thinks I am an adventuress," adding after a moment: "I have already lost everything for Alfred's sake, so it's silly of me to deprive myself of the joy of seeing him. At least at the ball I could watch him and study his character."

She sent for masks and dominoes; she put on the diamonds she had brought with her from Paris, either in order to make herself less recognizable to Alfred or to distinguish herself from the great crowd of other masks and perhaps entice him to

speak to her. Mina appeared at the ball on the arm of her companion, intriguing everybody by her silence. At last she caught
sight of Alfred, looking very sad. Mina's eyes never left him,
and she was beginning to feel happy when a voice behind her
whispered: "Love sees through Mademoiselle de Vanghel's disguise." She gave a start. She turned. It was Count de Ruppert.
Nothing could have been more disastrous than this encounter.

"I recognized the setting of your diamonds done in Berlin,"
he said. "I've been to Töplitz, to Spa, to Baden; I've rushed
from one watering-place to another looking for you."

"If you say another word," Mina answered, "I will never see
you again as long as I live. Tomorrow after dusk, at seven in
the evening, come to the rue de Chambéry and wait opposite
the house at number seventeen."

How was she to prevent Count de Ruppert from revealing her
secret to the de Larçays, whom he knew intimately? That was
the great problem that kept her awake all night. Several times,
in despair, she was on the point of ordering horses and leaving
on the instant.

"Then all his life Alfred will believe that the Aniken he loved
was nothing but a disreputable woman fleeing in disguise from
the consequences of some crime. And what's still worse, if I run
away now without telling Monsieur de Ruppert, in spite of his
respect for my money he is capable of betraying my secret. But
if I stay, how can I quiet Monsieur de Ruppert's suspicions?
What story can I invent?"

At the same masked ball where this unfortunate encounter
occurred, all the empty-headed society men who take their
boredom along with them to watering-places flocked as usual
around Mme de Larçay. Not knowing just what to say that
evening, as the commonplaces suitable to a drawing-room are
not admissible at a masked ball, they chattered to her of the
beauty of her German chambermaid. One of these idiots, a little
bolder than the others, even allowed himself an allusion, in
rather bad taste, to the supposed jealousy of Mme de Larçay.
Another mask coarsely suggested that she revenge herself on
her husband by taking a lover. This remark set off an explosion
in the mind of this highly respectable woman, whose eminent
position and great fortune accustomed her to an aureole of
flattery.

The next day there was an excursion on the lake. Mina was free and could go to Mme Cramer's, where she received M. de Ruppert. He had not yet got over his astonishment.

"A terrible misfortune, which has altered my situation," Mina told him, "has made me see your love in a different light. Would you be willing to marry a grass widow?"

"You were secretly married, then!" said the Count, growing pale.

"How could you have failed to guess it," Mina replied, "when you saw that I refused you—and not only you, but the best matches in France?"

"What a strange person you are, but wonderful!" cried the Count, trying to make up for his momentary show of consternation.

"I am bound to a man unworthy of me," continued Mlle de Vanghel; "but I am a Protestant, and my religion (which I should be happy to see you adopt) permits divorce. You must not think, however, that at this moment I can feel love for anyone, even for a man who inspires my highest esteem and confidence. All I can offer you is friendship. I like living in France; having once known France, who can forget it? I need a protector. You have a great name, you are clever—the very things that assure the highest position in society. A great fortune can make yours the foremost house in Paris. Will you obey me like a child? On these terms, and on these terms alone, I offer you my hand and will marry you in one year."

During this long speech Count de Ruppert weighed the pros and cons: there was not much pleasure to be had from such an affair; still, there was a fortune in it; and the woman, when you came right down to it, had real goodness. With much grace he swore obedience to Mina. He tried every possible means to ferret out more of her secrets.

"You are wasting your time," she replied, laughing. "And now, tell me, will you have the courage of a lion and the docility of a child?"

"I am your slave," replied the Count.

"I live hidden on the outskirts of Aix, but I know all that goes on there. In eight or nine days, when the church clock strikes midnight, look out over the lake; you will see a flare floating on the water. The next day at nine o'clock in the

evening I shall be here and will receive you. But, if you mention
my name or say a word to no matter whom, never in your life
will you see me again."

After the excursion on the lake, during which Aniken's
beauty was spoken of, and spoken of more than once, Mme de
Larçay came home in a highly irritated state quite foreign to a
character of such marked dignity and moderation. She promptly
snapped at Mina, who was stung to the heart because the words
were spoken in Alfred's presence and he did not come to her
defense. For the first time she gave a sharp and saucy rejoinder.
Thinking from this insolent tone that it was the girl's confidence in the love she had inspired that made her forget her
place, Mme de Larçay's anger knew no bounds. She accused
Mina of meeting certain persons at Mme Cramer's and of being, in spite of their pretended quarrel, hand and glove with the
woman.

"Could that blackguard Ruppert have betrayed me already?"
Mina wondered.

Alfred stared at her, as though trying to learn the truth. His
look was so boorish that it gave her the courage of despair. She
coldly denied Mme de Larçay's accusations and refused to add
another word. Mme de Larçay discharged her on the spot. It
was two o'clock in the morning; Mina had the faithful Dubois
take her to Mme Cramer's. Locking herself in her room, Mina
wept tears of rage to think that, because of the strange position
she was in by her own choice, she had so few ways of getting
her revenge.

"Oh, why don't I give up the whole thing," she thought, "and
go back to Paris? What I have undertaken is beyond me. But
then," she added, "Alfred will only remember me with scorn.
Alfred will despise me for the rest of his life." And she burst
into tears. She decided that, with this cruel thought eternally
plaguing her, she would be even unhappier in Paris than in
Aix.

"Madame de Larçay is slandering me; God knows what she
says about me at the Redoute! The malicious gossip of all these
people will poison Alfred's mind against me. How could a
Frenchman help thinking like *everybody else*? Wasn't he able
in my presence to listen to me being slandered without saying a
word to comfort me? But is it possible? Do I still love him?

Could anything make me so appallingly miserable except the last convulsions of an unhappy love? It is base not to get revenge." That was Mina's last thought.

The first thing in the morning, she sent for M. de Ruppert. Waiting for him, she paced feverishly up and down the garden. Little by little the bright summer sun rose and shone over the smiling hills around the lake. This gladness of nature redoubled Mina's rage. At last M. de Ruppert made his appearance.

"He's a conceited donkey," thought Mina as she saw him arrive. "I'll have to let him talk for an hour first."

She received M. de Ruppert in the drawing-room, and her bored eye kept watching the hands of the clock. The Count was enchanted; for the first time this little foreigner was listening to him with the attention his affability deserved.

"Tell me at least that you believe in my feeling for you," he said to her just as the hand of the clock reached the minute that would end her hour of patience.

"Revenge me and I'll believe everything," she said.

"What am I to do?"

"Make Madame de Larçay notice you, and manage it so that her husband thinks that she is deceiving him, believes it beyond a doubt. Then, through him, I'll be even with her for poisoning my life with her calumnies."

"Your little scheme is outrageous," the Count rejoined.

"Better say that it is difficult for you to carry into effect," Mina replied with a sarcastic smile.

"Difficult? Not at all!" cried the Count, his vanity piqued. "I'll ruin her," he added lightly. "It's a pity, for she's really a good woman."

"Take care, sir, that I don't force you to make a real conquest of Madame de Larçay. All I want is for her husband to have no doubts about her liking you."

The Count left; Mina felt less unhappy. To revenge oneself is to act; to act is to hope.

"If Alfred dies," she said to herself, "I shall die!" And she smiled. The joy she felt at that moment severed all her ties with virtue. What she had been through that night was more than a nature like hers could stomach; she had not been prepared to be slandered in front of Alfred and to have him lend credit to the slander. She might still talk of virtue in the future, but she would be deceiving herself; vengeance and love had taken entire possession of her heart.

Mina thought out a complete scheme of vengeance; was it practicable? That was her only worry. As means of action all she had, besides a great deal of money, was the devotion of a fool.

M. de Larçay appeared.

"What are you doing here?" Mina greeted him haughtily.

"I am very unhappy; I have come to weep with the best friend I have in the world."

"What! Your first word is not to tell me that you do not believe the calumny leveled against me! Go."

"My reply to your false imputations," Alfred replied with dignity, "is that I cannot conceive happiness away from you." And he added, with tears in his eyes: "Aniken, don't be angry with me. Find some reasonable way of bringing us together, and I am ready to do anything. Do with me as you like, if only you can get me out of this unlucky plight. For myself, I can see no way of doing it."

"Your presence here confirms all Madame de Larçay's calumnies; leave me. I never want to set eyes on you again."

Alfred left, feeling more anger than sorrow.

"He could find nothing to say to me," thought Mina; she was in despair; she was almost forced to despise the man she adored.

To think that he could find no way of bringing them together! And he was a man, a soldier! While she, a young girl, the moment she fell in love with him, had found a way, and a terrible way: this disguise which would ruin her if anyone discovered it! . . . But Alfred had said: *Do with me what you like, find some reasonable way. . . .*" There must still have been a little feeling of remorse in her heart, for these words consoled her: it was within her power to act.

"Just the same," insisted the voice of ill-omen, "Alfred never said: 'I do not believe in these calumnies.' "

"After all," she thought, "no matter how, in my folly, I exaggerated the difference between Germany and France, the fact remains that I do not look like a chambermaid. In that case, why should a girl of my age come to a watering-place in disguise? Such as he is . . . I can never be happy except with Alfred. 'Find a way of bringing us together,' he said. 'I am ready to do anything.' He is weak and entrusts me with the responsibility of our happiness. I accept the responsibility," she said, rising and walking feverishly about the room. "Let's first see if his passion can resist absence or if he is a man really to be despised in every way, a true child of France. In that case Mina de Vanghel will contrive to forget him."

An hour later she left for Chambéry, which is only a few leagues from Aix.

Alfred, without really believing in religion, thought it bad form not to profess any. On her arrival at Chambéry, Mme Cramer engaged a young theological student from Geneva to come every evening to expound the Bible to her and Aniken, whom, out of friendliness and to make up for her former burst of temper, she now called her niece. Mme Cramer was staying at the best inn and there was nothing in the least suspicious about her conduct. Thinking she was ill, she had sent for the best doctors in Chambéry and paid them very well. Mina would occasionally consult them about a skin disease that sometimes altered the color of her lovely complexion and made her look like a quadroon.

Mina's companion began to be much less scandalized by the name of Cramer, which she had been forced to assume, and by Mlle de Vanghel's conduct in general; she simply thought her mad. Mina rented a country house called Les Charmettes situated in a lonely valley about a quarter of an hour away from Chambéry, where Jean-Jacques Rousseau, from his own account, spent the happiest years of his life. This author's works were Mina's sole consolation. One day she had a moment of delicious happiness. At the turn of a path through the little chestnut wood opposite the modest house of Les Charmettes she came upon Alfred. It was two weeks since she had last seen him. With a timidity that enchanted Mina he proposed that she leave Mme Cramer's service and permit him to make her a small allowance.

"You will have a chambermaid instead of being one yourself, and I promise never to see you except in the presence of your maid."

Aniken refused for religious reasons. She told him that Mme Cramer was now very good to her and seemed to be sorry for the way she had acted when they first came to Aix.

"I have not forgotten," she finished by saying, "all Madame de Larçay's calumnies; I am therefore in duty bound to beg you most earnestly never to come to Les Charmettes again."

A few days later Mina went to Aix. She was very well pleased with M. de Ruppert. Mme de Larçay and her friends, taking advantage of the fine weather, made almost daily excursions through the surrounding countryside. On one such jaunt, to Haute-Combe (an abbey that is situated on the other side of Lake Bourget, opposite Aix, and is the Saint-Denis of the Dukes of Savoie), M. de Ruppert, who had followed Mina's instructions and made no attempt to seek Mme de Larçay's company, let himself be seen wandering through the surrounding woods. Mme de Larçay's friends were much interested by this display of timidity in a man notorious for his effrontery. It seemed evident that he had fallen desperately in love with Mme de Larçay.

From Dubois, Mina learned that his master was sunk in the deepest melancholy.

"He misses someone's charming company," said Dubois, adding, "and he has something else to worry him. Who would have thought it of such a sensible man? He is jealous of Count de Ruppert!"

This jealousy amused M. de Ruppert.

"Will you allow me," he asked Mlle de Vanghel, "to have him intercept a passionate letter that I shall write to his wife? Could anything be more comical than her denials, if he should decide to tell her?"

"Bravo!" replied Mina. "But," she added, her voice growing hard, "remember you are not to become involved in a duel with Monsieur de Larçay; if he dies, I will never marry you."

She quickly regretted her belligerent tone and began trying to make up for it. She perceived, however, that the harshness of her remark had completely escaped him, and her antipathy for him increased. M. de Ruppert told her that Mme de Larçay had perhaps not been altogether insensible of his attentions; but that, while assiduously courting her at a distance, he amused himself whenever he had occasion to speak with her alone by choosing the most colorless words to make the most harmless remarks.

Mina was satisfied with this way of proceeding. It was in keeping with her character (reasonable enough to all appearances, but in reality the antipode of reason) never to despise halfway. She boldly consulted M. de Ruppert about some investments in French government stocks that she was considering, and showed him letters from her attorney in Königsberg and from her banker in Paris. She noticed that the sight of these letters took his mind off a subject she wished to avoid: her interest in M. de Larçay.

"What a difference!" she thought while M. de Ruppert was giving his advice at great length on the investment of her money. "And there are people who find the Count more attractive and clever than Alfred! O nation of vulgarians! O nation of comedians! How I'd prefer the sober kindness of my dear Germans, except for the sad necessity of appearing at court and marrying the king's favorite aide-de-camp!"

Dubois came to tell her that Alfred had intercepted a singular letter from Count de Ruppert to Mme de Larçay; Alfred had showed it to his wife, who insisted that it was nothing but a ridiculous joke. After hearing this, Mina could no longer control her anxiety. M. de Ruppert was capable of playing any part except that of a patient man. She suggested he spend a week at Chambéry; he showed no enthusiasm.

"I behave in the most ridiculous way; I write a letter that may lead to insinuations against me. After that I can't let people think I'm trying to hide."

"On the contrary," replied Mina haughtily, "that is just what you must do. Do you want to avenge me or not? I don't wish Madame de Larçay to owe me the happiness of being a widow."

"You would prefer, I suspect, that her husband should be a widower!"

"And what's that to you?" rejoined Mina.

There ensued a violent scene, after which M. de Ruppert left in a fury. But on thinking it over he evidently decided that there was little danger of people inventing the accusation he dreaded. His vanity reminded him that his courage was well known. Moreover, here was his chance to repair by a single stroke all the follies of his youth and in one moment win for himself a superb position in Paris society. That, he decided, was better than a duel.

The first person Mina saw the day after her return to Les Charmettes was M. de Ruppert. She was delighted to have him there; but the same evening she was thrown into a state of extreme agitation: M. de Larçay came to see her.

"I shall not try to find any excuse or pretext," he said simply. "I cannot possibly remain two weeks without seeing you, and yesterday it was just two weeks since I saw you last."

Mina too had counted the days; never had she felt so irresistibly drawn to him; but she trembled in fear lest he and M. de Ruppert should meet. She did her best to get him to confide in her about the intercepted letter. He seemed preoccupied, but told her nothing; all she could wring from him was this:

"I have suffered a bitter blow. It has nothing to do with ambition or money, and the only good thing about my sad position is that it increases my passionate friendship for you. What is driving me to despair is that duty has no control over my heart. I simply cannot live without you."

"And I will never live without you," she rejoined, taking his hand and covering it with kisses while, at the same time, she prevented him from throwing his arms around her. "You must be very careful of your life, for I will not live one hour after you."

"Ah! then you know everything!" Alfred said, and had to struggle with himself not to continue.

The day after his return to Aix he received an anonymous letter telling him that during his absence in the mountains (it was the pretext he had used for going to Chambéry) his wife had received M. de Ruppert. This anonymous communication finished with:

> At midnight this evening M. de Ruppert has been given a rendezvous. . . . I hardly expect you to have confidence in me; so do not act hastily. Do not let anger, if you must be angry, get the better of you until you have seen for yourself. If I have been mistaken and if I am misleading you, it will cost you no more than a night in some hiding-place near Madame de Larçay's bedroom.

Alfred was very much upset by this letter. An instant later a note came from Aniken.

> We have just arrived at Aix; Madame Cramer has retired to her room. I am free; come.

M. de Larçay decided that, before concealing himself in the garden, he had time to spend ten minutes with Aniken. He was in a highly excited state when he arrived. But, though the night that had begun was to be as crucial for Mina as for him, she was unperturbed. To all the objections raised by her reason she had the same answer: death.

"You say nothing," Mina observed, "but it is plain that something extraordinary is happening to you. You shouldn't have given me the pain of seeing you like this. But since you have gone so far as to come, I refuse to leave you for the rest of the evening."

Against all Mina's expectations, Alfred agreed without difficulty. Under critical circumstances a strong mind sheds a sort of beneficent magnanimity.

"I am about to practice the idiotic profession of husband," Alfred told her at last. "I am going to conceal myself in my garden; that, it seems to me, is the least painful remedy for the mortification inflicted on me by an anonymous letter." And he showed her the letter.

"What right have you," Mina cried, "to bring disgrace upon Madame de Larçay? Aren't you virtually divorced? You abandon her and give up your right to keep her mind occupied; you barbarously leave her to the boredom that comes naturally to a young woman of thirty who is wealthy and without a care in the world.[3] Hasn't she the right to find someone to relieve her boredom? And you are the man who says he loves me, you who are more criminal than she is, for you were the first to break your common bonds; and you have the temerity to wish to condemn her to eternal boredom!"

This manner of thinking was too exalted for Alfred; but the tone of her voice gave him strength. He wondered at the power she had over him and was charmed by it.

"As long as you consent to let me stay near you," he replied at last, "I shall never know that boredom you speak of."

[3] Immoral in the eyes of 1830. (Manuscript note by Stendhal)

At midnight everything had long been quiet along the lake front; you could have heard a cat walking. Mina had followed Alfred behind one of those thick, wall-like hedges still to be seen in the gardens of Savoie. Suddenly a man jumped off the wall into the garden. Alfred started to run after him, but Mina restrained him forcibly.

"What will you find out if you kill him?" she whispered. "And how you would regret having killed him if he turned out to be only a burglar or some other woman's lover!"

Alfred had recognized the Count; he was beside himself with anger. Mina had some difficulty restraining him. The Count took a ladder lying on the ground beside the wall and hurriedly stood it up against a wooden balcony that ran along the first floor of the house eight or ten feet from the ground. One of Mme de Larçay's windows opened onto this balcony. M. de Ruppert entered the apartment through one of the drawing-room windows. Alfred rushed to a little door that gave access to the ground floor from the garden; Mina followed him. She gained a few moments by keeping him from finding his tinder-box and lighting a candle. She managed to take his pistols from him.

"Do you want to wake up the whole house with a pistol shot? That would make a nice scandal tomorrow morning! Even if you are bent on vengeance, which to me seems ridiculous, wouldn't it be better if an idle, malicious public only learned of the offense at the same time it learns of the vengeance?"

Alfred started up the stairs toward his wife's bedroom; Mina still followed him.

"It would be really too funny," she said to him, "if in my presence you should have the effrontery to maltreat your wife!"

When he reached the bedroom door Alfred opened it furiously. He saw M. de Ruppert escaping in his shirt sleeves from behind Mme de Larçay's bed at the far end of the room. M. de Ruppert was six paces from the door; he had time to open the window, rush out onto the balcony and from the balcony down the ladder into the garden. M. de Larçay speedily followed him; but when he reached the low wall that separated the garden from the lake, the boat in which M. de Ruppert was making his escape was already a cable-length from shore.

"Until tomorrow, Monsieur de Ruppert," M. de Larçay

shouted after him. There was no reply. M. de Larçay quickly returned to the apartment. He found Mina pacing excitedly up and down the drawing-room. She stopped him as he made a beeline for his wife's bedroom.

"What do you intend to do?" she asked. "Murder Madame de Larçay? And by what right? I won't let you. If you do not give me your dagger, I will shout at the top of my voice to warn her to escape. It is true that I shall be horribly compromised in the eyes of your servants."

Mina saw that this last remark had an effect, and quickly added:

"You say you love me and yet you are willing to dishonor me."

M. de Larçay tossed her the dagger and in a fury rushed into his wife's room. The scene was stormy. Perfectly innocent, Mme de Larçay thought there had been a burglar in the apartment; she had neither seen nor heard M. de Ruppert.

"You are quite mad," she finally said to her husband, "and I wish to God you were only mad! You apparently want a separation. You shall have it. At least have sense enough not to talk. Tomorrow I shall return to Paris; I shall say that you are traveling in Italy and that I did not care to go with you."

"What time are you going to fight tomorrow morning?" Mlle de Vanghel asked Alfred when she saw him later.

"What do you mean?" he rejoined.

"That it is useless to try to deceive me. Before you go to meet Monsieur de Ruppert I want you to take me down to the lake and put me in a boat; I want to go out on the lake. If you are stupid enough to get yourself killed, the waters of the lake will put an end to all my troubles."

"Well then, darling Aniken, make me a happy man tonight. Perhaps tomorrow this heart which, since I have known you, has beaten for you alone, and this lovely hand which I press against my breast, will both belong to corpses lighted by funeral candles in a corner of some church and watched over by two Savoyard priests. This beautiful day is the supreme moment of our lives, make it the happiest!"

Mina had a hard time resisting Alfred's transports.

"I shall be yours," she said to him at length, "I shall be yours if you live. At this moment the sacrifice would be too great; I prefer to be with you as we are."

That was the most wonderful day of her whole life. Probably the prospect of death and the generosity of the sacrifice she was making finally hushed the last stirrings of remorse.

Next day, long before sunrise, Alfred came to escort her to a charming little pleasure boat.

"Can you imagine a greater happiness than ours?" Mina said as they went toward the lake.

"From this moment you belong to me, you are my wife," Alfred replied, "and I promise you I will live to come down to the lake shore just where you see that cross, and signal you in your boat." She wanted to stay near the shore and was glad when the boatmen started fishing and paid no more attention to her. As eight o'clock was striking she saw Alfred coming down to the shore at a run. He was very pale. Mina got out of the boat.

"He is wounded," Alfred explained, "perhaps seriously."

"Take the boat, my love. This unhappy accident puts you at the mercy of the local authorities; disappear for a few days. Go to Lyon; I shall keep you informed of what happens."

Alfred hesitated.

"Think of what people will say!"

This remark decided Alfred; he pushed off.

Next day M. de Ruppert was out of danger; but he would probably have to stay in bed for a month or two. Mina saw him that night and was as charming and friendly as could be.

"Aren't you my 'intended'?" she said with a candor full of duplicity. She made him accept an order on her banker at Frankfurt for a considerable amount. "I must go to Lausanne," she informed him. "And before our marriage I want you to buy back your magnificent family estate, which your follies forced you to sell. Before that can be done I shall have to sell a large estate I own near Custrin. As soon as you are able to walk, you must go and sell this property for me; I shall send you the necessary procuration from Lausanne. Agree to lower the price if you have to, or discount the bills of exchange you will receive. Whatever you do, be sure to get cash. If I'm going to marry you, you ought to look as rich as I am in the marriage contract."

The Count had not the faintest suspicion that Mina was treating him as a humble agent whom one pays for his services.

At Lausanne Mina had the joy of receiving letters from Alfred by every post. M. de Larçay began to realize how his duel simplified his relations with Mina and his wife. "Madame de Larçay is guilty of no offense against you," Mina had said to him. "You were the first to abandon her, and, surrounded by a lot of attractive men, perhaps she may have been wrong in choosing Monsieur de Ruppert; but there is no reason why Madame de Larçay should be made to suffer financially." Alfred left his wife an allowance of fifty thousand francs; this was more than half his income.

"What will I need money for?" he wrote Mina. "I do not intend to return to Paris for several years, not until this ridiculous affair has been forgotten."

"That is just what I don't wish," Mina replied; "your return would make a great stir. Show yourself to the public while public opinion is still interested in you. Remember that your wife is in no way to blame."

A month later M. de Larçay joined Mina in the charming village of Belgirate on Lake Maggiore a few miles from the Borromean Islands. She was traveling under a false name. She was so much in love that she said to Alfred:

"If you like, you may tell Madame Cramer that you are my fiancé—my *intended*, as we say in Germany. I shall always receive you with joy, but only in the presence of Madame Cramer."

M. de Larçay felt that his happiness was not quite complete. Yet one could not have found a period in any man's life as happy as that month of September which Alfred spent with Mina on Lake Maggiore. Mina found his behavior so exemplary that little by little she had given up taking Mme Cramer with them on all their excursions.

One day when they were out sailing on the lake Alfred asked laughingly:

"Tell me, my little witch, who are you really? You can't expect me to believe you are a chambermaid—still less Madame Cramer's."

"Well," replied Mina, "let me see! What do you think I am? An actress who won an enormous prize in a lottery, and who wanted to spend a few years of her life in fairyland; or perhaps a kept mistress who, when her lover died, wanted to change character?"

"Even supposing you were much worse than that, if tomorrow I learned that Madame de Larçay was dead, day after tomorrow I would ask you to marry me."

Mina threw her arms around his neck.

"I am Mina de Vanghel, whom you once saw at Madame de Cély's. How could you have failed to recognize me? Ah, but I forget," she added, laughing, "love is blind."

No matter how happy this revelation made Alfred, Mina's happiness was deeper still. The only thing that had marred her happiness till now was having to keep a secret from him. When two people are in love, the one who deceives the other is miserable.

Nevertheless Mlle de Vanghel would have done well not to disclose her name to M. de Larçay. When a few months had passed, Mina began to notice some lurking melancholy in Alfred. They had gone to spend the winter at Naples with a passport that identified them as man and wife. Mina hid none of her thoughts from Alfred; her nature, so different from his, frightened him. She thought he missed Paris; she begged him on her knees to go and spend a week there. He swore he had no desire to. His melancholy persisted.

"Very well," Mina said to him one day. "It may be staking all my happiness on one grand throw, but seeing you melancholy like this is too much for my resolutions."

Alfred did not quite understand what she was driving at, but nothing could equal his wild delight when, in the afternoon, she said:

"Take me to Torre del Greco." [4]

After she had given herself to him Mina thought she had discovered the cause of his lurking sadness, for now he was completely happy. Mad with happiness and love herself, she forgot all her former ideas. ("Were death or a thousand deaths to strike me tomorrow," she thought, "it would not be too high

[4] A resort town at the base of Mount Vesuvius, built on lava from the volcanic eruptions that have repeatedly devastated it. (Editor)

a price to pay for what has happened to me since Alfred's duel.") She now found the most delicious pleasure in satisfying Alfred's every wish. Transported by her joy, she made the mistake of not trying to conceal from him her boldly unconventional way of thinking, which was the very essence of her character. Her manner of seeking happiness could not but seem strange, even shocking, to an ordinary soul. Until now Mina had been careful to humor what she called M. de Larçay's French prejudices; she was obliged to excuse what she could not admire in him by putting it down to the difference of nationality: in this she felt for the first time the disadvantage of the redoubtable education she had received from her father; such an education could easily make her odious.

In this rapturous state she threw caution to the winds and thought out loud before Alfred. When a woman reaches this stage of love, how much better for her to be *pitied* by her lover than envied! She was so madly in love, her lover in her eyes was so plainly the very prototype of everything that was most noble, handsome, agreeable, and adorable in the world, that even if she had wished to she could not have hidden any of her thoughts from him. To conceal from him the fateful plot that had provoked all the events of that night at Aix had for a long time now been almost too great an effort for her.

From the moment that the intoxication of her senses deprived her of the power to conceal anything from M. de Larçay, her rare qualities turned against her. Mina teased him about that trace of sadness she noticed in him. The love he inspired in her soon reached the last degree of folly.

"How silly of me to worry! It's because I love him more than he loves me. It is really foolish of me to fret and fume about something that happens in all the greatest joys on this earth! Unluckily I happen to be the sort of person who worries, and he isn't. Then, too, God is just," she added with a sigh (for, since her love had reached such a pitch, remorse sometimes troubled her happiness), "and I have done a great wrong: that night at Aix weighs on my conscience."

Mina accustomed herself to the idea that Alfred was destined by nature to love her less passionately than she loved him.

"But even if he were still less demonstrative," she told herself, "it is my fate to adore him. I am only thankful that he has no infamous vices. I feel perfectly certain that I'd think nothing of committing a crime if he wanted me to."

But at last Mina could delude herself no longer. She was struck one day by the somber anxiety that still seemed to be preying on Alfred's mind. For a long time he had had the idea of leaving Mme de Larçay his entire income, becoming a Protestant, and marrying Mina.

That day Prince de S—— was giving a monster fête, to which they of course had not been invited, and all Naples was in a frenzy of excitement. Mina imagined that her lover missed all the gaiety and glamour of a great fortune. She urged him to leave with her for Königsberg at the earliest possible moment. Alfred looked away and did not reply. At last he raised his eyes and in them Mina saw a look of painful suspicion, but no love. She was thunderstruck.

"Tell me something, Mina. The night that I surprised Monsieur de Ruppert in my wife's room, had you known of the Count's intentions? In other words, had you planned it together?"

"Yes," replied Mina without flinching. "Madame de Larçay had never given the Count a thought. I thought that you belonged to me because I loved you. *I* wrote the two anonymous letters."

"It was an infamous trick," Alfred rejoined coldly. "My eyes are opened, I am going back to my wife. I pity you and I no longer love you."

There was wounded pride in the tone of his voice. He left.

"And that," thought Mina, "is what greathearted souls lay themselves open to. But they have their own resources."

She crossed to the window and watched her lover till he reached the end of the street. When he had disappeared she went to Alfred's room and shot herself through the heart. Was her life a bad speculation? Her happiness had lasted eight months. She had too ardent a nature to be satisfied with things as they are.

Translated by Louise Varèse

THE OTHER DIANE

by Honoré de Balzac (1799–1850)

After the disasters of the July revolution, which wrecked a number of aristocratic fortunes backed by the court, Mme la Princesse de Cadignan was clever enough to foist on political events the blame for the total ruin she had brought on herself by her extravagance. The Prince had left France with the royal family; the Princess stayed on in Paris, the very fact of her husband's absence safeguarding her against arrest, for the responsibility of her debts—which were such that they could not be covered by the liquidation of all their salable property—fell on him alone. The income from their entailed property had been taken over by creditors; and the affairs of the great family were, in short, as badly off as those of the elder branch of the Bourbons. Things being at that pass, the Princess, notorious

---

Written soon after the second part of Les Illusions perdues, *"The Other Diane" was first published in periodical form, in 1839, under the title,* "Une Princesse parisienne." *In 1844, under the title* "Les Secrets de la Princesse de Cadignan," *it was incorporated as one of the* Scènes de la vie parisienne *into* La Comédie humaine. *Balzac called it* "a little pearl." *It is, and the fact that it is may be a reason why, in France as in America, it is often overlooked: one does not expect the architect and construction boss of a gigantic visionary universe to be also a dealer in gems.*

Then, too, among the ninety-seven novels of the Comédie humaine—*virtually all written in the eighteen-year period between the revolutions of 1830 and 1848—this short, rather "untypical" one is easily enough lost. And among the two thousand or so imaginary inhabitants of Balzac's universe, Diane, Duchess of Uxelles and Princess of Cadignan, has "secrets" ("secret motives" would be a more accurate translation) of a sort with which Balzac did not generally deal. By comparison, however, with the treacherous, shimmering abysses of ambiguity that*

under her maiden name of Duchesse de Maufrigneuse, resolved
on the prudent course of withdrawing completely from the public eye; she meant to make the world forget her. With such
speed was everything in Paris turned topsy-turvy that the
Duchesse de Maufrigneuse was in fact soon lost to sight under
the Princesse de Cadignan and became almost a stranger to
society; most of the new actors brought upon the stage by the
July Revolution knew nothing of her metamorphosis.

The title of duke takes precedence in France over all others,
even that of prince, though according to unadulterated heraldic
doctrine titles mean absolutely nothing and all the nobly born
are perfectly equal. This admirable principle of equality was in
former times scrupulously respected by the French royal house;
and nominally, at least, it still is, the kings of France being
careful to give their sons the simple title of count. By virtue of
the same system, Francis I, signing himself in reply to a letter
from Charles V "Francis, Lord of Vanves," reduced to nothing
the splendid array of titles assumed by that pompous monarch.
Louis XI had gone even further when he gave his daughter to
Pierre de Beaujeu, a nobleman with no title. The feudal system

*open up behind this perverse huntress bent on her erotic prey,
the realms of the supernatural on which Balzac made elsewhere
so many bearish frontal assaults tend to look like Emersonian
ponds. For the master stroke of the story, as Balzac put it, was
to have represented "falsehood"—the artifice of a wonderful
comédienne—as having a "soundness" and grandeur of its own,
as being "necessary," and as finding its "justification" in human need.*

*Of Balzac's own agitated love affairs, of his physical and
imaginative appetites, of his domestic and financial misadven-
tures, of the bric-a-brac that cluttered his houses and his
thoughts, it would be pointless to speak here. His life as a creator began when, at the age of thirty, after ten years devoted
to turning out high-flown or spicy pulp romances, he discovered
that the creatures swarming since childhood in his imagination
—none of whom (observed Baudelaire), down to the janitor,
but has some sort of genius, none of whom but is in some way
a man or woman "possessed," if by no more than insignificance
—were more at home in nineteenth-century France than in*

was so thoroughly broken up by Louis XIV that the title of duke in his reign became the supreme and most coveted honor.

Nevertheless, there are two or three families in France in which the princehood (involving considerable wealth at one time) is rated higher than the dukedom. The House of Cadignan is one of these exceptional families; the eldest son has the title of Duc de Maufrigneuse, while all the rest are called simply Chevaliers de Cadignan.

The Cadignans, like two princes of the House of Rohan in other times, have a right to a chair of state in their own house, and may keep a retinue of pages, and even gentlemen, in their service. (These details must be made clear, in part to anticipate the foolish carping of those who know nothing about the matter, in part to put on record an old stately order of things which is said to be passing away, and which so many people, not understanding it, are eager to abolish.) The Cadignans bear *or five fusils sable conjoined in fesse,* with the motto MEMINI, and a close crown, without supporters or lambrequins. What with the prevalent ignorance of heraldry and the great influx of foreigners to Paris, the title of prince is beginning to enjoy a

---

Ruritania. The revelation came to him a few years afterward (becoming an editorial and historical event in 1842) that this swarm made up a single, independent, organically coherent world of the imagination: a "human comedy."

Most of the characters who move through "The Other Diane" as if neither they nor their creator quite understood they were fictitious are old inhabitants of Balzac's books, and Balzac (like Faulkner nowadays) sometimes cavalierly takes for granted that the reader already knows them. Diane herself plays an important part in Le Cabinet des antiques (1838), where her affair with young d'Esgrignon is narrated in detail. As for the eminent doctor of the Comédie humaine, who here makes an appearance with his friend d'Arthez, the legend goes that Balzac's last words were: "Bianchon . . . Call Bianchon. . . . He's the only one who can save me!"

NOTE: *The historical events referred to in "The Other Diane" are those connected with the revolution or coup d'état of July 27–29, 1830, by which the elder branch of the house of Bourbon, restored to the French throne in 1814, was again*

certain vogue; but there are no real princes in France save
those who inherit domains with their name and are entitled to
be addressed as "Your Highness." The disdain felt for the title
by the old nobility, and the motives that led Louis XIV to give
supremacy to the rank of duke prevented France from claiming
the style of highness for the few princes in existence (those of
Napoleon's creation excepted). This is how the princes of
Cadignan happen to rank nominally below other Continental
princes.

The persons known collectively as the Faubourg Saint-Germain protected the Princess; treating her with the respectful
discretion that was due to her name, which will always be honored, to her misfortunes, which no longer gave rise to talk, and
to her beauty, which was the one treasure she had saved from
the general wreck. The world that she had adorned gave her
credit for taking the veil, as it were, by making a cloister of
her own house. For her, of all women, such a piece of good
taste involved an immense sacrifice; and in France anything
done in the grand style is always so keenly appreciated that the
Princess won back by her withdrawal whatever ground she had

*driven into exile after Charles X, its crowned head in 1830,
issued a set of drastically anti-liberal decrees. On August 9 a
coalition of liberal monarchists and empire-minded republicans
tried to reach a compromise settlement by installing in his place
the head of the younger branch, the Duke of Orleans, a man of
a supposedly liberal and bourgeois turn, who took the name of
Louis-Philippe I and was soon dubbed "The Citizen King."*

*Discontent remained strong on the part of the legitimists, or
adherents to the elder branch, and the more obstinate republicans. In 1832 the exiled Duchess of Berri, referred to as
Madame, came back to France in disguise and made an un-
successful attempt to set off a civil war in the royalist and Catholic Vendée region of the west. On June 5–6 of the same year
the funeral of Maximilien Lamarque, a former Napoleonic general who had become a popular liberal spokesman in the Chamber of Deputies, was the occasion in Paris of a large-scale
working-class and republican uprising, soon put down, which
centered around a bloody street battle at the church of Saint-
Merri.*

lost in public opinion while her splendor was at its height. Of her former women friends, she saw only the Marquise d'Espard; and as yet she did not appear either at important gatherings or at parties. The Princess and the Marquise called on each other in the early hours of the morning, rather like conspirators; when the Princess dined at her friend's house, the Marquise closed her doors to everyone else.

Mme d'Espard's behavior toward the Princess was admirable. She changed her box at the Italiens, coming down from the mezzanine to a *baignoire* [1] on the ground floor, so that Mme de Cadignan could come to the theater unseen and leave unrecognized. Not every woman would have been capable of a piece of delicacy which deprived her of the pleasure of dragging a former and fallen rival in her train and posing as her benefactress. Enabled as a consequence to dispense with ruinous wardrobes, the Princess went privately in the Marquise's carriage, which in public she would have refused to take. Nobody ever knew why Mme d'Espard behaved toward the Princess in this way; but her conduct was sublime, involving for a long period a host of little sacrifices that seem mere trifles in themselves, but which, taken as a whole, reach gigantic proportions.

In 1832 the snows of three years had covered the Duchesse de Maufrigneuse's adventures, whitening them so effectually that nothing short of a prodigious effort of memory could recall the heavy indictments formerly laid to her charge. Of the queen adored by so many courtiers, of the duchess whose levities might furnish a novelist with several volumes, there remained an enchantingly beautiful woman of thirty-six who might have passed for thirty, though she had a nineteen-year-old son. Georges, Duc de Maufrigneuse, beautiful as Antinous and poor as Job, was clearly cut out to do great things; and his mother had her heart set on marrying him into wealth. It may be that she meant to choose an heiress for him some day out of Mme d'Espard's salon, which was supposed to be the first in Paris, and that this was her private motive for remaining on close terms with the Marquise. The Princess, looking ahead, saw another five years of retirement before her—five desolate, lonely years; but if Georges was to marry well, her conduct must receive the hallmark of virtue.

[1] A closed box beside the stage.

The Princess lived in a modest ground-floor apartment in a mansion in the rue de Miromesnil, where relics of her bygone splendor had been turned to good account. A great lady's elegance still pervaded everything. She had surrounded herself with beautiful things, which told their own story of a life in high spheres. The magnificent miniature of Charles X above her chimney-piece had been painted by Mme de Mirbel, and bore engraved on the frame the legend "Given by the King." The companion picture was a portrait of Madame, who had been so singularly gracious to her. The album that shone conspicuous on one of the tables was an almost priceless treasure, which none of the bourgeoises who rule the niggling money-making society of nowadays would dare exhibit in public. It was a piece of audacity which paints the Princess's character to admiration. The album was full of portraits, some thirty among them belonging to intimate friends—lovers, the world said. The figure was a gross exaggeration; but where some ten of them were concerned there were perhaps, as the Marquise d'Espard said, pretty solid grounds for talk. However that might be, Maxime de Trailles, de Marsay, Rastignac, the Marquis d'Esgrignon, General Montriveau, the Marquis de Ronquerolles and d'Ajuda-Pinto, Prince Galathionne, the young dukes of Grandlieu and Rhétoré, the young Vicomte de Sérizy, and the handsome Lucien de Rubempré had all received most flattering treatment from the brushes of the famous portrait-painters of the day. As the Princess no longer received more than two or three of the individuals portrayed, she facetiously dubbed the book her "compendium of errors."

Adversity had made the Princess a good mother. During the fifteen years of the Restoration she had been too taken up with her own pleasure to think of her son; but now, when she took refuge in obscurity, this illustrious egoist bethought herself that maternal sentiment pushed to an extreme would win absolution for her; her past life would be condoned by the tenderhearted, who will forgive a fond mother anything. She loved her son all the more because she had nothing else left to love. Georges de Maufrigneuse was, for that matter, a son of whom any mother might have been proud. The Princess made all kinds of sacrifices for him. Georges had a stable and a coach house at her expense, and lived in three charmingly furnished rooms in the entresol above, which gave on the street. She stinted herself so that he could keep a saddle horse, a cab horse, and a little servant. She herself had only her chambermaid and a former kitchenmaid, who now served as cook. Her son's manservant, Toby, had his hands full. Formerly in the service of "the late Beaudenord" (as that ruined dandy was jestingly referred to in the world of fashion), Toby, now twenty-five but still taken for fourteen, had to groom the horses, keep the cabriolet or tilbury clean, follow his master about, keep his rooms in order, and be on hand in the Princess's antechamber to announce visitors, if by chance she was expecting someone to call.

When you considered the part that the beautiful Duchesse de Maufrigneuse had played under the Restoration—how she had been one of the queens of Paris, a radiant queen, leading a life so luxurious that even the wealthiest women of fashion in London might have taken lessons of her—it was strangely touching to see her in that mere nutshell of a place in the rue de Miromesnil, only a few doors away from the huge Cadignan mansion, which nobody was rich enough to live in. (The real-estate speculators have since demolished it.) The woman for whom thirty servants had barely sufficed, who had been mistress of the finest salons and most charming apartments in Paris, and who had entertained in them so splendidly, was now living in a suite of five rooms—antechamber, dining-room, drawing-room, bedroom, and dressing-room—with a couple of women servants for her whole establishment.

"Ah! she is an admirable mother," that shrewd busybody the Marquise d'Espard would remark, "and admirable without overdoing it; she knows just where to stop. Who would have thought that such a frivolous woman would be capable of taking a resolution and following it up so persistently? She has earned a pat on the shoulder from no less a man than our good Archbishop, who treats her now with the greatest consideration; he has just persuaded the dowager Comtesse de Cinq-Cygne to call on her."

The fact is (why deny it?) that a woman must *be* a queen to have the knack of abdicating with majesty, of coming down from high estate without quite losing her queenliness. It is only when people know they do not amount to anything in themselves that they bewail a fall, fret about it, and keep harping on the irrecoverable past (foreseeing correctly that they will not make the grade twice).

Being obliged to dispense with the rare flowers that had been the accustomed setting of her former life—a setting that showed her off in a most favorable light, as no one could help making the comparison between a flower and this beautiful woman—the Princess had chosen her ground-floor apartment with care, so as to have the use of a pretty little garden, full of shrubbery, and with a lawn whose year-round greenness brightened up the placidity of her retreat. Her annual income came to perhaps twelve thousand francs, but even that modest sum was made up of an allowance from the old Duchesse de Navarreins (the young Duke's paternal aunt) which would be kept up until the Duke was married, and of contributions from the Duchesse d'Uxelles, who was living on her estate in the country and saving as no one but an elderly duchess knows how (Harpagon was a mere tyro in comparison).

The Prince de Cadignan lived abroad, at the beck and call of his exiled sovereigns, sharing their adversity and serving them with unselfish devotion; he was perhaps the most intelligent man in their entourage. His position was even now a protection to his wife in Paris. In such obscurity did the Princess live, and so little did her destitution arouse the suspicions of the government, that a certain marshal, to whom France owes an African province, used to meet legitimist leaders at her house and confer with them at the very moment when Madame was making her attempt to win over the Vendée.

Taking stock of the fact that she would soon be forty—the age after which a woman has so little to look forward to—and that with the coming of that fearful moment her days of love would be over, the Princess had launched forth into the realm of philosophical studies. She took to reading—she who for the last sixteen years had showed the utmost abhorrence of anything serious! Literature and politics nowadays take the place of piety as the last refuge of feminine pretensions. It was said in fashionable circles that Diane meant to write a book. During this transition period, when the beautiful woman of other days was preparing to fade into a woman of intellect until such time as she should fade away for good, Diane made the privilege of being received at her house an honor in the highest degree flattering to the persons so favored. Under the cover of these occupations she contrived to hoodwink de Marsay, one of her early lovers and now the most influential member of the government of the Citizen King; several times she received visits from him in the evening while the legitimist leaders and the Marshal were actually assembled in her bedroom, discussing plans for winning back the kingdom. (The only thing the conspirators overlooked was that their schemes could get nowhere without the help of ideas.) It was a lovely revenge for a lovely woman thus to inveigle a prime minister and use him as a screen for a conspiracy against his own government. Of this adventure, which was worthy of the best days of the Fronde,[2] the Princess wrote Madame the sprightliest account imaginable.

The Duc de Maufrigneuse went to La Vendée and contrived to come back again in secret without having compromised himself, but not until he had shared Madame's perils. When all seemed lost, Madame sent him back—unfortunately perhaps, for the young man's impassioned vigilance might have prevented her being betrayed.

Great as Mme de Maufrigneuse's transgressions might have been in the eyes of the middle class, her son's behavior simply wiped them out so far as the aristocracy was concerned. It was something great and noble surely to risk in this way the life of an only son and the heir to a historic name. There are individuals—"shrewd" is the customary word for them—who think that by making themselves useful to the state they can whitewash their private lives; but the Princess had no such calculating purpose. Nor have many other people, perhaps, who act as she did, though things may work out so as to suggest otherwise.

On one of the first fine days in May 1833 the Marquise d'Espard and the Princess were taking a turn (they could scarcely be said to be taking a walk) along the garden path that circled the lawn. It was about two o'clock in the afternoon, the sun was taking leave of the garden for the day, the air was warm with heat reflected from the walls and fragrant with the scent of flowers brought by the Marquise.

[2] The civil war of 1648-53—serious enough, but slightly comical as well, in the style of an operetta, and notable for its devious factional intrigues.

"We shall lose de Marsay soon," Mme d'Espard was saying, "and with him goes your last hope of fortune for the Duc de Maufrigneuse; it is too bad, for since you played such a neat trick on that great politician he has become fond of you again."

"My son will never come to terms with the younger branch; I'd rather he starved; I'd rather go to work for him myself," returned the Princess. "But Berthe de Cinq-Cygne seems not to dislike him."

"The younger generation is not bound in the same way as the older—"

"Let us say nothing about that. If I fail to tame the Marquise de Cinq-Cygne, it will be quite bad enough when the time comes to be forced to marry my son to some blacksmith's daughter, like young d'Esgrignon."

"Did you love him?" asked the Marquise.

"No," the Princess answered gravely. "D'Esgrignon's naïveté was only a kind of provincial's callowness, as I found out a little too late, or too soon, if you prefer."

"And de Marsay?"

"De Marsay played with me as if I had been a doll. I was a mere child. A woman never falls in love with a man who takes it on himself to open her eyes; he rubs her precious little vanity the wrong way."

"And that wretched boy who hanged himself?"

"Lucien? An Antinous and a great poet. I worshipped him assiduously, and I might have been happy with him. But he was in love with a streetwalker; and I gave him up to Mme de Sérizy. If he had cared to love me, should I have given him up?"

"Of all things to happen—that you should come up against a creature like that Esther!" [3]

"She did have the edge on me where beauty was concerned," said the Princess.

There was a pause; then the Princess went on: "It is almost three years now that I have been living completely alone. Well, peace and quiet have not been hard to endure. Just between ourselves—I shouldn't dare say it to anyone else—I have been happy here. Adoration had begun to pall on me; I was too

[3] Esther Van Gobseck, the streetwalker of *Splendeurs et misères des courtisanes*.

jaded to find pleasure in anything; my feelings were never more than skin-deep. Every man I met seemed to me petty, small-minded, and shallow; not one of them did anything in the least unexpected; they had neither innocence, nor greatness, nor delicacy. I should have liked to find someone of whom I could stand in awe."

"Is your experience, then, my dear," asked the Marquise, "what mine has been—of going through the motions of love and never loving?"

"Never," replied the Princess, laying a hand on her friend's arm.

The two women went across to a rustic bench under a mass of jasmine in second flower. Both had spoken words full of solemn import for women at their age.

"Like you," resumed the Princess, "I have been more loved, perhaps, than other women; but, through so many adventures, I feel that I have never known happiness. I have done many reckless things, but always with an end in view, and that end receded as I advanced. My heart has grown old, and yet my innocence is still untouched. Yes, for all my experience of men, a man who knew how to make me love for the first time could lead me by the nose; just as, however wearing and blighting my life has been, I still feel beautiful and young. A woman may love and not be happy, or be happy and not love; but to have love and happiness both, to know at one and the same time these two supreme human joys—that is a miracle, and the miracle has not taken place for me."

"Nor for me," said Mme d'Espard.

"A dreadful regret haunts me in my retreat: I have had my fling, but I have not loved."

"What an incredible secret!"

"Ah! my dear, these are secrets that we can confide only to each other; nobody in Paris would believe us."

"And if we were not both over thirty-six, we might not be telling them to each other."

"True enough. What silly creatures we are about some things when we are young! We behave at times like those penniless young men who go about sucking on toothpicks to make people think they have just eaten their fill."

"Oh, well," came back the Marquise with an insinuating lilt

and a delightful girlish shrug, "at least we know better now; and there is life enough in us still, it strikes me, to have another fling."

"When you told me the other day that Béatrix [4] had gone off with Conti, I thought about it all night long," said the Princess after a pause. "A woman must be very happy indeed to be willing to sacrifice her position and her future and give up the world forever like that."

"She is a little fool," Mme d'Espard returned gravely. "Mademoiselle des Touches was only too delighted to be rid of Conti. Béatrix could not see that it was a strong proof there was nothing to him when a clever woman gave him up without making a defense of her so-called happiness for a single moment."

"Then is she going to be unhappy?"

"She is unhappy now. What was the good of leaving her husband? What is it but an admission of weakness in a wife?"

"Then you think that what Madame de Rochefide was after when she left him was not freedom to love and to be loved in earnest—in the way that for both of us is still a dream?"

"No. She was aping Madame de Beauséant and Madame de Langeais,[5] who, between ourselves, would have been (like you, incidentally) as great figures as La Vallière, or the Montespan, or Diane de Poitiers, or the duchesses d'Étampes or de Chateauroux, in any age less commonplace than ours."

"Except, my dear, that they wouldn't have had the King. Ah! how I should like to call up those women, and ask them if—"

"But there is no necessity to call up the dead," broke in the Marquise; "we know living women who are happy. A score of times I have begun intimate talks about this kind of thing with the Comtesse de Montcornet. For fifteen years she has been the happiest woman under the sun with that little Émile Blondet. Not an infidelity, not a thought for anyone else; and they are still as they were the first day. But somebody always comes to disturb us at the most interesting point. Then there are Rastignac and Madame de Nucingen, and your cousin Madame de Camps and that Octave of hers; there is some mystery behind these long attachments; these people know something, my dear, that neither of us knows. The world does us the exceeding

---

[4] The Marquise Béatrix de Rochefide in *Béatrix*.
[5] In *La Femme abandonnée* and *La Duchesse de Langeais* respectively.

honor to take us for *rouées* worthy of the court of the Regency, and we are as innocent as two little boarding-school misses."

"I should be glad to have even that innocence," the Princess mockingly exclaimed. "Ours is worse; it is positively humiliating. Ah well, there we are! Humiliation will just have to be the penance we offer up for our unrewarded pursuit of love. For it is scarcely likely, my dear, that in our Indian summer we shall find the glorious flower that did not bloom for us in May and June."

"That is not the real problem," rejoined the Marquise, after a pause given over by both to reflection. "We are still beautiful enough to make men fall in love with us; but we shall never convince anyone that we are either innocent or virtuous."

"If it were a falsehood, it would soon be garnished with commentaries, served up with the pretty art that makes a lie credible, and swallowed down like delicious fruit. But to make a truth credible! Ah! the greatest men have perished in that attempt," added the Princess, with a subtle smile that Leonardo's brush alone could render.

"There are always fools to be had," said the Marquise. "And sometimes they make good lovers. . . ."

"Yes; but not even fools are that simple-minded," pointed out the Princess.

"You are right," the Marquise said, laughing. "We ought not to look to a fool or a man of talent for the solution of the problem. There is nothing for it but genius. In genius alone do you find a child's trustfulness, a belief in love as a religion, and a willingness to be blindfolded. Look at Canalis and the Duchesse de Chaulieu. If you and I ever came across men of genius, they were too remote from our lives and too busy; we were too frivolous, too much carried away and taken up with other things."

"Ah! and yet I should not like to leave this world without knowing what it is really to love and to be loved," exclaimed the Princess.

"Provoking love in a man is easy enough," said Mme d'Espard. "The trick is to feel it oneself. How many women are mere pegs on which to hang a passion! They ought to be at once the source it flows from and the vessel to which it returns."

"The last passion that I inspired was something sacred and

noble," said the Princess. "A future lay before it. Chance, for this once, sent me the man of genius, our due—the due so hard to come by, for there are more pretty women than men of genius. But the devil took a hand in it."

"Do tell me about it, dear; this is quite new to me."

"I only discovered his fine passion in the winter of 1829. Every Friday at the opera I used to see a man of thirty or thereabouts sitting in the same place in the orchestra; he would look at me with eyes of fire, saddened at times by the thought of the distance between us and the impossibility of success."

"Poor fellow, we grow very stupid when we are in love," said the Marquise. The Princess smiled at the friendly epigram.

"He used to slip out into the corridor between the acts," she went on. "Once or twice, to see me or to be seen, he pressed his face against the pane of glass in the next box. If people came to my box, I used to see him glued in the doorway to steal a glance —he had got to know by sight all the people in my circle, and he would follow them so that when they opened my door he could take a look in. The poor fellow must have found out fairly soon who I was, as he knew the faces of de Maufrigneuse and my father-in-law. Afterward I used to see my mysterious stranger at the Italiens, sitting in a stall just opposite so that he could look up at me in unfeigned ecstasy. It was a pretty sight. After the opera or the Bouffons, I used to see him standing there motionless in the middle of the crush. People would elbow against him; he wouldn't budge. The light died out of his eyes when he saw me leaning on the arm of whoever happened to be in favor. As for anything else, not a word, not a letter, not a sign. It was in good taste, you must admit. Occasionally, when I came home after being out all night, I would find him sitting on one of the stone fenders of the gateway. He made a fine Unhappy Lover, with his wonderful eyes, his long, thick, fan-shaped beard cut like the King's, and his mustache and sideburns; you could see nothing of his face but the pale skin over the cheekbones and a noble forehead. All in all, a really classical head.

"The Prince, as you know," she continued, "defended the Tuileries, on the river side, during the July fighting. He came to Saint-Cloud the evening that all was lost. 'I was almost killed, my dear, at four o'clock,' he said. 'One of the insurgents had leveled his gun at me, when the leader of the attack, a young man with a long beard whom I have seen at the Italiens, I think, struck down the barrel.' The shot hit somebody else, a quarter-master, I believe, two steps away from my husband. So it was plain that the young fellow was a republican.

"In 1831, when I came to live here, I saw him leaning against the house wall. He seemed to rejoice over my calamities; per-haps he thought that they brought us closer together. But I never saw him again after the Saint-Merri affair; he was killed that day. The day before General Lamarque's funeral I went out walking with my son, and our republican went with us, sometimes behind, sometimes in front, from the Madeleine to the Passage des Panoramas, where I was going."

"And that was all?" asked the Marquise.

"All!" returned the Princess. "Oh, yes; the morning after Saint-Merri was taken, some boy came up and said he had to speak to me in person; he gave me a letter written on cheap paper and signed with the stranger's name."

"Do let me see it," said the Marquise.

"No, dear; the love in that man's heart was something so great and sacred that I cannot betray his confidence. It stirs my heart to think of that short, terrible letter, and the dead writer moves me more than any of the living men that I have singled out. He haunts me."

"What was his name?"

"Oh, quite a common one—Michel Chrestien."

"You did well to tell me of it," Mme d'Espard answered quickly. "I have often heard of him. Michel Chrestien was a friend of a well-known writer whom you have been wanting to meet—Daniel d'Arthez; he comes to my house once or twice in a winter. This Chrestien—who, as a matter of fact, died at Saint-Merri—did not lack friends. I have heard it said that he was one of those great politicians who, like de Marsay, need nothing but a turn of the wheel of chance to become at one stroke all that they ought to be."

"Then he is better off dead," said the Princess, hiding her thoughts beneath a melancholy expression.

"Would you care to meet d'Arthez some evening at my house?" asked the Marquise. "You could talk with him of your ghost."

"Gladly, my dear."

Some days after this conversation Blondet and Rastignac, who were acquainted with d'Arthez, promised Mme d'Espard that they would get him to dine with her. It would have been a rash promise, had they not been able to use the name of the Princess, whom the great man of letters was unlikely to refuse the chance of meeting.

Daniel d'Arthez is one of the very few men of our day who combine great natural gifts with great force of character. He had at that time won, not all the popularity that his work deserved, but a respectful esteem to which the chosen few could add nothing. His reputation will doubtless become even more widespread than it is, but in the eyes of connoisseurs it was already completely established; he is one of those writers whom the world may take its time about assigning to their true place, but who never afterward fall from it. Born of impoverished nobility, he had caught the drift of his age, and put all his stock not in birth but in personal merit. For many years he had fought his battle in the arena of Paris, to the annoyance of a rich uncle, who left the obscure writer to languish in the direst poverty. Afterward, when his nephew became famous, he left him all his money—a turnabout for which vanity was perhaps responsible. The sudden transition from poverty to wealth made no change whatever in Daniel d'Arthez's way of life. He continued his work with a simplicity worthy of ancient times, and laid new burdens upon himself by accepting a seat in the Chamber of Deputies, on the benches to the right.

Since his rise to fame he had occasionally gone into society. An old friend of his, the great doctor Horace Bianchon, had introduced him to the Baron de Rastignac, an Under-Secretary of State and a friend of de Marsay's. The two politicians had shown a certain high-mindedness in arranging authorization for Daniel, Horace, and a few other of Michel Chrestien's close friends to retrieve his body from the Church of Saint-Merri and to bury the republican with due honors. Gratitude for this favor (which stood out against the prevalent bureaucratic strictness of this period, when partisan feeling ran so high) formed a kind of bond between d'Arthez and Rastignac. The Under-Secretary of State and the illustrious Minister were too wily not to make good use of the incident for their own purposes;

thanks to it, they were able to win over several of Michel Chrestien's friends, who in any event did not share his political
views, and who now became supporters of the new government.
One of them, Léon Giraud, first received the appointment of
Master of Requests, and afterward became a Councilor of State.

Daniel d'Arthez's life was entirely devoted to his work. He
saw society by glimpses only; it was a sort of dream for him.
His house was a monastery in which he led the life of a Benedictine, with a Benedictine's sober rule and a Benedictine's
regularity of occupation. His friends knew that he had always
dreaded the accident of a woman's entry into his life; he had
observed women too closely not to fear them; but by studying
them overmuch he had lost all sense of what they were, resembling in this respect those profound students of military
tactics who, given circumstances not covered by their manuals,
are invariably beaten because their scientific axioms do not
apply. He presented to the world the face of an experienced observer, while at heart he was still a completely unsophisticated
boy. The seeming paradox is quite intelligible to anyone who
can appreciate the immense difference between mental faculties,
which proceed from the brain, and sentiments, which proceed
from the heart. A man may be great and yet a villain, just as a
fool may be a magnificent lover. D'Arthez was one of those
richly endowed beings in whom a keen brain and a wide range
of intellectual gifts have not excluded a capacity for deep and
powerful feeling. By a rare privilege he was both a man of action and a thinker. His private life was noble and pure. In keeping love at arm's length, he had known what he was about; he
knew beforehand in what a grip that passion would seize him.
For a long time, poverty, cold, and the exhausting labors that
went into laying a solid groundwork for those admirable books
of his had acted as marvelous safeguards. When his circumstances grew easier, he formed a commonplace and utterly incomprehensible connection; the woman certainly was good-
looking enough, but without manners or education, and socially
his inferior. She was kept carefully out of sight.

Michel Chrestien had maintained that men of genius possess
the power of transforming the most lumpish woman into a sylph,
the stupidest into a woman of wit, the peasant girl into a marquise; the more accomplished the woman, the more (according

to Chrestien) she loses in their eyes, because she leaves that much less play to the imagination. He also held that love, which for the lower order of beings is a mere physical craving, is for the higher among the most tremendous creations of the human spirit, and the most binding. By way of justifying d'Arthez, he instanced Raphael and the Fornarina. (He might have taken himself as a model of that kind—did he not see an angel in the Duchesse de Maufrigneuse?) But d'Arthez's strange fancy was explicable in many ways. Perhaps at the outset he lost all hope of finding a woman to correspond to the exquisite visionary ideal that is the fond dream of every intelligent man; perhaps his heart was too fastidiously sensitive for him to hand it over to the mercies of a woman of the world; perhaps he preferred, while giving nature its due, to keep his illusions and cultivate his ideal; or it may be that he had rejected love as incompatible with work and with the regularity of a cloistered life, in which passion would have upset everything.

For some months past, Blondet and Rastignac had twitted him on this score, reproaching him with knowing nothing of the world or of women. As they put it, his works were numerous enough and far enough along so that he might allow himself a little diversion; he had a fine fortune, yet he lived like a student; he had no pleasure from his fame or from his wealth; the whole subtle and exalted upper register of sensibility that comes into play for both partners to a love affair when one of them is a certain kind of highborn, highbred woman, was unknown to him. Was it not beneath him to know love only in its crudest forms? Love reduced to what nature made it was, in their eyes, the stupidest thing imaginable. It was the glory of civilization to have created Woman, whereas nature stopped short at the female; to have thought of perpetuating desire, where nature had aimed only at the perpetuation of the race; to have dreamed up, in short, the idea of love, the most attractive of mankind's religions.

D'Arthez knew nothing of the subtle charm that the words of this religion have, nothing of the ingenuity and feeling that go into proofs of love; nothing of the ceremonious forms by which desire is ennobled; nothing of the ways in which a woman of class can transform the grossest animalism into something unearthly. D'Arthez knew about women, perhaps, but not about

the spark of divinity they sometimes had in them. To make love
as it should be made, a woman needed to have a prodigious deal
of art and a wealth of resources for rigging out the spirit no less
than the flesh in proper finery. And so on. The tempters, ex-
patiating with relish on the breathtaking perversities of refinement that went into the art of love as Parisian women practiced
it, and pitying their friend, who lived on plain, wholesome, un-
seasoned fare, for not having savored the delights of Parisian
haute cuisine, worked on his curiosity. Dr. Bianchon, in whom
d'Arthez confided, knew that this curiosity was at last astir. The
great writer's liaison with a commonplace woman, far from
taking on for him the pleasantness of an old habit, had grown
intolerable; but the extreme shyness that afflicts solitary men
kept him from doing anything about it.

"Look here," said Rastignac, "the least a man can do when he
has an old Picard escutcheon like yours—what is it? *per bend
gules and or, a besant and a torteau counterchanged*—is to
show it off on a carriage. You have thirty thousand livres a year
plus what you make with your pen; you have one of those pun-
ning mottoes—ARS THES*aurusque virtu* [6]—for which our ancestors would have given their eyeteeth, and, after making it good,
you don't even trot it through the Bois de Boulogne! This is no
time for personal merit to hide itself under a bushel."

"If that cow you dote on," put in Blondet, "were at least
someone you could read your work to, I'd forgive you for holding on to her. But the fact is, old boy, if you live on dry bread,
physically speaking, intellectually you haven't so much as a
crust."

These friendly skirmishes between Daniel and his friends
had been going on for some months when Mme d'Espard asked
Rastignac and Blondet to induce d'Arthez to dine with her, saying as she did so that the Princesse de Cadignan was extremely
eager to make the famous man's acquaintance. Oddities of that
sort are for certain women what magic-lantern pictures are for
children—a treat for the eyes (and not much of a one at that)
which turns out to have been overrated. The more interesting a
clever man seems at a distance, the less he comes up to expectations on a nearer view; the more brilliant he is imagined to be,

[6] Loose translation: "Mastery and wealth through personal merit."

the less colorful the figure he cuts. And when people's curiosity is disappointed in this way, they are likely to resent it to the point of being unjust. D'Arthez was not a man to be fooled by Rastignac or Blondet, but they told him laughingly that here was a most alluring chance to rub the rust off his heart, to discover something of the supreme felicity that could be had through the love of a Parisian great lady. The Princess was positively smitten with him; there was nothing to fear; he had everything to gain from the interview; he could not possibly descend from the pedestal on which Mme de Cadignan had placed him. Neither Blondet nor Rastignac saw any harm in crediting the Princess with such sentiments; her past had furnished so many slanderous anecdotes that she could surely bear the weight of one more. For d'Arthez's benefit, they proceeded to relate the adventures of the Duchesse de Maufrigneuse. Beginning with her first flirtations with de Marsay, they told of her subsequent escapades with d'Ajuda-Pinto (whom she took from his wife, thereby avenging Mme de Beauséant); and of the affair (her third) with young d'Esgrignon, who went with her to Italy and got himself into a nasty scrape on her account. Then they told how wretched a certain well-known ambassador had made her; how happy she had been with a Russian general; how she had since played Egeria to two Ministers of Foreign Affairs; and so forth and so on. D'Arthez told them that he had heard more about her than they could tell him; their poor friend Michel Chrestien had secretly worshipped her for four years and had all but lost his wits because of her.

"I often used to go with him to the Italiens or the opera," Daniel said. "He and I used to rush along the streets to keep up with her horses while he threw admiring looks at the Princess through the windows of her brougham. The Prince de Cadignan owed his life to Michel's love for her; Michel prevented a street boy from killing him."

"Well, there you are, then; you have your subject of conversation ready-made," said Blondet with a smile. "There's just the sort of woman you need; if she's hard on you, it will be from nicety; she will initiate you into the mysteries of the fashionable life in the most gracious way. But watch out! She has a habit of running through people's fortunes. The fair Diane is one of these spendthrifts who don't cost a centime, but for

whom men spend millions. Give yourself body and soul if you
will, but hold on hard to your purse like the old man in Giro-
det's painting of the Flood."

This conversation invested the Princess with the grace of a
queen, the corruption of a diplomatist, the mystery of an initia-
tion, the danger of a siren, and the depth of an abyss. D'Arthez's ingenious friends, being quite unable to foresee the outcome of their hoax, ended by making Diane d'Uxelles out to be
the most prodigious of *parisiennes*, the cleverest of coquettes,
the most dazzling courtesan in the world. They were right; and
yet for d'Arthez the woman so lightly spoken of was sacred and
saintly. There was no need to excite his curiosity; he agreed to
meet her at the first asking, and that was all his friends wanted
of him.

Mme d'Espard went to see the Princess as soon as she had
her reply.

"My dear," she said, "if you feel in good form and disposed
to philander, come dine with me next week; I will serve you up
d'Arthez. Our man of genius is the shyest of the shy; he is
afraid of women; he has never been in love. There is something
for you to work on. He is extremely clever, and so simple that
he disarms suspicion and puts you at a disadvantage. His per-
spicacity is altogether of the retrospective kind; it acts after the
event, and throws off all your calculations. You may catch him
off guard on Monday, but on Tuesday he knows every trick in
your bag."

"Ah! if I were only thirty years old, I would have some
sport," said the Princess. "The one thing wanting in my life
till now has been a man intelligent enough to be worth out-
witting. I have always had partners, never an adversary. Love
was a game instead of a battle of minds."

"Admit that I am very generous, dear Princess; charity, they
say, ought to begin . . ."

The women looked laughingly into each other's faces, and
their hands met with a friendly pressure. What they had in the
back of their minds—a good deal—was, of course, something
else again. One favor more or less, one man more or less, probably did not make much difference in their accumulated private
accounts; for no friendship between women is sincere or lasting
unless it has been cemented together with petty crimes. Two

dear friends with murder in their hearts and poisoned daggers
in their hands present a touching picture of harmony—till the
moment when one of them, growing careless, drops her weapon.

When the week came round, the Marquise gave one of her
small evening parties, or *soirées de petits jours,* when a few intimate friends were invited by word of mouth and the hostess
shut her door to other visitors. Five people were asked to dinner: Émile Blondet and Mme de Montcornet, Daniel d'Arthez,
Rastignac, and the Princesse de Cadignan—three men and, including the mistress of the house, three women.

Never did chance deal from a more artfully shuffled deck
than when d'Arthez made the acquaintance of Mme de Cadignan.

Even at this day the Princess is supposed to be one of the
best-dressed women in Paris, and for women dress is the first of
arts. She wore a low-cut blue velvet gown with large white
hanging sleeves. A guimpe of slightly gathered tulle with a blue
fringe (such as one finds in some of Raphael's portraits) covered her shoulders and throat almost to the base of her neck. A
few sprigs of white heather, artfully arranged by her maid,
adorned the high-piled coils of her celebrated blond hair. She
did not look a day over twenty-five. Four years of solitude and
repose had restored a youthful clarity to her skin. And are there
not moments when a woman's desire to be thought beautiful
helps make her so? (For the physical changes that a face under-
goes are to some extent brought on by states of mind. It is
known that under the influence of strong emotion, people of a
sanguine or melancholy temper turn yellowish, while lymphatic
people tend to green. May not desire and hope and joy, by an
analogous power, work to freshen the skin, brighten the eye,
and add to natural beauty a shimmer as of morning sunlight?)
The lustrous white skin for which Diane was renowned had
taken on a rich coloring of maturity which gave her a majestic
air. Life had obliged her to reflect on her past and give serious
thought to her future; and her magnificent forehead, grown
pensive, harmonized to perfection with the slow, queenly gaze
of her blue eyes. No physiognomist, however skilled, could
have imagined that calculation and decision lay under these
preternaturally delicate features. Science breaks down and observation goes wrong before the impenetrable fineness and re-

pose of certain women's faces. To get anywhere, an observer would have to study them at moments when the passions speak, which is difficult; or after they have stopped speaking, which is no longer of any use, for the woman is old by then and no longer bothers to wear a mask.

The Princess was just such an impenetrable woman. Whatever she chose to be she could be. She was playful, childlike, distractingly innocent; or subtle, serious, and disquietingly profound. When she came to the Marquise's, it was with the idea of being a simple, sweet woman who had known life only by its deceptions; a soulful, much-slandered, but resigned victim —in a word, a cruelly used angel.

She came early so as to take her place beside Mme d'Espard on the settee by the fireside. She would be seen as she meant to be seen; she would arrange her attitude with an art concealed by an exquisite ease; her pose should be of the elaborate and studied kind that brings out all the beauty of the curving line that begins at the foot, rises gracefully to the hip, and continues through wonderful sinuous contours to the shoulder, outlining the whole length of the body. Nudity would be less dangerous than draperies so artfully arranged to cover yet reveal every line. With a subtlety beyond the reach of many women, Diane had brought her son with her. For a moment Mme d'Espard beheld the Duc de Maufrigneuse with blank amazement; then her eyes showed that she grasped the situation. She took the Princess's hand with: "I understand! D'Arthez is to be made to accept all the difficulties at the outset, so that you will have nothing to overcome afterward."

The Comtesse de Montcornet came with Blondet; Rastignac brought d'Arthez. The Princess paid the great man none of the compliments with which ordinary people are lavish on such occasions; but she treated him with a graciousness and deference that it was unlikely she would have carried further for anyone. Just so, no doubt, had she been with the King of France and with princes. She seemed pleased to see the great man of letters, and glad to have sought him out. People of taste (and the Princess's taste was excellent) are known by their manner as listeners; by an affability pure of derision, which is to mere politeness what continence is to virginity. Her attentive way of listening when d'Arthez spoke was a thousand times more flattering than the most highly seasoned compliments. The introduction was made by the Marquise simply and with no fuss.

Dinner was served. Where another woman would have put on a show of finicking about her food, the Princess ate heartily; she made a point of allowing the natural woman to appear without airs of any kind. D'Arthez sat next to her, and between courses she struck up a tête-à-tête with him under cover of the general conversation.

"I am particularly glad to be here with you," she said, "because of a hope that you may be able to tell me something of an unfortunate friend of yours who died for a cause other than ours. I was greatly indebted to him, but it was not in my power to acknowledge or to requite his services. The Prince de Cadignan shared my regrets. I heard that you were one of the poor fellow's most intimate friends; and the disinterested stanchness of your friendship was for me a high recommendation. So you will not think it strange that I should have wished to hear all that you could tell me of one so dear to you. I am attached to the exiled family, and of course hold monarchical opinions; but I am not of the number of those who think that it is impossible for a republican to be noble at heart. A monarchy and a republic are the only forms of government which do not stifle nobility of sentiment."

"Michel Chrestien was sublime, madame," Daniel answered with an unsteady voice. "I do not know of a greater man among the heroes of ancient times. You must not think that he was one of those narrow doctrinaire republicans who would like to re-establish the Convention and the Committee of Public Safety with its pretty ways. No, what Michel dreamed of was European federation on the Swiss model. If we set aside the magnificent monarchical system—which, in my opinion, is peculiarly suited to our country—we must admit that Michel's project would mean the abolition of war in the old world, and a Europe constituted afresh on a basis other than armed conquest, which was the underlying principle of the feudal system. The republicans were the people who, on this score, most nearly came up to his ideal; and for that reason he fought with them in July and at Saint-Merri. In politics we were diametrically opposed, but we were nevertheless the closest friends."

"It is the finest possible testimony to both your characters," Mme de Cadignan said timidly.

"During the last four years of his life he told me of his love for you. No one else knew about it," continued d'Arthez. "We had been like brothers; but that confidence bound us to each other even more closely than before. He was probably the only man who ever loved you as you deserve. How many times was I not soaked through as we accompanied your carriage home, racing to keep up with your horses so that we might look in and see you, feast our eyes on you. . . ."

"You make me feel, monsieur, that I owe you a great debt."

"If only Michel were still alive!" returned Daniel in a melancholy voice.

"Perhaps he might not have loved me for long," began the Princess with a sorrowful shake of the head. "Republicans are even more absolute in their ideas than we absolutists, who sin through indulgence. He dreamed of me as a perfect woman, no doubt; he would have been cruelly undeceived. A woman's life, you know, like a writer's, is plagued by slander; and, unlike you, we cannot defend ourselves against it by our fame and our achievements. People take us, not for the women we are, but simply as others make us out to be. Others would very soon have hidden the real, unknown self that there is in me by holding up a sham portrait of the imaginary woman who, in the eyes of the world, is the true Madame de Maufrigneuse. He would have thought me unworthy of the noble love he bore me and incapable of understanding him." Again the Princess shook her head with its coronet of heather among the bright golden curls. There was something sublime in the movement; it expressed sorrowful misgivings and hidden griefs that could not be uttered. Daniel understood all that it meant. He looked at her with quick sympathy in his eyes.

"Still," she said, "when I saw him again one day, a long while after the July uprising, I almost gave way to a wish that came over me to grasp him by the hand, then and there before everyone, in the peristyle of the Théâtre Italien, and to give him my bouquet. And then—I thought that such a demonstration of gratitude would be sure to be misconstrued, like so many generous acts that people call 'Madame de Maufrigneuse's follies'; it will never be in my power to explain them; nobody save God and my son will ever know me as I really am."

Her murmured words, spoken with an accent worthy of a great actress in tones so low that no one else would overhear them, could not help but move anyone; and they moved d'Arthez. He himself, the famous writer, counted for nothing in all this; it was for a dead man, his friend, that this woman was intent on rehabilitating herself. Perhaps people had slandered her to him; she wanted to know if anything had tarnished her name for this man who had loved her. Had he died with all his illusions?

"Michel was one of those men who love unconditionally," returned d'Arthez. "Such a man, if he makes an unwise choice, will sooner suffer for it than forsake the woman he has chosen."

"Then was I loved like that?" she cried, with beatific look.

"You were, madame."

"And he was happy through me?"

"For four years."

"No woman ever hears of such a thing without a feeling of proud satisfaction," she said, and there was a modest confusion in the noble, sweet face that she turned to him. (One of the cleverest maneuvers known to such actresses is a trick of blurring expression and gesture when words speak too clearly for themselves, and of making their eyes speak when language does not say enough; and these artful off-notes which they slip into the music of love have the same irresistible seductiveness whether the love is genuine or false.)

"Don't you think," she went on—her voice dropping lower and lower when she was sure of having produced the intended effect—"don't you think that when a woman has made a great man happy, and without wronging anyone, her destiny has been fulfilled?"

"Didn't he write to you?"

"Yes, but I wanted to be quite sure; for, believe me, monsieur, when he set me so high, he was not mistaken in me."

Women have an art of investing their utterances with a certain peculiar sacramental virtue; they can impart to their words an indescribable vibrance that gives them wider significance, greater depth; and, unless the charmed auditor subsequently takes it into his head to ask himself what those words really meant, the effect is attained—which is the special aim and object of eloquence. If the princess had worn the crown of France at that moment, instead of the high plaited coronet of bright hair and wreath of delicate heather, her brows could not have looked more queenly. She seemed to d'Arthez to be walking over the tide of slander as our Saviour walked over the Sea of Galilee; the shroud of her dead love wrapped her round as an aureole clings about an angel. There was not the remotest suggestion of her feeling that this was the one position left to her to take up; not a hint of a desire to seem great or loving; it was done simply and quietly. No living man could have done the Princess the service rendered by the dead.

D'Arthez, worker and recluse, had had no experience of the world; study had folded him beneath its sheltering wings. Her words, her tones, found a credulous listener. He had fallen under the spell of her exquisite ways; he was filled with admiration of her flawless beauty, matured by evil fortune, freshened by retirement; he bowed down before that rarest of combinations—a vivid intellect and a noble soul. He longed, in short, to be Michel Chrestien's heir and successor.

His love had its beginnings, as it usually does with men of a profoundly meditative cast, in an idea. While he looked at his neighbor, while his eyes grew familiar with the outlines of her head, the disposition of her delicate features, her figure, her foot, her finely modeled hands; while he saw her now on a closer view than in the days when he had accompanied his friend in wild pursuit of her carriage, he was thinking to himself that here was an instance of the wonderful faculty of moral insight which men have when they are under the exalting influence of love. How clearly Michel Chrestien had read this woman's heart and soul by love's blazing light! And she, on her side, had divined the federalist; he might, no doubt, have been happy! So it came about that the Princess was invested for d'Arthez with enchantment; an aureole of poetry shone about her.

In the course of the dinner d'Arthez remembered Michel's confidences, Michel's despair, Michel's hopes when he fancied that he was loved in return, and his passionate, lyrical outpourings to the one friend to whom he spoke of his love. That these chance preliminaries might work out to his own advantage had not occurred to Daniel. It is not often that a confidant can pass without remorse to the estate of rival; but as matters now stood, d'Arthez could do just that without wronging a soul. In one brief moment he realized the immense distance that separates the highbred lady, the flower of the great world, from the ordinary woman—whom, to be sure, he knew only by a single specimen. He had been approached on his weakest side, touched on the tenderest spots in his soul and genius. His simplicity and his impetuous imagination urged him to possess this woman; but he felt that the conventions of society held him back, and that the Princess's bearing, her majesty (to call it by its name), raised a barrier between him and her. It was something new to him to respect a woman he loved; and her charm was for him all the more potent, all the more corrosive, for the odd obligation under which he found himself to keep silent.

They talked of Michel Chrestien till dessert was served. It was an excuse for lowering their voices on either side. Love, sympathy, intuition—here was her opportunity of posing as a slandered, unappreciated woman! Here was his chance of stepping into the dead republican's shoes! Could it be (this soul of straightforwardness may have caught himself thinking) that he was becoming less sorry his friend was dead?

But when the dessert shone resplendent on the table, when the light of the candles in the sconces fell upon the rich colors of fruits and sweets among the bouquets of flowers, then, under shelter of the brilliant screen of blossoms that separated the guests, it pleased the Princess to put an end to confidences. With a word, a ravishing word, accompanied by one of those glances which seem to turn a fair-haired woman into a brunette, she found some subtle way of expressing the idea that Daniel and Michel were twin souls. Whereupon d'Arthez threw himself into the general conversation with childlike exuberance and a slightly fatuous air not unworthy of a schoolboy.

The Princess took d'Arthez's arm in the simplest way when they returned to the Marquise's little drawing-room. She held back a bit as they were going through the grand salon, till the Marquise, on Blondet's arm, was some distance ahead of them. There she stopped d'Arthez.

"I do not wish to be inaccessible to that poor republican's friend," she said. "I have made it a rule to receive no one, but you shall be the one exception. Do not think of this as a favor.

Favors are only possible between strangers, and it seems to me that we are old friends. I wish to look on you as Michel's brother."

D'Arthez could reply only by a pressure of the arm; he found nothing to say.

Coffee was served. Diane de Cadignan wrapped herself with coquettish grace in a large shawl and rose to go. Blondet and Rastignac, being diplomats and men of the world, made no motion to detain her by any ill-bred protest; but Mme d'Espard, taking the Princess by the hand, induced her to sit down again.

"Wait till the servants have dined," she whispered; "the carriage is not ready."

She made a sign to the footman, who carried out the coffee tray. Mme de Montcornet, guessing that Mme d'Espard wished to speak with the Princess, drew off d'Arthez, Rastignac, and Blondet by one of those wild paradoxical tirades at which *parisiennes* have so wonderful a knack.

"Well?" asked the Marquise. "What do you think of him?"

"He is just an adorable child; he is scarcely out of swaddling clothes. No, I can tell; it will be the same story all over again—a victory without a struggle."

"It is disheartening," said Mme d'Espard, "but there is one thing left to try."

"And that is?"

"Let me be your rival."

"As you please. My mind is made up. Genius is a certain way the mind works; I don't know what the heart gains by it. Suppose we talk about that another time."

Taking her cue from these indecipherable last words, Mme d'Espard plunged back into the general conversation. She gave no sign either of having been hurt by Diane's "As you please" or of being curious to know what would come of the interview. The Princess stayed nearly an hour longer on the settee by the fireside. She sat in a nonchalant and careless attitude, like Dido in the picture by Guérin; and while she seemed to be absorbed in listening, she glanced now and again at Daniel with undisguised yet well-controlled admiration. The carriage was announced. She grasped the Marquise d'Espard's hand, nodded to Mme de Montcornet, and slipped out.

No further mention was made of the Princess in the course of the evening. The rest of the party, however, reaped the benefit of d'Arthez's uplifted mood; he talked his best; and, indeed, in Rastignac and Blondet he had two supporters of the first rank for quickness and versatility of mind, while the two women had long since been counted among the wittiest great ladies in Paris. To them that evening was like a halt at an oasis, a blessed relief from the taut, tightly buttoned atmosphere of public stage, political arena, and fashionable salon; and they keenly appreciated it. Some people are privileged to shine like beneficent stars upon others, giving light to their minds and warmth to their hearts. D'Arthez was one of these finer natures. A man of letters, if he rises to the height of his position, is accustomed to think without restraint, and likely to forget in society that everything must not be said; still, as there is almost always a certain originality about his divagations, no one complains of them. It was this simple-minded freshness, this savor of originality (so rare in mere cleverness), that made d'Arthez's character something loftily apart; and therein lay the secret of that delightful evening.

D'Arthez came away with the Baron de Rastignac. As they drove home, the latter naturally spoke of the Princess and asked him what he thought of her.

"No wonder Michel loved her," returned d'Arthez. "She is a remarkable woman."

"Very remarkable," Rastignac returned dryly. "I can tell by the sound of your voice that you are in love with her already. You will call before three days are out; and I am too old a hand in Paris not to know what will pass between you. So, my dear Daniel, I beg you not to fall into any confusion of interests. Make love to the Princess if it is love that you feel for her; but keep an eye on your pocketbook. She has never asked or taken two centimes of any man whatsoever; she is far too much a Cadignan and a d'Uxelles for that; but to my certain knowledge she has not only squandered a very considerable fortune of her own, she has made others run through millions. How? Why? By what means? Nobody knows. She does not know herself. Thirteen years ago I saw her take a charming young fellow and, in the space of twenty months, swallow down every last penny he had, and an old notary's savings to boot."

"Thirteen years ago!" exclaimed d'Arthez. "Then how old is she?"

"Why, didn't you see her son?" Rastignac retorted, laughing. "That was her son at table—the Duc de Maufrigneuse, a young fellow of nineteen. And nineteen and seventeen make—"

"Thirty-six!" exclaimed the man of letters in amazement. "I took her for twenty."

"She won't object; but you need have no uneasiness on that score; she will never be more than twenty for you. You are setting foot in a world where nothing is impossible. Good night, here you are at home," added Rastignac, as the carriage turned into the rue de Bellefond, where d'Arthez lived in a trim little house of his own. "We shall meet at Mademoiselle des Touches's in the course of the week."

D'Arthez allowed love to invade his heart after the fashion of Uncle Toby.[7] Without the least attempt at resistance, he proceeded at once to uncritical adoration, admiring one woman to the exclusion of all others. The Princess—lovely creature that she was, and noteworthy even in a city like Paris, where no extreme of good or evil is lacking—became the "angel of his dreams" (worn out though the phrase may be). No one will understand the abrupt transformation that now took place in the illustrious author, who does not know for himself in what a state of innocence solitude and constant work can leave the heart. When love has consisted for a man merely in satisfying animal need with a woman of no account, and when this starvation diet has begun to wear on him, all sorts of extravagant fantasies and longings take possession of his mind; he becomes acutely aware that he has missed something; and there comes into play an exalted, fervent idealism of sentiment. D'Arthez was indeed the child, the schoolboy, that the Princess had at once made him out to be.

A very similar light had burst upon the fair Diane. At last she had found that man above other men whom every woman wants, if only to make game of him; that natural force to which (for once) a woman is willing to submit, if only so she may have the pleasure of bringing it under her control. Here at

[7] In Sterne's *Tristam Shandy*, of which Balzac, like Stendhal, was a devoted reader.

last was a great intellect joined with a simple heart—a heart never before touched by passion; and as if that were not enough, she saw (it was almost too good to be true) that the physical form in which these treasures lay was pleasing to her.

D'Arthez was handsome, she thought. Perhaps he was. He had reached the sober age of maturity; he had led a quiet, regular life that had preserved a certain bloom of youth through his thirty-eight years; and, like statesmen and men of sedentary life generally, he had attained a reasonable degree of stoutness. As a very young man he had borne a vague resemblance to the portraits of Bonaparte as a young general; and the likeness was still as strong as it might be between a dark-eyed man with thick brown hair and the Emperor with his blue eyes and chestnut locks. But all the high and burning ambition that once shone in d'Arthez's eyes had been softened, as it were, by success; the thoughts that swelled beneath the young man's forehead had blossomed; the hollows in his face had filled out. Prosperity had brought a glow into the sallow tints that once had told of a penurious life and of faculties braced to bear the strain of incessant and exhausting toil.

If you look carefully at the finest faces among ancient philosophers, you can always find that those deviations from the perfect type which give to each face a character of its own are rectified by the habit of meditation and the continual repose demanded by the intellectual life. The most crabbed visage among them—that of Socrates, for instance—acquires at last a well-nigh divine serenity. In the noble simplicity that adorned d'Arthez's imperial face there was something guileless, something of a child's unconsciousness of itself, and a kindliness that went to the heart. He had none of that surface polish in which there is always a tinge of insincerity, none of the art by which the best-bred and most amiable people can assume qualities that, much to the discomfiture of their belatedly enlightened dupes, often they do not have. He might sin against various social proprieties as a result of his solitary habits, but never so as to jar on anyone; and a tang of the undomesticated renders only the more ingratiating the natural affability that is peculiar to brilliant men. Such men have the knack of leaving their eminence at home and putting themselves on the same level as the people they are with. Like Henry IV, they are equally willing to let children climb on their backs and fools pick their brains.

It no more occurred to the Princess, as she went home, that there might be two ways about it than it occurred to d'Arthez that he might ward off her enchantment. There was no more to be said, so far as she was concerned; with all her knowledge and all her ignorance, she was in love. The only question she put to herself was whether she deserved such happiness. What had she done that heaven should send her such an angel? She would be worthy of this love; it should endure; it should be hers forever; her last years of youth and beauty should be sweet indeed in the promised land that now glimmered on the horizon. As for resisting, playing the coquette, quibbling about terms, no such thought crossed her mind. Far from it. She had sensed that genius had a grand way of its own; her instincts had rightly told her that a man of genius would not judge a woman in a thousand by common measures. Being such a woman, she made a swift estimate of the situation and promptly vowed to herself that she would surrender at the first summons. What she knew of d'Arthez from a single meeting led her to believe that there would be time to make what she wished of herself, to be what she meant to be in the eyes of this sublime lover, before that summons would be made.

And now began one of those recondite comedies—acted out in the private anterooms of consciousness by two personages, a man and a woman, of whom one is to be duped by the other—which push back the supposed limits of human perversity. By comparison with such dramas, made up in equal parts of the sinister and the comic, *Tartuffe* is the merest trifle; but they are not suited to the stage. Appalling as they are, they can not be called anything less than dramas of iniquity-turned-inside-out; and, as a final touch of the prodigious, they develop along perfectly conceivable natural lines and have their justification in human need.

The first thing the Princess did was to send for d'Arthez's books. She had not read a word of them; but had nevertheless talked about them for twenty minutes in the most flattering terms without once making a slip. She proceeded to read them through, and then tried to compare his work with that of the best contemporary writers. The result was a fit of mental in-

digestion on the day d'Arthez came. Every day that week she
had dressed with particular care, choosing her clothes in such
a way as to have them communicate, without his knowing how
or wherefore, a particular message. What she presented to his
eyes was a harmonious mingling of soft grays, the sort of
languid, graceful half-mourning that would befit a woman
weary of life and no longer attached to it except by one or two
natural ties (her son perhaps)—a woman whose elegant dis-
taste for living did not, to be sure, go to the point of suicide,
but who clearly felt herself to be rounding out her term in the
earthly prison-house.

She received d'Arthez as though she had been expecting him
and had seen him at her house a hundred times; she did him
the honor of treating him as an old acquaintance, putting him
at his ease in one stroke by the casualness with which she looked
up from a letter that she was in the midst of writing only long
enough to gesture him toward a settee. The conversation began
in the most commonplace way. They talked of the weather, of
the Cabinet, of de Marsay's bad health, of the hopes of the
legitimist party. D'Arthez was an absolutist. The Princess could
not but know the opinions of a man who sat among the fifteen
or twenty legitimist members of the Chamber of Deputies; so
she took occasion to tell the story of the trick she had played on
de Marsay; she touched on the Prince's devotion to the royal
family and to Madame; and thence, by an easy transition,
brought d'Arthez's attention to the Prince de Cadignan.

"There is this at least to be said for him," she observed: "he
is an attached and devoted servant of His Majesty. His public
character consoles me for all that I have suffered from him in
private life. But," she continued, adroitly disposing of the
Prince, "haven't you noticed (for nothing escapes you) that
men have two sides to their characters? One they show at
home, in private, to their wives—the true one; the mask is taken
off, dissimulation is dropped; they do not trouble to seem other
than they are; they are themselves—often they are horrible.
For the rest of the world, meanwhile, they are great, noble, and
generous; publicly, for the King and the court and the salons,
they wear a costume embroidered with virtues and bedizened
with fine language; they possess exquisite qualities in abundance. What a shocking farce it is! And yet there are people

who wonder at the smile some women wear, at their air of superiority over their husbands, their indifference. . . ."

She broke off, but allowed her hand to drop till it rested on the arm of her chair, a gesture that rounded off her little speech to admiration. D'Arthez's eyes were intent upon her slender figure; upon the lines so gracefully curved against the silken depths of her easy chair; upon the movements of her dress; upon a certain fascinating little gather of cloth over the waist— a brash touch that demanded a waist small enough to afford calling attention to itself. The Princess, watching him, picked up her thoughts a little further on, as though she were speaking to herself.

"But I shall say no more. Women who make a fuss about being 'misunderstood,' or who have married the wrong husbands and want to be thought dramatic and interesting because of it—women of that sort seem to me impossibly vulgar. And you literary people have ended by making them look thoroughly ridiculous besides. One must either submit, and there is no more to be said, or one resists and finds amusement elsewhere. In either case a woman should hold her tongue. It is true that I myself could not quite make up my mind to do either—which was all the more reason, perhaps, to say nothing. How stupid it is for a woman to complain! Women are never losers unless they have failed in tact or sense or finesse, and then they deserve to lose. Who but women rule France? They twist you men around their little fingers whenever they like, however they like, and as much as they like." And she gave a wonderfully feminine, impertinent, mocking, breezy little swing to her scent bottle.

"Often," she went on, "I have heard women—if you can call such creatures by that name—say they would give anything to have been born men; and I have always felt sorry for them. If it were up to me to choose, I'd still rather be a woman. Where in the world is the satisfaction of coming out on top when it is through mere natural strength and thanks to power put in your hands by a social code that you yourself have devised? But imagine the intoxicating joy it is for a woman, when men throw themselves at her feet and make perfect fools of themselves for her, to know in her heart that it is by her very weakness she triumphs! Obviously, then, a woman who succeeds should keep silent; if she doesn't, she is just playing into her captive's hands.

And if she fails, she should still keep it to herself: she owes it to her pride, for one thing; and, for another, it is by silence that the slave makes the master tremble."

These words were babbled forth in a voice of such sweet and gentle derisiveness, and with such pert little tosses of the head, that d'Arthez, to whom this species of woman was something absolutely new, sat there as if bewitched, exactly like some partridge hypnotized by a hunting-dog. What came from him at last was: "Tell me, madame, I beg of you, how any man could have made you suffer; and rest assured that what would be vulgarity in any other woman would in you be the height of good taste—not to mention that with your way of putting things you would make even a cookbook sound fascinating."

"You are rather hurrying matters, don't you think?" she said, so gravely that d'Arthez, perturbed, fell serious.

They talked about other things. It grew late. The man of genius, poor fellow, went away in a contrite frame of mind; he had seemed inquisitive; he had hurt her feelings; and he was convinced that she had known the rarest suffering. Suffering? Diane? She had spent her life looking for ways to keep herself entertained. A veritable Don Juan in skirts, she differed in one respect from the original: if she had tempted the stone statue, it would not have been with an invitation to supper, and not she but the statue would have come off second best.

A word must here be said about the Prince de Cadignan, better known as the Duc de Maufrigneuse; without it, the salt and savor of the Princess's marvelous machinations would be lost, and outsiders to Parisian life would miss the point of the sinister comedy that this woman was about to enact for the benefit of a man. In person, M. le duc de Maufrigneuse, like his father the Prince de Cadignan, was tall and spare; he was a complete fine gentleman, his urbanity never deserted him; he made charming speeches; he had become a colonel by the grace of God and a good soldier by accident. In other respects, the Prince was as brave as a Pole, showed his valor on all occasions without discrimination, and used the jargon of court circles to hide his mental vacuity. From thirty-six on, he had of necessity been as indifferent to the fair sex as his royal master King Charles X; for, like his master, he had found too much favor in his youth, and now he was paying the penalty. He had been the idol of the Faubourg Saint-Germain for eighteen years, during which time he led the dissipated, pleasure-filled life of an eldest son.

The Revolution had ruined his father; and though after the Restoration the elder Prince had recovered his post (including the governorship of a royal castle, with a salary and divers pensions), he had so insisted, during the brief gleam of prosperity, on keeping up the state of a great lord of the old days, and had squandered his fortune to such purpose, that all the sums repaid him by the law of indemnity went in a display of luxury in his immense old mansion. It was the only piece of property left him, and the greater part of it was occupied by his daughter-in-law. The old Prince de Cadignan died at the ripe age of eighty-seven, some years before the July Revolution. He had ruined his wife, and for a long time there had been a certain coolness between him and the Duc de Navarreins, his son-in-law by first marriage, to whom he could not satisfactorily account for the fortune of the bride.

The Prince's son (at that time Duc de Maufrigneuse) was the reigning lover of the Duchess d'Uxelles. Toward 1814, when M. de Maufrigneuse reached his thirty-sixth year, the Duchess, seeing that he was poor but stood very well at court, gave him her daughter, who had fifty or sixty thousand livres a year in her own right, besides what would be forthcoming from her mother. In this way Mlle d'Uxelles became a duchess, her mother knowing that in all probability the newly married wife would be allowed the greatest freedom. An heir was born, after which unexpected stroke of luck the Duke left his wife perfectly free to do as she wished, while he amused himself by going from garrison to garrison, spent the winters in Paris, contracted debts that his father paid, and professed the most complete unconcern about anything his wife might do. He always gave the Duchess a week's warning before returning to Paris. Adored by his regiment, in high favor with the Dauphin, an adroit courtier, and something of a gambler, the Duc de Maufrigneuse had no sort of affectation: the Duchess could not even persuade him (out of regard for appearances and consideration for her, as she so nicely put it) to take up with an Opéra girl. The Duke succeeded to his father's post at court and managed to please both Louis XVIII and Charles X, which

shows that he understood how to turn his vacuity to tolerably
good account. His life and behavior were covered by the most
elegant veneer; in language and fine manners he was a perfect
model; even the liberals liked him. The Cadignans, according to
the Prince his father, were famous for ruining their wives; in
this respect, however, he found it impossible to keep up the
family tradition, the Duchess contriving to go through her fortune unassisted.

These little details of the family history were public property
at court and in the Faubourg Saint-Germain; so much so, in
fact, that if anyone had begun to discuss them, he would have
been met with a smile. A man might as well have announced the
capture of Holland by the Dutch. No woman ever mentioned
the "charming Duke" without a word of praise. His conduct
toward his wife had been perfect; it was not a small thing for a
man to behave himself as well as de Maufrigneuse had done; he
had left the Duchess's fortune entirely at her disposal; he had
given her his support and countenance on every occasion. And,
indeed, from pride, or good nature, or from some sense of
chivalry, M. de Maufrigneuse had many a time come to the
Duchess's rescue on occasions when any other woman would
have gone under in spite of her connections, in spite of the combined credit of the old Duchesse d'Uxelles, the Duc de Navarreins, the old Prince de Cadignan, and her husband's aunt. The
present Prince is allowed to be one of the true nobles among
the nobility. To be loyal when his loyalty is needed is perhaps
one of the finest victories a courtier can win over himself.

The Duchesse d'Uxelles was a woman of forty-five when she
married her daughter to the Duc de Maufrigneuse, so it was
without jealousy, and even with a certain interest, that she
had for some time been a spectator of his other conquests. At
the time of the marriage she had acted with a high-mindedness
that offset the immorality of such an arrangement. But there
were people at court whose spiteful barbs fastened in that too;
according to them, the Duchess's magnanimity in making way
for her daughter did not represent much of a sacrifice; though
the fact was that she had just given some five years to the repentance and devoutness of a woman not lacking in things to be
forgiven for.

In the course of the next few days the Princess's accomplishments as a student of literature became increasingly impressive. Pursuing her studies day and night with an intrepidity worthy of all praise, she would venture with the utmost boldness, when d'Arthez came, into questions of the thorniest kind. D'Arthez was taken aback. Never dreaming that Diane (after the fashion of many writers) served up at night the pages she had read in the morning, he took her for a woman of really remarkable powers. In the course of these conversations they wandered further and further from the end that Diane had in view; she tried to return to the ground of confidential talk from which he had cautiously retreated; but it was not very easy to bring a man of his temper back to a subject after he had once been frightened away. However, after a month of literary forays and fine Platonic discourses, d'Arthez grew bolder and came every day at three o'clock. At six he took leave, only to return three hours later to stay till midnight or one o'clock in the morning; and this with the regularity of an impatient lover. The Princess, on her side, was always more or less artfully dressed at his hours. This mutual fidelity, the pains that they both took with themselves, everything about them, in fact, expressed feelings to which neither of them dared confess; and the Princess divined to perfection that the grown child feared the coming contest as much as she herself longed for it. And yet d'Arthez's manner was a constant declaration of love—a declaration made with a respect that gave the Princess no end of pleasure. Every day they felt all the more closely drawn together because the relation between them, never overtly defined, was free to develop unhampered by any explicit agreement as to where they stood; no barrier was raised, as frequently happens between lovers, by demands made for the sake of form on the one side and coquettish or sincere demurs on the other. Like most men whose youth lasts on into middle age, d'Arthez was consumed by a poignant irresolution caused by the vehemence of his desires and his dread of incurring his mistress's displeasure. A young woman understands nothing of all this while she shares the emotion, but the Princess had had too much experience of it in others not to linger over it appreciatively. So she delighted in his boyish fumbling, finding it all the more charming because she knew so well how to put an end to it. She was like a great artist, dwelling complacently on the vague outlines of a sketch, sure of the coming hour of inspiration that shall shape a masterpiece out of an idea that floats as yet in the limbo of things unborn. How many a time, when she saw d'Arthez ready to advance, she amused herself by checking him with her queenly air! She could control the tempest in the man's boyish heart, she could raise the storm and still it again, by a glance, by giving him her hand to kiss, by some commonplace word uttered in a soft, tremulous voice.

It was a cunning game, coldly thought out, sublimely played; her image more and more deeply etched itself upon his heart. It pleased her, when he was there, to transform the intelligent man of letters into a trustful, babbling, almost simple-minded child; yet there were moments when she had qualms and could not help but admire the sheer greatness that went along with all his innocence. The game imperceptibly bound the arch-coquette herself to her intended prey.

At length Diane grew impatient with her lovesick Epictetus; and as soon as she felt that she had brought him to the point where he would believe anything at all, she set about tying a thick blindfold over his eyes.

One evening Daniel found the Princess in a pensive mood. She was sitting with one elbow on the table, her bright golden head bathed in the lamplight while she toyed with a letter, absently tapping it upon the tablecloth. When d'Arthez had been allowed a full view of the letter, she folded it and thrust it into her sash.

"What is the matter?" asked d'Arthez. "You look troubled."

"I have heard from Monsieur de Cadignan," she replied. "Deeply as he has wronged me, I have been thinking, since I read this letter, that he is an exile, and alone; he is fond of his son, and his son is away from him."

Her soul seemed to vibrate through her voice; to d'Arthez it was a revelation of divine sensitiveness to another's pain. It touched him to the quick. His lover's curiosity passed over, as it were, into the curiosity of the literary man and student of the soul. If he could only know just how grand this woman really was, how deep the wrongs were that she had forgiven, how near the angels a woman of the world may rise while others accuse her of frivolity and selfishness and hardness of heart! Then he remembered that once before he had sought to know this angel's heart, and had been repulsed. He took up the slender, transparent hand with its tapered fingers, and said, with something like a tremor in his voice: "Are we friends enough now for you to tell me what you have suffered? Old troubles must count for something in your musings."

"Yes," said the fair Diane, prolonging the one syllable; Tulou's flute never sighed forth a sweeter sound. Then she drifted again into musings, her eyes clouded over; and as Daniel waited in anxious suspense, the solemnity of the moment penetrated his being. His poet's imagination beheld the cloud veiling the sanctuary; slowly the obscurity would clear away, and he should behold the wounded lamb lying at the feet of God.

"Well?" he said softly and quietly.

Diane looked into his face with its look of tender entreaty, then her eyes slowly fell, and the lashes drooped; the movement was a revelation of the noblest delicacy. A man would have had to be a monster to imagine that there could be a taint of hypocrisy in the sly grace with which Diane arched her throat as she lifted her head to direct another look deep into the great man's hungry eyes.

"Can I? And ought I?" she began, with a certain hesitation, and her face wore a sublime expression of dreamy tenderness as she gazed at d'Arthez. "Men keep faith so little in such things. They feel so little bound to secrecy."

"Ah! but if you cannot trust me, why am I here?" he cried.

"Oh! my friend, does a woman calculate when she binds herself to someone for life?" answered Diane, and there was all the charm of an involuntary confession about her words. "It is not a question of refusing you (what can I refuse to you?), but of what you would think of me if I spoke. I am more than willing to tell you of my position, a strange one at my age; but what would you think of a wife who should lay bare the wounds dealt her by her own husband and betray the secrets of another? Turenne kept his word with thieves;[8] ought I not to show the honor of a Turenne toward those who tortured me?"

[8] The Vicomte de Turenne (1611–75), a great French general to whom legend attributes this punctilious regard for his word of honor.

"Have you given your word to anyone?"

"Monsieur de Cadignan thought it unnecessary to ask for secrecy. Would you have more of me, then, than my heart and soul? Ah! Tyrant that you are, what you ask is no less than that I turn over my honor itself to your keeping." And her glance made the pretended confidence seem something greater than the gift of her person.

"You rate me rather too low if you can fear any wrong whatsoever from me," he said with ill-disguised bitterness.

"Forgive me, my friend," she said. She took his hand in hers, caressing it with the gentlest of fingers. "I know all your worth. You have told me the story of your life; it is a noble, a beautiful story; it is sublime, it is worthy of your name; perhaps I owe you mine in return. But at the moment, I am afraid of lowering myself in your eyes by telling secrets that are not mine only. And, poet and lonely thinker as you are, perhaps you may not believe in the horrors that the world contains. Does it ever occur to you writers, when you invent your tragedies for the stage, that tragedies far more terrible are being acted out within the most closely knit (or so it appears) of flesh-and-blood families? No, the amount of misery that lies hidden behind gilded fronts is something you know nothing about."

"I do know!" he cried. "All of it!"

"No, nothing," she answered. "Has a daughter ever the right to betray her mother?"

At these words of hers d'Arthez felt like a man who, having lost his way in darkness among the Alps, finds himself, at the first glimmer of dawn, on the brink of a bottomless abyss. He looked with dazed eyes at the Princess, and a cold chill crept over him. For a moment Diane thought that the man of genius was a weakling; but a flash in his eyes reassured her.

"And now you are almost like a judge for me," she said despairingly. "And I may speak; for every slandered creature has a right to prove its innocence. I have been—indeed, I am still, if anyone remembers a poor recluse, a woman forced by the world to renounce the world—accused of such scandalous conduct, of so many sins, that perhaps I have a right now, before a heart that has become for me a refuge from which I hope never to be driven forth, to show myself for what I am. Self-justification has always seemed to me to raise serious doubts of a person's innocence; for that reason I have always scorned to speak up in my own defense. And to whom, in any event, could I have spoken? Things so painful should not be confided to anyone but God, or to someone who seems very close to Him —to a priest, or to a second self. Ah, well, if my secrets are not as safe there," she added, laying a hand on d'Arthez's breast, "as they are here" (pressing so hard against the stiff rim of her bodice that it bent), "you will not be the great d'Arthez I took you for; I shall have been mistaken in you."

A tear rose to d'Arthez's eye; Diane seized upon it avidly, with a sidelong glance in which neither pupil nor eyelid seemed to flicker. It was as deft and neat as a cat's spring on a mouse. Then, for the first time, after sixty days of polite formalities, d'Arthez took the warm, scented hand, carried it to his lips, and set a kiss upon it—a slow, long kiss, from wrist to finger-tips, given with such exquisite rapture that the Princess, bending her head, augured very well of literature. In her opinion, men of genius ought to love more nearly perfectly than men of the world, coxcombs, diplomats, or even military men, though such people have nothing else to do. Connoisseur that she was, she knew that a man's character as a lover reveals itself by very small signs and tokens. A woman learned in this lore can tell from a mere gesture what she can look forward to, much as Cuvier could examine a fragment of a fossil foot and say: "This belonged to an animal that lived so many thousand years ago; it had (or had not) horns; it was amphibious, carnivorous, herbivorous," and so on. Sure that d'Arthez would put no less imagination into his love-making than into his literary style, she thought it essential to work him up to the highest pitch of passion and belief. Abruptly, with a gesture that was magnificent by the intensity of emotion it seemed to express, she drew back her hand. Had she said in so many words: "Stop! I can't bear it any longer!" she could not have expressed herself with greater force. For a moment her eyes rested on his; in the look she gave him were mingled joy, fear, prudery, trust, languor, vague longing, and a virgin's tremulous modesty. At that moment she was no more than twenty. She had prepared, you may be sure, for that hour's comedy of lies; never had a woman dressed herself with such art; and now, sitting there before him, she looked like some flower ready to open out at the first kiss

of the sun. Genuine or false, whichever she was, Daniel was
intoxicated by her. And why not? (I for one—if I may take
the liberty of speaking for myself—can think of no more agreeable way to be duped, and the longer the better.) To be sure,
the Princess was no Talma, whose histrionic artifice often left
nature far behind; but was she not the greatest actress of her
day? The only thing she lacked was an appreciative public.
For the unfortunate fact is that, in periods stormy with political
strife, women disappear from view; they are like water lilies,
which must have blue skies and the gentlest of warm breezes if
they are to blossom forth for our delight.

The hour had come. Diane was about to entangle the great
man in the inextricable toils of a cunningly worked-out fiction;
and he was to listen to it as a neophyte in the palmy days of
Christian faith might have listened to the message of an apostle.

"My mother, who is still living at Uxelles, married me in
1814 to Monsieur de Maufrigneuse when I was seventeen years
old (you see, my friend, how old I am). She made the match out
of love not for me but for him. He was the only man she had
ever cared for; so she repaid him in this way for all the happiness that he had given her. Oh, you needn't be horrified; ugly
as it may be, that sort of thing is done all the time. Many
women are better mistresses than mothers, and most are better
mothers than wives. The two kinds of love, sexual and maternal,
highly developed as they both are in the world we live in, often
conflict in a woman's heart. It is inevitable that one of them
should gain the upper hand, unless both are equally strong;
but that rarely happens—the few women in whom you find it
are the glory of our sex. A man of your genius surely will understand these things; fools wonder at them, yet they are none
the less true. I will go further: they are justifiable by differences
in character, temperament, situation, and the nature of the attachment. If I myself, for instance, at this moment—after
twenty years of misfortune, and disappointment, and heavy
trials, and hollow pleasures, and slander I could not refute—if
I were offered a true and lasting love, might I not feel ready to
fling myself at the feet of the man who offered it? And if I did,
would not the world condemn me? And yet, surely twenty years
of wretchedness ought to buy absolution for ten years or so
given to a pure and hallowed love—the ten years of life that

remain before I fade? But it will not be; I am not foolish
enough to diminish my merits in the eyes of God. I have borne
the burden and heat of the day until evening; I will finish my
day; I shall have earned my reward. . . ."

"What an angel!" thought d'Arthez.

"In short, though the Duchesse d'Uxelles cared more for de
Maufrigneuse than for the poor Diane whom you see before you,
I have never held it against her. My mother had scarcely seen
me; she had forgotten me; but her behavior to me, as between
woman and woman, was bad; and what is bad between woman
and woman becomes abominable between mother and daughter.
Mothers that lead such a life as the Duchesse d'Uxelles led keep
their daughters at a distance. I 'came out' only fourteen days
before my marriage. Judge for yourself what sort of innocent
I must have been! I knew nothing; I was incapable of guessing
what was behind the match. I had a fine fortune—sixty thousand livres a year from forests, which they either could not sell
or had forgotten to sell during the Revolution, and the Château
d'Anzy, in the Nivernais, to which the forests belonged; Monsieur de Maufrigneuse was head over ears in debt. If I afterward
came to understand what debts meant, I was too completely
ignorant of life at that time to suspect the significance of the
word. The accumulated interest of my fortune went to pacify
my husband's creditors.

"Monsieur de Maufrigneuse was thirty-eight years old when
I was married to him; but those years were like years of active
service for a soldier, they should have counted double. Oh, he
was far more than seventy-six years old. My mother at the age
of forty had not yet wholly done with men, and I found myself
caught between his jealousy and hers. What a life I led for the
next ten years! Ah! if people but knew how the poor, much-
suspected young wife suffered! To be watched over by a mother
who was jealous of her own daughter! Lord! You writers of
tragedies will never invent a drama so dark and so cruel! I
think, from the little I know of literature, that a play as a rule
is a series of events, speeches, and actions that lead up to the
catastrophe; but this thing of which I am speaking to you was
just a catastrophe without end. It was as if the avalanche that
fell this morning should fall again at night—and yet again next
morning. A cold shudder runs through me while I speak of it,

while I light up for you that cavern from which there was no escape, the cold, gloomy place that was my home. If you must know all, the birth of my child—altogether mine, indeed, for you must surely have been struck by his likeness to me?— he has my hair, my eyes, the outline of my face, my mouth, my smile, my chin, my teeth—well, my child's birth was owing either to chance or to some prearrangement between my mother and my husband. For a long time after my marriage I was the next thing to a virgin bride; I was abandoned, you might say, the morning after, to become a mother without really having become a woman. The Duchess was pleased to prolong the period of ignorance, and to attain this end a mother has horrible advantages. As for me, a poor little creature brought up like some mystic rose in a convent, I knew nothing of what marriage meant. I developed late, and felt very happy; I rejoiced over the good understanding and the harmony that prevailed in the family. I did not care much for my husband, and he took no pains to please me; and at length my thoughts were altogether diverted from him by the first joys of motherhood, which I felt all the more keenly because I had no suspicion that there could be joys of another sort. So much had been dinned into my ears about the respect that a mother owed herself! And besides, a girl always loves to 'play mama.' For a grown-up girl, which is what I was at the time, a baby takes the place of a doll. And I was so proud of him, he was such a lovely little thing—oh, wonderfully beautiful! How could one think of society while one had the pleasure of nursing and taking care of a little angel? I adore little children while they are tiny and pink and white. So I saw no one but my baby; I lived with him; I would not allow his nurse to dress or undress him or to change his diapers. The little cares that grow so wearisome to the mother of a regiment of babes were all pure pleasure to me. But after three or four years, as I am not altogether stupid, the light dawned on me in spite of all the pains they took to blindfold my eyes. Can you imagine me when the awakening came, four years afterward, in 1819? By comparison with the situation that arose then between the Duchess and myself—mother and daughter, mind you!—Racine's tragedy of fraternal hatred [9] is a mere bedtime story. I defied both her and my husband by

[9] Presumably *La Thébaïde ou les Frères ennemis.*

flirting publicly in a way that made people talk. Lord knows how they did talk! You can understand, my friend, that the men with whom I was accused of carrying on were for my purposes so many daggers to be wielded against an enemy. My thoughts were so full of revenge that I did not feel the wounds I inflicted on myself. I was innocent as a child; people looked upon me as a depraved woman, the most corrupt woman on the face of the earth; and I knew nothing.

"The world is very stupid, very ignorant, very blind. People only penetrate into the secrets that amuse them and serve their spite; but when the greatest and noblest things are to be seen, they put their hands before their eyes. And yet it seems to me that as I was in those days, with my fiery expressions, the surges of pride that used to run through my body, my gestures of outraged innocence, I would have been a godsend to some great painter. My storms of anger must have flashed like lightning through a ballroom; my disdain must have poured out like a flood. It was wasted passion. Nothing save the indignation of twenty years can rise to such sublime poetic heights. As we grow older we cannot feel indignant, we are tired; evil does not surprise us; we grow cowardly and afraid. What didn't I do then! I stopped at nothing. And—was there ever such a fool?— I brought blame on myself for wrongs I had never had the benefit of committing! I took such delight in compromising myself! I did things just from spite, the way children do.

"I went to Italy with a harebrained boy; he tried to make love to me, so I threw him over; but when I found out that he had got himself into a scrape on my account (he had forged a bill), I hurried to the rescue. My mother and my husband, who knew what I was really after, kept a tight hand over me as an extravagant wife. Oh! that time I went to the King. Louis XVIII, though he had no heart, was touched. He gave me a hundred thousand francs out of the privy purse. The Marquis d'Esgrignon (you may have met him in society, he married a very rich heiress afterward)—the Marquis d'Esgrignon was saved from the serious trouble he had got himself into for me. This adventure, brought about by my heedlessness, made me reflect. I saw then that the principal victim of my revenge was myself. My mother and husband and father-in-law had everyone on their side; they stood to all appearance between me and the consequences of my recklessness. My mother knew that I was far too proud, too great, too truly a d'Uxelles, to do anything commonplace; about this time she grew frightened by the mischief she had done. She was fifty-two years old. She left Paris and went to live at Uxelles. Now she repents of her sins toward me, and expiates them by the most extravagant piety and by a boundless affection for me. But in 1823 she left me to my own resources, face to face with de Maufrigneuse.

"Oh, my friend, you men have no idea what it is to live with a worn-out rake. You don't know what goes on in a house when a man accustomed to having society women fawn at his feet comes home and, because there is no one to lick his boots, because he himself has gone dead, decides to be jealous. When I at last had de Maufrigneuse to myself, I tried, I tried to be a good wife. But at every turn I came up against the crabbedness of a mind gone sour, against an impotent man's temperamental peevishness, against the driveling puerility and the smug vanity of a man who was, to tell truth, the most tedious, maundering grumbler in the world. He treated me like a little girl; it gave him pleasure to humiliate me on every occasion, to crush me with the bludgeon of his experience, and to show me how completely ignorant I was. He mortified me at every moment. He did everything, in fact, to make himself detestable and to give me a right to deceive him; but for three or four years I was the dupe of my own heart and my desire to do right.

"Do you know what infamous quip it was that drove me back to my wild ways? Could your imagination ever furnish you with a piece of slander to equal those which go the rounds of good society? 'The Duchesse de Maufrigneuse has gone back to her husband,' someone remarked.

" 'Pooh! out of sheer depravity; it is a triumph to quicken the dead; what else was left for her to do?' replied my best friend, the relative at whose house I had the pleasure of meeting you."

"Madame d'Espard!" exclaimed Daniel, aghast.

"Oh, I have forgiven her, my friend. The quip was extremely clever, to begin with; and I myself may very well have made even crueller epigrams about other unhappy women who were quite as pure as I was."

Again d'Arthez kissed her hand. The sainted woman had

chopped her mother in pieces and served her up to him; the Prince de Cadignan (whose acquaintance we have previously made) had been put forward as an Othello of the blackest dye; and now she was acknowledging her own faults and scourging herself vigorously—all to assume, for the eyes of this guileless man of letters, that virgin estate which the most benighted of women tries at all costs to offer to her lover.

"You can understand, my friend, that my going back into society made a considerable stir; and I meant to stir up society a good deal more before I had finished with it. There were fresh battles to be fought; I had to conquer my independence and put Monsieur de Maufrigneuse's guns out of action. So with other ends in view I began to lead a wild life. I wanted to stupefy myself, to forget the reality of my existence in a fantasmagoric whirl. I made myself conspicuous, I gave parties, I put on high and mighty airs, I piled up debts. When I went home, it was to sink oblivious into the sleep of exhaustion. The world saw in me a beautiful, high-spirited, reckless woman reborn. But in this weary struggle to hold off reality by the force of dreams, I went through my entire fortune.

"The revolt of 1830 came just as this chapter out of the *Arabian Nights* drew to an end; and just at that time I found the pure and sacred love that (I am frank with you!) I longed to know. It was a natural enough longing—won't you admit?— on the part of a woman whose heart, after being kept down by so many pressures from within and from without, had awakened at last, at the age when a woman sees that she has been cheated of her due? I saw that so many women about me were happy through love. Oh! why was Michel Chrestien so much in awe of me? As if there were not enough ironic twists to my life without that! Well, what can one expect? When the crash came, I lost everything; I had not a single illusion left; I had pressed out the last drops of all experience, but of one fruit I had not tasted, and now I have neither taste nor teeth left for it. In short, by the time I was obliged to leave the world I was disenchanted. There was something providential in this, as in the insensibility that prepares us for death," she added, with a gesture full of religious unction.

"Everything that happened just then was a help to me," she continued; "the downfall and ruin of the monarchy made it easier for me to bury myself out of sight. My son makes up to me for a great deal. Motherhood compensates a woman for all the other sentiments of which she has been thwarted. People are astonished by my retreat, but I have found happiness in it. Oh! if you but knew how happy the poor creature before you has grown. The joys which I have not known, and shall never know, are all forgotten in the joy of sacrificing myself for my son's sake. Who could believe that what life amounts to for the Princesse de Cadignan is a nasty wedding night, and that all the adventures with which she is credited come down, in effect, to a little girl's defiance of two people's sinister passion? No one, obviously. And at this late date there is nothing that does not frighten me off. If genuine feeling, true and sincere love, were offered to me now, I should probably be driven by the recollection of so much falsity and wretchedness to repulse it, in the same way that rich men repulse the deserving poor because some hypocritical knave has disgusted them with charity. All this is horrible, is it not? But, believe me, what I have told you is the story of many another woman."

She gave to these closing words an intonation of breezy pertness that recalled the flippant woman of fashion. D'Arthez was struck dumb. The convict sent to prison for robbery and murder with aggravating circumstances or for forging a signature on a bill had become in his eyes a saintly innocent compared with men and women of the world. Coming from the Princess, the monstrous threnody, forged in the arsenal of falsehood and tempered in the waters of the Parisian Styx, had the inimitable ring of truth. D'Arthez stared at her. The adorable woman, apparently crushed by her own revelations, had sunk back deep into her chair; from its arms her hands hung limp, like dewdrops on the petal of a flower. She seemed to have lived again through all her past sorrows as she spoke of them, and now they had overwhelmed her. Why, she was a veritable angel of melancholy!

Suddenly she sat bolt upright and, raising her hand, while from her eyes flashed the blaze of twenty years' self-imputed chastity, she cried out: "Judge for yourself then of the impression that your friend's love must have made on me! But by the savage irony of fate—or was it God's irony?—he died; he died just when (I confess it) I so thirsted for love that any man—

any real man, that is—who had been worthy of me might have had me for the asking; he died to save the life of another, and that other was—yes—Monsieur de Cadignan! Does it astonish you that I seem to have something on my mind?"

It was the last stroke. Poor d'Arthez could bear no more. He fell on his knees before her, he hid his face in her hands, and he wept—wept the bland tears that might be shed by angels, if angels cried. And since Daniel's face was hidden, Mme de Cadignan could allow a mischievous smile of triumph to steal across her mouth—a smile such as monkeys might summon up over a piece of superlative mischief, if monkeys laughed.

"I have him!" went through her mind. True enough, she had him.

"Why, you . . . you are . . ." he began, raising that fine head of his and gazing with adoration into her eyes.

"Virgin and martyr," she finished for him, smiling at the homely pompousness of the old tag-line, but lending to it, by the smile's acrid gaiety, the enchantment of a new sense. "I laugh," she said, "because I am thinking of the Princess as the world knows her, of that Duchesse de Maufrigneuse to whom the world assigns de Marsay as a lover; and that infamous cut-throat politician de Trailles; and harebrained little d'Esgrignon, and Rastignac, and Rubempré, and ambassadors and cabinet ministers and Russian generals—and all Europe, for anything I know. There has been much gossip about this album that I had made; people believe that all my admirers were my lovers. Oh! it is shocking! I cannot think how I can suffer a man at my feet; I ought to despise them all; that should be my creed."

She rose and went to the window; not a motion of her body but was magnificent in its eloquence.

D'Arthez started to get up from the hearth-stool where he was sitting, then sat down again. He did not dare go after the Princess, but he followed her with his eyes, he heard her use her handkerchief. Handkerchief? What princess ever blew her nose? Diane was doing the inconceivable to make d'Arthez believe she was a woman of great feeling. He thought his angel was in tears. He rushed to her, put his arms around her, pressed her to him.

"No, no, leave me," she murmured faintly. "I have too many

doubts to be good for anything. The task of reconciling me
with life is beyond a man's strength."

"Diane! Believe me, my love for you will more than make up
for all the life that you have lost!"

"No, do not talk to me like that," she answered. "I feel
ashamed; I am trembling as if I had committed the worst of
sins."

There was absolutely nothing now to hint that she was not
spotless as a babe; and yet she stood there before him grand
and august and noble as a queen. Her artifice had succeeded
beyond words; with such skill had she brought it off that now,
received into d'Arthez's fresh and unspoiled mind, it became
the purest truth. Great man of letters that he was, he stood
dumb with admiration, a passive spectator waiting for a word,
while the Princess waited for a kiss. But she had grown too
sacred to him for that. Diane felt cold in the window; her feet
were freezing; she went back to her chair.

"He will be a long while about it," she said to herself, looking at Daniel, her head high, her face sublime with virtue.

"Is she a woman?" the profound observer of human nature
was asking of himself. "How should one act with her?"

They spent till two o'clock in the morning in the fond, foolish
talk that women of genius like the Princess know how to make
enchanting. She was too old, she said, too faded, too much of a
wreck; d'Arthez proved to her (as if she were in any doubt!)
that she had the most delicate, soft, and fragrant skin, a delight
to touch and white and fair to see; she was young, she was in
her prime. Her beauty was disputed charm by charm, detail by
detail, with: "Do you think so? . . . Don't be ridiculous! . . .
You are blinded by love. . . . In a fortnight you will see me
as I am. No, really, I am close to forty. . . . How can a man
love a woman as old as I am? . . ."

D'Arthez was impetuous as a schoolboy, his eloquence was
bestrewn with the most extravagant words. Hearing the brilliant
man of letters babble like a lovesick second lieutenant, the
Princess, inwardly laughing, listened as if deeply moved, with
an air of rapt intentness.

Out in the street, d'Arthez asked himself whether he ought
not to have been more forward. He went over in his mind the
Princess's strange confidences (reported here, of course, in

much abridged form, for nothing less than a volume could do justice to them in all their mellifluous profusion and with all their intricate byplay). And the more closely this profound observer brought to bear on them in retrospect his keen eye for unsophisticated human truth, the more profound, humanly speaking, and the more plausible in its accents of sincerity, did he find the Princess's fiction.

"It is true," he said to himself as he lay sleepless, "it is true, then, that such dramas as this lie hidden within the life of society. What, if not masks covering just such horrors, are society's fine-feathered elegance, its ornate fabric of petty scandal, the hard, flashing surfaces of its talk? We writers think we dream up our stories, but they exist without us. Poor Diane! Michel's hunch was right when he said that beneath the enigmatic icecap there were volcanoes. And Bianchon and Rastignac are right too: what greater happiness indeed can there be for a man than to achieve, by loving a high-spirited, highbred, exquisite woman, the fulfillment in one and the same person of spiritual aspiration and physical desire?"

He tried to fathom the love that was in his heart, and he found it bottomless.

Toward two o'clock the next day Mme d'Espard, who had not seen or heard from the Princess in over a month and who could no longer contain her curiosity, came to call. The first half-hour of the conversation between this serpentine pair was a veritable treat. Diane steered clear of the subject of d'Arthez as sedulously as she would have avoided dressing in yellow; the Marquise circled about it like some Bedouin intent on a rich caravan. Diane lingered over the situation with relish; the Marquise fumed. Diane the huntress was waiting for her chance —she meant to turn her dear friend to account as a retriever. The fact is that, celebrated alike as these two women then were, they were unevenly matched. The Princess stood head and shoulders above the Marquise, and the Marquise, in the privacy of her own heart, knew it. Therein, perhaps, resided the secret of the bond between them. The weaker of the two, biding her time under cover of a feigned attachment, kept her eyes open for the chance so anxiously awaited by every underdog to leap at the stronger one's throat and sink into it an exultant fang.

Diane, for her part, was not fooled. So far as anyone else knew, they were the fondest of friends.

The Princess waited; and as soon as she saw the question rise to her friend's lips she said:

"Well, my dear, I can't tell you how wildly happy I am, and all because of you. It is tremendous, indescribable. There is no word for it but heavenly."

"What do you mean?"

"Do you remember the long talk we had three months ago, out in the garden, on the bench, under the jasmine, in the sun? Ah! it does take a man of genius to know how to love. I would say without hesitation of my great Daniel d'Arthez as Catherine de' Medici said of the Duke of Alba: 'One salmon's head is worth all the frogs' heads in the world.' "

"No wonder I no longer see anything of you."

"Promise me, my angel, if he goes to see you, that you won't say a word about me," continued the Princess, as she took the Marquise's hand. "I am happy—oh! happy beyond words—and you know how far an epigram or a jest may go in society. A word can be fatal; some people can put so much poison into a word. If you only knew how I have wished during the past week that you too might know a passion like this! How lovely it is, and what a glorious triumph, when we women can bring to a close our lives as women—lie down to sleep, as it were—in the warmth of a pure, complete, unstinting, and devoted love; especially when one has spent so much of one's life looking for just that."

"Why do you ask me to be true to my best friend?" said Mme d'Espard. "Surely you don't think me capable of doing anything to hurt you!"

"When a woman possesses such a treasure, she so instinctively worries about losing it that she begins to have the wild ideas that fear puts into people's heads. I am being absurd. Forgive me, my dear."

A few moments later the Marquise made her exit.

"What a pretty hash she'll set about making of me now!" thought the Princess, seeing her go. "I hope she doesn't leave anything out. But I'll save her the trouble of tearing Daniel away; I'll send him to her at once."

Daniel came a few minutes afterward, at three. In the middle of an interesting conversation the Princess suddenly interrupted him, laying her beautiful hand on his arm.

"Forgive me, dear friend, but I might forget to mention something; it seems a silly trifle, yet it is a matter of the utmost importance. You have not set foot in Madame d'Espard's house since that day—a thousand times blessed!—when I met you for the first time. Go to her; not out of politeness, not for your own sake, but for mine. What if, on your account, she has come to hate me? It is not impossible that she does, if by some chance or other she has found out that ever since her dinner party you have scarcely been out of my house. And besides, dear friend, I should not like you to give up your social life and the people you know, nor your books and the other things that occupy you. I should be more outrageously slandered than ever. What wouldn't people say of me? That I am keeping you on a leash, that I am monopolizing you, that I am afraid of comparisons, that I want to be talked about again, that I am taking good care to hold onto my conquest because I know that it will be the last, and Lord knows what else. Who could guess that you are the only friend I have? If you love me as you tell me you do, make people believe that we are to each other as brother and sister and nothing more. But go on with what you were saying."

There was an ineffable sweetness in the way in which this charming woman arranged her gowns so they would fall in lines of the utmost grace; it always schooled d'Arthez into obedience. And the fine, subtle delicacy of the words she had just spoken touched him to the point of tears. Other women might haggle and contest possession of themselves inch by inch on divans; the Princess rose at once above all ignoble and vulgar bargainings to unheard-of heights of greatness. It was understood between them, in the noblest way, that they should be joined; there was no need for her to say so. There was no question for them of its being yesterday or tomorrow or today; it should be when they willed it upon either side, and with none of the interminable piecemeal stripping off of veils that characterizes the ceremony that common women call a "sacrifice." Such women doubtless know how much, by revealing them-

selves, they stand to lose; while, for a woman sure that she
stands to gain by it, the accomplishment of the rite is a triumph.

Diane's words had been vague as a promise, sweet as hope,
and nevertheless binding as a pledge. It must be admitted that
the only women who can rise to such heights are illustrious and
supreme deceivers like Diane; they are queens still when other
women bow to a lord and master. By this time d'Arthez had
learned to measure the distance that separates these few women
from the common run. The Princess never showed herself otherwise than stately and beautiful. The secret of her majesty lay
perhaps in the art with which a great lady knows how to divest
herself of every stitch, standing forth at last in her nudity like
some antique statue, at a moment when, if she kept on a shred,
she would be indecent. The bourgeoise always tries to cover
something up.

Bearing the yoke of love and borne up by the loftiest virtues,
d'Arthez obediently went to Mme d'Espard's. The Marquise put
on for him her most inveigling show of charm. She was very
careful not to mention the Princess; she merely asked him to
dine with her in a few days' time.

When the day came, d'Arthez found a good many guests assembled. The Marquise had invited Rastignac, Blondet, the
Marquis d'Ajuda-Pinto, Maxime de Trailles, the Marquis d'Esgrignon, the two Vandenesses, du Tillet (one of the richest
bankers in Paris), the Baron de Nucingen, Nathan, Lady Dud-
ley, a couple of particularly underhanded embassy attachés,
and the Chevalier d'Espard. The Chevalier was one of the most
astute personages in the room, and counted for a good half in
the schemes of his sister-in-law.

Maxime de Trailles turned to d'Arthez.

"You see a good deal of the Princesse de Cadignan, don't
you?" he asked with a laugh.

D'Arthez replied with a curt nod. Maxime de Trailles was a
buccaneer of a superior order; he feared neither God nor man;
he shrank from nothing. Women had loved him, he had ruined
them and made them pawn their diamonds to pay his debts; but
whatever he did was covered by a brilliant veneer, by charming
manners, and a diabolical wit. Everybody feared him, everybody despised him; but, as nobody was bold enough to treat

him with anything short of extreme civility, he was quite un-aware of it; or else he was just playing along with the general pretense. Thanks to the Comte de Marsay, he had risen to the top of the ladder. De Marsay, who knew Maxime from far back, had seen that he was cut out for certain jobs of a confidential and diplomatic nature; and Maxime in fact brought them off to perfection. D'Arthez had for some time now been sufficiently mixed up in political affairs to see clear through the personage; and he was perhaps the only man with character enough to say aloud about him what others thought to themselves.

"Id is for her, no tout, dat you neklect de Champer," put in the Baron de Nucingen.

"Ah! a man could not set foot in the house of a more danger-ous woman," the Marquis d'Esgrignon softly exclaimed. "My disgraceful marriage is her doing."

"Dangerous?" repeated Mme d'Espard. "You must not say such things of my best friend. Anything that I have ever heard or seen of the Princess seemed to me to be prompted by the highest motives."

"Pray, let the Marquis have his say," put in Rastignac. "When a man has been thrown by a spirited horse, he will pick faults in the animal and sell it."

The Marquis d'Esgrignon, nettled by this quip, looked at Daniel d'Arthez and said:

"Monsieur is not, I trust, on such terms with the Princess that we may not speak of her?"

D'Arthez said nothing. D'Esgrignon, who did not lack wit, furnished at Rastignac's request an apologetic portrait of the Princess that set the table in high spirits. D'Arthez, extremely puzzled, leaned over to Mme de Montcornet, who was sitting next to him, and asked her to explain what the merriment was all about.

"Well, judging by the good opinion that you have of the Princess, you are an exception; but all the other guests, it would seem, have been in her good graces."

"I can assure you that that view is totally false," returned Daniel.

"Yet here is Monsieur d'Esgrignon, of a noble Perche family, who was utterly ruined for her twelve years ago, and all but went to the scaffold besides."

"I know about that," said d'Arthez. "Madame de Cadignan rescued Monsieur d'Esgrignon from the assize court, and this is how he shows his gratitude today."

Mme de Montcornet stared at him, all but openmouthed with astonishment and curiosity. Then she threw a look at Mme d'Espard, as much as to say: "She has bewitched him!"

Mme d'Espard, during this brief exchange, stood protection for the Princess—in the manner of a lightning rod, which elicits bolts from the blue. When d'Arthez turned back to the general conversation, it was to hear Maxime de Trailles getting off:

"In Diane's case, depravity is not an effect but a cause. That accounts perhaps for her air of exquisite naturalness—she does not have to go looking for those super-subtle refinements of hers; they cost her no effort of imagination; they come to her no less spontaneously than if they were promptings of the most artless love; and you can not help believing her."

The remark might have been made to order for a man of the caliber of d'Arthez. It left nothing more to say, and no one ventured a further thrust at the Princess, who was apparently polished off for good. D'Arthez turned to de Trailles and d'Esgrignon; he had a roguish look.

"The worst thing of all about her," he said, "is that she tries to play a man's game. Like a man, she squanders dowries and bridal portions, she drives her lovers to the moneylenders, she ruins orphans, she bankrupts old families, she instigates crimes and perhaps commits them herself; but—"

Never in their lives had either of the two individuals addressed heard a spade called quite so brutally a spade. When the *but* came, it was like a blow; everyone at the table sat transfixed—forks in mid-air, eyes darting back and forth between the intrepid man of letters and the would-be assassins of the Princess's character—waiting in appalled silence for what should follow.

"But," d'Arthez went on, derisive and jaunty, "there is one thing to be said for her that can not always be said of men: When a man gets himself into a scrape on her account, she pulls him out of it and speaks no ill of him afterward. Why should not one woman, among so many, have her sport of men as men have theirs of women? Why should not the fair sex now and then take its turn at that game? . . ."

"Cleverness is no match for genius," said Blondet, addressing Nathan.

And, indeed, d'Arthez's avalanche of epigrams was like a barrage of artillery fire turned loose in reply to a rattle of muskets. The subject was hastily changed. Neither the Comte de Trailles nor the Marquis d'Esgrignon appeared disposed to take d'Arthez up. When coffee was served, Blondet and Nathan went over to him with an alacrity that no one cared to imitate, so difficult was it to reconcile admiration of his behavior with the fear of making two powerful enemies.

"It is no news to us," said Blondet, "that your character is as great as your gifts; but I must say that the way you acted just now was more than manly, it was godlike. Not to let oneself be carried away by one's feelings or imagination, not to make the blunder of rushing to the defense of the woman one loves —which everyone was waiting for, and which would have meant a triumph for these people, eaten as they are with their resentment of literary eminence . . . Ah! permit me to say that this is the supreme application of diplomacy to private life."

"What a statesman you are!" put in Nathan. "To avenge a woman without coming to her defense is as artful as it is difficult."

"The Princess is one of the heroines of the legitimist party," d'Arthez returned coolly. "Surely it is the duty of every decent man to champion her, *no matter what?* Her services to the cause would excuse the most reckless life."

"He's keeping his cards to himself," said Nathan to Blondet.

"Yes," added Rastignac, as he joined the group; "for all the world as if the Princess were worth it."

D'Arthez went to the Princess. She was waiting for him in an agony of anxiety. She had promoted an experiment that might prove disastrous. For the first time in her life her heart knew what it was to suffer and her body to sweat. Others would tell d'Arthez the truth, she had told him lies; if he should believe the truth, she did not know what she would do; for a character so noble, a man so complete, a soul so pure, a conscience so ingenuous, had never before passed through her hands.

In weaving her tissue of ugly lies she had been prompted

by a longing to know love in all its truth. She felt in her heart the stirrings of such a love—for d'Arthez; and, wanting to remain for him the sublime actress whom he had watched perform, she was doomed to play him false. When she heard Daniel's step in the dining-room, a tremor ran through her that shook the very marrow of her bones. Never, throughout a career that had been (for a woman of her rank) adventurous in the extreme, had she been so profoundly shaken; she knew then that what was at stake for her was her entire happiness. Eyes staring, she took in d'Arthez with one all-enveloping look; she saw clear through his outward form into his innermost soul; and what she saw there was that the bat's wing of suspicion had not so much as brushed against him. From vertiginous fear, Diane, her gamble rewarded, swung on the instant to a vertiginous rapture that was almost too much for her to bear. (Is there anyone who does not more readily endure affliction than withstand the effects of extreme joy?)

"Daniel!" she cried, rising to her feet and holding out her arms. "I have been slandered, and you have avenged me!"

Daniel, dumfounded by these words issuing from he knew not what invisible source, felt his head grasped by two lovely hands; the Princess kissed him reverently on the forehead.

"How . . . how did you know . . . ?"

"Oh, magnificent simpleton! Can't you see that I am mad about you?"

Since that day, neither the Princesse de Cadignan nor d'Arthez has provided any food for gossip. The Princess has inherited a sizeable fortune from her mother; she spends her summers with the great man of letters in a villa at Geneva, returning to Paris for a few of the winter months. D'Arthez is no longer seen in public anywhere but at the chamber. He very rarely publishes anything.

Is this where the story ends? Yes, for the clever reader; not for the one who wants to know all there is to know.

Translated by Ellen Marriage and Stanley Geist

DEATH OF A HERO

by Charles Baudelaire (1821–67)

Fancioulle was an admirable jester, and practically a friend of the Prince. But for people professionally dedicated to the comic, serious matters have a fatal attraction, and, though it may seem queer that the notions of fatherland and freedom should take firm hold of an actor's mind, Fancioulle one day joined a conspiracy formed by some discontented noblemen.

The world is never lacking in upright men ready to denounce to the authorities those individuals of irritable disposition who seek to dethrone princes and to uproot society without consulting it. The lords in question were arrested and, together with Fancioulle, fated to certain death.

I should willingly believe that the Prince was almost sorry to find his favorite comedian among the rebels. This Prince was neither better nor worse than others; but hypersensitivity made him, in many cases, more cruel and more despotic than

---

Baudelaire himself did not know quite what to make of the hundred or so assorted pieces—fables, parables, sketches, prose-poems, anecdotes, tales, and yet finally none of these—that he planned and partly wrote, toward the end of his life, for the volume assembled after his death as Le Spleen de Paris, *or* Petits Poèmes en Prose.

"Death of a Hero," first published in 1863, tends toward the parable: parable, in this case, on the nature of the histrionic art. Baudelaire had been fascinated since childhood by the idea of the comédien, *or professional actor: the figure and the calling identified themselves for him with the poetic imagination, which, striking certain postures before the universe, in effect "gave itself," by a kind of "sacred prostitution," to various theatrical roles. The theatrical role became for him, on the one hand, a species of artificial enchantment or paradise "veiling the terrors of the abyss," and, on the other, a way of grappling with those terrors in symbolic form, a ritual celebration of "the*

all those of his sort. He was a passionate lover of the arts, a
great connoisseur to boot, and downright insatiable in his need
for pleasures. Rather indifferent toward men and morals, a
true artist in his own right, he knew no dangerous enemy but
Boredom, and the peculiar efforts that he made to escape from,
or to defeat, this tyrant of the universe would certainly have
induced some severe historian to hurl the epithet "monster"
at him, had it been permissible, in his realms, to write anything
that did not tend solely to give pleasure or surprise, which is
one of the most subtle kinds of pleasure. It was the misfortune
of this Prince never to have at his disposal a stage grand
enough to display his genius. Many a youthful Nero whose
name and alacrity the centuries to come will never know is
stifled by limits too narrow. Improvident Providence had endowed this particular one with gifts greater than his estates.

Suddenly it was rumored that the sovereign meant to pardon
all the conspirators. The source of this rumor was the announcement of a great command performance in which Fancioulle was to play one of his main and most successful roles,
and which was to be attended, so the talk went, by the condemned noblemen—a manifest token, superficial minds added,
of the offended Prince's generous inclinations.

---

mystery of life," a species of truth that called into question and
might put to shame the world's established powers.

"The Rope" (1864) belongs rather with those trivial and
sordid metropolitan episodes—tableaux parisiens—that had
gone into the poetic substance of Les Fleurs du mal (1857),
where they had added up to "the stripping bare of a soul in a
big city, the stripping bare of a big city's soul" (Thibaudet).
What such episodes lost in poetic force by being rendered in a
dry, precise, and haughty prose they sometimes gained in the
hardness and causticity that were the reverse of the Baudelaire
most often presented to American readers.

The Paris that he stripped bare he knew from birth; it became for him a phantasmagoric town where the mind shuttled
between its own abysses. He left it, except for brief excursions,
just twice, taking the abysses along. The first time, at twenty,
his authoritarian stepfather, exasperated by his refusal to adopt
any career but writing, and alarmed by the young man's bohe-

Everything was possible on the part of so naturally and deliberately eccentric a man, even virtue, even clemency, particularly should he hope to find in them some unforeseen pleasures.
But to those who, like myself, had been able to fathom more
profoundly the depths of this sick and curious soul, it seemed
infinitely more probable that the Prince wished to judge the
acting ability of a man sentenced to death. He wanted to take
advantage of the occasion to make a physiological test of *capital*
interest and determine to what extent an artist's usual gifts
might be altered or modified by the extraordinary circumstances in which he found himself. Beyond that, was there in
his soul a more or less clearly formulated intention to forgive?
It has never been possible to clear up this point.

At last the big day came, and the little court unfolded all its
pomp. It is difficult to conceive, unless one has seen it with one's
own eyes, how much splendor the privileged class in a state of
limited means can display on really solemn occasions. And this
one was doubly solemn, first by the magic of the luxury displayed, secondly because of the mysterious moral interest that
surrounded it.

Fancioulle was particularly outstanding in silent parts, or
those involving little talk, which are often the principal ones in

*mian excesses, sent him off on what was supposed to be a sober-
ing voyage to the Indies. Abandoning ship at a port of call,
Baudelaire came back all the more obsessed by the remote
places of the mind with which he was already familiar. The
second time he left, it was as an exhausted old man of forty-
two, rotted by syphilis, taking refuge in Belgium from his
private Furies, and dreaming of a conqueror's return. He was
brought back a couple of years later, paralyzed and mute, to
die. Between times he had (among other things) set the course
of French poetry for almost a hundred years and created a
fundamental type of modern sensibility.*

OTHER WORKS: *Collected critical writings:* Curiosités es-
thétiques (*1868*), L'Art romantique (*1869*). *Personal writings:*
Journaux intimes *and* Correspondence (*posthumous, various
dates*). *Translations: The* Tales *and other works of Poe* (*1856–
65*). *Imaginative "treatise" on opium and hashish:* Les Paradis
artificiels (*1860*).

that sort of fairy-like drama whose purpose is to represent symbolically life's mystery. He came onto the stage with lightness and perfect ease, and this fact contributed to strengthening in the distinguished spectators' minds the notion of gentleness and clemency.

When one says of an actor: "There is a good actor," one uses a formula that implies that the actor can still be made out under his part; in other words, that skill, effort, and intention are still apparent. Now, if an actor succeeded in being, with respect to the character he is to impersonate, what the best statues of antiquity, miraculously animated, brought to life, walking, seeing, would be with respect to the general and imprecise notion of beauty, that would assuredly be an unusual and thoroughly unforeseen event. That night Fancioulle embodied a perfect idealization that it was impossible not to suppose alive, possible, real. The jester stalked hither and thither, laughed, wept, writhed, an indestructible halo around his head—a halo invisible for all but myself—in which, strangely conjoined, blended the shining rays of Art and the glory of Martyrdom. By means of I know not what special grace, Fancioulle introduced the divine and the supernatural even into the most extravagant buffoonery. My pen trembles and the tears of an emotion still vivid blur my eyes as I try to describe this unforgettable evening to you. Fancioulle was giving me peremptory and irrefutable proof of the fact that the rapture of Art is more capable than any other of veiling the terrors of the abyss; that genius can play-act on the edge of the grave with a joy that prevents it from seeing the grave, being lost in a paradise that excludes all ideas of grave and destruction.

The public, frivolous and blasé as it may have been, soon fell under the artist's overpowering sway. No one any longer had a thought in his mind of death, of mourning, or of tortures. Everyone gave in, without uneasiness, to the manifold pleasures that the sight of a masterpiece of living art offers. Outbursts of joy and admiration several times shook the rafters of the building with the force of rolling thunder. The Prince himself, enraptured, joined in the applause of the court.

Yet, to a sharp eye, *his* rapture was not unmixed. Did he feel vanquished in his power as a despot? Humiliated in his skill at terrifying the hearts of men and numbing their wits?

Frustrated in his hopes and mocked in his expectations? Such hypotheses—not exactly justified, yet not entirely unjustifiable —went through my mind as I observed the Prince's face, on which a fresh pallor was steadily deepening the pallor it customarily had, as snow falls upon snow. His lips grew more and more pinched, and his eyes were lighted by an inner fire akin to that of jealousy and spite, even when he was ostensibly applauding the talented performance of his old friend, the queer jester, who made such splendid jest of death. At a certain moment I saw His Highness lean over toward a small page-boy standing behind him and whisper something into his ear. The pretty child's playful face was illuminated by a smile; then he quickly left the Prince's loge, as if to acquit himself of an urgent errand.

A few minutes later a sharp, prolonged blast of a whistle interrupted Fancioulle in one of his finest moments, shattering both eardrums and hearts. And from the part of the theater whence the unexpected disapproval had burst, a child dashed out into a corridor with muffled laughs.

Fancioulle, jolted, awoke from his dream, closed his eyes, opened them again almost immediately—and they were immeasurably wider—then opened his mouth as if to take a convulsive breath, reeled forward a little, then backward, and fell dead on the stage.

Had the whistle, quick as a sword, really frustrated the executioner? Had the Prince himself guessed the deadly effectiveness of his trick? It may be doubted. Did he miss his dear and inimitable Fancioulle? It is sweet and right to believe so.

The guilty nobles had enjoyed their last play. That very night they were blotted out of life.

Since then, several mummers, deservedly praised in various countries, have come to play before the court of ——; but none of them has succeeded in evoking Fancioulle's marvelous gifts or in rising to the same *favor*.

Translated by Pierre Schneider

THE ROPE

by Charles Baudelaire

Illusions (my friend was saying) are as countless as the relations among men or between men and things. And when the
illusion disappears—that is to say, when we see the person or
the fact as it exists outside of us—we experience a strange feeling, made up partly of regret for the vanished ghost, partly of
surprise before the new, before the real fact. If ever there was
a phenomenon evident, banal, always identical, and of such a
nature that it cannot be misinterpreted, it is maternal love. It
would be as difficult to imagine a mother lacking maternal love
as a flame devoid of heat. Is it not perfectly legitimate, therefore, to attribute to maternal love all the acts and words of a
mother which relate to her child? And yet, listen to this little
story, which saw me singularly mystified by the most natural
of illusions.

Being a painter, I am led to look attentively at the faces and
facial expressions that I meet on my way: you know what
pleasure we painters derive from a faculty that renders life for
our eyes more vivid and more meaningful than for those of our
fellow men. In the remote part of town where I live, and where
large vacant lots overgrown with grass still separate the houses,
I often noticed a boy whose fiery and playful expression appealed to me from the very first above all others. More than
once he modeled for me; sometimes I would make a little gypsy
out of him, sometimes an angel, sometimes a cupid. I made him
bear the vagabond's fiddle, the Crown of Thorns and the Nails
of the Cross, and Love's torch. I finally took such enjoyment in
the urchin's merriness that one day I begged his parents, poor
people, to let me have him on the promise that I would clothe
him, give him a bit of money, and impose no other chores on
him than cleaning my brushes and running my errands. The
child, once cleaned up, became quite charming, and the life he
led with me seemed to him like paradise compared to what he
would have had to undergo in his parents' hovel. In all fairness,

however, I am obliged to say that the little fellow sometimes puzzled me by peculiar fits of precocious sadness, and he quickly showed an immoderate fondness for sugar and liqueurs; so much so that one day, noticing that in spite of my numerous warnings he had again committed some such theft, I threatened to send him back to his parents. After that I went out, and my business kept me away from home for some time.

Imagine my horror and my stupefaction when, on my return, the first thing to meet my eye was my little fellow, the playful companion of my life, hanging from the closet door! His feet were almost touching the floor; a chair, which he must have kicked from under him, was overturned at his side; his twisted head rested on one of his shoulders; his swollen face and wide-open eyes, with their frightening stare, first gave me the illusion of life. Getting him down was not so easy as you may think. He was already quite stiff, and I felt an unexplainable repugnance at the thought of making him suddenly fall to the ground. I had to hold up his whole body with one arm while with the other hand I cut the rope. But once that was done, it was not all over; the little monster had used a very thin string, which had cut in deeply; and now, in order to set his neck free, I had to pry with a pair of small scissors between the two rings of swollen flesh.

I neglected to tell you that I had called promptly for help; but my neighbors all refused to come to my aid, in keeping with the customs of civilized human beings, who—I don't know why—never want to get mixed up in a hanged man's business. At last a doctor came; he declared that the child had been dead for several hours. Later, when we had to undress him to prepare him for burial, the corpse's rigidity was such that we gave up the attempt to bend his limbs and were forced to cut and slash his clothes to take them off.

The police inspector, to whom I was naturally obliged to report the accident, gave me a queer look and said: "There's something fishy about this!"—prompted, no doubt, by an inveterate desire and a routine habit of throwing scares—on the off chance—into the innocent as well as the guilty.

One final task remained to be performed, the mere thought of which caused me dire anguish; the parents had to be notified. My legs refused to take me to them. At last I gathered up sufficient courage. But, to my astonishment, the mother showed no sign of emotion; not a tear trickled from the corner of her eye. I attributed this strange behavior to the very horror that she must be feeling, and I remembered the old saying: "The most painful sufferings are dumb." As for the father, he merely said, half in stupor, half dreaming: "Well, maybe it's better like that; he would have come to a bad end anyhow."

Meanwhile the corpse lay stretched out on my couch. I was busy, with the help of a maid, taking care of the last details, when the mother entered my studio. She wanted to see her son's body, she said. I could not, in truth, prevent her from wallowing in her misery and refuse her this supreme and gloomy consolation. Afterward she begged me to show her the spot where her child had hanged himself. "Oh! no, madame," I replied, "that would upset you." And as my eyes involuntarily turned toward the sinister closet, I noticed, with a mixture of disgust, horror, and anger, that the nail had remained planted in the panel, and that a long piece of rope still dangled from it. I quickly ran over to tear off these last remnants of the catastrophe, and was about to throw them out the window, when the poor woman seized my arm and said to me in an irresistible tone of voice: "Oh! Monsieur, let me have it! I beg you! I implore you!" Despair, I gathered, had probably so crazed her that her love had fastened now upon the instrument of her son's death, and she wished to preserve it as a horrible and precious relic. She snatched the nail and the string from my hand.

At last! At last it was all over! There was nothing left for me to do but go back to work—more vigorously even than usual, so as to drive out bit by bit the little corpse that haunted the farthest corner of my brain and wore me down with his wide, staring eyes. The next day, though, I received a bundle of letters. Some were from the tenants in my house, others from neighboring houses; one came from the first floor, one from the second, one from the third, and so on; some were written in a half-joking manner, as if attempting to disguise under a bantering tone the earnestness of the request; others were bluntly insolent and badly spelled; all, however, were written with the same object: to obtain from me a piece of the sinister and luck-bearing rope. I must say that there were more women than men among my correspondents; but they were not all, by any means, from the lowest and commonest class. I kept the letters.

Then it was that, suddenly, a light dawned on me, and I understood why the mother was so eager to grab the string away from me and by what kind of trade she meant to console herself.

Translated by Pierre Schneider

THE RED HANDKERCHIEF

by Count Arthur de Gobineau (1816–82)

Cephalonia is a delightful island. I might, of course, recall what Homer said on the subject, but as his hero had nothing to do with Sophie, I shan't dwell on the opinions expressed by the author of the *Odyssey*. After the Venetians had completely conquered the land, they imported their laws and implanted their customs, both of which only grew all the hardier in consequence and in fact outlived the domination of Saint Mark's. Strolling along the principal street of Argostoli, one sees houses in which the style of Palladio has been reproduced at fifth or even sixth hand by some not too unskillful student of architecture, and though the arcades have not the majesty of the wide-open arcades on the ground floor of the Mocenigo and Vanier palaces; though the widely arched windows topped with heavy garlands haven't quite the sumptuousness of the originals on the Grand Canal; though, above all, the structures to be seen there have neither breadth nor spaciousness, being rarely more than one

---

Gobineau's charm and verve were an aristocrat's; and "aristocratic to his finger-tips" applies, for once, to the letter: M. de Gobineau took seriously, when he was alone with his pen, the supposed obligation that an ideal count has in the salon of an ideal countess to be witty, ironic, urbane, elegant without fuss, inelegant with assurance, worldly-wise without vulgar cynicism. There was something of the same fundamental naïveté—or good faith—or greenness of spirit—about everything he wrote and did, a fidelity toward the rather pure and simple image of himself he entertained which recalls the heroes of Stendhal (of whom, indeed, he was a premature admirer). "He died," writes one of his commentators, "without ever having savored the pleasure of treason"—treason, that is, to his idea of himself as a count, as a descendant of Viking warrior-nomads and kings, as an incorruptible.

Incorruptibles of this sort are apt to be dangerous; his superiors in the diplomatic service (which he entered at thirty-

story high, it is nevertheless true that here is a vivid and accurate, however reduced, reminder of the former Queen of the
Adriatic. Perpendicular to the street I am describing, the surface of which is striped in the Italian manner with two broad
lines of flagstones, are a number of little narrow, dark, rather
mysterious winding streets that are no less characteristic than
the broad thoroughfare into which they lead; the latter be-
speaking the gaiety and refinement of the Italians, the others
their trickery and dangerous secretiveness.

On the main street, at the corner of one of these little side
streets, stands a house that is among the finest in town. It belongs, as it has always belonged, to the Lanza family, distinguished by several generations of counts, and one of the most
famous on the island. I don't believe that this family is very
old; indeed, everything in this old land is new. But toward the
end of the seventeenth century a certain Michel Lanza, the
hero of his line, was raised to noble rank by the Grand Council
and even named a Knight of Saint Mark's. He engendered an
unbroken succession of lawyers and doctors who, from then on,
called themselves Count Lanza and piled up a fortune. They
were known for their sordid stinginess; they lent money at high
interest to the well-to-do, the working man, and the respectfully

---

*three, under the statesman-historian Tocqueville, after a career
given over till then to Oriental studies, journalism, and author-
ship) perhaps knew what they were about when they assigned
him to distant and exotic posts where he could do no great
harm. He had, luckily, a rare genius for travel; Persia, Greece,
Newfoundland, Brazil fed an incorrigibly youthful appetite for
alien sights and ways; from his many posts he brought back
manuscripts notable above all for the excitement of discovery
that informed them; and the title of the small volume published
in 1872 from which "The Red Handkerchief" is taken—*Souvenirs de voyage—*might serve as a generic title covering not
only such travel chronicles as* Trois Ans en Asie *(1859) and*
Voyage à Terre Neuve *(1861), but also his treatise on cunei-
form writings (1864), his work on the religions and philoso-
phies of central Asia (1865), his history of Persia (1869),
and his volume of admirable short stories,* Les Nouvelles asi-
atiques *(1876).*

impressed peasant, and were generally recognized as ranking with the five or six families pointed out as being the most respectable and the most illustrious in the Venetian islands. As long as the Republic reigned, these seigneurs—either doctors or lawyers, as the case might be—were always among the first to be welcomed to the table of the *provveditori* when the latter dignitaries entertained at supper. Ship captains felt honored by their presence at naval celebrations, and there was never a game of faro in good society to which they were not invited. For their own part, as far back as anyone could remember, they had never given so much as a glass of water to a living soul, a fact that only confirmed their well-deserved reputation of being prudent, circumspect patricians.

When the last doge had been shorn of his ducal horn and the Ionian islands no longer knew to whom to surrender, the hopes of his compatriots centered on Count Lanza. They looked to him, waiting to see what he would do, and the panicky fatherland sought his counsel. These hopes were not disappointed. Grave of countenance and tight-lipped, he went so far as to nod his head in a thoughtful manner that set people thinking.

He was loyal to the French, very loyal to the Russians, extremely loyal to the English, and always gave loud expression

---

Too much of a writer to be quite accepted as a diplomat (though he was a good one), too much of a diplomat and professional nobleman to be quite accepted as a writer (though his fiction was "rediscovered" not long ago and now even suffers from overpraise—an official French jury recently chose his sparkling novel, Les Pléiades *(1874), as one of the century's twelve "greatest"), Gobineau has labored for many years, thanks to his more or less Spenglerian* Essai sur l'inégalité des races humaines *(1853–5), under a dubiously founded reputation as a "racist philosopher."*

His last years were spent traveling in western Europe, chiefly in Italy, where he died.

OTHER WORKS: *Novels:* Ternove *(1847),* Mlle Irnois *(1847),* L'Abbaye de Typhaines *(1848). Story:* Adelaïde *(1914). Historical evocation:* La Renaissance *(1877). Letters:* Correspondence entre Tocqueville et Gobineau *(1908).*

to the opinion that the disastrous rule that had preceded the one under which he was speaking had been very felicitously replaced. The successive authorities regarded him as a man to be counted on and an outstanding citizen. He had received the Cross of the Legion of Honor from Emperor Napoleon the First; he was indebted to the esteem in which he was held by Emperor Alexander for the Cross of Saint Anne; and Queen Victoria had deemed it an honor for Saint George's Cross that it should have been conferred upon him. He had accepted it with modest pride. Indeed, he was a man of simple habits who went about the streets in a shabby black suit and dubious white tie, occasionally even in house slippers—faithful in this respect to Italian casualness—and with never the tiniest bit of ribbon in his buttonhole. People commended him for this.

Deep down in his heart Count Jerome Lanza was a man of strong passions, and, even though in reality he was rather indifferent where the affairs of others were concerned, he was not at all so, far from it, as regarded his own advantages, pleasures, and affections. A few weeks after his return from Padua, where he had received his degree, he had met at the home of a cousin a young bride, Countess Palazzi, by whom he had at once been singularly struck. It was, indeed, a case of love at first sight such as has been so often described by those who like to expatiate on love. At this period Lanza was most agreeable. He was a good talker, sang with more natural taste than knowledge, and, in short, seemed really to deserve to be liked, which he was. Hardly a year had passed, and Mme Palazzi had just had her first child, when, having become a close friend of her husband, he settled down to all the rights, obligations, prerogatives, enjoyments, immunities, and favors of a position that he was to occupy his entire lifetime. In this domain of his existence he showed a devotion that went well beyond the ordinary. He never wanted to marry, and twice paid debts incurred by Palazzi, who allowed himself to be led astray successively by a singer and by a certain Miss Julia Boyle, who had come to Cephalonia on the same ship as the General Staff of the 84th Highlanders, an extraordinary circumstance for which family troubles were responsible, according to the explanation given by poor Denys Palazzi. Palazzi had no misgivings as to the merits and virtues of his Julia until he met a lady from Paris under whose tutelage he made great progress. On these occasions Jerome Lanza showed a solicitude and patience equaled only by his generosity. He never lost his temper with his friend, and even assumed responsibility for the first-born son, Spiridion, a delightful young man who in time became an indispensable fixture of the principal café in Argostoli, from which he never moved, and where he was to be seen at all hours sitting over a cup of coffee or simply a glass of water. But Count Jerome's acknowledged favorite was Sophie Palazzi, who was two years younger than her brother. Everybody in town knew that her godfather had not married largely on her account, and it was believed that she would undoubtedly inherit his fortune, a fact that greatly enhanced the luster of her perfections in the eyes of all reasonable persons.

The mother of this young wonder, Mme Palazzi, had been very handsome; a bit stout, a bit heavy, with gazelle-like eyes that were more soft than bright and more bright than intelligent; but the combination had gone to make up a great beauty in the southern style, and Count Jerome had not lacked discernment. The close union of these two persons appeared to be of the happiest. Nevertheless, the gossips insisted that their sky was no more storm-free than the heavens above. Certain it is that around 1825, after long years of the most intense passion on the part of the two lovers, interested observers had noted a number of facts that, however, were discussed only with great circumspection, and which, once sifted of exaggerations, boiled down to something like this:

There had arrived one day from Paris, where he had just finished his education, a young man of the island. He was an extremely handsome fellow, and his name was Count César Tsalla. (Don't be surprised by all these counts; as it happened, the Venetians had settled their Ionian territories with them.) Count César had been brought up in a very select society composed of certain kind ladies who gave a warm welcome to young foreigners at the Grande Chaumière [1] and elsewhere. Having been especially singled out by persons of refinement, he had formed a rather good opinion of himself. Mme Palazzi seemed charming to him and he saw no reason to hide this fact from her. As a result, Jerome Lanza gave evidence of being

---

[1] A popular Parisian dance hall of the period.

somewhat disgruntled; César only became all the more attentive; and Mme Palazzi never stopped blushing when she met
him (whether from pleasure or fluster it would be hard to determine). But there might have been serious trouble in the
house of Denys Palazzi, who himself began to look askance at
his wife's new acquaintance, if, suddenly, all at once, and without anybody's being able to learn how or why, the handsome
César had not disappeared.

People wondered at it. The Venetians were a self-controlled,
prudent lot and the descendants of their former subjects are the
same. There were numerous comments, but they were made in
private. No one thought of questioning Jerome Lanza, whose
features had again taken on the most perfect serenity. Anyhow,
it was known that Count Tsalla was in St. Petersburg, where he
had enlisted in the Horse Guards. This news made Palazzi laugh
heartily when it was told him at the café, and he made such
open sport of the matter that all the suspicions reappeared.
They increased, even, when someone started the rumor that a
certain Apostolaki, a great, strapping fellow who was much
feared, and whose only profession was that of accompanying
Count Jerome at a distance when he went walking, and sleeping
in the Count's courtyard after having eaten in his kitchen, had
boasted of having accomplished a feat that was all the more admirable since nobody would ever know anything about it. Letters from St. Petersburg apprised all who cared to listen that
Count César had never been seen in that capital, in addition to
which the Horse Guards did not count him among their ranks.
Once the secret had gone the rounds of the Cephalonians, a few
Englishmen were allowed to share it—for indeed, like all great
men, Jerome Lanza had a few secret enemies—and finally, one
fine day, the Count was invited by the British High Commissioner to come and have a talk with him.

Europeans are accustomed to carrying on their affairs with a
scrupulousness that has always appeared to be highly ridiculous,
uncouth, even repugnant to Orientals; and it must be admitted
that there is nothing more disagreeable than a certain type of
questioning. Nevertheless, Count Jerome was quite able to cope
with the General's inquisitive insistence. He dismissed with the
indignation becoming a man of his station the abominable suspicions cast on his morals; he defied anybody to furnish a

single proof against him—and there was in fact none; he spoke
with feeling of how he had devoted his entire life to doing good,
and recalled tactfully the boundless devotion, so many times
exemplified, that he had shown for the throne of Great Britain
and Ireland. In a vehemently delivered peroration he ended by
pointing out to his solemn examiner that the people who were
trying to ruin his reputation all belonged to that despicable
party of anarchists and demagogues, so prevalent in Europe,
which was clearly bent, in the Ionian islands, on undermining
the legitimate authority of the Lord High Commissioner.
Whether our English civil servant was touched by his cry of
affronted honor, or whether, as is much more probable, in the
absence of all proof, he was bewildered by the oratory, emotion, indignation, and flood of words indulged in by Count Jerome, it is certain that he shook the latter's hand effusively and
invited him to dinner that very evening. As for Jerome, he displayed such nobility of soul that he won all hearts by having ten
thalers sent to one of Count César's distant relatives, who was
in a state of great poverty. It is none the less true that no one
ever knew what became of the too pleasant young man. Countess Caroline Palazzi remained as placid as before, began to take
on weight, became very stout in a few years, and continued to
show imperturbable devotion to Count Lanza, of whom people
claimed she was slightly afraid.

In 1835 the charms of this fair lady, now entirely submerged
by the exaggerations of her too flourishing health, were no
more than a memory in the faithful heart of her fortunate lover.
Sophie, however, had grown adorable, and only a Venus of
early times was more perfectly fashioned than she. She had her
mother's eyes, but with a dusky fire that they lacked; a great
deal of composure, but there was something beneath her silence; an aquiline nose, which, as time passed, grew slightly too
curved, but the nobility of which one could not but admire;
feet and hands that were nothing short of miraculous; and teeth
like two rows of pearls. Her mother viewed her with considerable satisfaction; her father Palazzi borrowed money from Jerome in order to be unable to say no to him; and Jerome, her
godfather, would sit and look at her for hours, in the throes of a
sort of ecstatic adoration.

This felicity might have lasted forever, had an accident not

occurred to disturb it. The entire smart set of Argostoli, as well
as the English officers, were regular visitors at the home of
Countess Palazzi. There was whist every evening, and occasionally the young people would dance or else play a number of
innocent games that involved whispering in one another's ears;
and generally the winter ended with several marriages. One
evening Jerome Lanza was in an especially good mood, almost
gay, in fact; he had just advanced their monthly pay to three
young lieutenants; it was the 24th of the month, and naturally
he felt satisfied with himself for having made this obliging gesture. He often did them this favor; the entire post knew him
well; everybody profited by it, he especially. He was therefore
feeling very expansive, when his glance happened to fall upon a
group of young men, one of whom seemed to be looking at his
beloved Sophie with undivided attention.

He was a tall, slender, rather distinguished-looking young
man, and, in spite of himself, his eyes betrayed the tenderest of
emotions. That was enough to make the old Count take notice;
but suddenly he grew slightly pale, his thin lips tightened, his
mind seemed to have clouded over.

"Who is that delightful young man?" he asked pleasantly,
addressing himself to a cavalryman, Alexander Paleocappa,
who was busy taking snuff at his side.

"You don't know him? Why, that's Gerasime Delfini, the son
of Catherine Delfini, the great beauty of fifteen years ago who
reigned over Zante's palmy days, and to whom our old friend
César Tsalla was so attached. Surely you remember César
Tsalla?" And he added, fool that he was: "Poor devil!" After
which he covered his face with an enormous blue cotton handkerchief in order to stifle—but it was too late—the noisiest of
sneezes.

While this bit of conversation was taking place, Gerasime
Delfini had seated himself at the piano and was singing a song
by the Zantian poet-composer Colomo in a voice that seemed
to Jerome Lanza to be making a very strong impression on the
fair Sophie. With a glance that could not err, he saw, as it were,
his goddaughter's very heart, he saw it beating, he even counted
its rapid palpitations. Without her noticing it, such was her absorption, this glance, than which no glance could have been
more penetrating and sharp, went straight into her eyes, which

it found to be filled with scalding tears; it entered into that charming head, which the wing of passion had touched and inclined slightly in the direction of the voice that lured; and there it discovered, it caught in the very act of existing, those swarming thoughts that love demands and youth holds in readiness. In short, Lanza became absolutely convinced that Gerasime loved Sophie, and that Sophie returned this love with all her heart.

One may question whether his suffering had been any greater on the day when the mother's faithfulness had seemed doubtful. After the last guest had gone and he found himself alone in the *salon* with Mme Palazzi, he began to question her.

"May I ask, my dear, what strange notion prompted you to invite young Gerasime Delfini to your house?"

"He was introduced to me a fortnight ago," replied the Countess, flushing slightly, which always happened to her when she imagined Jerome Lanza to be a bit angry. "He is a nephew of Madame Barretta, whose parents live in Zante, and he has come to spend a month here. That's all I know about him; I do believe, however, though I am not sure, that Sophie has met him occasionally at my sister's."

At these words, pronounced with the nonchalance that was peculiarly hers at all times, but which reached its climax at moments when she felt sleepy, her aging beau was seized with such a fit of impatience that, digging his hands into his trousers pockets, he began to stride up and down, his thoughts revolving about two harsh words: *Brutta bestia!* When he had calmed down somewhat, he took hold of a chair, set it down beside the easy chair into which Caroline had sunk, and, with a certain profusion of nervous gesticulation, had the following wingèd dialogue with her.

"You don't even know that your young Delfini is related to . . . let's be frank, the son . . . of your . . . of that wretch . . . I mean, Monsieur Tsalla?"

"What? What's that? What do you mean?"

"I mean what I say, and I am not talking at random. You didn't notice that this gentleman was making eyes at Sophie?"

"He's not the only one," the Countess murmured lackadaisically.

"And you haven't noticed that that scatterbrain, Sophie . . .

No! I don't want to believe it! I don't want to think about it! It would be too awful! To be betrayed twice in one's life in such an affection! And by whom, ye gods! Don't answer, my sweet, don't answer; and forget what I have just said! I am not accusing you, I am not accusing her; I know nothing, I believe nothing, I suspect nothing! Are you satisfied?"

"Not entirely," replied the Countess, a bit upset in the end by this display of acrimonious vehemence. "I don't know what you mean; you look daggers at me and beat your head and thighs. But what's to be done about it? How could I know that Monsieur Delfini would not meet with your approval?"

"Not meet with my approval? Lord God! She calls that not meeting with my approval! Who was it who said that women . . . I don't know who said it, but it's true! And that man, with his coal-black eyes and that frightening resemblance—for that was the first thing that struck me, it went through me like a dagger, I almost fell over in a faint, I swear it!—and that man doesn't make you ill? You're not horrified by him? What have you got in your veins, anyway? Boiled milk, or what?"

"Very well, what do you want? What are your orders? If you would only explain yourself, my dear, it might be possible to comply with your wishes."

"I don't want ever again to see that ghost in your house. And, beginning tomorrow morning, you must forbid your daughter ever to speak to him."

"Come, come, don't be so cross," said the Countess, as she rose and took up her candle. "Your orders will be obeyed."

Jerome, somewhat calmer, kissed her hand and left for home.

It was around noon when Sophie came to her mother's room to ask how she felt, and found her smoking a cigarette over her morning coffee. She seemed a bit more worried than usual or, at any rate, more thoughtful; for I am obliged to admit that our divine Sophie's opinion of her maternal parent's mental faculties was hardly flattering. She therefore began to wonder what unwonted thing was happening inside that head, when the head spoke.

"Sophie, my dear, I have something to say to you."

"Yes, mother?"

"But you are not going to like what I have to say."

"I don't know what you mean."

"Is Gerasime making love to you?"

Sophie stared at her mother and decided she was not obliged to honor her with her confidence.

"No more than to any of the other girls, I suppose," was her reply.

"Because your godfather doesn't want him to come here any more, and I have just written him that we are leaving for Corfu and that he needn't bother to call; since he will know that we haven't left, he will understand, and you won't see him again."

"I don't think that's very polite. What has he done that he shouldn't have?"

"He hasn't done anything, and I feel sure that he is an honest, deserving young man. However, between ourselves, your godfather doesn't like him. He comes from a family whose attitude toward our very excellent friend Lanza has been extremely ungrateful; the Count is upset by the presence of these people in our house, and we must not oppose him. His devotion to your father is above reproach; you know how much he has done for us, and you are his only heir. I urge you, therefore, if you have any liking for Gerasime, not to think about him any more, because it is of no use."

Sophie took up her tapestry, which represented an absolutely true-to-life green spaniel lying on a red cushion against a white background, and answered not a word. Caroline was in reality delighted to see that everything had gone off so smoothly.

I don't know whether the day seemed long or short to the young lady, but that evening, at dusk, she was to be seen half hidden in the frame of a narrow window giving onto one of those little winding streets I mentioned earlier. By chance, doubtless, Gerasime happened to pass by; all at once—and this could not have been by chance—a small object fell without warning into the middle of the room. Sophie ran to pick it up. It was a paper parcel with a string around it; inside were a letter, and a stone to give it weight. Sophie hurriedly bolted the door and read the following:

Mademoiselle, why are words only words, instead of being flames and swords, in order that I might give you a more faithful account of the tortures I am going through and the sorrow into which I have been

plunged! Not to see you, not to hear you, not to speak
to you again! Ah! Sophie! I should rather die a thousand deaths at once, at this very moment, the most
frightful kind of death, and not suffer such martyrdom
as this! Your cruel, heartless mother (excuse this blas-
phemy on my part, my beloved angel; it is wrung
from my embittered heart by an indignation that is
only too justified!), has your mother no notion of
what pity is, that she should thus drive me from you?
But what have I done? This very day I was going to
ask her for your hand, and I thought that there existed
a thousand reasons why my request would be granted
—my position, my wealth, a life devoted to love of my
suffering country, all the noble sentiments that I feel
burning in my soul and that your added virtues would
so greatly enhance! Why dismiss me with such violence? Ah, Sophie, my beloved Sophie, you let me love
you, you let me tell you that I loved you, you permitted
me to entertain high hopes: must I lose forever the
crown of glory I was about to don, and which would
have made me the happiest man on earth? . . .

There were eight pages in this vein, a natural mixture, in the
south, of a number of sentiments that are entirely genuine but
which overemphasis of expression renders slightly ridiculous to
people in the north. There were also a certain amount of verse,
protestations of undying love, the promise that he would write
again the following day and every day, a fervent prayer that she
should not forget him, and the solemn oath to overcome all obstacles with firmness and resolution; in short, Sophie was
pleased with Gerasime, told herself a thousand times that he
loved her, and said not a word on the subject.

Two days later Gerasime was down on the port's edge when
Count Lanza happened to pass by. The latter saw him, came up
to him, greeted him in a friendly manner, and, in a most affectionate tone, asked him why he never appeared any more at
Countess Palazzi's.

Gerasime began by giving the excuses usually given in such
cases, when suddenly some devilish prompting made him recall,
not the rumors that had gone the rounds concerning Count

Tsalla's disappearance, but the story about the ten thalers that had once been given to an aunt of his. The fact is that he needed hope in the same way that he needed air to breathe, and he sought to attach himself to anybody and anything. The slightest appearance of good will would have sufficed to make him believe in a friendliness for which he thirsted. He imagined, because he was dying for it to be so, that this very eminent Count Lanza, who had once given ten thalers to his aunt and now spoke with such unctuous affection, was a heaven-sent friend redolent of the best intentions; and so, out of the fullness of his heart, and without omitting anything, he told Lanza his story from beginning to end, using the floweriness of expression that characterized his epistolary style.

He told him that his fondness for Sophie had begun just a year ago to the day, in the country, at Zante, where she had gone for a three weeks' visit with her mother. The young lady had quickly allowed herself to be persuaded, Gerasime was obliged to admit, at the same time manifesting such raptures of gratitude and love that even the slightest suspicion of vanity on his part was unthinkable.

He repeated time and time again that his only idea was to beg for her hand on bended knee, in the hope of obtaining it, if he could, and that he didn't understand why Countess Palazzi had suddenly excluded him from her circle of friends without his having done anything whatsoever that he could reproach himself with.

"Nor do I understand it, my boy," said the elderly Jerome, shaking his head with an air of pained commiseration. "It's something I simply can't explain; however, I intend to plead your cause with Sophie's mother, and you are too well aware of my devoted friendship and boundless attachment for your family not to know in advance that I shall do everything in my power to defend your interests. But I should have to know the cause of your misfortune. Caroline Palazzi is not a woman of whims; someone must have been telling tales against you. Have you a rival, perhaps?"

Poor Gerasime shrugged his shoulders in expression of his profound ignorance, at the same time throwing his head back— a Turkish gesture that implies every possible kind of negation. Then, as his eyes fell again on his confidant, a thought came to him. He had the feeling that beneath all this friendly mummery Lanza was playing a game with him—and this frightened him. In a flash of suspicion he had the impression of treading on very dangerous ground, an impression that gripped him to such an extent that the conversation suddenly took an absolutely different turn.

"Well, my boy," Jerome went on, "you must not be discouraged. You love Sophie, she loves you, that's what's most important. I was young once myself, and victory always ends by being on the side of lovers. You have, of course, some means of corresponding with this young lady? I shan't insult you by believing you would neglect to take so necessary a precaution. And, indeed, what a delicious pleasure it is! How do you keep in touch with each other?"

"Alas! Thus far it has been quite impossible to get any word to her, nor have I received the slightest encouraging sign."

"Really!"

"I swear it. What reason would I have to pretend with you, who are the only person I have to lean on in the world?"

"That, indeed, I am, and you must never doubt it. But you do occasionally walk under Sophie's window?"

"I have only once dared to do so, and then I had not the good fortune to obtain a glimpse of her."

"That really is too bad. I cannot allow things to go on like this. Listen, let's go back to your house and, without losing a minute, you must write a few lines to set the poor child's mind at rest. Say nothing that a man like myself could not admit to having said. I'll find a way to slip this consoling word to her without her mother's knowing anything about it, and before the end of the week I hope to have arranged things in such a manner that the affair will have taken the turn we wish it to take."

By this time Gerasime was in a woeful state; on the one hand, he was passionately eager to tell Jerome everything, and, on the other, his distrust of a few minutes earlier was increasing. He had spoken with perfect frankness; but he had also told a number of fibs. If he had made a mistake in being sincere, what misfortunes might not result for Sophie herself? If, on the contrary, he had blundered in his mistrust, his lies would come home to roost, and, should Jerome become aware of them, he would be justified in taking offense, even—who could tell?—

in considering him as an enemy. Should he give him a letter? Should he not give it? What was he to believe, think, imagine, decide, do? There was more din and uproar in his head than in a blast furnace in which twenty fires are shooting up columns of flame, molten iron is sputtering, and twenty giant hammers are pounding at once against the beat of the deafeningly noisy waterfalls that keep them going. In the midst of his uncertainties he gave in, and, while debating with himself as to whether it was really prudent to write, he wrote. He had a regrettable native weakness for pen and ink and, after his own fashion, wrote eleven pages of lovers' ravings, promises to die, and fulminating exclamations. It was of course to be foreseen, with a temperament like his, that, overwrought as he might be, he was careful to say nothing that would necessarily imply the contrary of what he had last told Jerome—in which, as we know, there was not a word of truth. He had some doubts as to whether his confidant would deliver the letter; he was pretty certain that in any case he would read it; but writing it had given him intense pleasure; and even if it were never to reach Sophie's beloved hands, it was something to have been able once more to put on paper those romantic phrases that portrayed so well and so agreeably for their author the interesting state of his soul.

Count Jerome, who, while Gerasime was writing, had appeared to be reading with compunction the translation of a speech by General Foy on liberty for the masses, finally received the precious epistle from the hands of his *protégé*, whom he kissed with effusion on both cheeks as he held him close to his breast; and, in a peroration that the lover would have considered sublime had he not entertained such violent doubts as to the orator's honesty, the latter paraphrased the generous maxim according to which one must "win or die." He then called on Mme Palazzi, with whom he had an interview that lasted at least two hours, and following which Sophie was summoned to her mother's room.

The Count had left, and Mme Palazzi sat fingering her rosary, obviously very upset. She had hardly opened her mouth when, at the first words she spoke, Sophie decided that her mother was reciting a lesson.

"My dear child," said the handsome Caroline, "your godfather is very angry and he has, in fact, told me some frightful things. Apparently this young man, Delfini, speaks of you in the most offensive way, claiming that you adore him and that you gave him a watch-chain made of your own hair on which is hung an arrow-pierced heart engraved 'Sophie.' Your godfather also said that this very morning, in a café, Delfini read out loud to all the young men present a letter he had written to you that is a tissue of presumptuousness. In his recklessness he even went so far as to give the letter to one of his friends, in the hands of whom the Count discovered it and from whom he took it. My dear, you really shouldn't encourage this young man."

Caroline had stopped speaking and was looking out the window in order to relax after so great an effort; but her daughter understood that the ball of twine that had been placed in her mother's hands was not yet entirely unwound, and that the end was yet to come. So she sat down, took up her tapestry with the green dog, and began to pass the needle in and out with perfect self-control and in complete silence.

"As for myself," Caroline went on, after her gaze had followed for some time a group of donkey boys going down to the port, "I must say that I don't understand very well what the whole thing is about. Your godfather doesn't like Delfini, that much is certain, and this wretched letter has made him beside himself with rage. In point of fact, however, the letter is extremely well written, and I see nothing very wrong in it."

Sophie continued to embroider without lifting her eyes to look at the letter, which her mother was holding out to her, and which she could see perfectly well.

"The most annoying thing about it all," Mme Palazzi continued, "is that your godfather wants us to leave Cephalonia. He has taken it into his head to go and spend two or three years in Ancona, where he has a cousin in the customs service, and he has persuaded your father that it is the most delightful spot in the world. As you well know, your father never contradicts your godfather. My poor child! What will become of us in Ancona? How I wish the Count had never had any such idea!"

"Mother, don't you think the dog's tongue would be better if I made it a lighter green?"

"Yes, dear; but I believe I would make it purple, it's more natural. Can you imagine me living in Ancona for years? What is Ancona like, anyway? I am sure that they don't speak any-thing but English there, and I've never been able to remember a word of that language! I tell you we'll die of boredom. Surely you can find some way to keep us from going to Ancona."

The following day, at ten o'clock in the morning, Gerasime was seated in his usual café when he was accosted by a miserably clad little girl who said to him:

"Please, sir, my cousin Vasiliki has asked me to tell you that she would be grateful if you would see that her Uncle Yoryi gets this parcel."

Whereupon the child handed Gerasime a sort of scroll a few inches long, wrapped in a piece of cloth. Then, without waiting for an answer, she ran off.

Gerasime was somewhat taken aback. Three months before he had had in his employ a man named Yoryi who had left him to live on the coast in Acarnania, where there was every reason to believe that he was engaged in professional brigandry; but, having learned of this through conversations with friends of his, Gerasime had had nothing further to do with his former servant, nor did he understand why he should be asked to get in touch with him now. Thinking it over, however, he recalled that Vasiliki was employed as cook by Mme Palazzi. This brought with it a ray of light, or rather a gleam of hope, and, remem-bering his letter of the day before, he decided that Jerome had already kept his word, and that Sophie had probably discovered this means, with the assent of her godfather, of entering into correspondence with him. He leaped quickly from his chair and ran home. Using a pair of scissors, he cut open the scroll, which was very securely sewed together; in a second wrapper, made of an old newspaper, he discovered something that made so deep and so sharp an impression on him that he let the whole thing drop, and the contents of the parcel spilled out on the floor: a red silk handkerchief, a very pointed little dagger, and a faded bunch of violets.

The bunch of violets had nothing mysterious about it and left no doubt as to the sender. He himself had given it to Sophie a month before, and she had promised to keep it forever. The dagger, however, represented a type of object which is only sent to someone when it is to be used; and the red handkerchief indi-cated what was to be done with it. In the language of the country, thus far everything was as clear as the gold letters over a rue de la Paix shop.

What was less so was to know for whom it was intended. Seized by an exceedingly violent and entirely comprehensible emotion, Gerasime sat down with both elbows on the table. He was deathly pale, as any man would be who has just been ordered by the woman he loves to go out and kill somebody, who would feel dishonored if he refused, who considers that it is wise, useful, necessary, even indispensible to do it, but who hasn't the slightest notion as to who this somebody is, and who is unable to rid himself entirely of a dimly sensed fear of the police—a rather piquant touch in the midst of so many other feelings.

Whom was he supposed to kill? That was the question. And the more he thought about it, the more his perplexity increased. Because there was no sense that he could make out in going after just any innocent victim. The most important thing was to get the right man. But who was that? Within a few seconds his imagination had virtually strewn the ground with corpses; after which he brought each in turn back to life, in the fond hope that it was not that one whose life he had been ordered to take; for, unfortunately, his position was such that he was obliged to consider as possible, not to say probable, an entire series of the most appalling deeds.

"Let's see," he said to himself with a shiver, "could it be that my angel meant me to kill Palazzi?"

Palazzi! In his imagination he saw the tall, gaunt, battered figure of this now superannuated *bon vivant*. He saw his dyed hair, his hat over one ear, his velvet waistcoat, his gold chain, his little cornelian-topped cane; above all, he saw his twisted grin and heard his favorite jokes.

"Could Palazzi have offended her? Could it be that he is opposed to our love for each other? Ah! the wretch! . . . But why on earth? What does it matter to him? He has never meddled in anything. I've never done anything to him. For the two or three guineas he borrowed from me and which I never asked him to repay, he wouldn't have put me out of his house. It's not Palazzi, then, and furthermore, if I were to kill him and it turned out to be a mistake, Sophie might well think that it was no more than right for her not to forgive me. Whom, then, must I go for? Her mother? That great big lady? Nonsense! Paleocappa? Certainly not! It must be Lanza, and Lanza, despite the fact that I distrust him, has shown me nothing but kindness. Who, then, good Lord! Who could it be?"

Finally, he had an idea. It being Sunday morning, he hastened to the church and took his stand on the steps as the congregation filed out from Mass, the last bleats of the nasal-voiced priests still sounding in their ears. One person of his acquaintance, then a second, then a third, then a great number, passed out through the door. In the midst of this crowd he saw Sophie walking with an air that was as solemn as it was edifying. Her mother was on her right, her godfather on her left, and following behind was Palazzi giving a felicitous twist with his white hand to his heavily pomaded black curls. Gerasime stared at Sophie with a look that was more than eloquent. She understood and, as she passed in front of him with her escort, did not return his greeting. Instead, looking him straight in the eye, she suddenly shifted her gaze to Jerome Lanza, then back to her lover, as if waiting for something. It was all clear now; he made a sign of assent. At the same moment he felt himself being given a strong push from behind and, turning, noticed a black-guardly-looking fellow who, without excusing himself, showed him an open knife hidden in his sleeve, then disappeared.

"So that's how it is!" said Gerasime to himself. "Well, we'll see!" The thought of receiving a few inches of steel in his body set him into motion. That same evening he left for Acarnania, and a few days later he was dining peacefully in Missalonghi with Yoryi, whose good advice he had come to seek. Not that he would have been obliged to take all this trouble in order to do what he was about to do. Thank heavens, in Zante, in Cephalonia, in all the islands, in fact, it would have been easy, and I feel sure it will always be so, for anybody to find obliging young men ready to clear the way for their friends for a reasonable sum. But he had been ordered to deliver the red handkerchief to Yoryi and he felt obliged to carry out these instructions to the letter.

When our young swain had acquainted this gentleman with the case and given him all the facts about his own situation, Yoryi made a gesture of surprise. Gerasime noticed it and asked what it meant.

"What it means? It would be just as well for you not to know," replied his confidant. "All I can say is that you see some funny things in life. Fifteen years ago I did a job with old Apostolaki and four or five pals on orders from Count Lanza; he paid us well, I'll say that much for him. Today Apostolaki is on the retirement list, two of our fellow workers were hanged by the English—which was a shame—and now I'm about to take on Count Lanza, and, what's more, for you! It's a funny thing, but there does seem to be some justice in this world, though that doesn't concern me."

He refused to say more on this point and, being a practical man, turned immediately to analysis and discussion of the most satisfactory means of accomplishing the mission with which Gerasime had honored him.

A week later—it was during the night of Monday to Tuesday, and must have been around midnight—Count Jerome Lanza, preceded by a servant girl carrying a lantern, was turning into a narrow little street through which he generally passed on his way home from Mme Palazzi's, when he was suddenly surrounded by five men, four of whom were, or seemed to him to be, very tall. He was promptly knocked down by a sharp blow on the shoulder; this was followed almost immediately by a second, then a third; and at the very moment when he had succeeded in recognizing under its veil a face leaning over him that was thinner than the others, he fainted dead away.

The little servant had her lantern broken; but she had quite naturally let out several awful shrieks, in consequence of which a few windows were flung open. However, when people saw what was happening, nobody was in a hurry to interfere. Finally, the assassins having disappeared, they took the risk. The night watchman was called, then the policeman, who arrived with his side-partner. Somebody went to inform the English High Commissioner and to wake up Mme Palazzi, who appeared much astonished and shed copious tears before making up her mind to start out for the scene with her daughter. Palazzi would undoubtedly have come running right away, but he was nowhere to be found, and it was not until the next day that he heard about the event on his return from a trip to the country.

The aged Count lay stretched out in bed, his head cracked

open, both arms and legs fractured in several places, and his body stabbed by a well-aimed dagger. A bludgeon of gnarled wood with the points of heavy nails sticking out the top had been picked up on the scene of the crime. The judge presumed, and the clerk noted in his report, that the assassins had made use of this dangerous weapon on the person of the unfortunate Lanza. Lanza himself was of the same opinion, volunteering information in a weak voice. But when asked if he had recognized his slayers, he replied that he had been unable to distinguish anyone, and there was no getting him to say a word on this point—which was, nevertheless, an interesting one. Usually, in such cases, people who have been mishandled tend toward an excess rather than to a lack of suspicions; indeed, they suspect literally everybody, and, if they were to be taken at their word, the entire population would be put under arrest. But our old friend Lanza proved to be an exception to the rule, and refused to name anybody at all, which seemed very peculiar. The attending doctors stated that he had been mortally wounded and that it would surprise them if he were to live more than a few hours. It was decided, therefore, to leave him in peace.

When he found himself alone with Mme Palazzi and Sophie, both of whom were plunged in tears and sobbing, the Count said to his friend:

"My dear, it was Gerasime who did it. I recognized him as he leaned over me, despite the fact that his face was veiled. I don't want the law to mix into this affair, which doesn't concern it; on the contrary, if any compromising clues are discovered, I want you to promise me to do all in your power to clear Gerasime. You must swear under oath that you know him to be innocent. Then you must take what money you need from my house—which I am leaving to Sophie—and have Gerasime killed on the very same spot where he laid me out, in the same way, and with exactly the same sort of bludgeons. . . . I should very much like for his body to be stabbed with the same knife."

While he was expressing this quite natural desire, Mme Palazzi's tears and sobbing increased. The relatives began to arrive, followed by some priests, and the entire population was standing outside in the street as the aged Jerome breathed his last without having embraced either his dear Caroline or his adored Sophie. It was evident that he was thinking of one thing

only, and that was his ardent desire to be joined in the next
world by Gerasime in the manner he had arranged for.

There was a grand funeral. The archbishop himself offici-
ated in his most splendid clerical garb, escorted by all the
lesser *papas*, representing the various parish churches in the
city. The British High Commissioner made a speech in English
in which he paid deserved tribute to the political virtues of the
departed, who had been unfailingly devoted to the cause of
order and religion; the president of the Philhellenic Committee used modern Greek to praise the Count's generous efforts in
behalf of the cause of independence, specifying, however, only
the noblest of the aspirations involved. Speaking in Italian, the
Mayor wept for his city that it should have lost so enlightened
a member of its Municipal Council, and recalled the progress
made throughout Europe in the science of economics as a result
of Count Lanza's translation from the French, some thirty years
before, of a pamphlet on freedom of the cereal trade. Lastly,
the principal of the high school, speaking an ancient Greek of
the purest Athenian species (not a word of which was understood by those present), eulogized the literary genius of the
eminent Count Lanza, who, in his youth, had translated into
corrected Romaic a French novel entitled *La Dot de Suzette*,
by the eminent and well-known M. Fiévée, as a result of which
the entire Christian Orient had made great strides along the
path of civilization.

These speeches went on for eight consecutive hours, after
which everybody went home. The authorities carried out an
extremely able, well-directed investigation, but discovered nothing whatsoever. When they tried to find out whether Count
Lanza had any openly declared enemies whose interests might
have been served by his disappearance, they found nobody;
Count Lanza hadn't a single enemy. However, when they went
so far as to try to discover whether he had any friends, they
found that he was universally detested. This flagrant contradic-
tion only increased the general confusion, and they finally had
to give up and admit defeat. Merely as a matter of form, however, and in order to beat a more honorable retreat, they pretended for a while longer to be interested in an affair concerning which, from the very start, they had understood that they
would never understand anything.

Gerasime Delfini, who had not been in Cephalonia since at least a month before the Count's assassination, reappeared two months afterward, just back from Naples, about which he told marvelous tales and where he had greatly enjoyed himself.

Sophie, who was still very much taken up with embroidering her green dog, asked her mother:

"Mother, aren't you going to ask Monsieur Delfini to come and see you?"

Mme Palazzi uttered a sort of groan.

"You know quite well, my dear child," she murmured, "what your godfather told me."

"Do you believe that?" Sophie asked with her usual frankness, at the same time turning on her mother a gaze the steadiness of which had always been a source of wonder. "Do you really believe that? Didn't people at one time tell the most awful stories about my godfather in connection with Count Tsalla?"

"Poor Tsalla!" murmured the Countess, upon which, with a gesture that she would never have made during Jerome Lanza's lifetime, she drew her handkerchief across her eyes—which, as it happened, really did contain a few tears.

"Do you believe that my godfather had Count Tsalla assassinated?"

"My dear child," said the Countess, "that kind of thing should never be talked about. You are young and you don't know . . . Jerome was certainly incapable of doing such a thing, nor do I believe that Gerasime . . . I swear to you that I have nothing against the young man, if only he looked a little less like his mother, for I can assure you that Mme Delfini was nothing much to speak of; and, as I used to say to poor Tsalla, he made a great mistake to lower himself with such a creature. However, I swear to you that I have only the friendliest feelings for Gerasime, and if you don't think it would be disrespectful to your godfather's memory, it seems to me that I could let him come here."

A few weeks later Sophie and Gerasime were married. They lived happily ever after and had a great many children.

Translated by Maria Jolas

A SIMPLE HEART

by Gustave Flaubert (1821–80)

The housewives of Pont-l'Évêque were a half-century envying Mme Aubain her servant Félicité.

For one hundred francs a year she did the cooking and cleaning, sewed, washed, ironed, could bridle a horse, fatten poultry, or churn butter, and remained loyal to her mistress— not an easy woman to get along with.

Mme Aubain's husband, a dapper fellow with no money, had died at the beginning of 1809, leaving her with two very small children and a mass of debts. The upshot was that she sold her properties except for the farm at Toucques and the farm at Gefosses, which between them brought in five thousand francs a year at most, and gave up her Saint-Melaine house for another, less expensive to run, which had come down in the family and was located behind the market.

It was a house with slate shingles, set in between a thoroughfare and a path that went down to the river. Inside, between rooms, there were treacherous ups and downs. A cramped en-

---

For a brief period shortly before Flaubert's death the dense, tortuous, congested imagination that had worked half a lifetime over La Tentation de Saint Antoine *put on a show of blandness. It was not all show; but blandness has never been so cunning. And it might have been some Norman horse-dealer who, in "A Simple Heart," affected by such artful means the air of trusting simplicity, even of candor, that a face has when the mind behind it is soft or absent. Nothing could be less simple than the story that masquerades under the title of "A Simple Heart" as a little tale destined "to make sensitive souls cry."*

The subject is banal enough, to be sure. Had it been less banal, it would probably have lent itself less well to the half-mystical purpose that animated Flaubert's ferocious and solitary literary labors: to put words together in such a fashion as to "redeem" human existence from the insignificance or platitude

trance hall separated the kitchen from the "parlor" where Mme
Aubain used to spend the whole day, sitting by the window in a
wicker armchair. Against the paneling, which was painted
white, stood eight mahogany chairs in a row. Heaped on an old
piano, under a barometer, was a pyramid of boxes and cartons.
Two stuffed easy chairs with needlework upholstery flanked the
Louis XV fireplace of yellow marble. The clock on the mantel
was supposed to be a temple of Vesta; and the whole place had
a slightly musty smell about it, as it was on a lower level than
the garden.

Upstairs there was first of all "madame's" room—very large,
with pale, flowered walls and a portrait of "monsieur" in a
foppish get-up. A connecting door led into a smaller bedroom
where there were two children's cots without mattresses. Next
came the drawing-room, always kept closed, full of furniture
covered with sheets. From there a corridor led to a study;
books and papers lined three walls of bookcases around a broad
writing-table of dark wood. The panels on either side of the
door were half hidden under pen-and-ink drawings, water-color
landscapes, and engravings by Audran—mementoes of better
days and bygone affluence. A dormer window on the floor above
let daylight into Félicité's room, which looked out over the
fields.

---

*or plain monstrous absurdity that struck him as the characteris-
tics of its unredeemed state.*

*There was at last for him, as for James Joyce, nothing in the
world so insignificant, so platitudinous, so absurd, that contemplation and art together might not endow it with the mute
impersonal dignity—grave and humble, as in "A Simple Heart,"
or grotesque and humorous, as in* Bouvard et Pecuchet, *or
wryly tragi-comic, as in* Madame Bovary, *or disenchanted, as in*
L'Éducation sentimentale—*of a historical monument: a monument, that is, in the oddly "sacred" history of what his godson
Maupassant was to call* A Life.

*In "A Simple Heart" everything is banal, starting with the
language in which the story is written. Everything is "re-
deemed," banality passing over in each phrase (as no translation, however ungentlemanly, can quite make clear) to the sort
of luminous, hair-raising presence that Joyce later named*

She got up at the crack of dawn, so as to be in time for
Mass, and worked till nightfall without stopping; then, when
dinner was over, the dishes put away, and the door firmly shut,
she would bury the fireplace log under the ashes and doze off
in front of the hearth, holding onto her rosary. There was no
one more pigheaded when it came to bargaining. As for tidiness,
the way her pots gleamed drove other servants to despair. Of a
frugal nature, she ate slowly and gathered up off the table with
her fingers whatever crumbs fell from her bread—a twelve-
pound loaf, baked specially for her, that lasted her three weeks.

All year round she wore a calico kerchief fastened behind
with a pin, a bonnet covering her hair, gray stockings, a red
skirt, and, over her long-sleeved blouse, a high-fronted apron
like a nurse's.

Her face was thin and her voice sharp. At twenty-five she
looked forty. From fifty on, there was no telling her age; and,
silent as she was, with her erect figure and deliberate movements, she seemed to be made of wood and to run by clockwork.

II

Like the next woman, she had a love story in her life.

Her father, a mason, had been killed falling from a scaffold.

---

*"epiphany." And everything—a mother telling her daughter to
"be a big girl," a deaf old servant talking to a parrot, a verb
changing its tense—is momentous and monumental.*

*A complex private drama of literary creation so consumed
the other facts of Flaubert's life—his childhood in Rouen, his
youthful studies in Paris, his love affair with the poetess Louise
Colet, his travels in the Near East, his early withdrawal into the
monastic workroom of a "saint" dedicated to The Word—as to
transform into mere incidents all but the fact of his setting pen
to paper. Many of the "materials" that went into "A Simple
Heart" were incidents of his childhood until they became impersonal and luminous presences of his old age. The story is
from the volume brought out in 1877 under the mock-naïve
title of Three Tales.*

OTHER WORKS: *Novel:* Salammbô *(1862). Personal writings:* Correspondence *(1926–33).*

Then her mother died, her sisters scattered, and she was taken in by a farmer, who set her to work tending cows in the fields when she was a mere infant. She shivered in her rags, drank from puddles, lying on her belly, was beaten for anything or nothing, and at last was thrown out for stealing thirty sous, though it wasn't she who had stolen them. She found work on another farm, where she was given the chickens to take care of; and, as the people she worked for liked her, the other hired hands were jealous.

One August evening (she was eighteen at the time) they took her along to the annual Colleville fair. The din of the fiddles, the lights in the trees, the varicolored costumes, the laces, the gold crosses, the crowd of people jumping up and down together, all at once took her breath away, and her head swam. She was standing bashfully off by herself when a prosperous-looking young fellow who, elbows on the shaft of a cart, had been smoking his pipe came up and asked her to dance. He treated her to cider, coffee, cake, and a silk scarf; and, thinking she understood what he had in mind, offered to see her home. At the edge of a field of oats he threw her down roughly. She was frightened and began to scream. He left.

Another evening, on the Beaumont road, she caught up with a big hay wagon that was lumbering along; and, as she brushed past the wheels, there was Theodore.

He said hello as if there was nothing wrong, saying that she shouldn't hold it against him because "it was the drink that did it."

She couldn't think what to say, and wanted to run.

Straight off he began to talk about the crops and about the important people in the township—his father had left Colleville and taken over the farm at Les Écots, so that now he and she were neighbors. "Oh," she said. He added that his family wanted him to settle down. But he was in no hurry; he would wait for a wife who suited him. She dropped her eyes. After that he asked her if she had any notion of getting married. She came back, with a smile, that it was mean to make fun. "But I'm not, honest I'm not!" And he slipped his left arm around her waist. She let him hold her as she walked; they slowed down. There was a sultry breeze, the stars were glittering, the huge wagonload of hay rocked back and forth in front of them;

and the four horses, hoofs dragging, churned up dust. After a while, without waiting to be told, the horses turned off to the right. He kissed her once more. She disappeared into the darkness.

The following week Theodore got her to come out and meet him.

They met in the far corners of farmyards, behind a wall, under a solitary tree. She was no squeamish little miss—living among animals had opened her eyes; but she had too much innate good sense and self-respect to let herself go. Her resistance exasperated Theodore's desire to the point where, to satisfy it (or maybe in simple good faith), he offered to marry her. She was hesitant about taking him at his word. He swore up and down.

Not long afterward he came out with some disturbing news: the year before, his parents had bought him a substitute for the army; but any day now his number was likely to come up again; the thought of doing military service scared him. Félicité thought that his cowardliness proved how much he loved her, and she loved him for it all the more. She would steal out at night; and then, when they were at last together, Theodore would worry her and plead with her unbearably.

At last he declared that he would go to the Prefecture himself to find out where he stood, and would let her know the following Sunday, between eleven and midnight.

When the moment arrived, she ran to join her sweetheart. In his place she found a friend of his.

He told her that she would not be seeing Theodore any more. To make sure that he would not be drafted, he had married an old woman with a lot of money—Mme Lehoussais, from Toucques.

Félicité went wild with grief. She threw herself to the ground, screamed, cried out to God in Heaven, and lay moaning in the fields till daybreak. Then she went back to the farm and gave notice that she was going to leave; when the month was up and she had been given her wages, she tied all her belongings into a kerchief and made her way to Pont-l'Évêque.

In front of the inn she made inquiries of a lady wearing a widow's mantle, who, it just so happened, was trying to find a cook. The girl did not know much, but seemed to be so willing and to make so few demands that Mme Aubain finally said: "All right, I'll take you on."

A quarter of an hour later Félicité was installed at Mme Aubain's.

She was all a-flutter living there at first, because it was "such a high-class house" and on account of "monsieur," who, even if he was dead, was just everywhere. Paul and Virginie, the first aged seven and the other barely four, seemed to her to be made of some rare and precious substance; she carried them on her back like a horse, and Mme Aubain had to tell her not to be kissing them every other second, which mortified her. She found that she was happy, though. In these gentle surroundings her sorrow had melted away.

Every Thursday old acquaintances would drop in for a game of boston, and Félicité got the cards and footwarmers ready beforehand. They would arrive at eight on the dot and leave before eleven.

Monday mornings the junkman who lived down the street would lay out his old ironware under the trees. Then gradually the town would fill with voices buzzing, mingled with the whinnies of horses, the bleating of lambs, the grunting of pigs, and the clatter of carts through the streets. Toward noon, when the market was at its height, a tall old peasant with a hooked nose would appear at the door with his cap on the back of his head —that was Robelin, who ran the farm at Gefosses. A little while later it would be the turn of Liébard, the farmer at Toucques, short, fat, and ruddy, wearing a gray jacket and leggings fitted out with spurs.

Both of them would bring poultry or cheeses for their landlady. Félicité never failed to go them one better at canniness and they left with a very respectful opinion of her.

Off and on, Mme Aubain had a visit from the Marquis de Gremanville, an uncle of hers who had ruined himself by debauchery and now lived at Falaise on his last little scrap of land. He invariably showed up at lunch hour with an unsightly poodle that made a mess of all the furniture with its paws. Although he tried hard to keep up the appearance of a highborn gentleman, going so far as to tip his hat every time he said "my late father," habit was too strong for him, and, pouring himself one glass after another, he would let go with some pretty off-color remarks. Félicité would nudge him out politely, saying: "You've had enough for this time, Monsieur de Gremanville! Come again!" and close the door.

She opened it with pleasure to M. Bourais, a former attorney. His baldness and his white cravat, his frilled shirt front, his roomy brown frock coat, the way he flourished his arm when he took snuff—everything about him, in fact, threw her into the sort of nervous excitement people feel when they set eyes on remarkable men.

As he was the one who looked after "madame's" affairs, he would remain shut up with her in "monsieur's" study for hours on end, worried all the time about compromising himself; his respect for the magistracy knew no bounds, and he had some pretensions to Latin.

To further the children's education in an attractive way, he presented them with a geography in the form of pictures that showed scenes from various parts of the world—cannibals with feathers on their heads, an ape carrying off a young lady, Bedouins in the desert, a whale being harpooned, and so on.

Paul explained the prints to Félicité. That was all the book-learning she ever had.

The children received theirs from Guyot, a poor devil renowned for his fine hand who worked at the town hall, and who had a habit of stropping his penknife on his boots.

When the weather was good, they would get off to an early start and go to the Gefosses farm.

The farmstead is on a slope, with the house in the middle; and the sea in the distance looks like a gray smudge.

Félicité would dig into her basket for slices of cold meat, and they would eat lunch in a room next door to the dairy that was the only thing left of a country estate no longer in existence. The tatters of wallpaper quivered when they were caught by drafts. Mme Aubain, overcome by memories, would bow her head; the children would fall into an uncomfortable silence. When she said: "Why don't you go play?" they would scoot off.

Paul climbed into the hayloft, caught birds, skipped stones on the pond, or took a stick and made the big casks boom like drums.

Virginie fed the rabbits or dashed about picking cornflowers, her legs moving so fast that her little embroidered panties showed.

One autumn evening they went home by way of the meadows.

The new moon lit up part of the sky, and a thin layer of mist hung over the winding Toucques. Cattle lying out in the grass looked placidly at the four people going by. In the third pasture a few stood up, then formed a half-circle in front of them. "Don't be afraid," said Félicité; and, giving a kind of plaintive croon, she stroked the back of the one nearest her; he turned tail, and the others followed. But when they were crossing the next pasture, a fierce bellowing arose. It was a bull hidden by the mist. He came toward the two women. Mme Aubain was on the point of breaking into a run. "No! No! Slow down!" They walked fast anyhow, and heard snorts behind them coming closer and closer. The bull's hooves thudded on the grass like trip-hammers; he was galloping now! Félicité turned around, and with both hands she tore up clods of earth to throw into his eyes. He lowered his muzzle, shook his horns, and quivered with rage, giving fearful bellows. Mme Aubain, at the far end of the meadow with her two children, was looking frantically for a way to get over the high bank. Félicité kept backing away before the bull, all the while throwing handfuls of grass to blind him and crying out: "Hurry! Hurry!"

Mme Aubain got down into the ditch under the bank, pushed Virginie, then Paul, up ahead of her, fell several times trying to climb up herself, and by courageous efforts at last managed it.

The bull had driven Félicité against a rail fence; flecks of his slaver splattered into her face; another second and he would rip her open. She had just time to slip between two rails, and the huge beast, taken aback, stopped short.

The incident was talked about in Pont-l'Évêque for years afterward. Félicité was none the prouder for it; the notion that she had done something heroic did not even occur to her.

All she had time to think of was Virginie—who, as a result of the scare, came down with a nervous upset; M. Poupart, the doctor, recommended sea-bathing at Trouville.

Not many people went there in those days. Mme Aubain made inquiries, consulted Bourais, and got things ready as if for a long trip.

Her bags left a day beforehand in Liébard's cart. Next day

Liébard himself brought around two horses, on one of them a woman's saddle with a velvet back, while a coat rolled up on the crupper of the second made a kind of seat. Mme Aubain mounted on that, behind Liébard. Félicité took Virginie with her, and Paul straddled M. Lechaptois's donkey, lent on condition that it be given the best of care.

The road was so bad that it took two hours to cover the five miles. The horses sank in the mud up to their pasterns and gave jerks of their haunches pulling themselves free; or else they tripped in ruts; and other times they had to jump. Now and again Liébard's mare would just stop dead. He would wait patiently till she decided to go on again; and he would hold forth on the people whose properties were along the road, moralizing on their life stories. On the way through Toucques, for example, as they were passing under some windows bordered with hydrangea, he shrugged his shoulders and said: "That's a Mme Lehoussais lives there; she could have had herself a young man, but . . ." Félicité did not catch the rest; the horses were trotting now, and the donkey galloping; they turned single-file into a lane; a gate swung open, two boys appeared, and everyone dismounted in front of the manure heap, right in the doorway.

Granny Liébard, catching sight of her mistress, could not find words enough to say how delighted she was. For Mme Aubain's benefit she served up a lunch of sirloin, tripe, blood pudding, fricasseed chicken, sparkling cider, a fruit tart, and brandied plums, all the while passing out compliments to madame, who was looking better, to mademoiselle, who had become "a regular little lady," and to Monsieur Paul, who had "shot up so you wouldn't know him"; and she did not overlook, either, their late lamented grandparents, whom the Liébards had known well, being with the family as they had been for several generations. The farm, like themselves, bore the marks of great age. The ceiling beams were worm-eaten, the walls blackened by smoke, the windows gray with dust. An oak sideboard held all sorts of utensils—jugs, plates, pewter bowls, wolf-traps, clippers for sheep; a huge syringe made the children laugh. There was not a tree in the farm's three yards that did not have mushrooms at its base or a clump of mistletoe in its branches. The wind had blown down several of them. They had taken hold again from the middle, and they all drooped under the burden of their apples. The thatched roofs, of different thicknesses, and resembling brown velvet, withstood the sharpest gusts. But the cart shed was falling into ruins. Mme Aubain said that she would see to it, and gave orders for the horses to be resaddled.

It was another half-hour before they reached Trouville. The little caravan dismounted to pass the Écores—a cliff with boats down below; and three minutes later, at the far end of the quay, they entered the courtyard of "The Golden Lamb," kept by Mistress David.

Within a day or two Virginie was feeling less weak because of the change of air and the bracing effect of the baths. She went into the water in her chemise, as she had no bathing-costume; and her nanny dressed her in a customs shack that the bathers used.

Afternoons they took the donkey and went off past the Black Rocks, out Hennequeville way. The path climbed at first among smooth, grassy hummocks like the ones in parks, then came out on a plateau where meadows alternated with plowed fields. At the edge of the path, holly bushes sprouted from thickets of bramble; here and there a large dead tree made zigzags against the blue air with its branches.

Almost always they took a rest in a field, with Deauville on their left and Le Havre on their right; in front of them the open sea sparkled in the sun, smooth as a mirror and so still that its murmur barely reached them; invisible sparrows chirped; and all over everything was the immense dome of the sky. Mme Aubain sat and did her sewing; Virginie, beside her, braided reeds; Félicité rooted up sprigs of lavender; Paul would become restless and want to go.

Other times they crossed the Toucques in a boat and went looking for shells. When the tide went out, sea urchins, jellyfish, and starfish would be left stranded; and the children chased after bits of spume caught up by the breeze. The waves, dropping indolently to the sand, unrolled along the beach, which stretched away as far as the eye could see, though on the land side it was hemmed in by the dunes that separated it from the Marsh, a broad meadow shaped like an arena. When they came home that way, Trouville, on the far slope, grew bigger with every step, its assortment of houses seeming to dilate in lighthearted frowziness.

Days when it was too hot, they did not leave their rooms. The dazzle from outdoors made bright slashes between the slats of the shutters. There was not a sound in the village; and not a soul was on the sidewalk below. The pervading silence made things all the more peaceful. Far away, calking-hammers tapped against hulls, and a sluggish breeze wafted up the scent of tar.

What was most fun was to watch the fishing-boats come in. As soon as they rounded the buoys they would start tacking. The canvas would come down part way on the masts; and, with foresails ballooning, they would glide in through the slap of the waves to the middle of the port, then suddenly drop anchor. Afterward the boats would draw up against the quay. The sailors would heave squirming fish over the side; a row of carts would be waiting; and women in cotton caps would rush forward to take the baskets and give kisses to their men.

One of these women went up one day to Félicité, who a little while later came into the hotel room beaming. She had found a long-lost sister; and Nastasie Barette, now Mme Leroux, made her entrance, holding a baby at her breast and another child with her right hand, while at her left stood a little cabin boy with his fists doubled on his hips and a beret cocked over one ear.

Mme Aubain let her stay fifteen minutes.

They were forever turning up near the kitchen or on walks the family took. There was no sign of the husband.

Félicité took a fondness to them. She bought them a blanket, some shirts, and a cooking-stove; anyone could see they were making the most of her. Her softheartedness irritated Mme Aubain, who, moreover, did not like the nephew's familiar ways —he used *tu* with her son; so, as Virginie was coughing and the weather had turned, she went back to Pont-l'Évêque.

M. Bourais enlightened her on the matter of picking a school. The one at Caen was considered the best. Paul was packed off, and said his good-bys like a little man, pleased at going to live in a house where there would be other boys to play with.

Mme Aubain resigned herself to her son's being away from home, seeing that it was indispensable. Virginie thought about him less and less. Félicité missed the noise he made. But from

Christmas on, she had something else to do that took her mind off Paul: every day she took the little girl to catechism.

III

After bending her knee at the door, she would go down the high nave between the two banks of chairs, open Mme Aubain's pew, take her seat, and let her eyes wander.

Boys filled the right-hand choir stalls, girls the left; the curé stood by the lectern; on a stained-glass window in the apse, the Holy Ghost hovered over the Virgin; another window showed the Virgin on her knees before the infant Jesus; and behind the tabernacle a group carved in wood represented St. Michael slaying the dragon.

The priest started off with an outline of sacred history. In her mind's eye Félicité saw the Garden, the Flood, the Tower of Babel, cities all in flames, dying nations, idols overthrown; and these stunning visions left her awed by the Almighty and fearful of His wrath. She wept when she heard the story of the Passion. How could they have crucified Him like that? Didn't He love little children, feed the hungry multitudes, heal the blind? Hadn't He willed, in His meekness, to be born among the poor, on the dung heap of a stable? Sowings, harvests, wine-presses, all the everyday things the Gospel speaks of, had their place in her own life; God, by His passage, had sanctified them; and she came to love lambs more tenderly for love of the Lamb, and doves on account of the Holy Ghost.

She found it hard to visualize the Holy Ghost; for he was not only a bird, but a flame as well, and at other times a breath. It was his radiance, perhaps, that flitted at night along the edge of swamps, his breath that blew the clouds, his voice that gave bells their harmonious ring; and she would sit rapt in adoration, drinking in the coolness of the walls and the stillness inside the church.

Of dogma she understood nothing—did not even try to understand. The curé would expound the lesson, the children would recite, and in the end she would fall asleep, waking with a start to the clack of their wooden shoes on the flagstones as they filed out.

That was how, by hearing it over and over, she learned her catechism, for her religious education had been neglected when she was young; and from then on, whatever Virginie did, she did too, fasting the same way, and going with her to confession. At Corpus Christi they made a festal altar together.

Virginie's first communion had Félicité in a fret long beforehand. She fussed about the shoes, about the rosary, about the prayer book, about the gloves. She positively quaked as she helped Mme Aubain dress her.

She was in agonies all through Mass. M. Bourais blocked her view of one side of the choir; but directly to the front, the flock of little maids, white crowns over their lowered veils, formed a sort of snow patch; and she could pick out her own darling from far off by her prettier neck and the serious way she sat. The bell tinkled. The heads bowed; there was a silence. To peals of the organ, the choir and congregation intoned the *Agnus Dei;* then the procession of boys began; and, after them, the girls stood up. Step by step, and holding their palms together, they went toward the resplendent altar, knelt on the first step, received the sacrament one by one, and in the same order returned to their places. When it was Virginie's turn, Félicité leaned forward to see; and with the sense people have if they love someone very dearly of being in that person's place, she felt as if she herself were kneeling there; the child's face became her own; it was she who had on the child's dress; the heart pounding in her breast was the child's; and when Virginie's mouth opened, Félicité, eyes closing, nearly fainted.

Early the next morning she presented herself at the sacristy and asked M. le Curé to give her communion. She received it devoutly, but did not feel the same thrill.

Mme Aubain wanted her daughter to be an accomplished young lady; and as Guyot could not teach her music or English, she decided to send her away to the Ursuline convent in Honfleur.

Virginie made no objection. Félicité heaved sighs: madame must have no feelings at all. Then she wondered if her mistress might not be right. Things like that were beyond her.

One day, at last, an old spring van drew up in front of the door, and out stepped a nun who had come for mademoiselle. Félicité put the bags up top, gave some words of good advice to the driver, and tucked under the seat six jars of jam and a dozen pears, along with a bouquet of violets.

At the last minute Virginie burst into sobs; she threw her arms around her mother, who kissed her on the forehead, saying over and over: "Be a big girl now! Be a big girl!" The footboard went up and the carriage drove away.

Mme Aubain's strength failed her at that point; and in the evening all her friends—the Lormeaus, Mme Lechaptois, the Rochefeuille "girls," M. de Houppeville, and Bourais—dropped in to comfort her.

She missed her daughter terribly at first. But she heard from Virginie three times a week, wrote to her on the other days, walked in her garden, read a little, and in that way made the hours seem less empty.

Mornings, from habit, Félicité would go into Virginie's room and then just stand there staring. She felt lost with no little girl to comb, to lace boots for, to tuck into bed—and without her pretty face to look at all the time, or her hand to hold when they went out together. Not knowing what to do with herself, she tried making lace. But her fingers were too clumsy and broke the threads; she could not keep things straight in her mind, she no longer slept well, and was, as she put it, "all broken down."

To "get a hold on herself," she asked if her nephew Victor couldn't come see her.

He would arrive on Sundays after Mass, cheeks glowing, chest bare, fragrant with the scents of the countryside he had come through. She would immediately set her table, and they would have lunch facing each other. Eating as little as possible herself to save expense, she would stuff so much food into him that he eventually fell asleep. At the first stroke of Vespers she would wake him, brush off his trousers, knot his tie, and go off to church leaning on his arm like a proud mother.

His parents always sent him with instructions to get something out of her—a little brown sugar, it might be, or soap, or brandy, at times even money. He brought his things for her to mend; and she was glad to take on this chore, as that way he would be sure to come back.

When August came around, his father took him off on a coasting voyage.

It was vacation time. The arrival of the children made her feel better. But Paul was becoming moody, and Virginie was too big now to be called *tu,* which made things awkward and uncomfortable between them.

Victor went to Morlaix, then to Dunkirk, then to Brighton; he brought a present for Félicité after each trip. The first time it was a box made of sea shells; the second, a coffee cup; the third, a big gingerbread man. He was getting to be a good-looking boy, well built, with a faint mustache, clear, steady eyes, and a little leather cap that he wore pushed back the way pilots do. He kept her entertained by telling her stories sprinkled with sailor terms.

One Monday—it was July 14, 1819: she never forgot the date—Victor let her know that he had signed on for a long cruise, and would be leaving two nights later, by the Honfleur packet, to join his schooner, which was supposed to put out from Le Havre shortly. He might be gone for as much as two years.

Félicité's heart sank at the thought of him being away so long; and to say a last good-by to him, on Wednesday evening, after madame had had her dinner, she put on her clogs and covered the ten miles between Pont-l'Évêque and Honfleur as if they had been nothing.

When she reached the Calvary, instead of turning left she turned right, lost her way among the shipyards, and had to retrace her steps; some people she stopped to ask directions told her she had better hurry. She circled the whole harbor full of ships, and kept bumping into hawsers; then the ground took a sudden drop, lights crisscrossed in front of her, and she thought she had lost her wits, because she saw horses in the sky.

On the edge of the wharf, other horses were whinnying, frightened by the sea. A crane was lifting them up and lowering them into a ship on which passengers jostled one another among the casks of cider, the baskets of cheese, and the sacks of grain; there was a cackling of hens, and the captain was swearing; and a cabin boy stood leaning over the bow, paying no attention to what was going on. Félicité, who had not recognized him at first, cried out: "Victor! Victor!" and he looked up; as she rushed toward him, all at once the gangway was pulled back.

The packet moved out of the port, towed by women singing. Her timbers creaked, and the rollers smacked against her prow. The sail had shifted, no one could be made out any more; and against the sea, shimmering in the moonlight, the boat made a dark smudge that grew dimmer and dimmer, sank, and disappeared.

Passing the Calvary, Félicité had an urge to ask God to be good to the creature she held dearest in the world; she stood there praying a long time, her face wet with tears, her eyes turned toward the clouds. The town was asleep; a few customs officers were out strolling; and water poured on and on through the holes in the sluice gate, sounding like a torrent.

The convent parlor would not be open before daybreak. Madame wouldn't like it, anyhow, if she was late getting back; and in spite of wanting to kiss the other child, she started for home. The girls at the inn were just getting up as she came into Pont-l'Évêque.

So there was the poor little tyke going to toss about for months and months at sea! The trips he had made till then had not bothered her. People did come back from Brittany or England; but America, the Colonies, the Indies—all those were vague, dim places somewhere at the other end of the earth.

From then on, Félicité thought of nothing but her nephew. Days when the sun shone, she worried that he was thirsty; when it stormed, she was afraid lightning would strike him. Listening to the wind growl in the chimney and rip off slates, she saw him lashed by that very same storm, at the top of a broken mast, his whole body arched backward under a sheet of spray; or else—images from the pictorial geography coming to her mind —he was being eaten by savages, seized upon by apes in a wood, dying on some desolate shore. And she never once mentioned her worries.

Mme Aubain had worries of her own about her daughter.

The Sisters found she was a sweet child, but frail. The smallest excitement upset her. Her piano lessons had to be dropped.

Mme Aubain insisted on regular letters from the convent. One morning when the postman did not come, she began to fret, and paced back and forth in the parlor between her armchair and the window. She just didn't know what to think— not a word for four whole days!

To make her feel better, Félicité said:

"Look at me, madame—I haven't had one in six months!"

"Six . . . Who in the world from?"

The servant answered softly:

"Why . . . from my nephew!"

"Oh! Your nephew!" And Mme Aubain, with a shrug, went back to her pacing, as much as to say: "I had forgotten about him! . . . What do I care about him, anyhow? A cabin boy, a little brat . . . The idea! . . . You aren't comparing him to my daughter, I hope!"

Though Félicité had been brought up on curtness, she resented that, coming from madame. Then she forgot about it.

She could see how anyone might say foolish things when it was a question of Virginie.

One child meant as much to her as the other; bound together as they were in her heart, their two lives were for her the same life.

The druggist informed her that Victor's ship had reached Havana. He had seen it in a gazette.

On account of the cigars, she pictured Havana as a place where people did nothing but smoke; and there was Victor, with black men all around him, moving in a cloud of tobacco fumes. Could you come home by land "in case you had to"? How far was it from Pont-l'Éveque? To find out, she questioned M. Bourais.

He took out his atlas, then proceeded to explain about longitude and latitude; and his face broadened in a supercilious grin when he saw how flabbergasted Félicité was. Finally, with his pencil, he pointed to an all but invisible black speck among the indentations of an oval blob, commenting: "That's it." She bent over the map; the maze of colored lines strained her eyes but did not tell her anything; and when Bourais urged her to come out with what was troubling her, she begged him to show her the house Victor was staying in. Bourais threw up his arms, sneezed, and laughed immensely; it struck him as hilarious that anyone could be so simple. Félicité could not understand what he was laughing about—she had been expecting, it may be, such was the depth of her ignorance, to see nothing less than her nephew's portrait.

It was two weeks later that Liébard, coming into the kitchen as usual at market time, handed her a letter from her brother-in-law. As neither of them could read, she took it to her mistress.

Mme Aubain, who was counting stitches, put her knitting aside, broke the seal of the letter, gave a start, and said in a low voice, looking grave:

"It's to tell you . . . bad news. Your nephew . . ."

He was dead. The letter did not say any more than that.

Félicité dropped into a chair, her head sagging against the wall, and closed her eyes, which all at once turned pink. Then, with her head bent, her hands hanging limp, her eyes glassy, she kept repeating every few seconds:

"Poor little tyke! Poor little tyke!"

Liébard stood gawking and heaving sighs. Mme Aubain was trembling a bit.

She asked Félicité if she wouldn't like to go see her sister at Trouville.

Félicité gave a headshake that said no, it was useless.

There was a silence. Liébard decided he had best be getting along.

Then Félicité said:

"For all they care!"

Her head sagged again; and from time to time her fingers absently picked up the long needles on the worktable.

Some women crossed the yard with a barrow of dripping wash.

Catching sight of them through the window, she remembered her laundry; she had scalded it the day before; today it would have to be rinsed; and she left the room.

Her tub and board were down by the Toucques. She threw a pile of wash on the bank, pushed up her sleeves, and took her paddle; and the thwacks she gave resounded in the neighboring gardens. The meadows were empty, and the wind ruffled the surface of the river; on the bottom, long tufts of grass streamed out like the hair of submerged corpses. She held back her grief, and was very brave until nightfall; but, once in her room, she gave way to it, lying flat on her mattress, her face buried in the pillow and her fists pressed against her temples.

A long time afterward she heard from no less a person than Victor's captain how Victor had died. They had bled him too much, at the hospital, for yellow fever. There were four doctors holding on to him at once. He had gone just like that, and the head doctor had said:

"Hah! Another!"

His parents had always been horrible to him. She preferred not to see them again; and they, miserable creatures that they were, either forgot or were too heartless to get in touch with her.

Virginie was growing weaker.

The symptoms pointed to something serious—her breathing would come hard, she coughed, she was constantly having fever, her cheekbones were mottled. M. Poupart had advised that she be taken to Provence. Mme Aubain came around to his way of thinking, and would have brought her daughter home at once, if it hadn't been for the climate of Pont-l'Évêque. She arranged with a man who hired out carriages to be driven to the convent every Tuesday. In the garden there is a terrace from which you can see the Seine. Virginie, holding her mother's arm, would stroll there over the fallen vine leaves. Occasionally, when the sun broke through the clouds, she would have to squint as her eyes took in the faraway sails and the horizon stretching all the way from the chateau of Tancarville to the lighthouses at Le Havre. Afterward they would go to the arbor and rest. Mme Aubain had laid in a small cask of excellent Malaga, and Virginie, laughing at the idea of getting drunk, would sip a thimbleful, not a drop more.

Her strength seemed to come back. The autumn slipped away. Félicité kept telling Mme Aubain that things would work out all right. But one evening, on her return from an errand in the neighborhood, she found M. Poupart's buggy at the door; and he himself was in the hall. Mme Aubain was tying on her bonnet.

"Quick! My footwarmer! My purse! My gloves! Can't you move any faster?"

Virginie had inflammation of the lungs; it might be hopeless.

"Not yet!" said the doctor; and the two of them climbed into the carriage, snowflakes whirling around them. Night was coming on. It was very cold.

Félicité rushed into the church to light a taper. Then she ran after the buggy. When she caught up with it, an hour later, she leaped nimbly up behind and held on by the tassels. Then a thought struck her—the garden gate wasn't shut; what if thieves were to get in? And she jumped off.

Next day, at the crack of dawn, she went around to the doctor's. He had come in, then gone out again to the country-side. After that she waited at the inn, thinking that someone—she didn't know who—would come with a letter. At last, as day was breaking, she got onto the stagecoach from Lisieux.

The convent was at the bottom of a steep path. Part way down, she heard a strange tolling—a death bell. "It's for some-one else," she thought, and gave the clapper a violent jerk.

After a few minutes, slippers shuffled, the door opened a little, and a nun appeared.

The Sister, looking apologetic, said that Virginie had "just passed away." At the same moment St. Leonard's bell began tolling twice as fast.

Félicité found her way to the second floor.

From the door, she saw Virginie stretched out on her back, hands together, mouth open, head thrown backward under a black cross tilted toward her, with the curtains motionless on either side, less pale than her face. Mme Aubain, arms clutching the foot of the bed, was convulsed with agonized sobs. The Mother Superior was standing to the right. Three candlesticks on the chest of drawers made spots of red, and mist whitened the windows. Some nuns led Mme Aubain away.

For two whole nights Félicité did not leave the dead girl's side. She would say the same prayers over and over, sprinkle holy water on the sheets, come and sit down again, and just look at her. At the end of the first vigil she noticed that the face had gone yellow, the lips were turning blue, the nose was already pinched, and the eyes were sunken. She kissed the eyes several times, and would not have been greatly astonished if Virginie had opened them again; there is nothing complicated about the supernatural for such souls. She washed and combed her, wrapped her in her shroud, lifted her down into her coffin, placed a garland on her, and spread out her hair. It was blond, and unusually long for her age. Félicité cut off a thick lock and slipped half of it into her bosom, determined never to part with it.

The body was brought back to Pont-l'Évêque, in accordance with the wishes of Mme Aubain, who rode behind the hearse in a closed carriage.

After the Mass it took another three quarters of an hour to

reach the cemetery. Paul, sobbing, walked in front. Behind came M. Bourais, then the principal townspeople, the women-folk with black mantles on their heads, and Félicité. She was thinking of her nephew, and how she had not been able to pay this tribute to him, so she was doubly sorrowful, as if it had been his funeral too.

There was no end to the depths of Mme Aubain's despair.

She turned against God at first, finding it unjust of Him to have taken her child. What evil had she ever done? Was not her conscience pure of any stain? But no! She ought to have taken Virginie south. Other doctors would have saved her! She heaped accusations on herself, wanted to follow her daughter into the grave, and cried out in distress from the midst of her dreams. One dream obsessed her particularly. Her husband, dressed like a sailor, would come back from a long voyage and, in tears, tell her that he had been ordered to take Virginie. Then they would put their heads together to find a hiding-place somewhere.

She came in one day from the garden almost beside herself. A little while before (and she pointed to the spot) father and daughter had appeared to her, side by side—not doing anything at all, just looking at her.

For several months she remained in her room, inert. Félicité would lecture her gently: she must go on living for her son's sake, and for the other one's too, in remembrance of "her."

"Her?" groped Mme Aubain, as though just waking. "Oh! You mean . . . Yes. . . . It's not you who's forgetting her!" —alluding to the fact that she herself had been strictly forbidden to go to the cemetery.

Not a day went by that Félicité did not go.

At four o'clock sharp she would slip past the houses, go up the hill, open the gate, and come to a stop before Virginie's tomb. It was a little column of pink marble, with a slab underneath and chains all around enclosing a miniature garden. The flowers were so thick that they hid the beds. She sprinkled the leaves, smoothed out the gravel, and went down on her knees so she could break up the soil better. When Mme Aubain was finally able to come, it was a solace to her, a kind of consolation.

Then years passed, one like another, and uneventful except

for the recurrence of the Holy Days—Easter, Assumption, All Saints. Household occurrences became landmarks in time. 1825, for instance, was the year when two glaziers whitewashed the hall; in 1827 a piece of the roof fell into the yard and just missed killing a man. In the summer of 1828 madame's turn came to offer the consecrated bread; Bourais, about that period, went off somewhere on a mysterious visit; and the old familiar faces little by little disappeared: Guyot, Liébard, Mme Lechaptois, Robelin, and Uncle Gremanville, who had been paralyzed for some time.

One night the driver of the mail coach brought Pont-l'Évêque word of the July Revolution. A new sub-prefect was appointed a few days later—the Baron de Larsonnière, formerly a consul in America, who, in addition to his wife, had with him his sister-in-law and her three daughters, already quite grown-up young ladies. People would catch glimpses of them on their lawn, wearing billowy blouses; they owned a Negro and a parrot. They paid a call on Mme Aubain, who made a point of returning it. Whenever Félicité saw them coming, even far off, she would run to tell her. But there was only one thing that really made any difference to Mme Aubain, and that was her son's letters.

He could not stick to anything, as he spent all his time in cafés. She would no sooner pay off his debts than he made new ones; and the sighs that Mme Aubain heaved as she sat knitting by the window would be overheard by Félicité turning her spinning-wheel in the kitchen.

They took strolls together along the espalier wall, and they were forever talking about Virginie, wondering whether this or that would have pleased her, or what she would most likely have said about such and such.

All her little things were put away in a closet in the room with the two beds. Mme Aubain looked them over as rarely as possible. One summer day she decided it had to be done; and moths flew out.

Virginie's dresses were lined up under a shelf on which there were three dolls, a couple of hoops, a set of toy pots and pans, and the bowl she had used to wash in. They took down her petticoats and stockings and handkerchiefs as well, and laid them out on the two beds before folding them up again. The sun falling on these poor objects showed up the stains, and places where the body had made wrinkles. The air was warm and blue, a blackbird chittered, a profound sweetness seemed to be spread over everything. They turned up a little hat of thick brown plush; but the moths had got into it. Félicité asked if she couldn't take it to keep. The two women looked at each other, and their eyes filled; after a time the mistress opened her arms, and the servant threw herself into them; and they clung hard to each other, giving vent to their sorrow in a kiss that made them equals.

It was the first time that had ever happened, Mme Aubain not being a woman to show her feelings. Félicité was grateful to her as if for an act of kindness, and from then on she cherished her with the devotedness of a dumb brute and a religious veneration.

Her native goodness unfolded in her heart.

Whenever she heard the drums of a regiment marching through the street, she would go out front with a jug of cider and offer the soldiers drinks. She looked after people who had cholera. She took the Polish refugees under her wing—one of them even said he wanted to marry her. But they had a fight: one morning, when she came back from Angelus, she found him sitting uninvited in her kitchen calmly eating a *vinaigrette* that he had fixed for himself.

After the Poles it was Pappy Colmiche, an old duffer who was supposed to have done awful things back in '93. He lived down by the river in a ruined pigsty. The kids used to stare at him through gaps in the wall and throw stones that landed on his pallet, where he lay racked by coughing, his long hair hanging down, his eyes inflamed, and a growth on his arm bigger than his head. She got some linen for him, did what she could to clean up his hovel, and wondered if she couldn't somehow move him into the laundry without its being a bother to madame. After the abscess burst, she dressed it every day; now and then she brought him cake, and would put him where it was sunny on a heap of straw; the poor old fellow, slobbering and shaking, would croak his thanks; he was terrified of losing her, and would stretch out his hands as soon as he saw her start to leave. He died; she had a Mass said for the repose of his soul.

The same day a great happiness befell her. Just at dinner

time Mme de Larsonnière's Negro appeared, carrying the parrot in his cage, along with the perch, chain, and padlock. A note from the Baroness informed Mme Aubain that her husband had been made head of a prefecture, and they were leaving that night; she begged Mme Aubain to accept the bird as a memento and as a token of her esteem.

Félicité's thoughts had been full of him for a long time, because he came from America; and that name reminded her of Victor, so she was forever asking the Negro questions about him. Once she had even said: "Wouldn't madame love to have him, though!"

The Negro had repeated the remark to his mistress, who, as she could not take the bird with her, chose this way of getting him off her hands.

IV

His name was Loulou. His body was green, the tips of his wings were pink, his forehead was blue, and his throat golden.

But he had an irksome mania for gnawing at his perch, and he would tear out his feathers, strew his filth around, and splash his bath-water. Mme Aubain, finding him a nuisance, made a present of him to Félicité.

She set about training him; before long he was repeating: "Nice boy! Glad to, monsieur! Hello there, Marie!" He had a place by the door, and more than one visitor expressed surprise that he did not answer to the name of Polly, since parrots are always called Polly. They would say he looked like a turkey, or even like a chunk of wood—comparisons that cut Félicité to the heart. And it beat everything for stubbornness how if anyone was looking at him he wouldn't say a word.

But he did want attention; for on Sundays, when the Rochefeuille "girls" and M. de Houppeville, along with new members of madame's circle—Onfroy, the apothecary, M. Varin, Captain Mathieu—were busy at their cards, he would drum against the windowpanes with his wings and throw himself around so furiously that they could not hear themselves talk.

Bourais's face must have struck him as very funny. The moment he came in sight, Loulou would go off into positive gales of laughter. His raucous cackles would go echoing through the yard, then beyond; the neighbors would come to their windows and laugh too; and M. Bourais, to avoid being seen by the parrot, used to slink along the wall, concealing his profile behind his hat, down as far as the river, then come in by the door on the garden side; and the looks he threw at the bird were not exactly loving.

Loulou had once got himself flicked by the butcher boy for taking the liberty of poking his head into the boy's basket; and from then on he was always trying to take nips at the boy through his shirt. Fabu would threaten to wring his neck, though he was not really cruel, even if he did have tattooed arms and thick sideburns. In fact, he was rather fond of the parrot—so much so that he good-naturedly tried to teach him swear words. Félicité, aghast at such goings on, put Loulou in the kitchen. His chain was taken off, and he used to go roaming about the house.

To come down the stairs, he would prop his curved beak on the step below, then pick up his right foot, and after that his left. Félicité worried that these acrobatics would bring on dizzy spells. One day he fell sick and could no longer talk or eat. The trouble was a growth under his tongue, like the ones chickens have at times. She cured him by pulling off this scab with her fingernails. M. Paul was one day so thoughtless as to blow cigar smoke right into his nose; another time, when Mme Lormeau was teasing him with the end of her umbrella, he snatched the metal tip; finally, he got lost.

She had set him out on the grass to perk him up and left him alone for a minute; when she came back, there was no parrot anywhere in sight. She looked for him first in the bushes, by the river, and on the rooftops, paying no attention to her mistress's cries of "Be careful! You'll break your fool neck!" Then she scoured every garden in Pont-l'Évêque; and she stopped everyone she met with: "You didn't happen to see my parrot, did you, by any chance?" When people didn't know her parrot, she would describe it to them. All at once she thought she saw something green fluttering about behind the mills at the foot of the rise. But she went to the top without finding a thing. A peddler told her he had come across the parrot a little while before in Mère Simon's shop at Saint-Melaine. She ran. Nobody there knew what she was talking about. She finally came home, exhausted and heartsick, her slippers in shreds; and she was in the middle of telling Mme Aubain, seated on the bench beside her, about everything she had done, when something dropped lightly to her shoulder—Loulou! Where in the world had he been? Out for a little walk maybe!

She was a long time getting over this—never did get over it, in fact.

As a result of catching a chill, she came down with a bad chest cold, and a while after that with an ear infection. Three years later she was deaf; and she used to talk at the top of her voice, even in church. Though her sins might have been broadcast throughout the diocese without dishonoring her or offending anyone else, the curé decided it would be best not to confess her from then on anywhere but in the sacristy.

What addled her completely was hearing buzzing noises in her head. Often her mistress used to say to her: "For heaven's sake, how can you be so dumb?" And she would answer: "Yes, madame," looking all around her for something.

Her small circle of ideas shrank even more; and there was no longer for her the pealing of church bells or the lowing of cattle. All living things went through their motions silently as ghosts. Only one sound still reached her ear—the voice of the parrot.

As if to divert her, he would mimic the click of the roasting-jack, the sharp cry of a fish-vender, the saw of the carpenter who lived across the way; and when the doorbell rang, he would imitate Mme Aubain's "Félicité! The door! The door!"

They carried on conversations, he spilling out endlessly the three phrases in his repertoire, she replying to them in words that were no less incoherent, but that said what was in her heart. In her solitude, Loulou was almost a son to her, and a sweetheart. He scrambled up her fingers, nibbled at her lips, clung to her kerchief; and when she bent her head and wagged it, the way nannies do, the bird's wings and the big wings on her cap quivered in unison.

Whenever clouds gathered and the thunder rolled, Loulou would break into cries—remembering, it may be, the downpours of his native forests. The streaming of rain water would provoke him to frenzies; he would flap about wildly, dash against the ceiling, knock everything over, and go out the window to dabble in the garden; but he came right back in and perched on one of the andirons, where, hopping about to dry his feathers, he would exhibit his tail at one minute and his beak the next.

One morning during the terrible winter of 1837, when, because of the cold, she had put him in front of the fireplace, she came back and found him dead, hanging upside down in the middle of his cage, claws in the wires. Pneumonia had done it, the chances were. She had a notion he had been fed poisoned parsley; and, though there was not the slightest inkling of proof, her suspicions fell upon Fabu.

She had such a crying spell that her mistress said to her: "I tell you what—why don't you have him stuffed?"

She asked advice of the druggist, who had always been good to the parrot.

He wrote to Le Havre. A man named Fellacher agreed to do it. But, as packages sent by the stagecoach sometimes went astray, Félicité made up her mind to take the parrot as far as Honfleur herself.

One leafless apple tree after another lined the edges of the road. Ice covered the ditches. Dogs barked around the farms; and Félicité, hands under her short cape, with her little black clogs and her basket, strode briskly down the middle of the highway.

She crossed the forest, passed High Oak, and came to Saint-Gratien.

Behind her, plunging downhill in a cloud of dust, a stagecoach at full gallop swept toward her like a whirlwind. Seeing this woman who would not bother to move, the driver reared up in his seat, with the postilion shouting, while his four horses, now out of control, moved faster and faster; the two lead horses grazed against her; with a jerk of the reins he swerved them to one side; but then, infuriated, he raised his arm and, swinging his big whip at Félicité with all his might, gave her such a lash, from nape to belly, that she fell over on her back.

The first thing she did when she came to was to open her basket. Loulou was all right, thank heavens. Her right cheek burned; when she touched her hands to it they came away red. She was bleeding.

She sat down on a pile of stones and dabbed at her wounded cheek with her handkerchief. Then she ate a bread crust, which she had put in her basket just in case, and cheered herself up looking at the bird.

When she reached the top of Ecquemauville, she saw the lights of Honfleur glittering in the night like so many stars; farther off, the sea stretched out indistinctly. Faintness brought her up short then; and her wretched childhood, the disillusionment of her first love, her nephew's going away, and Virginie's death, all at once, like surges of a mounting tide, came flooding back and, rising to her throat, choked her.

Later she had to speak to the captain of the boat in person and make sure he would take good care of her package; she did not say what was in it, though.

Fellacher kept the parrot a long time. He kept promising it for the following week; when six months had passed, he sent word that a box was on its way; after that, not a sign. It looked as if Loulou would not be coming back. "They've gone and stolen him on me!" she thought to herself.

Eventually he came—and a splendid sight he was, too, perched up on a branch that screwed into a mahogany base, with one foot in the air, his head cocked, and his beak clamped on a nut which the taxidermist, heart set on the grandiose, had coated with gilt.

Félicité hustled him off to her room.

The place contained such an assortment of religious and other objects that it looked like a combination chapel and dry-goods emporium; not many people were allowed in.

A big cupboard made it hard to open the door. Facing the window over the garden, a small round one looked out into the yard; a table beside the cot held a water jug, two combs, and a cake of blue soap in a chipped dish. Hanging on the walls were rosaries, medallions, a few blessed Virgins, and a coconut holy-water vessel; on the chest of drawers, which was covered with a cloth like an altar, stood the box made of sea shells that Victor had given her, along with a watering-can and a ball, some copy-books, the pictorial geography, and a pair of girl's shoes; and there, tied by its ribbons to the nail holding up the mirror, was the little plush hat. Félicité carried this sort of piety to the point of keeping one of monsieur's frock coats. Whatever old things Mme Aubain had no more use for, she would take to put in her room. That accounted for the artificial flowers on the edge of the dresser and the portrait of the Comte d'Artois on the dormer wall.

A shelf was put up for Loulou against a jutting section of chimney. Every morning, when Félicité woke up, her eyes would fall on him there in the dawn light, and then, without sorrow, rather brimming over with peace, she would remember how things used to be; and the tiniest details of trivial incidents would come back to her.

Having no communication with anyone, she lived in a kind of sleepwalker's trance. The coming of the Corpus Christi processions brought her to life again, and she would go around among the neighbors collecting candlesticks and mats to decorate the altar that was being set up in the street.

In church she was forever scrutinizing the Holy Ghost, and it struck her that he looked a little like the parrot. A crude color print showing the baptism of Our Lord offered an even more convincing resemblance. There, with his purple wings and his emerald-green body, he was the very image of Loulou.

She bought him and hung him up in the place of the Comte d'Artois—that way she could have both birds in view at once. They became inseparable in her mind, so that the parrot was sanctified by his kinship with the Holy Ghost, who in turn became more real for her, and easier to grasp. It could not have been a dove that Our Heavenly Father had picked to be the bearer of His Word—nobody ever heard a dove talk; it must have been an ancestor of Loulou's. And Félicité would say her prayers looking at the picture, but now and then her eyes would stray in the direction of the bird.

Once she had a mind to go into the Sisters of Our Lady, but Mme Aubain talked her out of it.

An event of some importance came along: Paul's marriage.

After starting out as a notary's clerk, then trying his hand at business, the Customs Service, and the Internal Revenue, and even making efforts to get into Rivers and Forests, suddenly, at thirty-six, by an inspiration from heaven, he had found what he was cut out for—the Registrar's Office; and he had shown such aptitude in this line that an inspector had offered him his daughter's hand, promising to use his influence.

Paul, grown very earnest, brought her home to his mother's. She turned up her nose at the way things were done in Pont-l'Évêque, put on high and mighty airs, and hurt Félicité's feelings. When she left, Mme Aubain felt as if a weight had fallen from her shoulders.

The following week, word came that M. Bourais had died—somewhere in lower Brittany it was, at an inn. A rumor that he had killed himself turned out to be true; and doubts were raised as to his honesty. Mme Aubain went through his books, and in no time at all she had uncovered a whole long list of sins: embezzling arrears, selling timber on the sly, falsifying receipts, and so on. On top of everything, he had had an illegitimate child, and had been "carrying on with some woman in Dozulé."

These iniquities were a great blow to her. In March 1853 she came down with a pain in her chest; her tongue was coated with a smoky film; leeches failed to ease the pressure on her lungs; and on the ninth evening she died, aged just seventy-two.

Everyone had thought her younger because of her brown hair, which she wore parted in the middle and drawn back around her sallow, pock-marked face. She was not much missed, as her standoffish ways discouraged people from making friends.

Félicité's tears were not the tears a servant sheds for a master. That madame should die before she did seemed contrary to the natural order of things, out of keeping and monstrous; she did not know what to make of it.

Ten days afterward (just time enough for a quick trip from Besançon) the heirs turned up. The daughter-in-law rummaged through the drawers, picked out a few pieces of furniture and sold the rest; then the two of them went back to their registering.

Madame's armchair, her little round-topped table, her footwarmer—everything was gone. Where the prints had been there were yellow rectangles on the walls. They had taken away the two cots, as well as the mattresses for them, and in the closet not a single thing was left of Virginie's. Félicité went back upstairs, dazed with sorrow.

Next day there was a notice on the door; the apothecary shouted in her ear that the house was for sale.

She tottered, and had to sit down.

What distressed her most of all was the thought of giving up her room—it was so nice there for poor Loulou. Enveloping him in a look of anguish, she used to plead with the Holy Ghost, and she fell into the idolatrous habit of kneeling before the parrot to say her prayers. Now and then the sun coming in through the dormer window caught his glass eye, and the great beam of light that shot from it would send her into ecstasies.

She had a pension of three hundred and eighty francs a year, left by her mistress. The garden provided her with vegetables. As for clothes, she had enough to last her till the end of her days, and she economized on light by going to bed at dusk.

She hardly ever left the house, not wanting to pass the secondhand dealer's, where some of the old furniture was on display. Ever since the time she fell unconscious, one of her legs had dragged; and, because her strength was failing, Mère Simon, who had lost everything in the grocery business, came every morning to split wood and pump water for her.

She began to lose her sight. The shutters stopped opening. Many years passed. And nobody bought the house, and nobody rented it.

In dread lest she be put out, Félicité never asked for repairs. The roof laths rotted; one winter her bolster was damp all the time. After Easter she coughed up blood.

At that point Mère Simon called in a doctor. Félicité wanted to know what it was she had. But, being deaf, the only word she could make out was "pneumonia." It was a familiar word, and she replied softly: "Oh! Like madame," finding it natural that she should follow in her mistress's steps.

It would be time soon for the festal altars.

The first one was always at the foot of the hill, the second in front of the post office, the third somewhere halfway along the street. There was a dispute about where that one should go; the women of the parish settled it by picking Mme Aubain's yard.

Félicité's fever and the pressure on her lungs grew worse. She fretted about not doing anything for the altar. If there was just something she could put on it at least. Then she thought of the parrot. It would be out of place, the neighbors objected. But the curé gave her permission; she was so overjoyed that she asked him if, when she was dead, he wouldn't take Loulou, who was her only treasure.

Between Tuesday and Saturday, the day before Corpus Christi, she coughed more and more often. By evening her face was shriveled, her lips were sticking to her gums, and vomiting had set in; early the next day, feeling very low, she sent for a priest.

Three old women stood around her as she received extreme unction. Then she said that she had to speak to Fabu.

He arrived in his Sunday clothes, ill at ease in these gloomy surroundings.

"Forgive me," she said, trying to stretch out her arm; "I thought you were the one that killed him."

What was that nonsense all about? Suspect him of murder? Him? He flared up indignantly and was on the point of making a scene.

"But you can see for yourself, she's out of her head!"

Every once in a while Félicité would say something to a shadow. The old women left. Mère Simon ate breakfast.

A little while later she picked up Loulou and brought him close to Félicité.

"It's time. Say good-by to him now."

No matter that Loulou was not a corpse, the worms had gone to work on him anyhow; one of his wings was broken, and the stuffing was coming out of his belly. But she was blind by then; she kissed him on the forehead and held him against her cheek. Mère Simon took him away to put him on the altar.

V

Summer scents came in from the meadows; flies buzzed; the sun sparkled on the river and warmed the slates. Mère Simon, back upstairs, placidly dozed off.

Bells ringing woke her up; Vespers must be over. Félicité's delirium subsided. Her thoughts on the procession, she saw it as clearly as if she had been there.

All the school children, the choristers, and the firemen would be walking along the sidewalks, while down the middle of the street came first the verger with his halberd, then the beadle with a big cross, the schoolmaster keeping a watchful eye on his boys, the Sister nervous about her little girls; three of the prettiest, curly-headed as angels, were throwing rose petals up in the air; the deacon, arms outstretched, was keeping the musicians under control; and two censer-bearers turned around at every other step to face the Host, which M. le Curé, in his beautiful chasuble, was carrying under a canopy of scarlet velvet held up by four churchwardens. Behind, between the house walls draped with white, pushed a surging throng; and the procession reached the foot of the hill.

A cold sweat dampened Félicité's temples. Mère Simon wiped it away with a cloth, telling herself that it would be her turn some day.

The crowd's rumble swelled, was very loud for a minute, and went away again.

A fusillade rattled the windows. That would be the postilions firing a salute to the monstrance. Félicité rolled her eyes and, as audibly as she could, said:

"How does he look?" She was worried about the parrot.

The death throes began. Her sides heaved as, faster and faster, she gasped chokingly for breath. Froth bubbled at the corners of her mouth, and her whole body shuddered.

In a little while the hoarse blare of the ophicleides could be made out, along with the high voices of the children and the deep voices of the men. At intervals everything fell silent, and the tread of feet, muffled by flowers, sounded like cattle trooping across grass.

The clergy appeared in the yard. Mère Simon climbed up on a chair to reach the small round window, and in that way looked down onto the altar.

Green garlands hung from it, and it was trimmed with a flounce of English lace. In the middle was a small frame containing relics; an orange tree stood in each of the front corners; and all along were silver candlesticks and porcelain vases from which rose sunflowers, lilies, peonies, foxgloves, and clusters of hydrangea. The brilliantly colored mass sloped downward from the upper tier to the carpet extending out over the cobbles; and there were uncommon things to catch the eye—a silver-gilt sugar bowl with a crown of violets, pendants of Alençon stones gleaming against moss, two Chinese screens displaying their landscapes. Loulou, hidden under roses, was invisible except for his blue forehead, resembling a plaque of lapis lazuli.

Churchwardens, choristers, and children lined up along the three sides of the yard. The priest went slowly up the altar steps and deposited on the lace his great glowing golden sun. Every-one knelt. A deep silence fell. And the censers, swinging high, skidded along their chains.

A blue vapor rose to the room where Félicité was. Nostrils straining, she breathed it in with the voluptuousness of mystics; then she closed her eyes. Her lips were smiling. Her heartbeats slowed down, each softer and vaguer than the one before, as a fountain runs out, as an echo fades; and with her last breath there appeared to her, while the heavens opened, a gigantic parrot, hovering directly over her head.

Translated by Stanley Geist

JULIEN [1]

by *Émile Zola* (1840–1902)

The little town of P—— is built on a hill. By the old town wall there runs, deep and narrow between its steep banks, a stream called the Chanteclair, doubtless because of the crystalline music of its limpid waters. The traveler coming from Versailles arrives at the southern gate of the town and crosses the Chanteclair by a single-arched stone bridge, which has, on either side, a wide, low, rounded parapet, used as a seat by all the old men in the neighborhood. Straight ahead is the slope of the rue Beau Soleil, going up to a quiet square, the Place des Quatre Femmes, paved with big cobblestones so thickly overgrown with grass that the square is as green as a lawn. The houses are sunk in slumber. Every half-hour or so, a dog barks from behind a stable door on hearing the sluggish footsteps of some passer-by; the only excitement in this forsaken spot is provided by a group of army officers who go past regularly twice a day on their way to a boarding-house in the rue Beau Soleil, where they have their meals.

[1] The original idea for this story was taken from Casanova. (Zola)

Zola took himself to be rather a natural force, or an impersonal productive organism, than just a writer. He did produce— not less than a book a year, and usually several, for close on forty years. And he did have the rawness of natural forces, and a little of their power, and at times even something like their purity, which is not the same thing as innocence. He wrote with a blunt pen, which he used also as a club and an ax, but it was not half so blunt as literary mythology would like to have it: set it beside Dreiser's, and anyone might think it a stiletto. From his teens on, he was sure that the world needed to know about him; he made no secret of being after the world's fame and wealth (both of which he got); and he needed the world as a lion-tamer needs lions. He made no secret of that either; for if he was pugnacious and brash, he was also candid, calling the score as he saw it—whether about himself or about coal-

Julien Michon lived on the left, in a house belonging to a nursery-gardener. He rented a large room on the second floor; as his landlord occupied the other side of the house, overlooking the rue Catherine, where he had his garden, Julien lived in peace, with an entrance and a staircase to himself and, at twenty-five, the fussy, negative habits of a lower middle-class bachelor living in retirement.

He had lost his father and mother while still young. The Michons had formerly kept a saddler's shop at Alluets, near Mantes. When they died, one of Julien's uncles sent him to a boarding-school. Then the uncle himself had gone, and for the last five years Julien had been working as a copying-clerk in the post office at P——. His salary was fifteen hundred francs a month, and he had no hope of ever earning more. In any case, he managed to save on it, and it did not occur to him that anyone might lead a happier or more spacious life.

Julien was tall, strong, and angular, and his big hands were an embarrassment to him. He felt that he was ugly, with his square head that looked as if it had been roughly modeled by some careless sculptor and left in an unfinished state. This made him shy, especially with young ladies. One day a washerwoman had laughingly said to him that he wasn't as bad as all that, and the remark had filled him with confusion. In the street he let his arms hang limp; he bent his back, held his head low, and

---

miners or about prostitutes or about the accusers of Alfred Dreyfus—with his chin out, spoiling for a fight. Some of the scores he called now look dull-witted or absurd; and in fact Zola was often more unintelligent than imaginative writers are allowed to be, most of all when theorizing about his own work.

Though "Julien" was not published in book form until 1881 (in Le Capitaine Burle), it appears to have been written before Zola was much taken up with theorizing or had yet launched (in 1870) on his twenty-volume "natural and social history of a family under the Second Empire"—the best of which demonstrated that, where the imagination is concerned, poor theories make good-enough points of departure. The author of "Julien," then, was a young southerner, not very long in Paris, of mixed French and Italian parentage, who had served a feverish literary apprenticeship, and who, with Thérèse

strode along as if in a hurry to vanish again into the shadows. Because of his clumsiness, he lived in a continuous state of alarm and had a morbid longing for insignificance and obscurity. He seemed resigned to growing old in this way, never having had a friend or a sweetheart and having the tastes of a cloistered monk.

Yet this life did not weigh heavily on his broad shoulders. Julien was, at bottom, very happy. His was a calm, transparent soul. His daily round, lived according to fixed rules, was perfectly serene. Every morning he went to the office and took up his work where he had left off the day before; then he would eat his lunch, which consisted of a roll, and settle down to his copying again; then he had dinner, went to bed, and slept. The sun, rising the next morning, brought another identical day, and so it went on for weeks and months. This slow procession of days seemed, in the end, to produce a kind of sweet, gentle music that lulled him into the dreaminess of oxen ruminating at evening in fresh straw after their labors at the plow. He enjoyed all the charm of monotony. He would take pleasure, occasionally, in walking down the rue Beau Soleil after supper to sit on the bridge until nine o'clock should strike. He would dangle his legs above the stream and watch the Chanteclair flowing ceaselessly below with a pure tinkling of silver water. The willows on either bank would stand with pale faces downcast, their whole

---

Raquin (*1868*), *was shortly to reveal narrative gifts that had not many equals in the literature of the century. The imagination of this young man was soaked through by the harsh, hot sensuality of his native Provence; he had brought with him to Paris a larder of dreams, melodramatic fantasies, nightmares, hallucinations, and unfinished epic poems; and it was from these that he wrote for some years—progressing meanwhile from a garret to a publisher's stockroom to an upstairs office in the blurb department—before he discovered in the gross world about him enough matter to work on for a lifetime. What survives intact from the subsequent lifetime's work, which mistook itself by turns for social science and for prophetic revelation, is the thing his imagination did to the immense quantities of stuff that it took in and disgorged: the gross matter that Zola fed on became hallucinatory at his touch. Or,*

length reflected beneath them, while the fine gray ash of twilight drifted down through the sky. And he would remain there,
entranced and surrounded by utter calm, and thinking vaguely
that the Chanteclair must be as happy as he was, for it rolled on
forever over the same mosses and in the same delightful quiet.
When the stars came out, he would go home to bed, his lungs
filled with the cool freshness of evening.

He had other pleasures, too. At week-ends or on half-holidays
he would go off walking all on his own, quite happy to tramp
for miles and to come back utterly exhausted. He also made
friends with a deaf-mute, an engraver by trade; for whole afternoons together they would walk arm in arm up and down the
public promenade without exchanging as much as a sign. At
other times, sitting in the back of the Café des Voyageurs, they
would play endless games of checkers, interspersed with long,
motionless pauses for reflection. Julien had once had a dog that
had been run over by a carriage, and so religiously did he cultivate its memory that he had refused to have any other pet. His
colleagues at the post office used to tease him about a little
ragged, barefooted girl about ten years old who sold matches in
the street and whom he would ply with pennies though he never
took her matches. This annoyed him and he took pains to give
her the money when no one was watching. He had never been
seen out walking of an evening with a girl along by the old

---

as sometimes happened, it remained gross matter.

*In "Julien," Zola worked simply on an anecdote found in the
pages of a sophisticated adventurer; he transformed it into a
kind of nightmarish fairy tale whose characters are a bumpkin
with an almost magic flute, an inaccessible dark princess at her
window, and a perverse and sinister imp. The story has a freshness that is not always to be found in his later writings.*

OTHER WORKS: *Novels:* La Curée (*1872*), Le Ventre de
Paris (*1873*), L'Assommoir (*1877*), Nana (*1880*), Pot-Bouille
(*1881*), Germinal (*1885*), L'Oeuvre (*1886*), La Terre (*1887*),
La Bête humaine (*1890*), La Débâcle (*1892*). *Stories:* Naïs
Micoulin (*1884*), Madame Sourdis (*1929*). *Criticism:* Mes
Haines (*1866*), Le Roman experimental (*1880*), Les Roman-
ciers naturalistes (*1881*). *On the Dreyfus case:* La Vérité en
marche (*1901*).

town wall. Even the factory girls, who were brazen hussies, stopped bothering him when they saw that he took their encouraging giggles for jeers and remained speechless with embarrassment. Some of the townspeople thought him stupid; others claimed that quiet young fellows of this sort who live all alone are not to be trusted.

Julien's paradise, the place where he breathed freely, was his room. Only there did he feel himself safe from the world. As soon as he got home, he would straighten his back and laugh to himself; and when he caught sight of himself in the mirror, he would be surprised to see that he was still so young. It was a very big room; he had furnished it with a large sofa, a round table, two ordinary chairs, and an armchair. But there was still enough space for him to stretch his legs; the bed was tucked away in a huge recess; a small walnut chest of drawers stood between the two windows like a piece of toy furniture. Julien would walk up and down or stretch out on the bed; he never got bored with himself. Outside the office he did no writing, and reading tired him. The old lady who kept the boarding-house where he had his meals insisted on lending him novels to improve his mind, but he would bring them back without being any wiser as to their contents, because he could make neither head nor tail of their complicated plots. He would draw a little —always the same woman's profile, with a stern expression, hair parted in the middle and a string of pearls plaited into the bun. He had only one passion: music. For whole evenings together he would play the flute; that was by far his chief recreation.

He had taught himself to play. For a long time it had been one of his keenest desires to possess an old flute made of yellow wood which was offered for sale in the junk shop in the market place. He had the money, but the fear of looking ridiculous had prevented him from going in and buying it. At last, one evening he had had the courage to run off home with it, holding it pressed against his breast under his coat. Then he had spent two years—with doors and windows closed, and playing very quietly so that no one should hear—deciphering an old tutor he had found in a secondhand bookshop. Only during the last six months had he been bold enough to play with the windows open. He could manage only old, slow, simple tunes—love songs of the eighteenth century—which became infinitely tender when thus falteringly performed by a pupil so overcome by emotion. On warm evenings, when the whole neighborhood was asleep, and from the big room lit by a single candle there came this gentle piping, it was like a low, trembling, lovelorn voice confiding to solitude and to night secrets it would never have uttered in the light of day.

Knowing the tunes by heart, Julien would often put out his candle for economy's sake. Moreover, he liked being in the dark. He would play, sitting at the window and looking up at the sky. Passers-by would raise their heads to see where the music was coming from; it was thin and sweet, like the distant trilling of a nightingale. The old yellow flute was slightly cracked, and so its notes were a little muffled; it was the tiny charming voice of an old eighteenth-century marquise, still able to give a very good rendering of the minuets she had learned in her youth. One by one the notes would fly out, with the faint sound of rustling wings. The music seemed to be coming from the darkness itself, so closely did it blend with the hush of the night.

Julien was afraid that the neighbors might complain. But country people sleep soundly. Besides, the only other inhabitants of the Place des Quatre Femmes were M. Savournin, a lawyer, and Inspector Pidoux, a retired policeman; they were convenient neighbors to have, being always in bed and asleep by nine o'clock. Julien was more alarmed about the people who lived opposite, on the other side of the square—the aristocratic family of the Marsannes, whose house had the sad, gray, bleak look of a monastery. Five stone steps overgrown with grass led up to a door with a rounded top, forbiddingly studded with enormous nails. There was only one floor, with ten windows, the shutters of which were opened and closed regularly at the same times, though nothing could be seen of the rooms themselves because of thick curtains that were always kept drawn. On the left, the big chestnut trees in the garden formed a mass of greenery whose billowy leafiness stretched as far as the old town wall. The big, impressive house, with its gardens, its austere walls, and its look of majestic boredom, convinced Julien that if the Marsannes did not approve of his flute, they would only have to say the word to put an end to his playing.

He himself was filled with religious respect whenever he

leaned at his window to look out, so extensive did the grounds and the buildings appear. The big house was famous throughout the countryside, and it was said that strangers came from a great distance to visit it. There were also exciting stories about the wealth of the Marsannes. For a long time Julien had kept watch on the old place, trying to penetrate the mystery of their power and riches. He had spent hours lost in contemplation, but had seen nothing save the gray façade and the dark mass of the chestnut trees. No one ever climbed the five rickety steps, and the old door, green with moss, was never opened. The Marsannes did not use this entrance; they went in and out by a wrought-iron gate in the rue Saint-Anne; there was also another little door that Julien could not see; it led into the grounds at the end of a narrow street near the town wall. As far as Julien was concerned, the big house was dead, like a palace in a fairy tale inhabited by invisible creatures. All he could see was the arms of the servant who, morning and evening, dealt with the shutters. The rest of the time the house retained the noble, melancholy look of a tomb standing alone in the meditative silence of a graveyard. The chestnut trees were so thick that their branches hid the garden walks from sight. The thought of so proud and silent an existence, hermetically sealed off from the world, increased Julien's awe. Was this what wealth amounted to, a tranquil dreariness like the solemn atmosphere of a vast, empty church?

Many a time before going to bed he had blown out his candle and had remained watching for an hour at his window, in the hope of discovering the secrets of the Marsannes' house. At night it made a dark stain against the sky, and the chestnut trees were like a great pool of ink. The curtains must have been very carefully drawn on the inside because no ray of light escaped between the bars of the shutters. The house itself did not breathe as inhabited houses seem to breathe, with the breath of their sleeping inmates. It faded to nothingness in the dark. It was then that Julien made bold to take up his flute. He could play with impunity; the tiny rippling notes came echoing back from the empty house; some more languid cadences were lost in the darkness of the garden, where there was not even a rustle of wings to break the silence. The old yellow flute seemed to be playing its quaint tunes in front of Sleeping Beauty's castle.

On Sunday, outside the Church, one of Julien's fellow employees at the post office suddenly pointed out to him a tall old man and old woman who were, he said, M. and Mme de Marsanne. They stirred abroad so rarely that Julien had never seen them before. He was profoundly impressed; they seemed so gaunt and solemn, they walked so gravely and responded with only the slightest of nods to the deep bows of the people they passed. Julien's colleague added that they had a daughter, Mlle Thérèse de Marsanne, who was still at a convent boarding-school, and that little Colombel, clerk to Maître Savournin, the lawyer, was her foster brother. And it so happened, just as the old couple were about to turn into the rue Saint-Anne, that little Colombel appeared and went up to them; the Marquis held out his hand to him, an honor he had vouchsafed to no one else. It caused pain to Julien, because Colombel, a young fellow about twenty years old with sharp eyes and an unpleasant twist to his mouth, had for a long time been an enemy of his. Colombel had teased him about his shyness and had set the washerwoman of the rue Beau Soleil after him. The quarrel had ended in a bout of fisticuffs near the old town wall, and the lawyer's clerk had been given two black eyes. That evening, after learning these details about Thérèse and Colombel, Julien played his flute more softly still.

But, though the Marsannes' house disturbed him, it did not upset his habits, which were as regular as clockwork. He would go to his office, have lunch, have supper, and then go for his usual walk by the Chanteclair. The big house, with its profound peacefulness, came to have its place in his quiet daily round. Two years went by. He had become so used to the grass-covered steps, the gray façade, and the black shutters that it seemed to him that they must always remain the same and were a necessary part of that somnolent neighborhood.

Julien had been a tenant in the Place des Quatre Femmes for five years when, one July evening, an event occurred which upset his whole life. It was a very warm and starry night. He was playing his flute in the dark, rather absent-mindedly, at a very slow tempo, and even dozing over some of the notes, when suddenly a window of the Marsannes' house opposite was flung open and remained gaping wide, making a bright patch in the dark façade. A girl leaned against the sill and stood there, her slender form outlined against the light, lifting her head as if she was listening. Julien trembled and stopped playing. He could not see the girl's features, only her thick dark hair, which was already loose about her shoulders.

A lightly modulated voice came to him through the silence. "Didn't you hear it, Françoise? It sounded like music."

"Must have been a nightingale, miss," a gruff voice replied from inside the room. "Close the window or you'll let in moths or mosquitoes."

When the façade was all in darkness again, Julien could not leave his chair. His eyes were still dazzled by the bright gap that had opened in this wall, which had hitherto always been a lifeless black. And he was still trembling, wondering whether or not he ought to feel happy at the sudden vision. Then, an hour later, he began to play again, very softly. He smiled at the thought of the girl imagining that there must be a nightingale in the chestnut trees.

II

Next morning, at the post office, the great news was that Mlle Thérèse de Marsanne had returned from her convent school. Julien did not tell about seeing her with her hair down and her neck bare. He was very uneasy; he had an indefinable feeling of hostility toward Thérèse, for she was going to upset his habits. Without a doubt, he would be horribly bothered by the fact that at any moment the shutters of her window might fly open. He would no longer enjoy any privacy. He would have much preferred a man to a woman, for women are more given to mockery. How would he dare, from now on, to play the flute? He was too poor a player to perform within earshot of a young lady who must have studied music. So, by evening, after thus ruminating at length, he was convinced that he hated Thérèse.

Julien entered the house stealthily. He left his candle unlit, so that she would not see him. He intended to go to bed at once to prove to himself how put out he was. But he could not resist the craving to see what was happening opposite. The window did not open. Only later, about ten o'clock, did a faint glimmer show through the chinks in the shutters; it soon went out, and he was left watching the darkened window. From then on, every evening, he could not help spying on the house opposite in this

way. As in the beginning, he carefully noted the faintest breath-
ings that gave life to its old, mute stones. Nothing seemed to
have changed; the house slumbered on as before; practiced
eyes and ears were needed to catch the signs of new life. Sometimes a faint light would be seen moving from window to window; sometimes a fold of curtain would be drawn aside, giving
a rapid glimpse of some enormous room. On other occasions,
light footsteps could be heard crossing the garden, or there
would be the distant tinkle of a piano accompanying a song; or,
again, the sounds would be vaguer still; or there would be
merely a faint tremor revealing the throbbing of young blood
in the old mansion. Julien accounted for his curiosity by telling
himself that he was very upset by all this commotion. How he
regretted the days when the muted echoes of his flute came back
to him from the empty house!

Although he would not admit it, one of his most ardent desires was to see Thérèse again. He pictured her with rosy
cheeks, a mocking air, and shining eyes. But as he never ventured to appear at his window in the daytime, he caught sight of
her only after nightfall, and then she seemed all gray in the
darkness. One morning, as he was closing the shutters of one of
his windows to keep out the sun, he saw Thérèse standing in the
middle of her room. She seemed to be thinking of something as
she stood there, very tall and pale; her features were beautiful
and regular. She almost inspired him with fear, so different was
she from the gay person he had imagined. He was particularly
struck by her rather large mouth with its bright red lips, and
her black, deep-set, unsmiling eyes, which made her look like
some cruel queen. Slowly she came forward to the window, but
she did not appear to see him; it was as if he was too far away,
too imperceptible among so many other things. She turned
away, and her neck rippled with so strong, so graceful, and so
rhythmical a movement that, in spite of his broad shoulders, he
felt as weak as a child compared with her. Now that he had seen
her, she alarmed him still more.

After this, Julien led a miserable existence. The noble, serious, beautiful young lady who lived so near him reduced him to
despair. She never looked at him; she was unaware of his existence. But that did not prevent him from feeling faint at the
thought that she might notice him and consider him ridiculous.

His morbid shyness made him think that she was spying on
every one of his movements to mock at him. He would slink
home and would take care not to move about in his room. Then,
when a month or so had passed, he began to suffer because she
disregarded him. Why did she never look at him? She would
come to the window; her black eyes would gaze over the deserted square, then she would withdraw without ever guessing
his anxious presence opposite her. And just as he had trembled
at the thought of being seen by her, so now he quivered with the
craving to feel her eyes fixed on him. She filled every hour of
his life.

When it was time for Thérèse to get up in the morning, Julien, who had always been so punctual, would forget about his
work. He was still afraid of her white face and scarlet lips, but
his fear was delicious; he enjoyed feeling it. Hiding behind a
curtain, he allowed the terror she inspired to flow into him until
he felt ill and his legs were as shaky as if he had just been
for a long walk. He would dream that she had suddenly taken
notice of him, had smiled at him, and that he was no longer
afraid.

Then it occurred to him to woo her by means of his flute.
During warm evenings he began to play again. He would leave
the two windows open, and in the darkness he would play his
oldest tunes—pastoral airs that were as sweet and innocent as
little girls dancing in a ring. Sometimes the notes were tremulous and long drawn out, and followed one another in a simple
rhythm, like lovelorn ladies of the past spreading out their
skirts. He would choose moonless nights; the square was dark,
and it was impossible to tell the source of the gentle music that
rose up past the sleeping houses, skimming the walls like the
soft wing of some night bird. The very first evening he had the
excitement of seeing Thérèse, on the point of getting into bed,
come to the window all in white and lean out, astonished to
hear once more the music she had noticed the day she had come
home.

"Listen, Françoise," she said in her deep voice, turning inward from the window. "It's not a bird."

"Oh," replied the old woman, of whom Julien could see nothing but her shadow. "It must be some player amusing himself
in a house a long way off."

"Yes, a very long way off," repeated the girl, after a pause, as she cooled her bare arms in the night air.

Thereafter, every evening, Julien played louder and louder. And as the sound swelled, his excitement passed from his lips into the old yellow wood flute. And Thérèse, as she listened every evening, was astonished at the music; it waited until darkness fell before coming toward her, and then the lively cascades echoed from roof to roof. She realized that the serenade was addressed to her window, and she would sometimes stand on tiptoe as if to look over the housetops. Then one night the notes burst forth so near that they seemed to touch her; she guessed that they were coming from somewhere in the square, from one of the slumbering old houses. Julien breathed all his passion into the instrument, which throbbed with a sound of crystal. The darkness made him so bold that he hoped to draw her to him by means of his music. And indeed Thérèse leaned out from her window as if caught and charmed.

"Come inside," said the old woman's voice. "There's thunder about, and you'll have nightmares."

The whole night through, Julien did not sleep. He imagined that Thérèse must have guessed who he was or must have seen him. He lay on his bed, hot with passion, wondering whether he should not reveal himself the next day. Undoubtedly it would be ridiculous of him to remain in hiding any longer. Yet he decided that he would not show himself, and at six o'clock in the morning he was standing at his window, putting his flute back into its case, when Thérèse's shutters suddenly flew open.

Usually she did not get up until eight o'clock, but now she appeared in a dressing-gown, with her hair carelessly tied about her neck. Julien stood there stupidly, looking up at her, unable to turn away, and all the while his clumsy hands were vainly struggling to take the flute to pieces. As for Thérèse, she examined him with a steady, imperious look. For a few moments she seemed to be studying his heavy bones, his great, lumpish body—in short, the whole appearance of the shy and ugly giant. And she was no longer the ardent girl of the night before; she was haughty and very pale, with black eyes and scarlet lips. When she had made up her mind about him, with as calm an air as if she were wondering whether or not she liked a dog in the street, she condemned him with a slight pout. Then, taking her time about it, she closed the window and turned her back on him.

Julien, feeling weak at the knees, dropped into his armchair, and strangled phrases broke from his lips. "She doesn't like me! . . . And I love her. . . . It'll kill me."

He held his head in his hands and sobbed. Why, oh why, had he shown himself? A misshapen fellow like him ought to keep in hiding and not come out to frighten the girls. He cursed himself, furious at his ugliness. Ought he not to have gone on playing his flute in the shadows like some night bird that wins all hearts by its song but must never appear in daylight, on pain of displeasing? He would have remained forever a gentle air that she listened to, an old-fashioned tune expressing mysterious love. She would have adored him without knowing him, as if he had been some Prince Charming come from afar to die of love beneath her windows. But he, rough fool that he was, had broken the spell. And now she knew that he was as clumsy as an ox at the plow, and she would never like his music again!

He was right. In vain he repeated his tenderest tunes, choosing warm nights scented with the fragrance of flowers and trees; Thérèse neither listened nor even heard. She came and went in her room or leaned out at her window as if he had not been there opposite her, trying to express his love in humble little notes. One day she even exclaimed: "Oh, how irritating to hear that flute playing out of tune!"

Filled with despair, he put his flute away in a drawer and never played again.

It should be mentioned that little Colombel also mocked at Julien. One day, on his way to Maître Savournin's, he had seen Julien busy practicing a piece at the window, and every time he crossed the square he would laugh his jeering laugh. Julien knew that the lawyer's clerk was a frequent visitor at the Marsannes' house, and this cut him to the quick; he was not jealous of the stunted little fellow, but he would have given his life's blood to be in his shoes for an hour. Colombel's mother, Françoise, had been in service with the Marsannes for years; she had begun as Thérèse's wet nurse and was now her maid. The young aristocrat and the little peasant boy had grown up together, and it seemed natural that something of their early relationship should have survived. Nevertheless, it was painful for Julien to

meet Colombel in the street, his lips twisted in a thin smile.
Julien's dislike became keener when he noticed that his stunted
rival was not ill-featured; Colombel's head was round, like a
cat's, but delicate, handsome, and diabolical; he had green eyes
and wisps of curly beard on his soft, round chin. Oh, if Julien
could have got him again in a corner near the old town wall,
how he would have made him pay for the pleasure of seeing
Thérèse in her own home!

A year went by. Julien was very unhappy. He lived only for
Thérèse. His heart was in the cold house, in whose shadow he
was wasting away with shyness and love. All his leisure moments were spent in the same spot; he remained there with his
eyes fixed on the stretch of gray wall, every mossy stone of
which he knew by heart. For months he had watched and listened in vain; he still knew nothing of the inner life of the
solemn mansion, where his whole being was in bondage. Vague
sounds and stray glimmerings confused him. Did they indicate
celebrations or funerals? He could not tell, because it was on
the other side of the house that life was lived; he could imagine
whatever he chose according to the sadness or the gaiety of his
mood; Thérèse and Colombel, boisterously amusing each
other; the young girl strolling under the chestnut trees, or
swaying in the arms of her dancing-partners, or, again, suddenly overwhelmed by unhappiness and weeping in cheerless
rooms. At other times he thought he heard only the faint footsteps of the Marquis and the Marquise pattering mouse-like
over the old polished wooden floors. And so he lived in ignorance, Thérèse's window being the only gap in the mysterious
wall. The young woman came daily into view, as silent as a
statue, but her appearance never brought the slightest hope. He
was profoundly distressed by her remoteness and his ignorance
of her life.

His happiest moments were when the window was left open.
Then he could peer into the corners of the room during
Thérèse's absence. It took him six months to discover that her
bed, which had curtains of pink silk, was on the left in a recess.
It took him six more months to make out, opposite the bed, a
Louis Quinze chest of drawers, on which stood a porcelain-
framed mirror. Facing the window was a white marble fire-
place. The room was his dream of paradise.

The course of his love was marked by tremendous struggles. For weeks he would remain hidden, ashamed of his ugliness. Then he would be seized by fits of rage. He would feel a craving to display his heavy limbs and to force upon her the sight of his knobbly, feverish face. And so he would remain for weeks at his window to harass her with his gaze. On two occasions, even, he threw her burning kisses, with the savagery of a shy man consumed with a frenzy of boldness.

Thérèse did not even get annoyed. When he remained hidden, he could see her moving about with her regal mien, and when he forced himself upon her, she became, if anything, only more cold and imperious. He never caught her in a relaxed moment. If she happened to set eyes on him, she was in no hurry to turn away. When he heard them saying at the post office that Mlle de Marsanne was very pious and charitable, he sometimes protested violently under his breath. No, she was not religious; she was fond of blood, for her lips were blood-red and the pallor of her complexion was a result of her contempt for the world. And then he would weep at the thought of having insulted her, and he would ask her pardon as if she were a saint enfolded in the purity of her wings.

During this first year, day after day went by without bringing the slightest change. When summer came round again, he experienced a strange sensation. Thérèse seemed to him to be living in a different atmosphere. The same little things continued to happen: her shutters were opened in the morning and closed in the evening, and she appeared regularly at the usual times. But from her window there came a breath of something new, and she herself seemed paler and taller. One day, when he was beside himself with love, he ventured a third time to raise a feverish hand and blow her a kiss. She remained at the window and looked at him steadily, with her usual disconcerting gravity. It was he who drew back, his cheeks crimson.

There was only one new occurrence, toward the end of the summer. It was a very simple matter, but it affected him deeply. Almost every day, at dusk, Thérèse's window, which had been left ajar, was closed so violently that the woodwork creaked and the click of the catch could be clearly heard. The sound always gave Julien a painful start, and, without knowing why, he would be gripped by anguish and his heart would ache.

After this brutal jolt the house would relapse into a deathlike silence that filled him with fear. For a long time he could not make out who closed the window in this way. But one evening he saw Thérèse's pale hands; it was she who turned the catch with such furious energy. And when she opened the window again an hour later, she would do so unhurriedly, with measured dignity, and she would lean out for a few moments with an air of lassitude; then she would move about her virginal bedroom, absorbed in some unimportant feminine task. Julien's mind would be a blank, except for the sound of the window catch still ringing in his ears.

One autumn evening, when the weather was mild and over-cast, the window was shut with a terrible grating noise. Julien shivered and tears started from his eyes as he sat watching the gloomy house, now obscured by the oncoming dusk. It had rained that morning, and the chestnut trees, which had lost half their leaves, gave off a funereal odor.

Meanwhile, Julien was waiting for the window to open again. It did so all of a sudden and just as noisily as it had been shut. Thérèse appeared, very pale, large-eyed, and with her hair loose on her shoulders. She stood right in the middle of the window, put the fingers of both hands to her red lips, and blew Julien a kiss.

Julien, bewildered, pressed his two fists to his chest, as if to ask whether the kiss was meant for him.

This made Thérèse think he was backing away. She leaned farther out, again put her fingers to her red lips, and threw him a second kiss. And then a third. It was as if she were returning the three he had given her. Julien gaped with astonishment. Through the twilight he could see her quite clearly, framed in the darkness of the window.

When she thought that she had convinced him, she glanced round the little square, and in a muffled voice pronounced the one word: "Come!"

He went—downstairs and across to the house. As he looked up, the door at the top of the steps was opened—the door that had been bolted for half a century perhaps, so that its two leaves were sealed with moss. But he moved on in a kind of stupor, no longer surprised at anything. As soon as he was inside, the door was closed again and he followed a small, icy hand that led the way. He went up a flight of stairs, along a corridor, through one room, and then found himself in another, which he recognized. It was the earthly paradise he had dreamed of, the room with the pink silk curtains. Daylight was fading there slowly and gently. He felt an impulse to fall on his knees. But Thérèse was standing upright in front of him; her hands were clasped together and she was so resolute that she managed to control the trembling of her body.

"Do you love me?" she asked in a low voice.

"Oh, yes, yes," he stammered.

But she made a gesture as if to cut short any useless talk. With a haughty air that seemed to make the words natural and chaste on her young lips, she continued: "And if I gave myself to you, you would do anything for me?"

He was incapable of answering; he could only press his hands together. To be kissed by her he would have sold himself into captivity.

"Well, I want you to do something for me."

He remained as imbecilic as before. As she felt that her strength was so exhausted that she might not dare make her request, she burst out with sudden violence: "Come! You must give me your word! I swear to keep my part of the bargain. Swear! Swear!"

"I swear . . . anything you like," he said in a rush of complete abandon.

The pure fragrance of the room intoxicated him. The curtains of the alcove were drawn, and the thought of her virginal bed in the soft half-light filtering through the pink silk was enough to fill him with a religious ecstasy. Then, with hands that had become suddenly rough and brutal, she wrenched aside the curtains and revealed the alcove in the sinister glimmering of twilight. The bed was untidy; the bedclothes were hanging half off it, and a pillow, lying on the floor, seemed to have been bitten right through. And, sprawling across the bed among the crushed lace covers, lay the body of a man. His feet were bare.

"You see," she explained in a strangled voice, "he was my lover. I pushed him and he fell. I don't know exactly what happened. But he is dead, and you must carry him away."

III

Thérèse de Marsanne had begun to bully Colombel when she was still a little girl. He was her elder by a little under six months, and from the time of Thérèse's birth, his mother, Françoise, had reared him on the bottle in order to suckle her. He grew up in the house and came to occupy an ambiguous position there, being half servant and half playmate to the little girl.

Thérèse was a terrible child. Not that she was tomboyish or noisy. On the contrary, she always maintained an attitude of exceptional gravity, so that visitors, to whom she curtsied very prettily, thought her a well-mannered child. But at times she behaved very strangely. When she was alone, she would burst into inarticulate cries or stamp and rage madly; or she would lie down flat on her back in the middle of a garden path and remain stretched out there, obstinately refusing to get up, in spite of the whippings she sometimes received.

No one ever knew what she was thinking. Even when she was a child, she kept every revealing gleam out of her wide eyes, which, unlike those clear mirrors in which the souls of little girls are so accurately reflected, were two dark pools, as black as ink, which gave nothing away.

At the age of six she began to torment Colombel. He was small and weakly. So she would take him to the far end of the garden under the chestnut trees, to a spot where the shade was thickest, and there she would jump on his back and make him carry her. For an hour at a time she would gallop him round and round a clear space where the paths met, hugging him tightly, digging her heels into his ribs, and never allowing him to get his breath. He was the horse; she was the lady. When he was dizzy to the point of collapse, she would bite his ear till it bled or would cling to him with so fierce an embrace that her tiny nails pierced his flesh. And off again they would gallop— the cruel six-year-old queen riding through the trees with her hair flying and the little boy she was using as her mount.

Later, in her parents' presence, she would nip him, having first forbidden him to make a sound. She continually threatened to have him thrown out of the house if he spoke about their games. They had, therefore, a secret life and a different relationship in public. When they were alone, she treated him like a doll and, every now and again, had a sudden desire to break him, to see what was inside. Was she not a marquise, and did not everyone bow to her will? They had given her a little man to play with, and she could surely do what she liked with him. And when she tired of ruling over Colombel in private, she would give herself the keener pleasure of kicking him or sticking a pin into his arm when they were in a room full of people, at the same time hypnotizing him with her dark eyes so that he did not even give a start.

Colombel put up with his martyrdom, but he had moments of silent rebellion when he would stand trembling, with downcast eyes, so as not to be tempted to strangle his young mistress. He himself had a sly nature. It did not displease him to be beaten. He took a bitter pleasure in it. Sometimes he would provoke Thérèse into pricking him and would wait for the prick with a thrill of rage; he would be satisfied when he felt the point of the needle; he could then abandon himself to the delights of resentment. In any case, he was already taking his revenge. He would fall down deliberately on stony ground, taking Thérèse with him; he had no fear of breaking his own limbs and was delighted when she acquired a bruise or two. The reason he did not cry out when she pricked him in the presence of grownups was that he did not want anyone to come between them. Their relationship was their own affair, and he intended to get the upper hand later.

Meanwhile, Thérèse's violent outbursts disturbed the Marquis. One of her uncles had led a most disorderly life, which had ended by his being murdered in a brothel in a remote part of the town, and Thérèse was said to be like him. A tragic thread ran through the family history of the Marsannes. While most of them were austerely dignified, in every generation or so one member of the family would be afflicted with a strange malady. It took the form of a kind of craziness, a perversion of the feelings; it was like some evil scum by means of which the family was purged for a time of its impurities. Therefore, the Marquis prudently decided that Thérèse must have a stern upbringing. He sent her to a convent, where, he hoped, the discipline might tame her wild nature. She stayed there until the age of eighteen.

When she came home again, she was a tall, very well-behaved girl. Her parents were happy to notice that she was profoundly pious. In church she would remain kneeling for a long time with her head between her hands. At home she filled the atmosphere with a fragrance of innocence and peace. She had only one weakness—a fondness for sweets. She would eat them from morning till evening, sucking them with half-closed eyes and slightly trembling red lips. No one would have recognized her as the silent, stubborn child who had used to come in from the garden with her dress torn to ribbons and refuse to tell what had happened. The Marquis and his wife, who for the last fifteen years had remained shut up in their big, empty house, felt that they must begin to hold receptions again. They gave a number of dinners, and even a ball, to which neighboring aristocrats were invited. Their aim was to marry Thérèse off. In spite of her chilliness of manner, she fell in with their wishes, dressed and danced—but with so pale a face that she alarmed the young men who ventured to fall in love with her.

Since returning home, Thérèse had not mentioned Colombel. The Marquis, who had taken an interest in him and seen to his education, had recently found him a job with Maître Savournin, the lawyer. One day Françoise brought her son to the house and pushed him forward to greet Thérèse, at the same time reminding her that he was her former playmate. Colombel was neatly turned out, all smiles and not in the least embarrassed. Thérèse looked at him calmly, said that she remembered him, and then turned away. But Colombel came back a week later, and was soon established on the old footing. He would come to the house every evening after work, bringing with him sheets of music, books, and picture albums. The Marsannes treated him in an offhand manner, making him do their errands as if he were a servant or a poor relation. He was regarded as a hanger-on of the family. So no one thought it peculiar that Thérèse and he should be left alone together. As in the old days, they would shut themselves up alone in the big rooms and spend hours together under the trees in the garden. To tell the truth, they no longer played the same games. Thérèse would walk slowly along, her dress rustling lightly over the grass. Colombel, dressed like one of the wealthy young men of the town, would stroll at her side, flicking the ground with a flexible cane, from which he was never parted.

However, Thérèse had become the queen again, and he was reverting to the position of her slave. She no longer bit him, it is true, but she had a way of walking beside him which made him smaller than he actually was and transformed him into a court lackey, acting as train-bearer to a sovereign. She tormented him with her sudden changes of mood. At one moment she would be all confiding and affectionate and then, the next, all harshness—simply for her own amusement. When she was looking the other way, Colombel, with glistening eye, would steal a furtive glance at her, a glance as cutting as a sword, and his whole vicious body would strain into watchfulness as he wondered how he could catch her out.

They had been walking for a long while one summer evening, under the thick shade of the chestnut trees, when Thérèse, after a moment's silence, gravely remarked: "I say, Colombel, I feel rather tired. What about carrying me, as you used to? You remember?"

He gave a slight laugh, then replied, very seriously: "If you like."

But she walked on, merely saying: "Good! I only wanted to know."

They continued their stroll. Night was falling, and the shadows were black under the trees. They were talking about a young woman who had just married an officer stationed in the town. As they turned to go along a narrower path, Colombel stepped aside to allow Thérèse to go first; but she bumped violently against him, forcing him to walk ahead. Then they both fell silent.

Suddenly Thérèse jumped onto Colombel's back with all her old vicious, tomboyish suppleness.

"Come on, gallop!" she said, and her voice was strained and distorted by her childhood passion.

She had snatched his cane from him and was belaboring his thighs. Clamped to his shoulders and squeezing his flanks between her wiry, amazon's legs, she drove him madly into the dark shadows under the trees. For a long time she went on whipping him and urging him forward. The sound of Colombel's galloping feet was muffled by the grass. He did not utter a word, but, breathing heavily, he tensed himself on his short legs to carry the warm burden of the big girl, who was pressing down on the nape of his neck.

But when she shouted: "That's enough!" he did not stop. He galloped on more quickly still, as if carried along by his own impetus. His hands were clasped behind his back, and her legs were so tightly caught that she could not jump down. The horse was bolting now and running off with its mistress. Suddenly, disregarding the thrashing cane and her clawing fingernails, he headed for a shed where the gardener kept his implements. There he threw her down on a heap of straw and raped her. At long last his turn had come to be the master.

Thérèse became paler still, her lips more scarlet, her eyes blacker. She behaved as piously as before. A few days later the scene was repeated; she jumped onto Colombel's back, tried to get the better of him, and was thrown down onto the straw in the shed. When other people were present, she continued to treat Colombel with gentle condescension, as if she were his elder sister. He too remained calm and smiling. They were still, as they had been at the age of six, like spiteful animals, taking pleasure in biting each other on the sly when they were let loose. Only it was the male who triumphed now, at the turbid climax of desire.

Theirs was a ferocious love affair. So that Colombel might come to her room, Thérèse gave him a key to the little garden gate opening onto the narrow street by the old town wall. At night Colombel had to pass through another room, which, as it happened, was his mother's bedroom. But the two lovers displayed such tranquil audacity that they were never caught. They boldly arranged meetings in broad daylight. Colombel would come to the house before dinner, and Thérèse, expecting him, would close the window to shield herself from prying eyes. They had a constant longing to be together, not to bill and coo in the usual manner of sweethearts of twenty, but to match pride against pride. Often a quarrel would break out between them and they would abuse each other in undertones and shake with anger because they could not strike each other and shout.

On this particular evening Colombel had come before dinner. As he was moving about the room, with bare feet and still in his shirt sleeves, he had a sudden impulse to grasp Thérèse round the waist and lift her up, as wrestlers do at the beginning of a bout.

Thérèse tried to release herself, saying: "Let me go. You know I'm stronger than you are. I'll only hurt you."

Colombel gave a slight laugh. "Go on. Hurt me!" he whispered.

He was shaking her, trying to force her down. She gripped him. It was a game they often played to satisfy their zest for conflict. Usually Colombel was tossed backward onto the carpet, winded, limp, and exhausted. He was too small; Thérèse could pick him up and smother him, like a giantess embracing a pygmy.

But on this occasion Thérèse slipped to her knees, and Colombel, with a quick movement, pulled her over. Then, standing over her, he said triumphantly, with an insulting laugh: "You are not stronger, you see."

She was white with rage. She got up slowly and silently and grasped him again. She was trembling so violently with anger that he felt a thrill of panic. She wanted to choke him, to make an end of him, to see him lying inert at her feet, vanquished once and for all. For a minute or two they struggled without a word, panting hard, their joints cracking as they gripped and swayed. They were no longer playing a game. A cold, homicidal breath blew around them. He began to gasp audibly. Fearing that they might be overheard, she threw him with one last terrible heave. His temple caught the corner of the chest of drawers and he slumped heavily to the floor.

It took Thérèse a moment or two to get her breath back. Then she tidied her hair in front of the mirror and smoothed her skirt, affecting to pay no attention to her beaten adversary. He could pick himself up. Then she prodded him with her foot. As he still did not move, she finally bent over him, feeling a chill at the nape of her neck under the curling wisps of hair. She saw that Colombel's face was as pale as wax, his eyes glazed, and his mouth twisted. There was a hole in his right temple where he had hit himself against the corner of the chest of drawers. Colombel was dead.

Horror-stricken, Thérèse stood up again. She spoke aloud in the quiet room. "Dead! So he's dead, then!"

And suddenly the realization of what had happened filled her with terrible anguish. Of course, for a few seconds she had wanted to kill him, but the angry thought had been mere stupidity. Anyone who fights wants to kill the other person, but in fact never does so, because a dead person is too much of an embarrassment. No! No! She wasn't guilty. She had not intended to kill him. In her bedroom—it was unthinkable!

She continued to speak aloud in disjointed phrases. "Well, it's all over. . . . He's dead. . . . He will not get out of here alone."

Then the first cold stupor gave way to hot feverishness, which rose from her bowels to her throat like a wave of fire. There was a dead man in her bedroom. She would never be able to explain how he came to be there, with bare feet, in his shirt sleeves, and with a hole in his temple. She was lost.

Thérèse stooped down and looked at the wound. But terror made her stand motionless over the body. She could hear Françoise, Colombel's mother, going along the corridor. There were other noises, too; footsteps, voices, sounds of preparation for the reception that was to take place that evening. At any moment someone might call her or come to fetch her. And the dead man was lying there. She was suddenly conscious of the burden of her lover's death and of the great weight of their sin.

Then, bewildered by the increasing commotion in her mind, she stood up and began to walk round and round the room. She was looking for a hole in which to throw the corpse, which now lay between her and the future; she looked under the furniture and into corners, shaking with tremulous rage at being so powerless. There was no hole to be found; the alcove did not go back far enough; the cupboards were too narrow; no part of the room would come to her aid. Yet this same room had concealed their love-making! Colombel would come in stealthily, wickedly, like a cat, and depart in the same manner. She would never have believed that he could become so heavy.

Thérèse was still pattering round and round the room with the crazy, leaping movements of a cornered animal, when she had a sudden inspiration. Could she not throw the body out of the window? But it would be found, and it would be easy to guess where it had come from. However, she had lifted the curtain to look out into the street; suddenly she saw the young man opposite, the stupid young man who played the flute, leaning out of his window, with his usual meek, dog-like expression. His pasty face was familiar to her; it was always gazing in her direction, and she was tired of it, so clearly did it express cowardly adoration. But she stopped short at the sight of Julien, at once so humble and so loving. A smile lit up her pale face. She was saved. Her stupid neighbor loved her with the fidelity of a watchdog and would commit a crime for her sake if told to do so. Moreover, she would repay him with all her heart and all her body. She had not loved him before, because he was too meek; but she would love him; if, for her sake, he stained his hands with blood, she would silence him forever by keeping her word and yielding her body to him. Her scarlet lips quivered slightly as if she were already tasting his terror-stricken love; the prospect attracted her by its novelty.

Then, swiftly, as if she were lifting a bundle of clothes, she picked Colombel's body up from the floor and carried it to the bed; after which, opening the window, she threw three kisses to Julien.

IV

Julien moved as if in a nightmare. He was not astonished to see that the man on the bed was Colombel. It seemed a simple and natural fact. No one but Colombel could have been lying there in the alcove with a gash in his temple and his legs sprawled out in a horribly obscene posture.

But Thérèse was speaking to him; she had been for some time. At first he did not hear what she was saying. The words dripped through his confused mind in an indistinct murmur. Then he realized that she was giving him instructions, and he listened. He was on no account to leave the bedroom, but was to stay there until midnight, when the house would be dark and empty. The reception her father was giving made it impossible for them to do anything before then; but on the whole it was a help. Everyone would be too busy to think of coming up to Thérèse's room. When the time came, Julien would hoist the corpse onto his back, carry it downstairs and along the rue Beau Soleil, and then throw it into the Chanteclair. Nothing could be easier, judging by the calm with which Thérèse explained all the details of the plan.

She paused; then, putting both hands on Julien's shoulders, she asked: "Have you understood? Are we agreed?"

He trembled from head to foot. "Yes, I'll do whatever you like. I'm yours to command."

Then, very gravely, she leaned toward him. He did not understand what she wanted, so she said: "Kiss me."

With a shiver, he deposited a kiss on her cold brow, and they both fell silent.

Thérèse had drawn the bed curtains again. She sank into an armchair and, hidden by the shadows, relaxed for the first time. Julien remained standing for a few moments; then he too sat down. Françoise had left the next room; only muffled sounds came from the rest of the house; the room seemed to fall asleep as darkness gradually stole over it.

For almost an hour nothing stirred. Inside Julien's head, a great throbbing prevented him from following any line of thought. He was in Thérèse's bedroom, and the realization filled him with delight. Then suddenly he would remember that the corpse of a man was lying in the alcove behind those curtains that caused him such a thrill when he brushed against them; and he would feel faint. Was it possible that she could have loved the puny little wretch? He forgave her for having killed him; what made his blood boil was the sight of Colombel's bare feet among the lace covers of the bed. With what glee he would throw him into the Chanteclair. He knew of a deep, dark pool at the end of the bridge. They would both be rid of him then, and could enjoy each other. And suddenly, at the thought of such happiness—a happiness such as he had not dared dream of that morning—Julien imagined himself lying on the bed in exactly the same place as the corpse; but it was cold there, and he was filled with terror and revulsion.

Lying back in her chair, Thérèse remained motionless. He could see only the outline of her head, topped by its bun, against the vague brightness of the window. Her face was buried in her hands, and it was impossible to tell what she was feeling as she lay there, sunk in oblivion. Was it simply the physical reaction after the horrible crisis that she had just gone through? Was it stifled remorse or regret for her lover, now sleeping his last sleep? Was she calmly settling the final details of her plan, or was she hiding her face in the shadows to conceal the marks of terrible fear? He could not guess.

In the heavy silence the clock struck the hour. Thérèse rose slowly from her chair and lit the candles on her dressing-table. They showed her to be as beautifully composed as ever, relaxed and strong. She seemed to have forgotten about the body lying behind the pink silk curtains. She moved hither and thither with the tranquil step of a woman busy about some task in the sheltered privacy of her room. Then, as she was letting down her hair, she remarked, without even turning round: "I am going to dress for the reception. If anyone comes, you will, of course, hide at the back of the alcove."

He remained seated, watching her. She was already treating him like a lover, as if the bloody collusion into which she had brought him had accustomed them to each other like a long liaison.

She lifted her arms and arranged her hair. He watched her, trembling, so desirable did she appear with her bare back and her delicate elbows and slender hands lazily moving in the air as she adjusted her ringlets. Was she already trying her wiles on him and, to give him courage, showing him what sort of mistress he was about to win?

She had just finished putting on her shoes when there was a sound of approaching footsteps.

"Hide in the alcove," she whispered.

With a quick gesture she covered Colombel's stiffening corpse with the underclothes she had just taken off; they were still warm and scented with the smell of her body.

Françoise came in and said: "They are waiting for you, mademoiselle."

"I'm coming, Françoise," Thérèse calmly replied. "Since you are here, you can help me on with my dress."

Julien could see them through a gap in the curtain, and Thérèse's audacity made him tremble. His teeth were chattering so hard that he had to grasp his jaw with his hand to stop the noise. By his side he could see one of Colombel's feet, now ice-cold, projecting from under Thérèse's petticoat. What if Françoise were to draw the curtains and to bump against the foot that was sticking out, her son's foot!

"Be careful," Thérèse was saying. "Handle it gently or you'll loosen the flowers."

There was no trace of alarm in her voice. She was smiling now, like any girl happy to be going to a ball. Her dress was of white silk decorated with white wild roses, each of which had a tiny splash of red at the center. And when she stood up in the middle of the room, she was like a mass of blossom, virginal in its whiteness. The snowy whiteness of her bare arms and neck continued the whiteness of the silk.

"Oh, how beautiful you look, how beautiful!" Françoise went on repeating with satisfaction. "Wait! You need the spray of roses for your hair."

She glanced round the room to find it, and put out her hand toward the curtains, as if she were going to look on the bed. Julien stifled a cry of anguish. But Thérèse answered unhurriedly, still smiling to herself in the mirror: "It's on the chest of drawers. Hand it to me. But don't touch my bed. I've put my things there and you'll disarrange them."

Françoise helped her to place in position the long spray of wild briar which served as a headdress, with one wavy strand hanging down behind. Then Thérèse stood for a moment looking at herself with satisfaction. She was all ready now and was putting on her gloves.

"Well, I'll say this," Françoise exclaimed. "No Madonna in a church was ever whiter than you."

The compliment brought another smile to Thérèse's face. She looked at herself for the last time and went toward the door, saying: "Come along. Let's go down. You may blow out the candles."

In the sudden darkness that invaded the room Julien heard the door close behind them and Thérèse's dress move away with a silken rustling along the corridor. He sat down on the floor at the back of the alcove, not yet daring to emerge. The blackness of night had dropped a veil over his eyes, but near him he could still feel the presence of the bare foot; it seemed to chill the whole room. He had sat like that for a long time—how long he did not know—and so weighted down with confused thoughts that he might have been in a doze, when the door opened again. A faint rustle of silk told him it was Thérèse. She did not come near him, but placed something on the chest of drawers, saying in a low voice: "You can't have had any dinner. . . . You must eat. Do you hear?"

Again there was a faint rustle, and for the second time the dress moved off down the corridor. Julien, shaken out of his torpor, got up. He felt he could no longer breathe in the alcove. He could not bear to stay near the bed, next to Colombel. The clock struck eight. He still had four hours to wait. So he began to walk backward and forward, stepping gingerly so as to make no noise.

A dim light coming from the starry sky helped him to make out the dark masses of the furniture. Some corners of the room were lost in shadow. Only the mirror retained a dull sheen, like old silver. He was not easily frightened, yet every now and again, in that bedroom, beads of perspiration would run down his face. Around him the dark shapes of the furniture seemed to move and adopt menacing attitudes. Thrice he thought he heard sighs coming from the alcove. Each time he stopped, terrified. Then, on listening more intently, he realized that the sounds were coming from the reception below; he could hear a snatch of music or the merry chatter of the crowd of guests. He would close his eyes, and suddenly, escaping from the black pit of the bedroom, he would find himself in a blaze of light in a dazzling ballroom, and Thérèse would waltz past in her virginal dress, swirling amorously in her partner's arms. The whole house resounded with gay music. He was alone and shaking with fear in the horrible room. At one moment he started back with his hair standing on end. He thought he saw a light appear on one of the chairs. When he nerved himself to go up to it and touch it, he realized that it was a white satin corset. He picked it up, buried his face in the material, which had been softened by the pressure of her amazon's breasts, and, to forget his anguish, inhaled the scent of her body.

What bliss it was! He would have liked to forget everything. He was not keeping a vigil for the dead, but a vigil of love. He drew near to the window and, with his forehead resting against the pane and the satin corset still at his lips, he went through the story of his love from the beginning. Opposite, on the other side of the street, he could see his room with its casements still open. It was there that he had won Thérèse's heart by devotedly playing his music during the long evenings. His flute had breathed his adoration and confessed his tenderness with the voice of a shy lover, a voice so sweet and tremulous that, in the end, Thérèse had been touched and had given him a smile. The satin he was kissing belonged to her; it was part of her satiny skin that she had left with him to help him to be patient. His dream became so distinct that he turned from the window and ran to the door, thinking he heard her.

The chilly atmosphere of the room enfolded him once again and, disillusioned, he remembered where he was. Furiously he made a resolution; he would not hesitate; he would come back that very night. She was too beautiful and he loved her too fiercely. Lovers linked by crime must embrace with a passion that makes their bones crack. Yes, he would come back; he would run back without losing a minute as soon as he had thrown the bundle into the river. In a fit of hysteria he bit madly at the satin corset and rolled his head in its folds to stifle his sobs of desire.

Ten o'clock struck. He listened. He felt as if he had been in the room for years. By now he was stupefied with waiting. Finding bread and fruit within reach of his hand, he ate standing, greedily, and with an ache in his stomach which refused to be calmed. Perhaps the food would strengthen him. But when he had finished he was overcome by an immense weariness. It seemed as if the night would go on forever. The sound of music came more clearly now from the far side of the house. At times the floor boards shook to the rhythm of a dance. Carriages could be heard rolling away from the gates. As he gazed steadily at the door, he seemed to see a star at the key hole. He did not even bother to hide. What if someone did come in!

"No thank you, Françoise," Thérèse was saying, when she appeared with a candle. "I can easily undress myself. . . . Go to bed. You must be tired."

She closed the door behind her and slipped the bolt home. Then she remained motionless for a second or two, with a finger on her lips and the candlestick still in her hand. Dancing had not brought the slightest color to her cheeks. She did not speak, but put the candle on the dressing-table and sat down facing Julien. For another half-hour they waited, looking at each other.

Doors could be heard closing as the house settled down to

sleep. But Thérèse was worried by the proximity of Françoise in her room next door. For a few minutes she could be heard walking about. Then her bed creaked; she had lain down. For a long time she tossed from side to side as if she could not get to sleep. At last, deep, regular breathing could be heard through the partition wall.

Thérèse, who was still looking gravely at Julien, uttered only two words: "Come on."

They drew back the curtains and set about dressing Colombel's corpse, which had now stiffened in a sinister, puppet-like attitude. By the time the job was finished, both their brows were wet with perspiration.

"Come on!" she said again.

Julien, without hesitation and with a single heave, caught up Colombel's small body and threw it over his shoulder like a butcher carrying a calf's carcass. His tall frame was bent forward and Colombel's feet were a yard from the ground.

"I'll go in front," Thérèse whispered quickly. "I'll hold on to your jacket. Move gently and let yourself be guided by me."

First of all they had to go through Françoise's room. That was the terrible part of the expedition. They had got safely across when one of the corpse's legs knocked against a chair. The noise woke Françoise up. They heard her raise her head and mutter indistinctly. They stopped dead, Thérèse against the door and Julien bending under the weight of the body, and both afraid that the mother was going to catch them in the act of conveying her son to the river. It was a moment of appalling anguish. Then Françoise seemed to drop off to sleep again and they edged cautiously out into the corridor.

But another scare was in store for them. Thérèse's mother was not yet in bed. Her door was ajar, and a beam of light was shining into the corridor. They dared neither go on nor turn back. Julien felt that Colombel would slip right off his back if they were forced to retrace their steps through Françoise's room. For almost a quarter of an hour they stood stock still, and Thérèse had the fearful courage to hold up the corpse so that Julien should not get tired. At last the beam of light disappeared and they were able to reach the ground floor. They were saved.

For the second time that evening Thérèse opened the big door that had remained shut for so long. And when Julien, carrying his burden, reached the middle of the square, he could see her standing at the top of the steps, with bare arms, white from head to foot in her ball dress. She was waiting for him.

V

Julien was as strong as a horse. As a boy he had enjoyed helping the woodcutters in the forests near his native village and hoisting tree trunks onto his young back. Colombel therefore seemed to him as light as a feather. The puny little corpse was no heavier around his neck than a bird would have been. He could hardly feel its weight, and he took a vicious pleasure in its lightness, its flimsiness, its insubstantiality. Never again would little Colombel jeer at Julien's flute-playing as he went past his window; never again would he make jokes at Julien's expense in public. The thought that his fortunate rival was now lying stiff and cold in his grasp sent a thrill of satisfaction down Julien's spine. He hitched the corpse further up, clenched his teeth, and hurried on.

The town was in darkness. However, in the square a light was showing at Inspector Pidoux's window; the Inspector was apparently indisposed; the swollen outline of his belly could be seen moving back and forth behind the curtains. Julien was stealing along anxiously, keeping close to the houses opposite, when a slight cough froze him in his tracks. From the shelter of a doorway he saw Mme Savournin, the lawyer's wife; she had come to her window for a breath of fresh air and was heaving great sighs as she looked at the stars. This was a piece of very bad luck; usually, at that time of night, the Place des Quatre Femmes was fast asleep. Fortunately Mme Savournin decided in the end to return to the conjugal bed and to her husband, whose snores, coming through the open window, were clearly audible in the street. When she had shut the window, Julien quickly crossed the square, keeping an eye all the time on Inspector Pidoux's anguished, agitated silhouette.

He felt safer in the narrow cleft of the rue Beau Soleil. There the houses leaned so close together and the steep road twisted and turned so much that the starlight did not penetrate all the way down; at ground level there was a thick sediment of shadow. As soon as he felt himself sheltered there, Julien had an irresistible desire to run, and he set off suddenly at a wild gallop. It was a stupid and a dangerous thing to do, as he realized quite clearly. But he could not help it; he could still feel behind him the light, empty expanse of the Place des Quatre Femmes and Mme Savournin's and Inspector Pidoux's windows shining in the night like two great eyes watching him. His shoes made such a clatter on the paving-stones that he imagined he was being followed. Then, suddenly, he stopped again. Thirty yards away he could hear the voices of the officers who took their meals at the fair-haired widow's house in the rue Beau Soleil. They must have ordered a bowl of punch that evening to celebrate the transfer of one of their number. Julien reflected that if they came up the street, he was lost. There was no side street in which to take refuge, and he would certainly not have time now to go back. Choking with anxiety, he listened to the rhythmical thudding of their boots and the faint jingling of their swords. For a few seconds he could not tell whether the noise was approaching or receding. However, it slowly died away. He waited a little longer, then decided to walk on, treading as softly as possible. He would have gone barefoot if he had dared spare the time to take his shoes off.

At last he came out at the old town gate.

There is no toll-house there or sentry box of any kind, so he was able to go freely ahead. But as he emerged from the narrow rue Beau Soleil, the sudden openness of the countryside terrified him. Before him stretched a soft blue landscape traversed by the cool breath of night. He had the impression that an immense crowd was waiting for him and breathing in his face. They would see him; a huge shout would go up and bring him to a halt.

However, the bridge lay ahead. He could make out the white road and the parapets on either side, squat and gray like two parallel seats of granite; he could hear the gentle, crystalline music of the Chanteclair running through the long grasses. He ventured out, bent double and avoiding the open spaces, so as not to be seen by the thousands of silent spectators whose presence he could feel around him. The most alarming stretch of road was on the bridge itself, where he would be entirely exposed and in full view of the town, which was built in a curve above the river. His goal was the far end of the bridge—the spot where, on fine evenings, he would come to dangle his legs above the river as he drank in the cool air. There the Chanteclair formed a deep pool whose sluggish black surface was dimpled by rapid little whirls revealing the inner commotion of some violent current. How often Julien had whiled away the time by throwing stones into the water to gauge the depth of the pool from the kind of bubbles they made. With a last effort of will he crossed the bridge.

Yes, that was the place. Julien recognized the stone that his long sessions there had rubbed smooth. He leaned over the edge and saw the level surface of the water dimpling merrily. That was the place. He unloaded his burden onto the parapet. He had an irresistible craving to take a last look at Colombel before throwing him in. Had the eyes of all the townspeople been fixed on him at that moment, they would not have prevented him from satisfying his desire. For a few seconds he remained face to face with the dead man. The hole in Colombel's temple had gone black. Far away, somewhere in the sleeping countryside, a cart was moving with a harsh, sobbing sound. Then Julien made haste and, to avoid too noisy a splash, he picked the body up again and leaned over with it as far as possible. But somehow the dead man's arms got caught around his neck and pulled at him so roughly that he fell forward. By a miracle, he was able to hang on to a projecting stone. Colombel had tried to drag him into the river.

When he was seated again on the parapet, he felt faint. He remained there, drained of energy, his back bent and his legs dangling, in the relaxed posture he had so often assumed on returning from a long walk. And he gazed at the sluggish surface of the water twinkling again with dimples. Colombel, dead though he was, had grabbed him round the neck and had tried to pull him in. But all that was forgotten now. Julien inhaled the cool scent of the countryside in deep drafts; his gaze followed the silvery gleam of the river between the velvety shadows of the trees; here nature seemed to be offering him peace—lulling, endless peace and discreet, secret pleasure.

Then he remembered Thérèse. She was waiting for him; of that he was sure. He could still see her at the top of the dilapidated steps, on the threshold of the moss-invaded doorway. She was standing erect in her white silk dress trimmed with scarlet-centered briar roses. But perhaps she had begun to feel cold; if so, she must have gone back to her room to wait for him there. She had left the door open and had slipped between the sheets like a bride on her wedding night.

The prospect was sweet; no woman had ever waited for him that way. In a few minutes he would be back as he had promised. But his legs were growing numb, and he was afraid of falling asleep. Was he, after all, a coward? To rouse himself, he thought of Thérèse at her dressing-table after she had thrown off her clothes. He saw her with uplifted arms and pointed breasts, her delicate elbows and pale hands weaving through the air. He tried to whip up his emotions by remembering the scent of her body, the suppleness of her skin, and the frighteningly sensuous room where he had experienced such mad intoxication. Was he going to renounce all the passion that was now offered him while the foretaste he had had of it was still burning his lips? No, rather than that, he would drag himself along on his knees, if his legs refused to carry him.

But the battle was already lost, and his defeated love was in its death throes. He had only one feeling left—an irresistible longing to go to sleep and sleep forever. Thérèse's image was fading; a great black wall was rising and cutting him off from her. He was convinced now that the slightest touch of his finger on her shoulder would kill him. His desire flickered out, leaving a deathlike odor. All love appeared impossible between them; the ceiling would crash down on their heads if he went back into the room and clasped Thérèse against his body.

Sleep, everlasting sleep; how pleasant it must be when there was nothing within oneself worth keeping awake for. He would not return to work at the post office next morning; what was the point? He would never play the flute again, never sit at the window. Then why not sleep forever? His life was finished; he could lie down. He gazed again at the river, trying to see if Colombel was still there. Colombel was a very clever fellow; he must have known what he was doing when he tried to pull him in.

The surface of the pool was broad and level, though pricked here and there with rapid whirls. The Chanteclair was now gently musical, and the countryside, spreading far and wide under the night sky, was utterly at peace. Thrice Julien stammered out Thérèse's name. Then, with his head tucked into his chest, he dropped like a bundle, and there was a great splash. After which the Chanteclair continued its music among the grasses.

When the two bodies were discovered, it was supposed that there must have been a fight, and a suitable story was invented. Julien had lain in wait for Colombel to pay him back for his teasing; then, after striking him on the temple with a stone and killing him, he had thrown himself into the river. Three months later Mlle Thérèse de Marsanne married the young Comte de Véteuil. She was dressed in white, and her calm, beautiful face wore a look of stern and noble purity.

Translated by J. G. Weightman

MONSIEUR FOLANTIN

by Joris-Karl Huysmans (1848–1907)

The waiter placed his left hand on his hip, supported his right hand on the back of a chair, balanced on one foot, and compressed his lips.

"Well, it's a matter of taste," he said, "but if I were monsieur, I'd order Roquefort."

"All right, make it Roquefort."

The table was cluttered with plates full of congealed scraps and with bottles that left blue rings on the cloth. M. Jean Folantin made a long face, confident that he was about to eat a heartbreaking piece of cheese, and his expectation was fully realized. The waiter brought in a white, lacy substance with indigo blotches; it looked as if it had been cut out of a cake of laundry soap.

M. Folantin pecked at the cheese, folded his napkin, and arose; the waiter bade good evening to his back and closed the door behind him.

Outside, M. Folantin opened his umbrella and hastened his

"There is some ugliness, some flaw, at the origin of things," *Huysmans once wrote. "The world is an ignoble and disgusting place." The sentiment, like the sullen ferocity with which it is expressed, was common to all of Huysmans's work, from the "naturalistic" novels of his earlier years, through the "symbolist" novel, A Rebours (1884), which became a touchstone for an entire literary generation, to the long succession of "Catholic" writings which followed his conversion in 1892. The sentiment was not particularly remarkable, except by its persistence; nor, in merely personal terms, was the cantankerous, bilious, lugubrious, hypersensitive, scrawny little man who entertained it—and who looked after the integrity of his disgust and horror as a cranky spinster might have looked after a pair of pet Siamese. It was genuine enough, however; and it had on his strongest pages something of the grim poetic and visionary force that one finds in medieval Dances of Death.*

step. The blades of frost that had nipped his ears and nose had given way to the thin lashes of a driving rain. The bitter cold spell that had congealed Paris for three days was broken, and melting snow sloshed down the gutters beneath a swollen, water-soaked sky.

M. Folantin began to trot, thinking of the fire he had kindled at home before going out to his restaurant. Yet he was not without misgivings; that evening he had been too lazy to re-build from top to bottom, as he usually did, the fire laid by his concierge. "Coke doesn't catch easily," he reflected; he climbed the stairs four at a time and, on entering, could not detect the slightest flame in the fireplace.

"Why is it," he grumbled, "that no cleaning-woman or con-cierge knows how to make a fire?" He set a candle on the floor; then, without taking off his hat or coat, he overturned the grate and refilled it methodically, leaving plenty of gaps for air in the edifice. He lowered the curtain, kindled the paper, and took off his things.

Suddenly he heaved a sigh, for when he tried to light his lamp, all it would do was belch loudly.

"Looks like there's no oil. That's all I needed." He turned up the wick and contemplated it desolately, a worn-out yellow af-fair, blackened and jagged at the top.

The "subject" of Monsieur Folantin *(published in 1882 un-der the title* A Vau-l'Eau, *which loses its sense when translated) could not be less promising: a shabby bachelor with stomach trouble in search of a decent meal. Huysmans applied to this dismal subject no less truculence, ferocity of humor, and cruel closeness of observation—to say nothing of his gamy, intricate prose—than if the subject had in fact been for him a Dance of Death. It was; and by the time he had finished with it, what was in question was no longer just a meal, but* la mort dans l'âme, *or the ashes in Everyman's mouth.*

M. Folantin occupies a niche in the national pantheon of legendary personages about halfway between the Frédéric of Flaubert's Éducation sentimentale *and the Roquentin of Sartre's* Nausée. *Like the other heroes (if they can be called that) of Huysmans's books, all of whom are variations on a single one, he is more or less a caricatural self-portrait with*

"This life is unbearable," he muttered to himself as he looked for the scissors; he trimmed the lamp as best he could, flung himself into an easy chair, and was soon sunk in his thoughts.

It had been a bad day; he had been deep in gloom since morning; the chief clerk in the office where he had worked for twenty years had rudely reproved him for coming in late. M. Folantin had bristled, pulled out his old watch, and replied dryly: "Eleven o'clock on the dot."

The chief clerk had drawn an impressive stem-winder from his pocket. "Eleven twenty," he countered. "I set mine by the Stock Exchange." And contemptuously he had deigned to pardon his underling, evidently out of pity for his antique timepiece.

In this ironic indulgence M. Folantin saw an allusion to his poverty, and replied sharply to his superior, who, no longer accepting the senile transgressions of a watch as an excuse, drew himself up and again reproved M. Folantin in menacing terms for his lack of punctuality.

After this beginning, things had gone from bad to worse. Under a dismal light that turned the paper gray, he had copied interminable letters and drawn up voluminous lists, all the while subjected to the chatter of his colleague, a little old man who stood, hands in pockets, enjoying the sound of his own voice.

The old man rattled off the whole newspaper and added

---

the literary genius left out.

Huysmans's father was a Dutch artisan of small means, his mother a Frenchwoman; he was born and grew up in Paris, to some of whose lesser-known quarters he devoted several volumes; he worked for most of his life as a minor civil servant, earning for himself meanwhile a well-deserved reputation as an avant-garde art critic, and provoking with his books critical and imaginative furors that have not yet wholly abated.

OTHER WORKS: *Novels:* Marthe (*1876*), Les Sœurs Vatard (*1879*), En Ménage (*1881*), En Rade (*1887*), Là-Bas (*1891*), En Route (*1895*), La Cathédrale (*1898*); *Art Criticism:* L'Art moderne (*1883*), Certains (*1889*); *Miscellaneous:* Croquis parisiens (*1880*), Les Vieux Quartiers de Paris (*1890*), De tout (*1902*).

opinions of his own; he found fault with phrases in the articles and brought forth others that he would have liked to see in their place; and he punctuated these observations with details on the poor state of his health, which, however, was improving just a little, thanks to constant applications of Populeum Ointment and frequent cold baths.

Listening to these fascinating remarks, M. Folantin had begun making mistakes; the lines in his accounts swerved and the columns of figures ran riot; he had been obliged to scratch out whole pages and overload some of the lines, but this effort was quite wasted—the chief clerk had returned his work with orders to do it over.

At last the day had ended; under a low sky, amid squalls of rain, M. Folantin had plodded through mud melbas and snow sherbets on his way to his home and his restaurant. Then, to complete his misery, the dinner had been wretched and the wine had tasted like ink.

Squeezed into shoes warped by the rain, his feet were frozen; his head was aglow with the heat of the gas jet above it. He had eaten next to nothing for dinner, and his ill luck was still with him; the fire refused to take, the lamp smoked, and his tobacco was damp and went out, staining the cigarette paper with its yellow juice.

A vast discouragement took hold of him; he saw the emptiness of his walled-in life. Leaning forward in his chair and resting his head against the mantelpiece, M. Folantin began to poke the fire and review the calvary of his forty years, pausing in despair at each station of his cross.

His childhood had not been graced by prosperity. From father to son, the Folantins were an impecunious lot; in the remote past, it is true, the family annals mentioned one Gaspard Folantin, who had made nearly a million in the leather business; but the chronicle added that he had run through his fortune and gone bankrupt. The memory of this man was still vivid in the minds of his descendants, who cursed him and cited him to their sons as an example not to be followed, and who never wearied of predicting that they would die in the poorhouse unless they kept away from cafés and women.

Be that as it may, Jean Folantin had been born under appalling circumstances; on the day of his birth, his father had only a few coppers to his name. An aunt, who, though not a midwife, was versed in that kind of work, delivered the child, wiped him off with butter, and, by way of economy, powdered his behind with flour scraped from a loaf of bread in place of lycopodium powder. "So you see, my boy, that your birth was humble," said Aunt Eudore, who had informed him of these little details. And even in earliest childhood Jean dared cherish no hopes of future prosperity.

His father died young and his stationery store in the rue du Four was sold to pay the debts incurred during his illness; mother and child found themselves on the street. Mme Folantin went to work, becoming first a salesgirl, then cashier, in a dry-goods store, while the child was sent to the *lycée* as a boarder. Despite the wretchedness of her own situation, Mme Folantin obtained a scholarship for her son and, by depriving herself of everything, put enough aside from her meager wages to meet the future expense of examinations and diplomas.

Aware of his mother's sacrifices, Jean worked hard, carrying off all the first prizes. The principal's pleasure over his success at the big competitive examinations made up to him in some measure for the general contempt inspired by his poverty. He was a very bright boy, mature for his years. He saw the wretched life his mother led, shut up from morning to night in a glass cage, coughing into her hand as she sat over her books, timid and gentle in the midst of the bustling shoppers, and he realized that he could expect no mercy from fate, no justice from destiny. Thus he had the good sense to ignore the suggestions of his teachers, who tried to push him with a view to enhancing their own reputations and gaining promotion. He plodded along and took his baccalaureate a year earlier than usual.

He was determined to find a job and so lighten his mother's burden; for a long time he found nothing, for his sickly look did not predispose people in his favor and he limped with his left leg as a result of an accident in school. At last his luck seemed to change; he passed an examination for a position in one of the ministries and was appointed at a salary of fifteen hundred francs.

When her son announced the good news, Mme Folantin smiled gently. "Now you are your own master," she said. "Now

you can take care of yourself, my poor boy; it was high time."
And indeed her health was fast declining; a month later she
died from the aftereffects of a heavy cold she had caught in
the drafty cage where she had spent her days, winter and summer alike.

Jean was left alone; Aunt Eudore was long since dead and
buried; his other relatives were scattered or dead, and, anyway, he had never known them; he barely remembered the
name of a girl cousin who had gone into a convent somewhere
in the provinces.

He made a few friends and acquaintances, but then some left
Paris and others married; he had no heart to make new friends;
he gave up little by little and resigned himself to living in
solitude.

"Any way you look at it, it's miserable to be alone," he reflected, as he added pieces of coke to the fire one by one. And
he thought of his old friends. "Marriage broke up everything.
We were intimate, we lived the same life, we couldn't do without one another, and now we barely exchange a greeting when
we meet. A married friend is always a little embarrassed because he's the one who has broken off relations; he thinks you
ridicule the life he leads. And besides, he is convinced, in all
good faith, that he occupies a more honorable position in life
than a bachelor"—and M. Folantin recalled the embarrassment,
tinged with disdain, of the old friends he had seen since their
marriage. How absurd! And he smiled, for the recollection of
these friends of his youth carried him back to the days of their
friendship.

He had been twenty-two, and everything had delighted him.
The theater seemed a place of joy, the cafés were an enchantment; and at Bullier's the girls arching their backs to the sound
of the cymbals, kicking their feet in the air and shrieking, fired
his imagination, for in his ardor he pictured them undressed
and saw their flesh grow taut and moist beneath their drawers
and petticoats. An aroma of femininity rose in the clouds of
dust, and he sat there blissfully, envying the men in soft hats
who beat time on their thighs as they trooped past. As for him,
he was shy, he limped, and he had no money. But, even so, the
torment was sweet, and, like so many a poor devil, he found
happiness in trifles. A passing word or a sidelong smile en-

tranced him; he would go home and dream of these women, imagining that those who had given him a look or a smile were more desirable than the others.

Ah! if his wages had only been higher. Poor as he was, he could not aspire to dance-hall pickups. He had recourse to the women who lurked in dark alleys, wretched creatures with great bellies that hung nearly to the ground. He would plunge into an alley, trying to make out a face in the shadow. And nothing could deter him, neither gross face-paint, nor hideous old age, nor sordid dress, nor the squalor of the rooms. Just as his healthy appetite impelled him to devour the vilest food in the restaurants he frequented, so his carnal hunger enabled him to accept the leftovers of love. There were even nights when, penniless, and consequently without hope of satisfying himself, he would saunter through the rue de l'Egout, the rue du Dragon, the rue Neuve-Guillemin, the rue Beurrière, just to be close to women; he took pleasure in being accosted, and when he knew one of the girls, he would chat with her, pass the time of day, and then retire discreetly for fear of scaring away her customers. And he would long for the end of the month, promising himself rare joys as soon as he drew his wages.

The good old days! And to think that now when he was a little better off, now that he could graze on greener pastures and spend his passions on cleaner beds, all desire had left him. Money had come too late, when pleasure had lost its lure.

But there had been an intermediate stage, when he was no longer overwhelmed by the turbulence of his blood, but had not yet become the incurious, almost impotent old fellow who spent his evenings by the fireside. By the time he was twenty-seven he had grown sick of the prostitutes sprinkled round his quarter; he wished for a little fondling and caressing and dreamed of situations in which, instead of rushing straight for the couch, he would be able to take his time and sit down for a while. As he hadn't enough money to keep a mistress, as he was sickly and lacked social talent, glibness of tongue, and jovial rakishness, he had all the time in the world to reflect on the kindness of a providence that to some gives money, position, health, and women, and to others nothing. He still had to content himself with unprepossessing fare, but as he paid more, he was expedited in cleaner rooms and on whiter sheets.

Once he thought that happiness had come to him; he met a girl who worked for a living, and she showed him something approaching tenderness; but suddenly, for no particular reason, she left him—with a memory that was not easily cured. He shuddered as he recalled that period of misery when, in spite of it all, he had had to go on working and living. True, he was still young, and instead of consulting a doctor he had gone to a quack, disregarding the warnings scrawled over their ads in the public urinals; truthful comments such as: "Depurative remedy . . . yes, for the pocketbook"; dire prognostications: "You'll lose your hair"; or, on a note of philosophical resignation: "Better sleep with your wife." Everywhere the adjective *free* coupled with the word *treatment* was crossed out, gouged out, slashed out, and you could feel that this work had been done with fury and conviction.

Now his love-life had ended; his ardors were quelled; breathless fevers had given way to continence, to profound peace; but what an abominable emptiness had descended on his existence the moment sexual problems had gone out of it!

"It's no joke," thought M. Folantin, shaking his head and poking the fire. "Freezing in here," he muttered. "Too bad that wood's so expensive, what a fine blaze I'd make!" And this reflection led him to think of the wood that was distributed so freely at the ministry, then of the government service, and finally of his office.

There again his illusions had been short-lived. After imagining that promotion was gained by good behavior and hard work, he discovered that pull was everything; the clerks born in the provinces were backed by their deputies, they got ahead despite their provincial origin. He, who had been born in Paris, had no one to help him; he remained a common pen-pusher, copying and recopying mounds of dispatches year in and year out, tracing innumerable lines, drawing up mountains of lists, thousands of times repeating the invariable formulas of salutation. His enthusiasm had waned, and now, having lost all hope of bonuses or advancement, he had become careless and indifferent.

With his 237 francs, 40 centimes, per month, he had never been able to rent comfortable lodgings, hire a maid, and enjoy the comforts of a well-ordered household. On a day of discouragement he had attempted an unfortunate experiment in defiance of all realism or good sense. Its failure had been decisive; at the end of two months he was once again steering his course from restaurant to restaurant, esteeming himself happy to be rid of Mme Chabanel, his housekeeper, an old woman six feet tall, with hairy lips and obscene eyes surmounting flabby cheeks. She was a kind of *vivandière* who ate like a teamster and drank for four; she was a wretched cook; and her familiarity surpassed all bounds. She tossed the dishes on the table every which way, sat down opposite her master, hiked up her skirts, and snickered insolently at him, her bonnet askew and her hands on her hips.

There was no hope of getting her to wait on him properly; but M. Folantin might still have put up with her humiliating nonchalance if she hadn't robbed him right and left; his flannel vests and his socks kept disappearing, his slippers were nowhere to be found, the liquor evaporated, and even the matches burned all by themselves.

This state of affairs could not go on. M. Folantin summoned up all his courage. For fear that she would pillage all his belongings while he was out, he brought things to a head one evening and fired her out of hand. Mme Chabanel turned crimson and her toothless mouth gaped; then she began to jump up and down and flap her wings, until M. Folantin said in an amiable tone: "As long as I won't be eating here any more, I might as well give you what provisions are left rather than waste them; so if it's all right with you, let's go over them together."

And he had opened the cupboards.

"This is a bag of coffee and this bottle contains *eau de vie*. Right?"

"Yes, monsieur, that's right," Mme Chabanel had wheezed.

"Well, they're worth keeping, so I'll keep them," said M. Folantin, and so on with everything. In the end Mme Chabanel inherited nothing but two sous worth of vinegar, a handful of cooking-salt, and a little glassful of lamp oil.

"Oof!" M. Folantin had exclaimed as the woman stumbled down the stairs; but his joy was short-lived; ever since then his insides had been all twisted. Widow Chabanel had been replaced by the concierge, who pummeled the bed with his fist

and made pets of the spiders, taking good care not to disturb
their webs.

Ever since then his fare had been strange and nondescript,
his stations at the neighborhood restaurants had never ceased,
and his stomach was corroded; now began the days of mineral
water to settle the stomach, and of mustard to mask the putrid
taste of the meat and lend savor to the cold dishwater served up
as sauce.

From calling up these memories, M. Folantin fell into the
blackest gloom. For years he had bravely endured his loneli-
ness, but on this night he admitted defeat; he regretted not
having married, and refuted one by one the arguments with
which he had formerly preached celibacy for the poor. "Children? Oh, well, you bring them up, even if it means taking
another notch in your belt. Goodness, I'd manage like everyone
else, I'd do extra copying at night so my wife could dress a little
better; we'd eat meat only for lunch, and, like most poor families, we'd content ourselves with a dish of soup for supper.
What are all these little privations beside the orderly life, the
evenings spent with your wife and children, the scanty but
wholesome food, the mended clothes, the laundry brought back
clean and at regular intervals? Ah, the laundry, what a head-
ache for a bachelor! They call for it when they feel like it,
and they bring back limp, bluish shirts, handkerchiefs in tatters, socks full of holes; and if I complain, they just laugh.
And how will it all end for me? At the hospital or charity home
in case of prolonged illness, or, if death comes quickly, here
in my lodgings, hoping for a kind word from a sick-nurse.

"It's too late. I've lost my virility, marriage is out of the
question. No doubt about it, I've been a failure. Oh, well,"
M. Folantin sighed, "the best thing I can do is go to bed and
sleep." As he drew down the covers and arranged his pillows,
he gave thanks in his heart for the merciful blessing of his bed.

II

Neither on the next day nor the next did M. Folantin's gloom
leave him; unable to fight off his crushing depression, he let
himself drift. Beneath the rainy sky he went mechanically to
his office, left it, ate dinner, and went to bed at nine o'clock,

only to repeat the same routine the next day; little by little he slipped into a state of total apathy.

Then, one fine morning, there was an awakening; he seemed to throw off his lethargy. The weather was bright and the sun beat on the windowpanes curtained with frost; it was winter again, but luminous and dry. M. Folantin arose, muttering: "My, there's a bite in the air," and he felt cheered. "And now," he told himself, "I'd better find some cure for these fits of gloom."

After long deliberation he decided to go out more and to vary his restaurants. But though these resolutions were easily conceived, they were hard to put into practice. He lived in the rue des Saints-Pères, and there weren't many restaurants near by. The sixth *arrondissement* was hard on bachelors. You had to be a priest to be able to live in the streets surrounding Saint-Sulpice; then you could eat at the refectories reserved for the clergy. Outside the precincts of religion, there was nothing fit to eat unless you were rich enough to frequent the high-class restaurants; failing to meet these conditions, M. Folantin was reduced to a handful of restaurants in different parts of the neighborhood. This section really seemed to be inhabited exclusively by people who were officially or unofficially married. "If I only had the courage to leave it," M. Folantin would sigh from time to time. But his office was near by, here he had been born, and here his family had always lived; all his memories were attached to this quiet old quarter already disfigured by new streets, by dismal boulevards, sweltering in summer and glacial in winter, by dreary avenues that had Americanized the aspect of the quarter and destroyed forever its air of intimacy without having brought comfort, life, or gaiety in exchange.

"I ought to eat dinner across the river," he kept telling himself, but a profound disgust would seize him whenever he departed from the Left Bank; besides, it was painful for him to walk with his limp, and he hated buses. Above all, the idea of undertaking a long journey in search of dinner was repugnant to him, and he preferred to explore those neighborhood wineries and soup-houses that were still unknown to him.

He at once abandoned the hashery where he usually ate; first he tried the soup-houses, with their waitresses in nun-like cos-

tumes that made him think of a hospital dining-room. He ate
there for several days, and his appetite, already discouraged
by the greasy effluvia of the place, left him completely at the
sight of the insipid-looking meat, made still less appetizing by
poultices of chicory and spinach. What gloom emanated from
the cold marble tops of those dolls' tables, from the unalterable
menu, the infinitesimal portions, the tiny slabs of bread! Packed
into two rows, face to face, the diners seemed to be engaged
in a game of chess as, for lack of space, they moved their knives
and forks, their bottles and glasses into one another's territory.
With his nose in his newspaper, M. Folantin envied his companions their powerful jaws, which could crunch through the
sinews of steaks that defied knife and fork. Nauseated by the
roasts, he had recourse to eggs, which he ordered fried and
very well done. Usually they were brought in almost raw, and
he did his best to spoon up and sop up the yolk swimming in a
morass of whites. It was bad, it was expensive, and, above all,
it was depressing. "Enough of that," said M. Folantin to himself, "it's time to try something else."

But everywhere it was the same; the drawbacks varied with
the type of restaurant; at the high-class wineries the food was
better, the wine was less acrid, the portions were more plentiful,
but in general the meal took two hours, for the waiter was busy
serving the tipplers stationed downstairs at the bar; besides,
in this miserable neighborhood the menu didn't vary; there
were always the same chops or steak for which you paid ex-
orbitantly because, to avoid seating you with the workmen, the
proprietor shut you up in a separate room and lighted two gas
jets.

Further down the scale were the low-class bistros and wineries; here the company was repulsive and the filth incredible;
the meat was fetid, the glasses bore lip marks, the knives were
tarnished and greasy, and the tablecloths were spotted with
egg yolks.

M. Folantin began to wonder if all this changing-about had
been worth while, as the wine was always watered and adul-
terated, the eggs were never done the way you wanted them, the
meat was always dry, and the boiled vegetables reminded you of
garbage from the municipal jail. But he persisted: "If I keep
on looking, maybe I'll find something." Resuming his wander-

ings, he explored hasheries and creameries; but, far from being appeased, his dissatisfaction only grew, especially when, descending the stairs from his lodgings, he breathed in the savor of soup, saw the light shining beneath the doors, passed men coming up from the cellar bearing bottles, heard the bustle of activity in the rooms. All this—even to the aroma escaping from the lodge of his concierge as he sat with his elbows on the table, the visor of his cap clouded by the steam rising from his soup—added to his regrets. He almost came to feel sorry he had fired Mme Chabanel, the old battle-ax. "If I'd been able to afford it, I'd have kept her," he thought, "in spite of her revolting ways."

He was desperate, because in addition to his moral difficulties he now began to suffer from physical weakness. Undernourishment was playing havoc with his already delicate constitution. He began taking iron, but all the body-builders he consumed merely blackened his insides without any appreciable effect. He tried arsenic; Fowler's prescription only wrecked his digestion and gave him no added strength; finally, as a last resort, he took to quinquina, which created a fire in his insides; then he mixed these substances and took them all together, to no avail; his wages went for masses of bottles, tubes, phials; his home pharmacy contained every variety of citrate, phosphate, percarbonate, lactate, sulphate of protoxyde, iron iodide and periodide, Pearson's liquor, Devergie's solution, Dioscoridian salts, pills of sodium arsenate and arsenate of gold, tonic wines containing gentian and quinine, coca and colombo.

"To think that it's all a hoax! The money I've wasted!" M. Folantin sighed, as he dolefully reviewed his useless purchases. And the concierge, though not consulted, was of the same opinion; he felt a healthy man's contempt for this anemic tenant who could only keep body and soul together with the help of all these medicines, and his dusting became more perfunctory than ever.

Meanwhile, M. Folantin's monotonous existence went on. He could not bring himself to go back to his original restaurant; once he went as far as the door, but then the smell of the fried meats and the sight of a bowlful of purplish chocolate cream put him to flight. Now he alternated between wineries and soup-houses, and one day a week he would try a bouillabaisse factory. Here the soup and fish were bearable, but it was not a good idea to order anything else: the meat was like shoe leather and everything tasted like lamp oil.

To revive his appetite, further dulled by the abject aperitifs of the cafés—the absinthe that stank of copper; the vermouth: sour leftovers of white wine; the madeira: alcohol cut with caramel and molasses; the malaga: prune juice flavored with wine; the bitters: made from heaven knows what venomous herbs—M. Folantin had recourse to a measure that had been successful in his childhood; every other day he went to the public baths. The idea appealed to him first of all because it helped him kill the two hours between work and the evening meal, and saved him from sitting at home with his coat and shoes on, watching the clock and waiting for the dinner hour. And the first few times he enjoyed some delicious moments. He would bask in the warm water and amuse himself by creating tempests and whirlpools with his hands. He would gently doze off to the silvery sound of the water dripping from the faucets, creating great rings that broke against the walls of the tub; now and then he would start at the furious ringing of bells in the corridors, followed by the sound of steps and the slamming of doors. And then the silence would resume, with the gentle dripping of the faucets, and all his troubles would melt away in the steam; he would lie and dream, and his thoughts became as hazy and pleasant as the vapor. Oh, well, it was all for the best. He had his troubles, but who doesn't? At any rate, he had avoided the worst calamities, those which come with marriage. "I must have been feeling pretty low," he said to himself, "that night when I wished I had married. Imagine a fellow like me, who likes to stretch out in bed, forced to lie still with a woman beside me every single night, and having to satisfy her when I just wanted to sleep.

"And even then it wouldn't be so bad if we didn't have children—if the woman were sterile, or knew how to manage. But how can you be sure of such things? Worry, worry, and sleepless nights. One day the kid yells because a tooth's coming in, another day because it isn't coming in; and the whole place stinks of sour milk and pee-pee. If at least you could be sure of marrying a sweet, good-natured girl—fat chance; with my luck,

I'd have gotten a harridan, an old bag who'd blame me for her afterpains as long as she lived.

"No, may as well face it, married or single, we all have our troubles; and it's a crime putting children into the world if you're not rich. It's dooming them to general contempt when they grow up; it's sending them unarmed into a heartbreaking struggle; it's persecuting poor innocent creatures by making them start their father's miserable life all over again. Ah, at least the pitiful race of the Folantins will die with me." And, comforted by his bath, M. Folantin would repair to his soup-house with new courage to lap up the dishwater and hack away at the moist sponge set before him as meat.

Somehow or other he worried through the winter, and life became more bearable; the season of home comforts was ended, and M. Folantin no longer hankered so much after sheltered evenings spent sleepily by the fireside. Once again he began to take long walks along the quays.

Already the trees were covered with a lace of little yellow leaves; the Seine flowed by, reflecting the mottled blue of the sky in great blue and white blotches, which the *bateaux-mouches* broke and churned into foam. The setting in which he lived seemed to have been refurbished. The two vast stage-flats, one representing the Pavillon de Flore and the entire façade of the Louvre, the other the line of tall buildings extending as far as the Palais de l'Institut, had brightened, as though done over, and on the restretched backdrop the turrets of the Palais de Justice, the spire of the Sainte-Chapelle, and the steeple and towers of Notre Dame stood out against a softened, fresh-painted ultramarine.

M. Folantin loved this part of the quay, between the rue du Bac and the rue Dauphine; he selected a cigar in the tobacco store near the rue de Beaune and sauntered along, one day on the left side, rummaging in the boxes on the parapet, and another on the right side, examining the books displayed on the open stands.

Most of the volumes piled in the cases were castoffs from bookstores, worthless junk, stillborn novels about women of high society, written in the language of the concierge, and relating the trials of tragic love, the duels, murders, and suicides.

Others contained a message, all evil being imputed to the aristocrats, all virtue to the common people; still others had a religious purpose; they were sponsored by Monsignor So-and-so,
and their sticky prose was diluted with spoonfuls of holy water.

Unquestionably these novels had been written by imbeciles,
and M. Folantin would hurry past, pausing only at the volumes
of poetry whose pages lay fluttering in the breeze. These were
less tattered and soiled than the rest because no one opened
them. M. Folantin was filled with compassion at the sight of
these forsaken volumes. There were plenty of them, old ones
dating from Malekadel's entrance into literature, recent ones
sprung from the school of Victor Hugo, singing the praises of
gentle Messidor, the shady wood, the divine charms of a young
person who in private life was probably a streetwalker. They
had all been read in little gatherings of friends, and the poor
authors had been so hopeful. Lord knows, they had expected no
brilliant success, no mass sales, but only a little encouragement
from the more sensitive readers; and nothing had come of it,
not even a modest bit of prestige. Here and there a few words
of faint praise in a third-rate paper, a ridiculous letter from
the Grand Master, piously preserved, and that was all.

"The saddest part of it," thought M. Folantin, "is that those
poor fellows have every justification for loathing the public;
there's no such thing as literary justice; their verses are neither
better nor worse than the ones that have sold, and even gained
their authors admission to the Institute."

Thus dreaming, M. Folantin relit his cigar. He recognized
the weather-beaten, loquacious booksellers who stood beside
their stalls as in previous years. He even recognized the biblio-
maniacs he had seen plodding the whole length of the parapets
the previous spring, and the sight of these men he did not know
delighted him. He liked them all; he guessed them to be good-
natured eccentrics, easy-going fellows passing quietly through
life, and he envied them. "If I could only be like them," he had
thought, and he had tried to imitate them, to become a biblio-
phile. He had consulted catalogues, thumbed through diction-
aries and scholarly tomes, but he had never made any sensa-
tional finds, and he felt sure that, even if he did, it would not
dispel the boredom that was gradually hollowing out his soul.
Alas, a taste for books could not be cultivated, and, aside from

the collectors' items that his poverty could not afford, there were few books he desired. He had no liking for novels of adventure, and he destested such slush as Cherbuliez and Feuillet. He cared for works reflecting the realities of life, and consequently his own library was limited, containing only some fifty volumes that he knew by heart. And this dearth of reading matter was not one of his least sorrows. In vain he had attempted to take an interest in history; all these complicated explanations of simple things failed to fascinate or convince him. His browsings had become haphazard, for he had given up hope that he would find anything to add to his collection. But the walk distracted him, and when he was tired of disturbing the dust on books, he would lean over the parapet and look at the barges with their tarred hulls, their cabins painted leek-green, and their lowered mainmasts. He stood there delighted, watching the kettle simmer on the cast-iron stove, the eternal black-and-white dog running about the deck, tail in air; the very blond children sitting near the helm with their hair over their eyes and their fingers in their mouths.

"It would be merry to live like that," he thought, smiling in spite of himself at these childish desires, and he even felt a pang of sympathy for the fishermen sitting like a row of onions, separated from one another only by their little boxes of worms.

On these afternoons he felt younger and livelier. He would consult his watch, and, if it was still far to dinner time, he would cross the street and make his way back on the opposite side. He would idle along, browsing some more among the books lined up outside the shops and going into raptures over old morocco bindings lined with gold crests; but these last were shut up in glass cases like precious objects that only the initiate may touch. And he would start off again, examining shops full of antique oak furniture, so skillfully repaired that not one splinter of the original wood remained; old Rouen china manufactured at Les Batignolles, great Moustiers platters made in Versailles, Hobbema paintings, the brook, the water mill, the house roofed with red tiles, shaded by a clump of trees bathed in yellow light; astonishing imitations done by a painter who had crawled into old Minderhout's skin, but was incapable of absorbing the manner of any other master or of producing the

slightest original work; and peering through the doors of the
shops, M. Folantin would try to make out the inside; he never
saw any customers; usually an old woman sat there alone in a
little nest she had made for herself amid the chaos of bric-a-
brac, her mouth wide open in a protracted yawn of boredom
which communicated itself to the cat lying on a console table.

"It's odd," said M. Folantin to himself, "how the antique
dealers vary from place to place. The few times that I've passed
through the Right Bank quarters, I've never seen nice old ladies
like these in the shops; when I looked through the windows, I
always saw tall, handsome women between thirty and forty,
with carefully pomaded hair and smoothly made-up faces.

"These shops gave off a vague scent of prostitution; the
ladies in charge were experts in the significant glance calcu-
lated to discourage any attempts to bargain. Ah, the dear old
ladies are dying out and the neighborhoods are shifting; nowadays the rare-book and antique dealers just vegetate in this
quarter, and the moment their lease expires they move over to
the Right Bank. Ten years from now this whole quay will be
full of cafés and restaurants. Yes, there's no doubt about it,
Paris is turning into a sinister Chicago." And, overcome by
melancholy, M. Folantin would say to himself: "We'd better
make the best of the little time that's left before the final invasion of New World boorishness!" And he went on, pausing
outside windows displaying eighteenth-century prints; but actually he cared little for the colored engravings of that period
or for the black-and-white ones in the dark English manner
which usually accompanied them, and he missed the Flemish
interiors, which had been relegated to the folders as a result of
the collectors' new craze for the French school.

When he was tired of shopwindows, he would stroll into the
dispatch room of a newspaper. Here the walls were hung with
drawings and paintings representing Italian women and Oriental dancing-girls, babies being kissed by mothers, medieval
pages strumming mandolins beneath balconies (evidently a
series intended for the decoration of lamp shades); and he
turned aside, preferring to inspect the photographs of murder-
ers, generals, actresses, and others whom a crime, a massacre,
or a popular song had made famous for a week.

But, all in all, these displays were not very amusing, and, making his way to the rue de Beaune, M. Folantin would be more impressed by the dauntless appetite—which communicated itself to him—of the coachmen sitting in the wineries. Those platefuls of beef lying on thick beds of cabbage, those massive platters piled high with beans and mutton, those triangles of *brie*, those full glasses, sent pangs of hunger through him; those men with their cheeks swollen by enormous mouthfuls of bread, their great hands clutching knives, points in air, their boiled-leather caps rising and falling with their jaws, made him ravenous, and he dashed off, trying to preserve this impression of voracity along the way. Unfortunately his stomach shriveled the moment he sat down in his restaurant, and he would gaze dolefully at his meat, wondering what was the good of the quassia chips he kept marinating in a bottle at his office.

Even so, these walks dispelled his darkest thoughts. And so he passed the summer, strolling along the Seine before dinner, and sitting afterward outside a café to smoke and enjoy a bit of fresh air, despite his revulsion at the Vienna beer brewed from boxwood and colicroot in the northern suburbs of Paris. And he would sip two *bocks* of it to put off his bedtime.

At this season even the day was easier to get through. He sat in his shirt sleeves and dozed, only vaguely hearing his colleague's stories, waking up to fan himself with a calendar, working as little as possible, planning his walks. Gone was his dread of leaving his heated office, of taking his wet, cold feet out to dinner, and of returning home to his cold room. Quite the contrary, it was a relief to escape from the office with its dusty, musty smell of files and inkpots.

And now his room was in better shape because the concierge no longer had to build the fire. The bed was still roughly pummeled, and the covers were not tucked in, but it didn't matter, for M. Folantin lay down naked on top of the blankets. And he was happy to stretch out all alone on these sultry nights when most people were sweating like pigs between their sticky sheets. "I feel sorry for couples," he said to himself as he rolled about on his bed, seeking the coolest spot. And in those moments fate seemed a bit more kindly.

III

Soon the heat became less oppressive, the days grew shorter, the air freshened, the smoldering sky lost its blue and began to look fuzzy and mildewed. Autumn returned with its rains and fogs. Alarmed at the thought of inexorable evenings, M. Folantin began to make new plans.

First he decided to come out of his shell, to try the tables d'hôte, to make friends with his table companions, even to go to the theater.

Fate played into his hands; one day, on leaving his office, he met an acquaintance. For a whole year they had eaten side by side, warning each other about inedible dishes, lending each other the newspaper, discussing the virtues of the various iron preparations they were taking, for a month drinking tar water together, exchanging weather prophecies, and guiding the foreign policy of France.

Here their relations had stopped. Once outside, they shook hands and went their separate ways. Yet M. Folantin had been sorry to lose sight of this fellow sufferer.

Now he was glad to see him. "Well, if it isn't Monsieur Martinet! How goes it?"

"Why, Monsieur Folantin, what have *you* been doing all this time?"

"Deserter!" said M. Folantin. "Where have you been keeping yourself?"

And they exchanged confidences. M. Martinet had taken to dining at a table d'hôte that he now began to praise fulsomely. Ninety to a hundred francs a month, neat and clean; plenty to eat and good company. "I'm on my way there now; why don't you come along?"

"I'm not very fond of tables d'hôte," said M. Folantin. "I'm a bit of a bear, as you remember; I can't bring myself to talk to people I don't know."

"But you don't have to talk. You do just as you please. We're not all at one table, it's like in a big restaurant. Come, give it a try."

M. Folantin hesitated, torn between the pleasant prospect of not eating alone and his dread of regimented meals.

"Come, come. You can't refuse," M. Martinet insisted. "You'll be the deserter if you run out on me now."

Not wishing to be rude, M. Folantin meekly followed his companion through the streets. "Here we are. It's upstairs." And M. Martinet stopped on the landing outside a door with a green tambour.

From within, a great clatter of dishes could be heard above the unbroken hum of voices. The door opened, there was a deafening uproar, and a number of men in hats rushed down the stairs, tapping their canes on the banister.

M. Folantin and his friend moved to one side, then pushed the door in their turn and found themselves in a billiard room. M. Folantin recoiled, choking, from the dense cloud of tobacco smoke vibrant with the clicking of billiard balls; thence M. Martinet drew his guest into another room where the smoke was still thicker; amid the sound of clogged pipes, tumbling dominoes, and laughter, dim shapes passed to and fro, discernible only by the eddies they created in the smoke. M. Folantin stood bewildered, groping for a chair.

M. Martinet had left him. Through the clouds M. Folantin vaguely saw him passing through a door. "We'll have to wait a bit," said M. Martinet. "All the tables are taken. Oh, it won't be long."

Half an hour passed. M. Folantin would have given anything in the world never to have set foot in this wretched place, where you could smoke but couldn't get anything to eat. From time to time M. Martinet slipped away to make sure that all the places were still occupied. At last he reported with an air of satisfaction: "I've found two gentlemen who have started on their cheese course, and I've reserved their places."

Another half-hour passed. M. Folantin wondered if it mightn't be a good idea to head for the stairs while his friend was reconnoitering the tables. Finally M. Martinet returned, announcing the departure of the two cheese-eaters, and they passed into a third room, where they sat down, squeezed like herring in a keg.

Plates were set on the still tepid tablecloth amid bread crumbs and puddles of sauce. The meal consisted of leathery cold meat, tasteless vegetables, a slice of rubbery roast beef that merely contracted beneath the pressure of a knife, salad, and dessert. The room reminded M. Folantin of the dining-hall in a run-down boarding-school where the children are allowed to bellow at table. Nothing was missing but the tin cups stained red with the special school wine and the plates overturned to provide a cleaner repository for prunes or jam.

The food and wine were certainly wretched, but worse than the food or wine was the company. First, the skinny, desiccated waitresses with sharp, stern features and hostile eyes. One look at them gave you a feeling of utter helplessness; feeling watched, you ate with a discouraged caution, not daring to leave skin or gristle for fear of a lecture, or to take a second helping beneath those eyes which seemed to appraise your appetite and hurl it back into the bottom of your stomach.

"Well, what did I tell you?" said M. Martinet. "Isn't it cheerful? And they give you real meat."

M. Folantin made no reply; around him the uproar was terrifying. All the races of southern France sat there, spitting, sprawling, and bellowing. Men from Provence, Auvergne, Gascony, Languedoc, with their black side-whiskers, their hairy nostrils and fingers, their booming voices, sat laughing like lunatics. Their southern accent, emphasized by epileptic gestures, chopped up their sentences and flung the fragments into your eardrums.

Nearly all of them were students, members of that glorious youth whose slavish ideas assure the ruling class of suitable heirs to their imbecility; M. Folantin was subjected to a parade of every cliché, every inanity, every outmoded literary opinion, every paradox exhausted by a century of hard use. "A ditch-digger would show more sensibility," he thought, "and a salesman more wit."

On top of it all, the heat was stifling. Steam condensed on the plates and glasses; every time the door opened, clouds of tobacco smoke were wafted in; flocks of students were still arriving, and their impatience impelled the diners to hurry. As in a station restaurant, you had to take two mouthfuls at once and gulp down your wine.

"So this is the famous table d'hôte where our politicians broke bread in their humble beginnings," mused M. Folantin, revolted at the thought that these louts who were filling the room with their uproar would one day be solemn gentlemen, glutted with honor and position.

"Better to take a sausage and a glass of water at home," he said to himself, "than to dine in places like this."

"Will you have coffee?" asked M. Martinet amiably.

"No, thank you. I'm stifling. I think I'll slip out for a breath of air."

But M. Martinet was in no mood to let him go. He caught up with him on the landing and took him by the arm.

"Where are you taking me?" asked M. Folantin glumly.

"Look here, old man," said M. Martinet. "I can see that you didn't like my table d'hôte. . . ."

"Oh, but I did . . . it's amazing for the price . . . only it was so hot," M. Folantin replied timidly, fearing to have wounded his host by his forlorn look and his flight.

"Well, we see each other so seldom that I wouldn't like to leave you with a poor impression," said M. Martinet cordially. "Why don't we make an evening of it? If you like the theater, I suggest that we go to the Opéra-Comique." He looked at his watch and added: "We have time. They're playing *Richard Cœur-de-Lion* and the *Pré-aux-Clercs*. What do you say?"

"Anything you like." ("After all," thought M. Folantin, "I might enjoy myself, and how can I say no to this good fellow after pouring cold water on all his enthusiasms?") "Will you have a cigar?" he suggested, and entered a tobacco shop.

In vain they did their utmost to activate the combustion of the genuine havanas that tasted like cabbage and didn't draw. "Another pleasure gone," said M. Folantin to himself; "even if you're willing to pay for it, you can't get a decent cigar any more."

"We'd better give it up," he said aloud, turning toward M. Martinet, who was sucking with all his might at his havana, which gave off the barest wisp of smoke from its cracked wrapper. "Anyway, here we are." He ran to the box office and brought back two seats in the orchestra.

Richard began, to an empty house. During the first act M. Folantin experienced a strange sensation. The series of songs for the spinet reminded him of the hurdy-gurdy in a winery he had formerly frequented. When somebody turned the crank, there was a tinkling of old-fashioned tunes, very low and sweet, with now and then a piercing, crystalline note ringing out above the mechanical strumming of the refrains.

The second act brought a different impression. The "Burning Fever" aria evoked the image of his grandmother sitting in her velvet easy chair and singing it in a quavering voice; and for a time he had in his mouth the taste of the rusk she gave him when he had been good.

In the end he stopped listening; the singers had no voices; all they did was to project their rounded mouths over the foot-lights, while the orchestra became increasingly somnolent, weary of trying to brush the dust off this music.

Then in the third act M. Folantin thought neither of the hurdy-gurdy in the winery nor of his grandmother; suddenly his nostrils were filled with the smell of an old box he had at home, a vague, musty smell with a faint suggestion of stale cinnamon. "Good Lord, how old it is!"

"Good show, eh?" said M. Martinet, poking him with his elbow.

M. Folantin fell from the clouds. The spell was broken. They arose as the curtain fell amid the applause of the claque.

M. Folantin was utterly crushed by *Le Pré-aux-Clercs,* which followed *Richard.* Long ago he had swooned with delight at these familiar airs; now all these romanzas seemed fusty and old-hat, and the singers got on his nerves. The tenor had the stage-presence of a floor-polisher and sang through his nose when he produced any sound at all. Costumes, sets, and every-thing else were in keeping; they would have been hissed in any other city in France or abroad, for nowhere else would so ab-surd a performance have been tolerated. And yet the hall had filled, and the audience had applauded when so directed by the relentless claque.

M. Folantin was truly unhappy. He had cherished so fond a memory of *Le Pré-aux-Clercs,* and now that too had crumbled.

"Everything's going sour," he said to himself with a deep sigh.

And when M. Martinet, very much pleased with his evening, suggested that they renew these little pleasures from time to time, that if he wished they might go to the Comédie Française together, M. Folantin became quite incensed and, forgetting that he had resolved to be tactful, declared in no uncertain terms that he never set foot in the place any more.

"But why not?" M. Martinet asked.

"Why not? First of all, because if there were a well-written play with a spark of life in it—and personally I know of none—I'd read it at home in an armchair; and second, because I don't need those ham actors, total ignoramuses most of them, trying to interpret the playwright's ideas."

"But you must admit," said M. Martinet, "that the actors of the Comédie Française—"

"Those contemptible creatures!" cried M. Folantin. "Why, they're nothing but cooks, sauce-makers. All they know how to do is pour the invariable white sauce on the portions if it's a comedy and brown sauce if it's a tragedy. They're incapable of inventing a third sauce; and even if they were, tradition wouldn't allow it. They're just vulgar troupers, that's all. But you've got to do them justice: they do know how to advertise. The department stores have taught them the trick of the man with the Legion of Honor in his buttonhole who exhibits himself around the counters to give the house a good name and bring in customers."

"Come now, Monsieur Folantin—"

"There's no 'come now' about it, and, to tell the truth, I am not displeased with this opportunity to state my opinion of Monsieur Coquelin's store. And now, dear monsieur, I must be leaving you. I am enchanted with our meeting. Good-by, and I hope I shall soon have the pleasure of seeing you again."

This evening had salutary consequences. The memory of his weariness, his embarrassment, made M. Folantin esteem himself happy to dine where he saw fit and to spend whole evenings in his room; he judged that solitude was not without its advantages, that to mull over his memories and entertain himself with his own nonsense was preferable to associating with people whose convictions and sympathies he did not share; his desire to come closer to his fellow men, to rub elbows with his neighbors, left him, and once more he repeated to himself the heartbreaking truth that when old friends are gone you had better make up your mind not to look for new ones, to live alone and get used to it.

After this he attempted to narrow his scope, to take an interest in little things and draw comforting deductions from his observation of life as seen from his table. For a time he ate dinner at a little soup-house near the Croix Rouge. This establishment was frequented chiefly by old people who arrived day after day at quarter to six, and the tranquillity of the little dining-room compensated in his eyes for the monotony of the fare. It seemed to him that these were people without family, without friends, seeking a dark corner in which to perform an unpleasant duty in silence; and he felt at his ease in this world of the disinherited, of discreet, well-mannered folk who had no doubt seen better days and busier evenings. He knew almost all of them by sight, and he felt a sort of kinship with these strangers who hesitated to choose a dish from the menu, who crumbled up their bread and drank little, suffering both from the dilapidation of their stomachs and from the weariness of lives that dragged on without hope or aim.

Here there were no loud cries, no uproar; the waitresses spoke softly. But though these ladies and gentlemen entered into no conversation with one another, they always exchanged the most gracious greetings, bringing the manners of the drawing-room into this humble place.

"They are even worse off than I am," thought M. Folantin. "They no doubt have something to mourn for—children, wives, lost fortunes, a life that once hung together and that now is wrecked."

By feeling sorry for others, he began to feel less sorry for himself; he went home and reflected that, after all, his worries were very slight, his sorrows very trivial. "How many people," he thought, "right now are walking the streets with nowhere to go; how many would envy me my big armchair, my fire, my package of tobacco which I can take as much of as I please!" And he stirred up his fire, toasted his slippered feet, and prepared hot, honey-colored grogs. If any really good books ever came out, life would be quite bearable.

Some weeks passed in this manner, and his office colleague declared that M. Folantin seemed positively younger. He entered into the conversation now, listened with angelic patience to all the chatter, even took an interest in his companion's ailments. As the cold set in, his appetite became more regular, and he attributed this improvement to the creosote tonics and manganese preparations he was taking. "At last," he thought, "my experiments have unearthed a treatment less disappointing than the others." And he recommended it to everyone he met.

Things went on in this way until winter, but his melancholy returned with the first snow. He grew sick of the soup-house to which he had clung since the fall and began to try his luck at random, here and there. On several occasions he crossed the bridges and tried new restaurants; but the waiters would dash busily about, ignoring his calls, or else they would toss his dish down on the table and disappear when he asked for bread.

The food was no better than on the Left Bank, and the waiters were disdainful and negligent. M. Folantin learned his lesson; henceforth he remained in his own district, determined to leave it no more.

Once more his appetite left him. Once more he recognized the futility of tonics and stomachics, and the remedies he had so much touted joined the others in the closet.

And what was he to do with his free time? The weekdays slipped by after a fashion; it was Sunday that really weighed on him. In the old days he had explored out-of-the-way neighborhoods; he had taken pleasure in strolling down the forgotten little alleys and the poor, provincial-looking streets, in peering into ground-floor windows and surprising the secrets of the humble families who lived there. But today the calm, quiet streets had been demolished, the quaint little passages had vanished. You could no longer look in through the half-opened doors of old houses and see a bit of a garden, the lip of a well, a bench corner. It was no longer possible to imagine that life would be less crabbed, less unfriendly in this courtyard, to dream of the day when you might retire to this silence and warm your old age in this milder air.

Everything had vanished; there were no more clumps of greenery, no more trees, but only interminable barracks as far as the eye could see. This new Paris filled M. Folantin with a sense of anguish and malaise. He was the kind of man who hated the luxury stores; nothing in the world would have made him set foot in a fashionable barber shop or one of those modern grocery stores with their windows flooded with gaslight. He liked only the simple old shops where you were made to feel at home, where the proprietor didn't try to bamboozle you or humiliate you with his prosperity.

All this luxury and bad taste, which had spread even to the suburbs, had led him to abandon his Sunday walks. Strolling round Paris no longer had its old tonic effect; these tall buildings with their marble-faced entrances and their arrogant concierge's lodges that gave themselves the airs of bourgeois drawing-rooms, made him feel punier, more lost, and more alone than ever.

And yet a part of his quarter remained intact. It seemed to him that the Place Saint-Sulpice, not far from the mutilated Luxembourg, still preserved its kindly, intimate air. Sometimes he ate lunch in a tavern on the corner of the rue du Vieux-Colombier and the rue Bonaparte; and there, sitting by the window on the second floor, he looked out over the square, watched the people coming out of church, the children with their books descending the steps a little ahead of the fathers and mothers, and the crowds around the fountain with its bishops sitting in niches and its crouching lions.

Leaning out a little over the balustrade, he could see the corner of the rue Saint-Sulpice, a terrible corner swept by the wind blowing down the rue Férou, and likewise occupied by a tavern, frequented by thirsty choristers. He loved to look down on this part of the square and watch the people clutching their hats in the wind as they reeled past the big red-brown La Villette buses, drawn up by the curb in front of the church.

The square grew lively, but without merriment or bustle; the cabs lay dormant at their station in front of a five-centime toilet and a drinking fountain; the great yellow Batignolles buses lurched down the street, passing on their way the little Pantheon bus and the pallid two-horse vehicle bound for Auteuil; at noon the seminarists filed past like mannequins, two by two, with downcast eyes, in a long black-and-white band running from Saint-Sulpice to the seminary.

When the sun shone on it, the square was charming; the unequal church towers turned golden; the gilded signs on the shops selling religious articles glittered; the colors in a furniture-mover's huge sign became brighter and louder than ever; and in this neighborhood of sacristans and pious old ladies, a cleaner's advertisement posted on the outside of a urinal—two scarlet hats against a black background—evoked an atmosphere of ritual solemnity and priestly dignity.

But for M. Folantin there was no novelty in this spectacle. How many times as a young man he had crossed this square to see the aged wild boar that in those days was displayed in the window at Bailly's; how many evenings he had listened to the plaint of a street singer beside the fountain; how often he had sauntered about the seminary on the days of the flower market. He had long ago worn out the charm of this quiet spot; only by limiting his visits to rare intervals could he savor it anew.

Thus the Place Saint-Sulpice was no longer of any help to him on Sundays. He preferred the days of the week when he went to his office and was not so much at loose ends; ah, yes, the Sundays were growing interminable. On Sunday he would eat lunch later than usual and linger at table to give the concierge time to clean his room, but when he returned, it was never done. He would stumble over the rolled carpets and grope his way through a cloud of dust stirred up by the broom. One, two, three, the concierge would straighten the sheets, spread the carpets, and take his leave on the pretext that he didn't wish to disturb monsieur.

M. Folantin would run his fingers over the furniture and find dust everywhere, put away his clothes that were piled high on an armchair, make a few motions with the feather duster, and put fresh ashes in his spittoon. Then he would count his laundry, which was now and then brought back to him, and such disgust would assail him at the sight of his threadbare shirts that he would toss the whole pile into a drawer without further scrutiny.

The day would trickle by quite easily until four o'clock. He would reread old letters from relatives and friends long dead; he would thumb through some of his books, savoring a passage here and there; but at about five o'clock he began to feel wretched; the time was coming when he would have to put on his coat and hat. The mere idea of going out spoiled his appetite, and on some Sundays he didn't stir—or sometimes, fearing that hunger might set in later, he would go down in his slippers and buy two rolls, a pâté, or some sardines. He always kept a little chocolate and wine in a closet, and he would enjoy his little

meal, happy to be at home with plenty of elbow-room, to avoid
for once the hemmed-in feeling he had at restaurants. But then
the nights were bad; he would wake with a start, hungry and
shivering; sometimes he would lie awake for an hour or more;
the darkness quickened his gloomy thoughts, and he would
mull over the same grievances as in the daytime, going so far as
to deplore the absence of a woman in his life. "Marriage is out
of the question at my age," he would tell himself. "Ah, if I had
had a mistress in my youth and held on to her, I should end my
days with her; when I came home, my lamp would be lit and
my dinner ready. If I had my life to begin all over again, I'd
do things differently; I'd make sure of having a companion for
my old age; I've overestimated my strength, and now I'm done
for." And when he arose in the morning, his legs would ache
and his head would feel dull and faint.

Altogether, it was a bad time. The wintry wind made one's
fireside so desirable and the restaurants with their constantly
opening doors doubly hateful. Suddenly a great hope dawned
for M. Folantin. One morning, in the rue de Grenelle, he ran
across a pastry shop that had just opened. On its windows these
words were inscribed in flaming copper letters: "Dinners delivered."

A dazzling light burst upon M. Folantin. For years he had
dreamed of having his dinner brought him at home—was this
dream to be realized at last? But he lost heart when he remembered his vain searches in the quarter for an establishment that
would agree to send up his meals.

"It won't cost anything to ask," he told himself finally, and he
went in.

"Why, certainly, monsieur," replied a young lady ensconced
behind a counter, her bosom hemmed in by saint-honorés and
tarts. "It will be perfectly simple since you live so close by.
What time would you like us to send it?"

"At six," said M. Folantin, trembling with excitement.

"Very well."

M. Folantin's brow clouded over.

"Now what I would like," he said, stammering a little, "is
some soup, a meat dish, and a vegetable. How much would
that be?"

The lady seemed to lose herself in thought. "Soup . . . meat

. . . vegetable," she murmured, gazing aloft. "You don't wish any wine?"

"No, I have wine at home."

"Well, monsieur, in that case it will be two francs."

M. Folantin's features brightened. "Good," he said. "Then it's settled; when can we begin?"

"Whenever you like. This evening if you wish."

"This evening it is." His nod was answered by so much bowing and scraping behind the counter that the lady's nose almost collided with the saint-honorés and the tarts.

Out in the street M. Folantin came to a stop after a few steps. "At last!" he thought. "What luck!" But then his joy subsided. "If only the stuff is no worse than middling! Oh, well, I've put up with so much execrable food in my wretched life, I've no right to be difficult. And the lady is nice; not that she's exactly pretty, but she has expressive eyes. I only hope she does a good business." And he trotted along, wishing the pastry shop all prosperity.

Next, he did everything he could think of to prepare for this first evening; he ordered six bottles of wine from a grocery store, and on reaching his office drew up a little list of provisions that he would buy on the way home:

Jam	Pepper
Cheese	Mustard
Biscuits	Vinegar
Salt	Oil

"Every day I'll have the concierge bring up some bread; my God," he thought, "if this works out, I'm saved."

He longed for the end of the day; thinking of the solitary contentment he would enjoy that evening made the hours drag even more than usual.

From time to time he consulted his watch. Startled at the ecstatic air with which M. Folantin sat dreaming, his colleague smiled. "Admit that she's waiting for you," he said.

"Who, she?" M. Folantin asked in astonishment.

"Come, come. You wouldn't try to teach an old monkey how to make faces. Joking aside, is she blonde or brunette?"

"I can assure you, my friend," said M. Folantin, "that I have other things to think about besides women."

"Yes, yes, so they say. You faker, you. You're just an old Lothario, that's what you are."

"Here, gentlemen, will you copy this immediately. I must have these two letters ready to sign before leaving," and the chief clerk had come and gone.

"It's outrageous," M. Folantin grumbled. "Four closely written pages, I won't be done before five o'clock. It's perfectly absurd," he added, turning to his colleague, who only grinned and muttered: "My dear fellow, you can't expect the administration to worry about little things like that."

Grumbling all the while, he somehow completed his task, and then returned home by the shortest route, his arms laden with bundles, his pockets bulging with paper bags; having closed the door behind him, he heaved a sigh of relief, put on his slippers, ran a napkin over the few dishes he possessed, wiped the glasses, and finding neither board nor sandstone with which to polish the blades of his knives, plunged them into the earth in an old flower pot and managed to make them shine a little.

"Oof," he said, moving the table closer to the fire. "I'm ready." The clock struck six.

He awaited the delivery boy impatiently, with a little of that fever which in his younger days had prevented him from sitting still when a friend of his was late for an appointment.

Finally at a quarter past six the bell chimed and a young fellow lurched in head first, dragged down by the weight of a large tin pail; M. Folantin helped him lay the plates on the table, but did not uncover them until he was alone. There was tapioca broth, braised veal, and cauliflower with white sauce.

"Why, it's not bad," he said, tasting each of the dishes. He ate heartily, drank a little more than usual, then fell into a gentle reverie and looked about his room.

For years he had thought of having it decorated, but he kept telling himself: "What's the use? I'm never here; if later I can arrange to live my life differently, I'll do something about my living quarters." Still, though he bought nothing, he had his designs on a number of knickknacks that he ogled whenever he went walking on the quays or the rue de Rennes.

The idea of covering the cold walls of his room suddenly seized him as he was tossing off a last glass of wine. Gone was his indecision; he resolved to spend the few sous he had accumulated over the years, and he passed a delightful evening mulling over the changes he would make. "Tomorrow," he decided, "I'll get up early and start with a little tour of the yard-goods stores and antique shops."

He no longer had time on his hands; a new interest took possession of him; his eagerness to unearth a few engravings, a few pieces of pottery, yet without spending too much money, kept him going through the day; and after work he moved with feverish haste, leaping up the stairs of the Bon Marché and the Petit Saint-Thomas, plowing through masses of material, finding some too dark or too light, some too wide or too narrow, rejecting the remnants and bargains that the salespeople tried to palm off on him, and making them bring out the goods they were holding back. After hours of goading and pestering he managed to make them produce some rugs and ready-made curtains that really appealed to him.

After these purchases and various ferocious arguments with sellers of curios and prints, he was flat broke; all his savings were gone; but, like a child who has just been given new toys, M. Folantin merely turned over his purchases, examining them from every angle. He climbed on chairs to hang his prints, and he rearranged his books. "It's good to have a home," he said to himself; and, indeed, his room was no longer recognizable. The old nail-holes in the wallpaper vanished beneath the engravings of Ostade and Teniers and the other realistic painters he was so fond of. A collector would certainly have been very contemptuous of these unbordered prints, but he was neither a connoisseur nor wealthy; he liked scenes from humble life, and these represented most of his purchases. He cared little whether they were authentic or not, provided the colors were bright and lent cheer to his room.

"It would have been nice to get rid of all this mahogany furniture," he told himself, contemplating his boat-shaped bed, his two arm chairs done in russet damask, his cracked marble washstand, his table with its reddish veneer, but that would be too expensive. "Besides," he thought, "the curtains and rugs brighten up this old furniture, which, like my old clothes, fits in with my movements and habits."

And what a hurry he was in now to go home, to light the lamp and sink into his chair. The cold seemed to have been left outside, repulsed by this sheltered intimacy, and the falling snow that muffled the sounds of the street added to his well-being. How delightful it was in the evening silence to dine with his feet by the fire, as the plates and wine warmed beside the grate; office cares and the sorrows of bachelordom all vanished in this sweet peace.

Yet before a week had passed, the shop's service began to fall off. The invariable tapioca was full of lumps, and the broth was chemically produced; the sauce on the meats reeked of sour restaurant madeira; all the dishes had a unique but indefinable taste, suggesting rancid library paste and stale, tepid vinegar. M. Folantin energetically peppered his meat and added mustard to the sauces; "Bah!" he muttered. "The stuff can be gotten down. The whole thing is to get used to it."

But the poor quality of the dishes did not remain static; little by little it became accentuated, and the tardiness of the delivery boy made matters worse. He arrived at seven o'clock covered with snow, with black eyes and lacerated cheeks. M. Folantin had no doubt that the youthful apprentice was setting his bucket down on the sidewalk for the pleasure of getting himself thrashed in brawls with his contemporaries. He gently suggested as much; the boy whimpered and, spitting on the floor, advancing one foot, and raising his arms to heaven, swore that this was not so. But there was no improvement. Generously, M. Folantin said nothing, not daring to complain at the pastry shop for fear of injuring the boy's prospects.

For a whole month he bravely put up with this disheartening situation, though his courage flagged when he had to recover his meat from the bottom of the tin, for on some days a tempest seemed to have struck the bucket, everything was topsy-turvy, and the tapioca was full of white sauce and cinders.

Then, fortunately, there was a brief respite: the little apprentice was fired, doubtless as a result of complaints from less indulgent customers. His successor was a gangling simpleton with a pasty complexion and enormous red hands. He at least was punctual, arriving on the stroke of six o'clock, but his filth was repellent; he was clad in dishcloths caked with grease and grime, his cheeks were smeared with flour and soot, and from his unwiped nose two green streams flowed around his mouth.

M. Folantin stanchly parried this new blow; abandoning the

sauces and soiled plates, he transferred the meat to a plate of his own, scraped it, and ate it with nothing but salt. But despite his resignation, a moment came when certain dishes turned his stomach. Now all the spoiled meatballs, all the burned pastry came his way; and in everything he found crusty remnants of patty shells. Encouraged by his forbearance, the cook put the last remnant of shame aside and sent him all the leftovers from his kitchen.

"Poisoner!" M. Folantin muttered as he passed the woman's shop; he no longer thought her so attractive, and as he cast a sidelong glance in her direction, he no longer wished her the slightest prosperity.

He took refuge in hard-boiled eggs. Every day he bought a few out of fear that the dinner would be inedible. And often he filled up on salads; but the eggs were rotten, for the grocery woman, regarding him as a man unversed in these matters, sold him her worst and oldest.

"If I can only hold out till spring," thought M. Folantin to give himself courage; but from week to week his strength waned as his woefully underfed body moaned beneath this cruel treatment. His gaiety vanished, his home lost its brightness; and all his old troubles assailed his forlorn existence. "If only I had some overpowering passion," he reflected; "if I loved women or my office; if I loved cafés, dominoes, cards, I could eat out, for then I should never be home. But alas, nothing diverts me, nothing interests me; and my stomach is going to ruin. Ah, it's a funny thing, people who have the money for food but can't eat for want of an appetite are just as much to be pitied as the poor devils who can't afford a meal."

VI

One evening as he was nibbling at his flatulent eggs, the concierge brought him a communication that ran as follows:

✝

M——

The nuns of the society of Saint Agatha beg you most humbly to commend to God in your prayers and at the Holy Sacrifice of the Mass, the soul of their be-

loved sister Ursule-Aurélie Bougeard, who passed away
on September 7, 1880, in the sixty-second year of her
life and the thirty-fifth year of her Holy Profession, fortified by the Sacraments of our Holy Mother Church.

De profundis!
Sweet heart of Mary, save me.
(300 days ind.)

She was a cousin whom he had known briefly in his childhood; for twenty years he had not given her a thought, and yet
the death of this woman affected him deeply; she was his last
surviving relative, and he felt more alone than ever now that
she was dead in her faraway province. He envied her calm and
silent life and regretted the faith he had lost. "What better occupation," he thought, "than prayer, what better pastime than
confession, what better outlet for your energies than religious
practice? When evening comes, you go to church, you immerse
yourself in contemplation, and life's miseries are as nothing;
and the Sundays slip away in long services, in the sweet languor
of hymns and vespers, for the pious soul doesn't know the
meaning of depression.

"Yes, yes, but why are the consolations of religion fit only for
the feeble-minded? Why has the Church made dogma of the
most absurd beliefs? It is true that if you have faith . . . but I
haven't." Besides, the intolerance of the clergy revolted him.
"And yet," he reflected, "religion is the only thing that might
heal the wound that torments me. It's wrong to tell the faithful
how inane their beliefs are. They are fortunate if they can accept all the calamities and afflictions of this life as a passing
trial. Yes, Cousin Ursule must have died without regrets, convinced that she was entering into everlasting bliss."

He thought of her, tried to recall her features, but his memory had preserved no trace of her; then, to bring her a little
closer, to share a little in the life she had led, he reread the
mysterious and penetrating chapter of *Les Misérables* about
the convent of Le Petit-Picpus.

"Lord," he thought, "it's a heavy price to pay for the unlikely
blessings of a future life." The convent struck him as a kind of
jail, a place of terror and desolation. "No, none of that. I'm
done with envying Cousin Ursule her lot; but other people's

troubles are no consolation, and in the meantime the swill from the pastry shop is becoming insufferable."

Two days later another rude blow fell. As a change from his dinners of salads and desserts, he went to a restaurant. The place was empty, but the service was slow and the wine smelled of benzine.

"Well, at least no one steps on you, and that's something," M. Folantin consoled himself. At this point the door opened, and a cold wind buffeted his back. There was a great rustling of skirts, and a shadow fell across his table. A woman stood before him, moved the chair on whose bars he was resting his feet, and sat down, depositing her veil and gloves beside his glass.

"Devil take her," he grumbled; "with all the tables in the place to choose from, she has to settle down at mine." He raised his eyes mechanically from his plate and, in spite of himself, examined his neighbor. She looked rather like an organ-grinder's monkey with her squashed-in face and her ample, faintly mustached mouth beneath a turned-up nose; but despite her impish look, she struck him as well-mannered and reserved.

From time to time she turned to him and asked him in a soft voice to pass the water or the bread. Despite his timidity, M. Folantin could not help replying to some of her questions; little by little a conversation started, and by the time the dessert came they were deploring, for want of anything better to say, the bitter wind outside, which froze one to the bone.

"It's bad weather for sleeping alone," said the woman dreamily.

This remark flummoxed M. Folantin, who did not feel called upon to reply.

"Don't you think so, monsieur?" she insisted.

"Goodness, mademoiselle . . ." And, like a coward who throws away his weapons to avoid battle, M. Folantin confessed that he led a continent, unassuming life, eschewing the molestations of the flesh.

"Would you be trying to fool me?" she said, looking him straight in the eye.

He grew flustered, all the more so because her advancing bosom gave off a scent of amber and "New-Mown Hay."

"I'm not as young as I used to be," he said, "and I'm not much of a one for women any more—if I ever was; it doesn't go with my age." And he indicated his baldness, his sallow complexion, and his clothes that no longer belonged to any fashion.

"Oh, stop! You're not as old as all that." And she added that she didn't like boys, but preferred mature men because they knew how to act with a woman.

"Yes, of course . . ." M. Folantin stammered, and asked for the check; the woman made no move toward her purse, and he realized that it was up to him. He paid the ironical waiter for two dinners, and was preparing to say good-by to the woman when, at the door, she calmly took his arm.

"Shall we go to your place, eh, monsieur?"

He sought frantically for an excuse, for some way out of this fix, but he became confused, and weakened beneath the assault of the woman's eyes and her perfume that tightened round his temples.

"It's not possible," he finally answered. "I'm not allowed to take women to my room."

"Then come to mine"—and she pressed close to him, prattling away and alleging that there was a good fire in her room. Then, remarking M. Folantin's attitude of gloom, she sighed: "Don't you like me?"

"Why yes, madame . . . of course I do. But it's quite possible to like a woman, and not . . ."

She began to laugh. "Isn't he the funny one!" she said, and kissed him.

M. Folantin was dreadfully embarrassed to be kissed like this in the street; he saw the absurdity of the scene—a lame old man being publicly fondled by a whore. He quickened his pace, seeking to escape these caresses, yet at the same time fearing, should he attempt to flee, a ridiculous scene that would attract a crowd.

"Here it is," she said, giving him a slight push and walking behind him to cut off his retreat. He climbed to the fourth floor and, contrary to the woman's claims, he saw no sign of a fire in her room.

He looked sheepishly round him. The walls seemed to tremble in the flickering candlelight; the chairs had blue wool covers, and over the divan lay a bedspread of Algerian stripe. Under one of the chairs he discerned a muddy shoe, and across from it, under the table, a pair of fire tongs. The walls were hung with

farina advertisements, chaste chromos representing babies
smeared with soup; the curtain of the fireplace had not been
pulled down all the way and revealed the base of a footwarmer.
On the false marble mantelpiece lay an alarm clock, a half-
empty glass, some pomade on a playing card, some tobacco, and
some hair on a newspaper.

"Make yourself at home," said the woman, and, though he
declined to take his things off, she seized his overcoat and hat.

"J. F.," she said, glancing at the initials in his hatband. "I bet
your name is Jules."

He admitted that his name was Jean.

"That's a lovely name. . . ." She made him sit on the divan
and jumped up on his knees.

"Well, dearie, what's my little present going to be?"

With difficulty M. Folantin brought forth a five-franc piece,
which she nimbly spirited away.

"You could spare another," she said. "I'll undress all the
way. I'll be very nice, you'll see."

M. Folantin gave in, but said he'd rather she didn't undress.
Whereupon she kissed him so adroitly that a little of his youthful ardor returned, he forgot his resolutions and lost his head.
Later, as he was attentively lingering, she said: "Don't worry
about me. Do your business."

M. Folantin went down the stairs feeling utterly sick at heart.
As he made his way homeward, he took in at a glance the whole
desolate horizon of his life. He saw the futility of any changes
of course, of any enthusiasm or effort. "There's nothing to do
but drift with the stream," he said to himself. "Schopenhauer is
right: 'the life of man swings like a pendulum between suffering
and boredom.' It's no use trying to speed it up or slow it down;
the only thing to do is to fold your arms and try to sleep; nothing but trouble has come of my attempts to repeat the past, to
enjoy the theater or a good cigar, take tonics, and go to bed
with a woman. Nothing but trouble has come of leaving one bad
restaurant for others that were equally bad, not to mention those
filthy *vol-aux-vents* from the pastry shop."

Thus meditating, he arrived in front of his house. "Goodness,
I'm out of matches," he said to himself, fumbling in his pockets

as he mounted the stairs. He entered his room and an icy wind struck him in the face. Groping his way in the darkness, he sighed: "The simplest thing is just to go back to the wretched old slop-house, to return to the fold. Improvements are not for the poor. If you're poor, you may as well expect the worst."

Translated by Ralph Manheim

THE DESIRE TO BE A MAN

by Villiers de l'Isle-Adam (1838–89)

Midnight struck at the Bourse; the sky was filled with stars. Those were the days when the rigors of martial law still weighed on the city; to comply with curfew regulations, waiters were hurrying to close down the establishments where lights still showed.

In the cafés along the boulevards the last gas-butterflies were rising from the chandeliers and taking quick flight, one by one, into the darkness. Outside, there was the noise of chairs being stacked in clusters of four on marble tables. The psychological moment had come when every bar-keeper deems it fitting to point out to his last customers, with a flourish of his napkined arm, the straight and narrow path leading to the street.

The October wind was whistling that Sunday. A few seared leaves, dusty and rustling, raced along with the gusts, slapping against stones and scraping the pavement; then, like bats, they vanished into the night, bringing to mind humdrum days forever gone. The theatres of the boulevard du Crime, on whose

---

Villiers de l'Isle-Adam, who had five Christian names as well, was descended from a line of Breton Catholic nobility dating back to the Middle Ages. He was born and grew up in the Breton seaport of Saint-Brieuc; he took over from his quixotic father—a ruined marquis forever in pursuit of phantom fortunes—a pride of race and caste which was all the crustier and more extravagant in him for his sense of being, like some French Roderick Usher, the last, superfluous survivor of a once mighty house. (And in fact Poe, to whose work he was introduced by Baudelaire, inspired many of his stories.) Villiers was not unaware, in his ironic way, of the archaic figure that he cut in a world whose catchwords were Progress, Democracy, Science; and his irony, like everything else about him, was in a measure histrionic—but this in a country where histrionics, long since accepted as one of the useful public aspects of the

stages Medicis, Salviatis, and Montefeltres had stabbed one another all evening long to their hearts' content, now loomed like
the very hide-outs of silence, mute doors guarded by their
caryatids. Carriages and pedestrians became fewer by the minute. Here and there, a skeptical rag-picker's lantern already
gleamed, like phosphorescence from the piled-up filth over
which it hovered.

At the corner of the rue Hauteville, under a lamp post by a
fairly sumptuous-looking café, a tall passer-by with a saturnine
face, a smooth chin, and the gait of a sleepwalker—long, gray-
ing hair covered by a felt hat in the style of Louis XIII, black-
gloved hands gripping an ivory-headed cane, figure wrapped in
an old blue cloak lined with questionable Persian lamb—had
paused as if absent-mindedly hesitating to cross the street that
separated him from the boulevard Bonne-Nouvelle.

Was this belated personage on his way home? Or had he been
guided to that street corner merely by the vagaries of a noc-
turnal stroll? It would have been hard to tell by the look of
him. The fact remains that, noticing suddenly on his right one
of those public mirrors—long and narrow in shape like himself
—which one sometimes finds flanking the windows of more important bars, he came to an abrupt stop, planted himself
squarely in front of his reflection, and scrutinized it with deliberation from head to toe. Whereupon, without warning, he

literary life, receive due honor also as a form of truth, involving, like any other, certain perils. One such peril is the subject
of "The Desire to Be a Man."

Villiers, the young provincial poet, reciting his brilliant
monologues in Parisian literary cafés, more or less corresponds
to the standard American notion of the long-haired Left Bank
Bohemian. This convenient notion, however, does not quite account for the formidable quantity of time and labor which he
spent in jealously guarded solitude composing his volumes of
elaborately wrought (sometimes overwrought as well as over-
worked) verse and prose.

The rather unkempt, semi-nomadic existence that Villiers led
in a succession of furnished (or unfurnished) rooms contrasted
strikingly with his art, which was elegant to the point of being
dandified, and with a personal manner that Mallarmé called

raised his hat and, with a gesture that seemed to come from out of the past, gave himself a by no means unceremonious salute.

The head thus unexpectedly bared proved to belong to the celebrated tragic actor, Esprit Chaudval, originally Lepeinteur, known as Monanteuil, offspring of a very worthy family of Saint-Malo pilots, whom the mysterious ways of Fate had induced to play leading rôles in out-of-town productions, heading casts abroad, and rivaling (often with success) our one and only Frédéric Lemaître.

While he stared at himself in a kind of stupor, the waiters of the café were helping the last clients into their overcoats and handing them their hats. Others noisily turned over their money boxes and made cylindrical piles of the day's change on a tray. The cause of all this haste and fluster was the ominous presence of two unlooked-for policemen who, standing in the doorway with their arms crossed, harried the laggard bar-keeper with a cold stare. Soon the shutters were locked tight in their iron frames—all but the one for the mirror, which by a strange oversight was neglected in the rush.

Then the boulevard grew very quiet. Chaudval, alone now and heedless of things' disappearance all around him, had remained in his ecstatic attitude on the sidewalk at the corner of the rue Hauteville in front of the forgotten glass.

"princely." Contrasts *of various sorts—most of all between abject realities and exalted ideals, which he rendered in terms almost equally theatrical—underlay much of his work. Common to all his best work was the ceremonious, sardonic, "affected" haughtiness that constitutes at times for professional tragic comedians (Barrymore was another) that point in the register of personal expression where truth and artifice have the same falsetto voice.*

"The Desire to Be a Man" was first published in Contes Cruels *in 1883.*

OTHER WORKS: *Stories:* Tribulat Bonhomet (*1887*), Histoires insolites (*1888*), Nouveaux Contes cruels (*1888*), Derniers Contes (*1909*). *Novels:* L'Ève future (*1886*), Axël (*1890*). *Plays:* La Révolte (*1870*), Le Nouveau Monde (*1880*), L'Évasion (*1891*).

This pallid, lunar mirror seemed to give the artist the same sensation as bathing in a pond: Chaudval shivered.

Alas! let us admit it: in that cruel and somber crystal the actor had just seen himself growing old.

He found that his hair, which only yesterday had been just sprinkled with gray, was turning silver. That, then, was that! Good-by curtain calls and wreaths, good-by roses of Thalia and Melpomene's laurels! He must take leave forever, with handshakes and tears, of beaux and grisettes, of noble liveries and shapely curves, of comedy valets and ingénues.

The time had come for him hastily to scramble down from the chariot of Thespis and watch it carry off his companions! Time to watch the tinsel and streamers that, in the morning sun, like playthings of the lighthearted breeze of Hopes, had fluttered from the chariot's very wheels—to watch them disappear into twilight at the faraway bend of the road.

Chaudval (a good fellow, really) sighed, rudely awakened to the fact of his fifty years. His eyes clouded, a kind of wintry fever seized upon him, and hallucination dilated his pupils.

The distraught fixity with which he peered into the mirror that providence had placed on his road gave to those pupils at last the faculty of magnifying objects and of suffusing them with solemnity—a trait that physiologists have often noted in persons affected by intense emotion.

So it was that, under those eyes filled with murky and turbid thoughts, the long mirror underwent changes of form. Memories of his childhood, of beaches and silvery waves, danced up and down in Chaudval's brain. And the mirror, probably because of the stars that lent depth to its surface, gave him a feeling at first of somnolent bay-water. Then, expanding farther still by virtue of his sighs, it assumed the appearance of the sea and the night, those age-old friends of desolate hearts.

He feasted for some time on this vision, but the street lamp overhead, casting a reddish glow on the drizzle behind him, came back to him from the depths of that awesome glass as the blood-colored flare of a lighthouse pointing the path of shipwreck to the lost vessel of his future.

He shook the nightmare off and drew himself up to his full height, giving vent to a burst of forced, bitter laughter that startled the two policemen patrolling under the trees. Supposing the artist—fortunately for him—to be some harmless drunkard or, perhaps, a disappointed lover, they continued on their round without giving the unhappy Chaudval a second thought.

"All right, then, let's face it: that's that," he said, simply and softly, as the prisoner sentenced to die says to the executioner who abruptly wakes him: "I am all yours, my friend."

Whereupon, dazed and prostrate, the old actor went off into a monologue:

"I acted wisely the other night when I requested my good friend Mlle Pinson—who has access to the Minister's ear, to say nothing of his pillow—to obtain for me, between two avowals of burning passion, that post as lighthouse-keeper which my forebears held on the Breton coast. . . . Hah! Now I begin to understand why the reflection of this street lamp in the mirror affected me so strangely: it expressed what was in the back of my mind. No question about it, Pinson is going to send me my appointment. And no sooner do I have it than I withdraw into my lighthouse like a rat into a cheese. I shall light the way for ships far out to sea. A lighthouse! There's always something of a stage-set about a lighthouse. Alone in the world as I am, what better refuge for my old age could I ask?"

Suddenly Chaudval broke off his reverie.

"Well, I'll be . . . !" he said, feeling his chest beneath his cloak. "That letter—that letter the mailman brought as I was leaving—it must be my reply! . . . But what in—? There I was on the point of stepping into this café to read it, and then it completely slips my mind! I really am in a bad way. Ah! Here we are."

Chaudval had extracted from his pocket a large envelope from which fell out, as soon as he broke the seal, a sheet of official stationery. He picked it up with feverish haste and ran his eyes through it under the red glare of the street lamp.

"My lighthouse! My appointment!" he cried. "Saved, ye gods above!" he added mechanically, as if prompted by an old habit, and in a falsetto so sudden, so different from his own voice, that he looked all around, imagining there must be a third person present. "Come now, hold on to your self and . . . be a man!" he went on after a moment.

At these words, however, Esprit Chaudval, originally Lepeinteur, known as Monanteuil, stopped as if he had been turned to a pillar of salt. The phrase seemed to have paralyzed him.

"What was that?" he went on after a pause. "What was it I just wished? To be a Man? . . . Come to think of it, why not?"

He folded his arms and lost himself in thought.

"For nearly half a century now I have been *aping*, I have been *acting out* other people's passions without ever feeling them myself—for, at heart, I have never felt a thing. What am I, then, but a mere play-likeness of 'other people'? What more am I than a *shadow?* Passions! Feelings! Real acts! REALITY! That's what makes a MAN, in the word's true sense. So then, since old age forces me to return to the human fold, I must find some passions for myself, some *real* feeling or other—that being the *sine qua non* of any claim to the title of Man. There's solid reasoning for you: it's as clear as day. Now then, what emotion would be best suited to this true character of mine which has at last come back to life?"

He meditated awhile, and then went on sadly: "Love? Too late. Glory? I have tasted it. Ambition? We can leave that rubbish to politicians."

Suddenly a cry broke from him:

"I've got it! REMORSE! Now there's something that goes with my dramatic temperament."

He looked at himself in the mirror, putting on a face contorted and convulsed as if by some unearthly horror.

"That's it!" he concluded. "Nero! Macbeth! Orestes! Hamlet! Erostratus! Ghosts! . . . Yes! I too want to see ghosts, the same way those lucky people did who couldn't make a move without having ghosts around them."

He struck his forehead.

"But *how?* I am as innocent as an unborn lamb."

And, after another pause between lines, he went on:

"Ah! but no matter; where there's a will there's a way! I have ample right, after all, to become what I *ought* to be. I am entitled to my Humanity! To feel remorse, you say, one must have committed crimes? Well then, let us have crimes: what does it matter, so long as they are perpetrated for . . . for the good cause? Yes. . . . Very good." (And he fell into dialogue:) "I shall commit hideous ones." "When?" "At once. Let's not put it off until tomorrow!" "What crimes?" "Just one! But a great one, an extravagantly hideous one, that shall unleash all Hell's Furies!" "What crime is that?" "Why, the most dazzling. . . . Bravo! I've got it! ARSON! There we are, then; I'll have just time. I start a fire, pack my trunks, return duly skulking behind the window of some cab, gloat on my triumph in the midst of the frantic crowd, carefully gather up the curses of the dying—then catch the Northwest Express, with enough pangs of conscience stocked up to last me for the rest of my days. After that, I go into hiding in my lighthouse. In the very heart of the spotlight! Surrounded by the ocean! Where, as a result, my crime having *no interested motive*, the police will never track me down. And there, in solitude, I shall writhe." (At this point Chaudval straightened up and improvised a line worthy of Corneille:

Saved from suspicion by the dark deed's grandeur!)

" 'Tis said! And now," the great artist concluded, picking up a cobblestone after having made sure there was no one else around, "and now, as for you, never again shall you reflect another man."

And he hurled the stone against the glass, which broke into a thousand gleaming splinters.

This initial duty carried out, Chaudval made off hurriedly and—as if satisfied with this preliminary but energetic feat of derring-do—hastened toward the boulevards, where, a few minutes later, he signaled a carriage to a stop, jumped in, and disappeared.

Two hours later the flames of an immense conflagration, bursting from great storehouses of kerosene, oil, and matches, reddened all the windowpanes of the Faubourg du Temple. Soon companies of firemen, pushing and pulling their engines, converged from every side, and the sinister blasts of their horns roused the startled inhabitants of this thickly settled district. Innumerable hurrying footsteps rang out on the sidewalks; the great Place du Château d'Eau and the adjoining streets were crammed with people. Bucket brigades were already hastily forming. In less than a quarter of an hour a detachment of soldiers had formed a cordon around the scene of the fire. Policemen, working by the blood-red glare of torches, held back the crowd.

Carriages were trapped and could no longer move. Everyone was shouting. Distant cries could be made out amidst the fearful crackling of the fire. The victims caught in this inferno screamed, and the roofs of the houses crashed in on them. A hundred families, those of the workmen employed by the blazing factories, were left, sad to say, destitute and homeless.

Over yonder, a solitary carriage, laden with two large trunks, stood motionless behind the crowd milling in the square. And in that carriage sat Esprit Chaudval, originally Lepeinteur, known as Monanteuil. From time to time he raised the blind and contemplated his handiwork: "Ah!" he whispered. "Am I not an object of horror in the sight of God and Man? Yes, that's it; there's the mark of your true outcast!"

The good old actor's face was beaming.

"Oh, wretch that I am!" he muttered. "What vengeful insomnias I shall taste, besieged by the ghosts of my victims! I feel surging within me the soul of Nero, burning Rome from sheer artistic exaltation! Of Erostratus burning the temple of Ephesus for the sake of glory! Of Rostopchin burning Moscow out of patriotism! Of Alexander burning Persepolis as a gesture of gallantry for his immortal Thaïs! But I, I burn for *Duty's* sake, having no other means of *existence!* I burn because I owe myself to myself! I am squaring up my accounts! What a Man I shall be! How I shall live! Yes, I am going to know at last what it feels like to be tortured by remorse. What exquisite, what magnificently horrible nights I shall pass! Ah! I am breathing now! I am reborn! I exist! To think that I was once an actor! Now, since in the gross eyes of mortals I am nothing but a scoundrel fit for the gallows, let us flee with the speed of light! Let us shut ourselves up in our lighthouse, that we may enjoy our remorse in peace."

Two days later, at nightfall, Chaudval reached his destination without incident and took possession of his lonely old beacon, located on our western coast: a flame fallen into disuse at the top of a ruined building, which an official's compassion had stirred up for him.

There was small chance of the signal's being of any use whatever: it was a mere superfluity, a sinecure, a dwelling with a blaze on top, which no one in the world but Chaudval would ever have missed.

So our worthy actor, having brought thither his bed, a supply of food, and a tall mirror in which to study his facial expressions, shut himself up, then and there, far from all human suspicion.

About him moaned the sea, wherein the age-old abyss of the heavens bathed its starry light. He watched the waves lashed by the winds fling themselves against his tower, as Simeon Stylites might have contemplated the sands swirling about his column under the hot breath of the desert wind.

Off in the distance he followed with an empty stare the sails of fishing-boats or the smoke of steamers.

Every two seconds the fire he had set slipped this dreamer's mind. He went up and down his stone staircase.

On the evening of the third day Lepeinteur sat in his room, sixty feet above the water, rereading a Paris newspaper in which was recounted the story of the great disaster that had occurred two days before.

An unknown criminal, the article said, had thrown some matches into the vaults where kerosene was kept. An enormous fire, which had kept firemen and residents of the neighboring districts up all through the night, had broken out in the Faubourg du Temple.

Nearly one hundred persons had perished; whole families of unfortunates had been plunged into darkest misery.

The entire square, still smoking, was in mourning.

The identity of the wretch who had perpetrated this foul deed was not known, and still less was his *motive.*

When he read these words, Chaudval jumped with joy and rubbed his hands excitedly, exclaiming: "What a success! What an admirable scoundrel I am! How I shall be haunted now! What ghosts I shall see! I was sure that I would become a Man! Ah! the means were drastic, I must admit, but it had to be done! It had to be done!"

Reading over the Paris paper again, he found a mention of a benefit performance to be given on behalf of those hit by the fire.

"Ah!" he murmured, "I should have offered my talented services for the benefit of the victims! It would have been my farewell performance. I would have recited *Orestes.* I'd have been thoroughly convincing. . . ."

Whereupon Chaudval began life in the lighthouse.

Evenings came and went; nights passed.

Something happened that startled the artist. Something atrocious!

Contrary to all his hopes and expectations, his conscience gave him no pangs. Not a single ghost appeared! He felt *nothing, absolutely nothing!*

The silence was beyond belief. He could not get over it.

Every once in a while, as he looked into the mirror, he noticed that the easy-going expression on his face had not changed. Infuriated, he would thereupon rush to his signals and mix them up, in the fervent hope that he might cause some far-off ship to sink and thus help along, quicken, stimulate his refractory remorse—that he might arouse the ghosts!

In vain!

Fruitless crimes! Wasted efforts! He felt *nothing.* Not one menacing phantom did he behold. He no longer slept, so stifled was he by despair and *shame.* So much so that one night, cerebral congestion having struck him in his glowing solitude, he cried out, in his death struggle, amidst the noise of the sea, and while the great ocean winds lashed against his tower lost there in the infinite:

"Ghosts! For the love of God, let me see a ghost, were it but one! *Haven't I earned it?*"

But the God whom he invoked did not grant him this favor, and the old player died still declaiming with futile emphasis his great wish to set eyes on a ghost, *not realizing that what he was after, he himself already was.*

Translated by Pierre Schneider

AT SEA

by Guy de Maupassant (1850–93)

The following news item recently appeared in the press:

> From our own correspondent, Boulogne-sur-Mer, 22nd
> January. An appalling disaster has brought grief to our
> fisherfolk, who have suffered so much during the last
> two years. A fishing smack, commanded by its owner,
> M. Javel, was carried westward as it was entering the
> harbor, and was dashed to pieces against the rocks of
> the breakwater.
>
> In spite of the efforts of the lifeboat and the use of
> rocket apparatus, four members of the crew and the
> cabin boy lost their lives.
>
> Heavy seas are still running and further wrecks are
> feared.

I wonder who this Javel is. Perhaps he is the brother of one-
armed Javel. If so, the poor fellow, whose drowned body is now

---

*Among authors one comes to the end of, whom one some-
times has the illusion of seeing through, Maupassant lasts. The
hard, spare cleanness of his best work (not often visible in
translation) helps preserve it from rot: writing stripped so
nearly to the bone has few excrescences for rot to attack.
Literary virtues of this sort come high, of course, in merely
human terms; they have non-literary origins that cannot always be looked into by the pure of heart. Just that is the
reason why Maupassant does last: he did pay the price: the
origins were terrible. And what lasts in him is more than
the hard, spare cleanness of certain pages; it is also the massive terror (complemented by a massive frozen pity) behind
them.*

*He was born of a remarkable mother and a no-account, skirt-
chasing father, in Normandy, a region to which he "belonged"
—and which he knew and loved—somewhat as Mark Twain belonged to and knew and loved the Mississippi Valley. The region
produces, along with the race of tight-fisted peasants and tough*

being tossed about by the waves or is lying at the bottom under
the wreckage of his boat, was once involved in another terrible
event, as simple and frightening as these great dramas of the
deep always are.

It happened eighteen years ago now. In those days the elder
Javel already had his own trawler.

The trawler is the typical fishing-boat. Broad in the beam and
built to withstand all weathers, she bobs up and down in the
waves like a cork. She is out at all times and, under the constant
battering of the harsh, salt Channel winds, she plows un-
wearyingly through the water, with bellying sail, dragging over
the side a big net that scours the bottom of the sea, picking up
the creatures snoozing in the crannies of the rocks, the flatfish
sticking to the sandy bottom, heavy crabs with crooked claws,
and lobsters with pointed whiskers.

Fishing begins when the wind freshens and the sea is choppy.
The net is attached to a long, wooden bar strengthened by iron
braces, and is lowered by means of two cables working on two
windlasses placed one at either end of the boat. Then the
trawler, drifting with the wind and the currents, drags this contraption along with her, stripping and ransacking the sea bed.

---

*fishermen who fill so many of his stories, a race of artists for
whom the standard epithets are somber, powerful, virile, sen-
sual, robust—Corneille and Flaubert are other examples among
writers, Poussin among painters. Flaubert was a kind of adop-
tive father to Maupassant (as well as his official godfather); it
was from Flaubert, and later from Turgenev, that he learned
the discipline of his art. Maupassant published little before he
was thirty, earning his livelihood as a clerk in government of-
fices in Paris (he knew, also, the race of petty bureaucrats
which fills so many of his other tales). Boule de Suif, in 1880,
brought him instant fame; with it began the literary career on
which he entered, as he put it, "like a meteor," and from which
he made his exit, a few years afterward, "in a flash of lightning." With success and wealth, Maupassant, the vigorous young
sportsman, avid of air and water and freshly spilled blood, became to some extent the man-about-town and inexhaustible lady-
killer of Maupassant legend. There was more than a little cold,
loveless savagery about his lady-killing; but the ladies, who*

Javel had on board with him his younger brother, four men, and a cabin boy. He had left Boulogne in fine, clear weather to go trawling.

But soon the wind rose and a squall forced the trawler to run before it. She came within reach of the English coast, but heavy seas were dashing against the cliffs and pounding the shore, so that it was impossible to enter harbor. The little boat put out again and headed back to the French coast. There, too, the storm made it impossible to come into harbor. The approaches to all the ports were dangerous, being surrounded by roaring, foaming waves.

The trawler set off again, rising to the rollers, tossing and bumping, dripping from stem to stern, smacked from time to time by great masses of water, but still perky, for she was quite used to rough weather, which kept her on the move for five or six days at a time and prevented her from drawing in either to the French or to the English coast.

When, eventually, the gale died down, the trawler was out in the open sea, and though there was a strong swell, the skipper gave orders to lower the dragnet.

And so the big trawl was let down over the side and the ropes

---

were wild about him, had their revenge—they killed him in turn. An undiagnosed case of hereditary (plus acquired) syphilis had begun to destroy him before he was thirty-six; he was dead at forty-three, in a madhouse, howling, raving, "down on all fours licking the walls of his cell" (Paul Morand).

The view from Maupassant's window is blocked by a hedge he planted to keep out demons and wild beasts—wilder, that is, than the ones already in. The hedge has been given various names—pessimism, naturalism, determinism, cynicism, skepticism; and at times he himself mistook it for the horizon at the far edge of the world.

The two stories that follow are from Contes de la Bécasse *(1883), written when Maupassant was in his best form.*

OTHER WORKS: *Stories:* La Maison Tellier *(1881)*, Miss Harriet *(1884)*, Toine *(1885)*, Contes et Nouvelles *(1885)*, La Horla *(1887)*. *Novels:* Une Vie *(1883)*, Bel-Ami *(1885)*, Pierre et Jean *(1888)*, Fort comme la mort *(1889)*. *Travel books:* Au soleil *(1884)*, Sur l'eau *(1888)*.

holding it were fed out from the windlasses by two men standing in the bows and two others at the stern. Suddenly the net touched bottom, but at that moment a big wave tipped the trawler, and young Javel, who was in the bows directing the lowering of the net, lost his footing. His arm was caught between the cable, which the movement of the boat had slackened for a second, and the wood of the gunwale over which it passed. He made a desperate effort to lift the rope up with his other arm, but—the trawl being already in operation—the cable was taut and would not move.

Twisted with pain, he gave a shout. The others rushed to his aid, and his brother left the helm. They threw themselves against the rope to free the arm that was being crushed. The rope would not move. "Cut it!" said one of the men, drawing from his pocket a broad-bladed knife that, in a couple of strokes, could free young Javel's arm.

But to cut the rope was to lose the trawl, and the trawl was worth money, a lot of money—fifteen hundred francs. And it belonged to the elder Javel, who was strongly attached to his possessions.

In an agony of anxiety he cried: "Wait! Don't cut! I'll pull her round." And he ran to the tiller and put it hard over.

The boat scarcely responded at all, being paralyzed by the net, which put her out of control; she was, in any case, drifting with the wind and the waves.

Young Javel had dropped to his knees with clenched teeth and wild eyes. He did not utter a word. His brother came back, still afraid that one of the sailors might use a knife. "Wait! Wait! Don't cut it! We'll drop anchor."

The anchor went overboard and the whole length of the chain was run out. Then they began to heave at the capstan to slacken the ropes holding the trawl. The ropes did eventually relax, and the limp arm, in its blood-soaked woolen sleeve, was set free.

Young Javel seemed to have gone stupid. They took his jersey off and saw a horrible sight—a mass of pulped flesh from which blood was starting in spurts as if ejected by a pump. Young Javel looked at his arm and muttered: "Done for."

Then, as the blood was forming a pool on the deck, one of

the sailors cried: "He'll have none left soon. Bind his arm."

They took a piece of twine—thick, brown, tarry twine—put it round his arm above the wound, and pulled it as tight as they could. The spurting of the blood gradually diminished and finally stopped altogether.

Young Javel stood up, with his arm dangling at his side. He took hold of it with his other hand, lifted it up, turned it round, and shook it. It was completely broken; the bones were cut right through; the arm was hanging only by the sinews. He looked at it mournfully, deep in thought. Then he sat down on a pile of folded sail, and his shipmates advised him to keep moistening the wound to prevent gangrene.

They put a bucket beside him, and every few minutes he would dip a glass into it and bathe the horrible wound by letting a little clear water trickle over it.

"You'd be better down in the cabin," his brother said to him. He went below, but after an hour came up again, not feeling comfortable on his own. Also, he preferred to be in the fresh air. He sat down on the sail again and continued to bathe his arm.

The catch was a good one. Broad, white-bellied fish lay beside him, flapping in the throes of death. He watched them as he went on bathing his torn flesh.

The trawler had almost reached Boulogne when a fresh wind sprang up. The little boat started racing along madly as before, tipping and bouncing, shaking the despondent young Javel.

Night fell and the wild weather lasted until dawn. At sunrise the English coast was again visible, but, as the sea was now less rough, they turned back toward France and began beating up against the wind.

Toward evening Javel called his shipmates and showed them black marks that had appeared on the lower part of his arm; all this part now displayed sinister signs of putrefaction.

The sailors looked at it, and each gave his opinion.

"It might be gangrene," said one.

"You need some salt water on that," said another.

So they brought salt water and poured it over the wounded arm. Young Javel went white, ground his teeth, and writhed; but he uttered no cry.

Then, when the stinging had stopped, he said to his brother: "Give me your knife."

The brother handed it over.

"Hold my arm up, straight out, and pull."

They did as he told them.

He then set about cutting off the arm himself. He did so gently and thoughtfully, severing the last tendons with a blade as sharp as a razor; soon he had only the stump left. He heaved a deep sigh and remarked: "Had to. Otherwise I was done for."

Seeming relieved, he was breathing deeply. He resumed his bathing of the stump.

The next night was wild, too, and they could not put into harbor. When it was daylight again, young Javel picked up his severed arm and examined it at great length. Putrefaction had set in. His shipmates came to have a look at it as well. They passed it round from hand to hand, felt it, turned it over, sniffed it.

His brother said: "Better throw it overboard now."

But young Javel was indignant. "Not likely. I'm not having that. It's my arm, isn't it?"

He took it back and placed it between his legs.

"It'll go rotten, all the same," said his elder brother. Then young Javel had an idea. When the boat was a long time out, they put the fish into barrels, between layers of salt, to keep it fresh.

"Couldn't I put it in salt?"

"So he could," remarked the others.

And they emptied one of the barrels that had been filled during the last few days. They put the arm in at the bottom, scattered salt over it, and then replaced the fish one by one.

One of the sailors cracked a joke: "Let's hope we don't auction it with the rest!"

Everybody laughed except the two brothers.

The wind was still blowing, and they tacked about outside Boulogne until ten o'clock the next morning. The injured man went on pouring water over his wound.

Every now and again he would get up and walk from one end of the boat to the other.

· His brother, standing at the helm, would watch him and shake his head.

Eventually they were able to put in to land.

The doctor examined the wound and said that it was healing nicely. He dressed it thoroughly and told his patient to rest. But Javel would not go to bed until he had recovered his arm; he hurried back to the harbor to look for the barrel he had marked with a cross.

They emptied it in front of him and he retrieved his severed limb, which came out wrinkled and fresher-looking, having been well preserved by the salt. He wrapped it in a towel he had brought for the purpose and went home again.

His wife and children carefully examined the dead fragment of their husband and father, feeling the fingers and removing the grains of salt which remained under the nails. Then the carpenter was sent for to make a little coffin.

The next day the entire crew of the trawler attended the funeral of young Javel's arm. The chief mourners were the two brothers, who walked in front side by side. The sacristan had the corpse tucked under his arm.

Young Javel did not go to sea again. He found a light job ashore, and, whenever he spoke about his accident later, he would say in a confidential whisper: "If that brother of mine had been willing to cut away the trawl, I'd still have my arm, to be sure. But he never could part with his belongings."

Translated by J. G. Weightman

MINUET

by Guy de Maupassant

Great calamities have little effect on me (said Jean Bridelle; he was a bachelor and, it was thought, of a skeptical turn of mind). I have seen a battlefield at close quarters; I stepped over the dead bodies without compunction. Great acts of brutality by nature or mankind can wring cries of horror or indignation from us, but they do not tug at the heart, they do not send a shiver down the spine, like some tiny but distressing events.

The greatest of all possible griefs is, for a mother, to lose her child, or, for a man, to lose his mother. The pain is violent and terrible; it rends and devastates the sufferer. But one recovers from such disasters, just as gaping, bleeding wounds eventually heal. There are, however, some encounters with people, some half-glimpsed, half-guessed-at realities or secret sorrows or treacherous blows of fate that awaken within us a whole painful world of thought, that suddenly open up a mysterious vista of mental suffering—complex, incurable suffering, which goes all the deeper because it seems so slight, which is all the more acute for being so indefinable and all the more stubborn through appearing so imaginary. Such things leave a trail of sadness in the heart, a taste of bitterness in the mouth, and a feeling of disillusionment from which we are slow to recover.

I still have clearly present to mind two or three things that other people very possibly would not have noticed but which pierced me like long, slender, incurable stings.

You may not understand why such brief experiences should have left such feelings. I will give you just one example, a very old one, but as fresh as if it had happened yesterday. Perhaps the emotion it arouses in me is owing entirely to my imagination.

I'm fifty now. It happened when I was young. I was a sad and rather dreamy law student imbued with philosophic melancholy. I had no liking for noisy cafés or for my rowdy fellow students or for stupid girls. I was an early riser, and one of my great delights was to go for a solitary walk at about eight o'clock in the morning through the nursery garden in the Jardin du Luxembourg.

This nursery garden was before your time, of course. It was like some forgotten eighteenth-century garden, as pretty as a smile on an old, gentle face. Narrow, regular paths ran between thick hedges, calm paths between walls of methodically pruned foliage. The gardener's big shears were always cutting back these leafy partitions. At intervals there were banks of flowers or beds planted with rows of saplings, like schoolgirls walking in double file, or communities of magnificent rosebushes, or whole regiments of fruit trees.

One corner of this delightful grove was inhabited by bees. Their thatched hives were carefully set out on planks, with the entrances (each about the size of a thimble) turned toward the sun; and all along the garden walks one came across the golden, humming insects, the real owners of that peaceful place and the true occupants of those quiet, corridor-like paths.

I used to go there almost every morning. I would settle on a bench to read. Sometimes I would let the book drop to my knees and I would sit day-dreaming, listening to the sounds of Paris around me and enjoying the deep restfulness of those old-world arbors.

But I was not long in noticing that I was not the only person who frequented the place as soon as the gates were opened. On turning a bushy corner, I would sometimes find myself face to face with a strange little old man. He wore buckled shoes, full-fall knee breeches, a snuff-colored frock coat, a lace cravat, and an unbelievable broad-brimmed beaver hat that might have come out of the ark.

He was thin, very thin and angular, and always grimacing and smiling. His bright eyes twinkled and raced under his constantly twitching lids, and he always carried a magnificent gold-topped cane, which must have been a souvenir of former splendor.

At first I was astonished by the old fellow, and then I became extraordinarily interested in him. I would watch for him through the leafy walls, follow him at a distance, and pause at the corners so that he should not see me.

Finally, one morning, when he thought himself quite alone, he began to make very peculiar movements. First he gave a series of little leaps, followed by a deep bow. Then his spindly legs performed a still sprightly *entrechat*, after which he began to twirl seductively, hopping and quivering in the oddest way, smiling to an imaginary audience, making graceful, rounded gestures with his arms, twisting his poor, puppet-like body, and waving pathetic and ridiculous little greetings to the empty air. He was dancing!

I stood dumfounded, wondering which of us was mad.

But suddenly he stopped, came forward like an actor advancing to the front of the stage, bowed, and then backed away, smiling with the graciousness of a leading lady and throwing kisses with his trembling hands to two lengths of pruned hedge.

Then he gravely resumed his walk.

From then on I did not let him out of my sight, and every morning he repeated his incredible performance.

I felt an irresistible desire to speak to him, so one morning, raising my hat, I ventured to remark: "A lovely day, monsieur."

He bowed. "Yes, monsieur. Quite like the weather we used to have."

A week later we were friends, and he told me his story. He had been dancing-master at the Opéra in Louis XV's time. His handsome cane was a present from the Comte de Clermont. And on the subject of dancing he talked inexhaustibly.

Then one day he took me into his confidence: "My wife is La Castris, monsieur. I will introduce you to her if you wish, but she comes here only in the afternoons. This garden, you must understand, is our only entertainment; indeed, our whole life. It is all that remains of the past, and we feel that, were it not here, we could no longer go on living. It is old and has distinction, don't you think? Here I seem to breathe an air that has not changed since I was young. My wife and I spend all our afternoons here. But I come in the mornings too because I am an early riser."

As soon as I had finished lunch, I returned to the Luxembourg, and it was not long before I saw my friend advancing ceremoniously, arm in arm with a tiny old woman dressed in black. I was introduced. She was the great dancer, La Castris, the toast of princes, a favorite of the King, and the idol of that whole amorous century which seems to have perfumed the world with love.

We sat down on a bench. It was May. The scent of flowers was wafted along the trim walks; warm, comforting sunshine slipped through the leaves and splashed us with brightness. La Castris's black dress seemed to be steeped in light.

The garden was empty, but cabs could be heard rolling in the distance.

"Tell me," I said to the old ballet master, "what exactly was a minuet?"

He gave a slight start.

"You must understand, monsieur, that the minuet was the queen of dances and the dance of queens. Now that we have no king, the minuet has ceased to exist."

And he began a long, incomprehensible eulogy, couched in pompous dithyrambic terms. I asked him to describe the steps, the movements, the attitudes. He got confused, was annoyed at his inability to explain, and became exasperated and depressed.

Then suddenly, turning toward his aged wife, who had remained silent and serious, he asked: "Élise, would you agree— it would be most kind of you—would you agree to show monsieur what it was like?"

After glancing anxiously around, she rose without saying a word and took up her position in front of him.

Then I saw a sight I shall never forget.

They moved to and fro with mincing, childish ceremoniousness, smiled to each other, swayed and bowed and hopped like two little old dolls worked by some antique mechanism, now slightly out of order but made originally by a very clever craftsman skilled in the methods of his day.

As I watched them, my heart was troubled by extraordinary sensations and my soul was moved with inexpressible melancholy. I seemed to be contemplating a vision at once pathetic and ridiculous, the ghostly survival of a vanished century. I wanted to laugh and cry at the same time.

Suddenly they stopped; they had completed the dance. For a few seconds they stood facing each other, making astonishing grimaces; then they fell into each other's arms and sobbed.

I was to leave three days later for the provinces. I did not see them again. When I returned to Paris after two years' absence, the nursery garden had disappeared. I wonder what has become of them without the old-fashioned garden of which they were so fond, with its maze, its scent of the past, and its graciously winding walks.

Perhaps they are dead, or perhaps they are wandering through our modern streets like hopeless exiles. Or have they become pale specters, dancing a fantastic minuet in some moon-lit churchyard, among cypresses and along paths edged by tombs?

Their memory haunts me still; it is a torturing obsession, like an unhealed wound. I cannot tell why, and you probably think me ridiculous.

Translated by J. G. Weightman

A ROMANCE

by Jules Renard (1864–1910)

PART ONE: CHICKEN EGG

Mme Lérin's son had said to the hired girl: "Françoise, there's another hen in the garden!"

And Françoise had replied: "I'll go, Monsieur Émile. It's always the same one. But this time I'll show her a thing or two!"

She lifted her arms and cried: "Hen! Hen!" and ran red-faced through the network of garden paths.

The hen was in among the green peas, resting comfortably in a crater of warm earth she had dug, but still on the alert for whatever might come. Sure enough, something came: a stone.

The hen got up, sang out raucously, jumped up onto the wall, turned about to face Françoise, and shook her dust-grayed feathers; then, settling down comfortably, her eyes half shut, her tail-feathers jauntily uplifted, she stood her ground in bravado. By now, however, Françoise was rounding the pease patch, whooshing with her lips and resoundingly flapping her skirt. With one hop the hen was out in the road. That should

The two very different stories by Jules Renard on the following pages will at least hint at the range of notes and tones that this willfully "small" artist was able to elicit from his flute. Both stories are from the volume entitled La Lanterne sourde *(1893), published three years after his fine "novel"* L'Écornifleur, *and, like it, notable for a mixture of dryness, sharpness, purity, acidity, acridity, and tight-mouthed lyricism. A man of undistinguished intellect, Renard was a stubborn and fanatically scrupulous literary artisan who examined the small, the common, the commonplace with such an intensity of poetic exactitude as sometimes to endow it with the imaginative force of the big. The big—whether the Big Idea, the Big Word, or the Grand Style—he distrusted profoundly; and he would have no truck with it.*

have been the end of it. The road was chicken territory, and
nothing they might do there should make any difference to
Françoise. But the hired girl opened the garden gate and stood
there whirling and snapping her dishcloth. She was carried away
by indignation, perhaps also by the pleasure of the chase. The
hen grasped her danger and proceeded struttingly to travel the
length of the house, then turned into the large courtyard, where,
whenever she had the time, she paused to take a peck at some
herb or plant. For a moment it seemed to her that the game was
up. She had imprudently strayed into an angle of the wall near
the barn, and already Françoise, with skirt spread wide, was
blocking her escape. Terrified, she lifted herself from the ground
with one violent flap of her wings, found herself perched on a
round of the ladder which rose to the hayloft, and, her spread
wings serving to balance her, went on up it in little sharp hops,
unhurriedly, rung by rung—and disappeared. Françoise climbed
after her; at the door to the hayloft she paused.

It was full of shadow: the hay was stowed there in matted
courses like stacked pancakes. A small gust of heady, fuddling
fragrances caressed the girl's sweaty face.

"Well, I'll go in for a second," she said. "Anyway, there may
be eggs, since the hens seem to come in here."

The hay, jammed up against the rafters and crowding against
them with all its weight, tumbled down toward Françoise's feet

*Born to a family of peasant origins and brought up in the
Nivernais region of central France, Renard went to Paris as a
young man, settled down early to a quiet marriage and an active literary career, and thereafter lived a life that was almost
devoid of such external events as go to make up a biography.
The internal events of that life, equally lacking in the grandiose,
are recorded in a pungent Journal. The spareness and meager-
ness of his person, suggesting some thrifty peasant fined down,
corresponded pretty much, like his slightly reptilian eyes and
his taciturnity, to the general character of his work, in which
the principle of economy was carried to a point just short of
mutism. He belonged to no school, group, or tendency, though
he overlapped several, nor did he found any of his own; but his
writings have exerted on recent French literature a powerful*

in irregular ramps and stairs. The hen had settled on the heights, in a nest that might have been made especially for her. Anyone who wanted to reach her would have to brave dangers, tumble into pits, take risky jumps, and generally go to all sorts of trouble. The hen didn't worry in the least as she watched the hired girl's attempts to storm her position—watched her feel out the layers of hay with the tip of her shoe, pull back from suspected chasms, waver, prudently halt, ponder, and then recommence the assault.

"You wait, you wait . . ." said Françoise. "I'm going to teach you, I am."

What was she going to teach her?

Her foot struck something solid, the handle of a pitchfork that was buried to the teeth in the hay.

Françoise fell down on her back; her arms beat the air.

She felt all her anger dissolve like a piece of maple candy, and under the serious eye of the hen she burst into a long fit of laughter.

It was soft as a featherbed, softer. The hay tickled her with all its little prickles, playing with her, nestling all about her and watching for a chance to surprise an ear lobe. She rolled over from one cheek to the other, feeling as if she were holding a pincushion in either hand; and when she stirred her soft calves, her stocking were filled with knitting-needles. She closed her

fascination; and young Jean-Paul Sartre, intent on literature of another kind, regarded him as an author whom it was essential to demolish.

If a place had to be found for Renard in a historical catalogue, it would be with the long line of French artists who have believed that a glass of water is a likelier poetic subject than the sea—a view that has something to be said for it, and for which the arts in France (the poems of La Fontaine, for example, or the paintings of Chardin) offer some striking justifications.

OTHER WORKS: *Stories and sketches:* Coquecigrües (*1893*), Histoires naturelles (*1896*), Nos Frères farouches (*1908*), Les Cloportes (*1919*). *Novel:* Poil de Carotte (*1894*). *Plays:* Le Plaisir de rompre (*1898*), Le Pain de ménage (*1899*). *Miscellany:* L'Oeil clair (*1913*).

eyes, opened them again, observed the hen still sitting there
grave and absorbed, and cried again, her voice strangled with
laughter: "Hen! Hen! Oh, you hussy!"

Now she was lying in a perfect shower of hay. A cascade of
dry grasses was pouring down from the rafters. Billows broke
over her arms and her face as if the hayloft had suddenly been
changed into a sort of tumultuous pond. Only now and then,
through rifts, did she glimpse the motionless hen. The hay
surges kept on coming in regular rhythm. Abruptly, Françoise's
laughter was cut short.

Mme Lérin's son was kneeling close to her.

"Oh, it's you, Monsieur Émile, it was you!"

She was amazed to find him there, practically on top of her,
she not having suspected a thing; he seemed to have risen from
the hay or dropped from the tiles by magic. He was smiling in
an embarrassed way and chewing on a straw. Now, with the
pitchfork, he began again to cover her, as with a blanket of
hay—her breast, her legs, all her body.

"It was the hen," said Françoise. "I fell, Monsieur Émile, but
now I'll get up again."

She tried to, and failed.

"Oh, Lordy, I'll never be able to get up, now!"

She began again to laugh helplessly, her arms held out.

"No, I can see I'll just have to stay here forever!"

M. Émile tossed his pitchfork high up on the hay slopes and
took Françoise by both hands. They were plump and moist. He
stiffened, leaning backward with legs braced, and raised her
up. But then things misfired; he had to let go, and Françoise
fell back.

"Try again!" she said.

M. Émile seized her hands once more. Painstakingly he spread
her fingers apart in order to lock his own between them; then
he tried to take her by the wrists, but that was too slippery; at
last he returned, by way of the palms, to the fingers.

"One, two: are you ready?"

He was ready; he clasped her, enfolded her, kissed her hotly,
and held her against him, hard: all this very quickly and without a word.

From the high corner into which M. Émile had thrown it,
the pitchfork plunged down, its three sharp prongs foremost,

and stung him. He could not hold back a cry of pain, and, with a backhand toss, he returned the fork higher yet.

It came remorselessly back down again: but slyly now, with prongs outthrust, in dulcet slips and glides—and arrived without a sound, unexpected, surprising.

This time it was Françoise who cried out, violated in all her flesh.

M. Émile thrust the fork away with such vigor that it sank its three prongs deep into the hay and, standing upright, was still, like some surly beast subdued.

The hen in her nest remained loftily indifferent, wholly engrossed in her own business.

Roundabout them the infinite labors of the hayloft went on and on. The spiny universe of straw and hay rustled faintly like a sleetfall. From tiles and laths and beams the stubborn spiders hung their fragile mazes. Several of these were coalesced into a single delicate tent, without rip or wrinkle. Other isolated webs resembled remnants of a wallpaper peeled off by the dampness in some uninhabited room. A solitary spider was gliding along a thread, suspicious, oblique in his traveling. A swallow entered rocketing, swept up web and spider together, and left, all in one swoop.

Suddenly the hen, aghast, pecked several times at the void and, heavily unfolding her wings, passed cackling over the two intertwined bodies to fall fluttering into the middle of the courtyard.

One of her distracted feathers, carried along in her wake, whirled indolently, was caught by invisible fingers of wind, and, so enlivened, rose up and faded away, vanishing like a bird, a living thing.

Françoise raised her head. Mme Lérin was calling. "Françoise, Françoise, where are you?"

"Coming! Coming!" But in her grogginess she did not stir, and was going to remain just where she was, until M. Émile, with great presence of mind, clambered up to the hen's nest, thrust his hand into it, took out the egg, and offered it to Françoise.

She went quickly down the ladder.

"Now what on earth have you been doing," said Mme Lérin, "to get yourself all covered with hay?"

"It's full of eggs up there," said Françoise. "I even broke one. Look, here's the other."

It seemed to her that Mme Lérin was looking at her hard, and in a funny way.

"It must show," she thought.

But Mme Lérin, weighing the egg in her hand and trying it against the sunlight, said to her in a natural tone of voice: "You must be careful, Françoise. Eggs are rare this year, much rarer than last."

Never have they been so rare.

PART TWO: THE BUCKET

During the night there is a scream out in the garden; and about five o'clock in the morning, feeling bolder now because of the sunlight, I jump out of bed to have a look around. My father and mother are still sleeping; so is our maid Françoise, who has been getting pretty lazy lately.

I try to remember what the cries were like, or the wails, more exactly; but I'm not at all like those gifted people who can hear a tune once and hold on to it. The sounds my memory keeps are faded, vague, lighter than hollow eggs.

I slowly cross the garden, looking for footprints.

The paths are too dry. A great many white threads are stretched across them. One path, though, has less than the others, and these few seem to have been rigged up in a hurry at the last minute.

I walk down this path, questioning myself about what all these threads are good for.

Do the spiders secrete them to use as laundry lines?

Spider laundry!

My imagination is in good form today, and leads me to anticipate important discoveries.

First, I note that a pear tree has got several of its branches broken.

Did some animal do it?

But a goat doesn't scream, it bleats.

Furthermore, it would have stripped the branches.

A thief, then?

I know how many pears there were: twenty-eight. Not one is missing. They are shining with dew. They would be pleasant to kiss, like cheeks. In two or three weeks they will be ripe enough to gather.

I pick up some twigs from down among the strawberry plants. Whoever broke these off did not do so idly or absently. They have been chewed on as if to ease some pain, a violent toothache for instance. Myself, I would eat leaves!

From the number of chewed-up twigs I conclude that the person in question was suffering considerably, and that this person remained for some time near the pear tree.

A little farther on *she* leaned against another tree, a tall apple tree whose small gray apples satisfy my most violent summer appetites.

I say *she* because the bark has plucked out, between two of its scales, a long, blond, woman's hair. I would feel better if it were black or auburn hair, and I begin to sense now that there is unpleasantness ahead.

Beyond the apple tree the prints of feet become visible. The steps become gradually heavier. The foot remains a long time pressing into the gravel, making a sharp impression; then it is laboriously removed. The prints are closer together now, almost touching.

I come to the end of the path. It loses itself in a thick clump of hazel trees beneath which, for my siestas, I have arranged some faggots in the shape of an armchair. "Armchair" is by no means too luxurious a word; no seat has ever given me more pleasure, and nowhere could I hope to find a more comfortable refuge from the heat.

That's where the thing must have happened.

The faggots are tossed around like bedclothes after a restless night. Mosses, sorrels, and pinks have been torn up by the handful, and the earth, scarred with heel-marks and damp here and there, has not yet drunk up all the spilled blood. Squatting down, I examine the ground closely, minutely; mechanically I straighten the trampled grass-blades and efface the stains; with the flat of my hand I stroke and smooth the ground.

It's no use trying not to understand; I have understood for a long time.

Now wave after wave of the truth breaks over me. With intense concentration I review the series of clues I have just observed, reading their meaning now at sight; I reconstruct the scene, and bring to mind the month, the day, when Françoise, tapping me on the shoulder, hastily said to me: "I've gotten caught, you know."

Never did she dare to use the familiar *tu* with me. She was not one of those peasant girls who grow conceited over any intimacy with a bourgeois.

I reassemble the armchair and then, having gone a little distance away, I come back again, pretending to be some casual stroller who suspects nothing and is passing this hazel grove quite by chance; and I persuade myself that the scene wears its everyday, natural aspect. Then, too, some cats could have had a squabble there or a stray dog have taken a roll.

I glance at the gradually rising sun, and I shift my shadow aside so that the telltale wet patches may be exposed to the heat and this whole slimy mess be quickly scorched away. To tell the honest truth, I don't feel easy in my mind at all.

Afterward, when the painful struggle was over (they say that it's a very nasty business), what had she done?

I've got to keep on understanding things, whether I want to or not.

I'm so lucid that it scares me. All I have to do is to follow this path; it's as plain as a dotted line on a map. I rake it smooth behind me as I go; and here I am at the well. My legs wish to retreat, but I deal severely with their craven cowardice, while at the same time a painful light is breaking in my mind.

Françoise didn't just throw the baby in. She put it in the tin bucket and lowered away gently, because of the squeaking pulley—gently and maternally. Then she lost her head. She hadn't the stomach to pull the bucket up again. It's hanging down there, at the bottom. To my confused eyes the chain seems still to be shivering; it's completely unreeled, and all the links have gone through the pulley except the last one, which is bigger than the rest.

I take hold of it and pull. The nearer it comes to the well-rim, the heavier it is. I pull without looking, fearful that I may be hauling up . . .

For two cents I'd let go altogether.

Nothing!

Of course: the bucket tipped over when it hit the water, the

way buckets always do, and the baby is far, far away. I make
the chain fast, and then something makes me lean down over
the well-edge. For an instant my head feels packed in ice.

A piece of cement breaks off, plummets down through echoing strata of darkness, fills the well with dull, overlapping
sounds. I keep my ear cocked for a long time.

I straighten up again, my forehead refreshingly chilled. A
comforting thought strikes me: "Françoise has committed murder; she won't talk."

She has been very decent. The rest is up to me. First I want
her to make a good recovery, and I shall ask my mother to let
her have a week, two weeks, of rest. Mother never refuses me
anything. She will hire a cleaning-woman until Françoise is
feeling better. Even if it should be necessary to confess things,
I suspect that mother will be no more troublesome than any
discreet accomplice.

By golly, I'm in luck; the thing could very easily have turned
out badly. But let's not start that again, old man! Forget it.

Feeling every minute more tranquil and innocent, I look behind and before me. The path is neat and in order; my soul
likewise. Of course, there are one or two bad moments ahead of
me: for example, unless I can find some excuse, I'll have to
drink our well-water at the table without betraying any disgust.
Also, there is the question of how I'm to behave in the presence
of Françoise, at our first meeting—our confrontation.

Will she lower her eyes?

It is seven o'clock. My mother and father are waking up, and
Françoise, lying there exhausted, is choosing what words to say
so that she won't have to get out of bed. I won't forget in a
hurry the two hours of successive emotions which I've just gone
through; and now I could do with a breath of fresh air; I need
to relax.

Usually, when the sun is like this, the fish run close to the
surface, leaping with open jaws upon the flies; and they are just
as eager for artificial bait. A man might have very good luck
this morning. I know a corner near the raspberry bushes where
the thatch, with all its little gutters, keeps the ground in just
that state of cool dampness which little yellow worms adore.

I take a pickax, raise it high with stiff arms, bring it down,

and with the first blow I disinter—I *deliver*—a limp little
bundle, a red muddy rag you wouldn't touch with a pair of
tongs, the slimy envelope of my castoff delight, looking like
nothing so much as a greasy, crumpled picnic paper. . . .

Translated by Richard Wilbur

THE SPOILED CAKE

by Jules Renard

Mme Bornet tore open the telegram along the dotted line and read:

"CANNOT COME TONIGHT. INDISPOSED. REGARDS. LAFOY."

"How revolting!" she said. *"Indisposed!* I ask you, what kind of an excuse is that? After all my preparations."

"Such things only happen to us," said M. Bornet.

Mme Bornet reflected. "Now that I think of it, there is a solution. The Nolots are coming tomorrow. The cake will still be fresh. We can give it to them."

But next day, just as she was lighting the candles, she received a second telegram:

"IMPOSSIBLE FOR THIS EVENING. APOLOGIES. NOLOT."

"It's a conspiracy," said M. Bornet.

Livid and well-nigh prostrate, Mme Bornet could not bring herself to accept the relentlessness of fate. She opened her mouth wide to let the bitter words escape: "At nine o'clock they notify us. What ill-breeding!"

"Better late than never," said M. Bornet. "Anyway, you'd better calm down, old thing, or you'll curdle."

"Oh, you can laugh. It's a fine thing. This time the cake is really a total loss."

"We'll have it for lunch tomorrow."

"If you think I buy cakes just for us to eat! . . ."

"No, of course not. But there's nothing else to do. We may as well resign ourselves."

"Very well," said Mme Bornet, "we'll throw our money out the window."

Vexed in her role of housewife, she spent a bad night, tossing and turning, while her husband slept very well, dreaming perhaps of vanilla frosting.

"He's looking forward to that cake," she thought.

As agreed, the maid, not without due precaution, brought in the cake at lunch. M. and Mme Bornet contemplated it. It had caved in, the cream had turned yellow and was seeping out through the crevices, slowly submerging the eclairs. What had once resembled a fortified castle now recalled no known construction, at least not among those which are still standing. M. Bornet kept these observations to himself, and Mme Bornet began to cut the cake. Preoccupied with turning out equal portions, she said to her husband:

"You're making eyes at the bigger one. Pig!"

Her knife vanished beneath the flood of collapsing cream and scratched the plate, setting their teeth on edge. But she couldn't manage to establish limits, to trace dry pathways; the portions persisted in merging. Exasperated, she took the plate, spilled half the cake into her husband's dish, and said: "Here. Stuff yourself."

M. Bornet took a soup-spoonful, blowing upon it, for the cream had a very cold look. Then he thrust it into his mouth. But his tongue had its reservations and his lips refused to smack. He made a wry face, then grinned. "I think it's a little sour," he said.

"That's a good one," said madame. "Aren't we picky and choosy? My word, I don't know how to please you any more. God in heaven, what did I do to deserve this?"

"You try it," said M. Bornet simply.

"There's no need for me to try it. I am sure in advance that it isn't the least bit sour."

"Try it anyway. Just take one spoonful, just one."

"Two if you like," said Mme Bornet.

True to her word, she gulped them down in quick succession and said: "See! There's nothing the matter with this cake. Oh, maybe it's a tiny bit ripe. . . ."

But she took no more. She was on the point of tears when M. Bornet had an idea.

"Listen! You haven't given the concierge anything for a long time, and I've noticed that since New Year's Day his attentions have been falling off. Why not sacrifice ourselves? Let's give him the cake. We have a whole lifetime ahead of us to eat cake in."

"Well, at least put your share back," said Mme Bornet.

They sent for the concierge. After the usual compliments M. Bornet held out the plate and said: "We should like to make you a present of this."

"You are too kind," said the concierge. "But won't you miss it?"

"No, no," said M. Bornet. "I've got it up to here." He pressed his Adam's apple and stuck out his tongue.

"Take it," said Mme Bornet. "Don't give it a thought. It's yours."

The concierge eyed the cake, sniffing ever so slightly, hesitated, then suddenly asked: "Has your cake got eggs in it?"

"Of course!" said M. Bornet. "You can't make a good cake without eggs."

"Then I'm very sorry. I don't like eggs."

"What are you telling him, my dear?" said Mme Bornet. "There's one egg yolk at the very most, just enough to bind the dough."

"Oh, madame, it makes me sick to my stomach just to hear a hen cluck."

"I assure you," said monsieur, "that the cake is exquisite. It will be a treat for you."

By way of proof, he dipped the tip of his finger into the cake and sucked it bravely.

"Maybe," said the concierge. "I wouldn't know. Anyway, I don't want it. I'd throw up. I beg your pardon and thank you just the same."

"But for your wife?"

"My wife is like me. She doesn't like eggs. She can't keep them down either. In a way, that's what brought us together."

"You could give it to your charming babies?"

"My kids? Oh, madame, the big one has trouble with his teeth, they've been falling out all over the place. Sweets are no good for him. And the little one, poor little fellow, isn't much of an eater yet."

"That's enough," said Mme Bornet coldly. "Let him be. We won't force you. We haven't the right. So sorry, my good man."

"Yes, it's quite enough," said M. Bornet in the tone he might have taken to repulse a beggar.

It was too humiliating. The concierge saw that they were displeased. Taken with scruples of delicacy, he did not wish to leave them with this unpleasant impression. "Monsieur," he said politely. "You are a scholar, you wouldn't happen to have a book with letters written in it, printed, you know, to wish somebody a happy name day, somebody called Honorine for instance? Now there's something that would give me pleasure and come in very handy. I'd bring it back."

They didn't so much as reply. Abashed, he retreated backward, feeling sure that he had offended them, and resolved to make up for his conduct by favors in his own province.

"Idiot!" said M. Bornet. "Why, those people are starving. Recently I saw their baby sucking a lettuce leaf."

"It was pride," said Mme Bornet. "You could see he was dying to take it."

She couldn't get over it. Her feverish fingers beat like little drumsticks on her temples. Elbows on table, monsieur studied one of his coat sleeves. No, really, it was too hard to find a taker for this cake. Pretty soon they would wash their hands of the whole thing."

"How stupid we are!" madame said at length, and sharply pressed the electric bell.

The maid appeared.

"Louise," said Mme Bornet crisply, "eat this. You will save your cheese for tomorrow."

Louise carried away the cake.

"She is certainly getting her fill of dessert. I can see her gobbling it up."

"It all depends," said monsieur, "I wouldn't be too sure. She's not the bumpkin she was, you know. Paris is making its mark. She's been wearing glass diamonds in her ears."

"I know. Ever since mistaken generosity made us take her to the circus, she's been juggling with the dishes. But she's not that refined. She's not going to be finicky when it's a question of her stomach."

"Eh, I've got my suspicions. She may bolt it down and she may not touch it."

"That is something I would like to see."

They waited; then, for one reason or another, Mme Bornet slipped quietly into the kitchen. She returned grinding her teeth with rage.

"Guess where our cake is now?"

M. Bornet reared up in his chair, swaying like a giant question mark.

"Guess. I'll give you a hundred guesses."

"Oh! I'm beginning to see red."

"In the garbage pail."

"That's too much!"

"Sacrifice yourself for strumpets like that. Lift them out of the gutter. There's your reward: 'Madame, I didn't come here to eat your rotten cakes!' But I call God to witness that she paid for her insolence."

Disdaining human speech, Mme Bornet held up the five fingers of her right hand and three fingers of her left hand.

"Eight days' notice," he muttered. "I should think so!" And his jowls grew leaden.

Face to face, they stirred one another to vengeance. She, holding up her eight fingers as though transfixed, felt the glow of her red ears, her inflamed forehead, her feverish cheeks, while his countenance grew blacker and blacker, like a window in the shadow of a slowly lowered awning.

Translated by Ralph Manheim

CRATES

by Marcel Schwob (1867–1905)

He was born at Thebes, became a disciple of Diogenes, and also met Alexander. His father, Ascondas, was rich and left him two hundred talents. One day, while watching a performance of a tragedy by Euripides, he felt a sudden inspiration at the sight of Telephos, King of Mysia, dressed in beggar's rags and holding a basket in his hand. He rose to his feet and announced in a loud voice that he would hand over his inheritance of two hundred talents to anyone who wanted it, and that henceforth he would be content to be dressed like Telephos. The people of Thebes laughed at him and assembled outside his house; yet he laughed harder than they did. He threw his money and his furniture to them out of the windows, took a cloak of sackcloth and a beggar's pouch, and departed.

When he got to Athens, he wandered about the streets or rested with his back against a wall, sitting among turds. He practiced all that Diogenes preached. He thought Diogenes's tub superfluous. In Crates's opinion, man was neither a snail nor a

---

"Literature," in the term's more as in its less disreputable meanings, saturated Marcel Schwob's sense of the world as it had saturated Emma Bovary's. The fact that it was "good" literature—Baudelaire, Poe, Whitman, Twain, Shakespeare, Villon, Dostoevsky (all of whom left their mark); the fact that his imaginative and "sentimental" devotion to it was ballasted by linguistic and scholarly accomplishments of a fairly impressive kind; the fact that he brought to it a cosmopolitan, French-Jewish family tradition many centuries old of erudition, cultivation, intellectual and moral ardor;—all these made the danger only the more great. Whatever he touched turned under his hands to Literature; a sort of Midas curse was on him; and the exquisitely worked gold of this Midas was not always solid.

Just because it was not solid, his best pages—those in which

hermit crab. He dwelled naked in filth and picked up crusts of bread, rotten olives, and the bones of dried fish to fill his pouch. He used to say that this pouch of his was a spacious and opulent city where neither parasites nor prostitutes were to be found, and which produced enough thyme, garlic, figs, and bread for its king. And so Crates carried his country about with him on his back and lived on it.

He did not concern himself with public affairs, not even to jest about them, and he did not make a show of insulting kings. He did not approve of the behavior of Diogenes, who, having called out one day: "Men, draw near!" had taken his stick and belabored those who came, saying: "I called for men, not turds." Crates was indulgent toward mankind. Nothing worried him. He was quite used to sores. He deeply regretted that his body was not supple enough to allow him to lick them as dogs do. He also deplored the necessity of eating solid food and of drinking water. He thought that man should be self-sufficient, with no need of external aid. For his own part, he did not fetch water to wash himself. When he was so dirty as to be uncomfortable, he merely rubbed his body against a wall, having noticed that asses behave in this way. He rarely spoke about the gods and did not trouble his head about them; it was of no consequence to him whether they existed or not, for he knew quite well that they could do him no harm. Moreover, he com-

---

he brought off a total transformation of learned fact into tenuous fiction—have the charm of perfect fairy tales: fairy tales, however, in which the "adventures" (as this lover of Jules Verne and Stevenson called them) are those of the mind (or imagination, if one prefers) dealing with human experience and coming to special terms with it. They have, as a result, in addition to their charm, a singular poetic gravity; and, like those dreams in which everything suddenly if falsely becomes clear, they preserve, long after one has recognized their frailness, a power to enchant, even to haunt, which refuses to be reasoned down.

The two stories that follow are from Schwob's Vies imaginaires (1896), a collection of such "adventures" attributed to actual persons of whom more orthodox biographies can sometimes be found on library shelves. They were among Schwob's

plained that they had deliberately made man unhappy by lifting
his gaze toward the sky and so depriving him of a faculty common to most animals who walk on all fours. Since the gods
have decided that man must eat to live, said Crates, they ought
to have made him look downward at the ground where roots
grow; man cannot feed on air or stars.

Life did not treat him generously. The bitter dust of Attica
made him rheumy-eyed. Some unknown skin-disease covered
him with ulcers. He scratched himself with his uncut nails and
remarked that by so doing he achieved a twofold benefit, as
he trimmed them at the same time as he eased his irritation.
His long hair became like thick felt which he arranged on his
head to protect himself from the rain and the sun.

When Alexander came to see him, Crates proffered no interesting remarks, but looked at the King without making any
distinction between him and the rest of the crowd. Crates had
no opinions about important people. They meant no more to
him than did the gods. Only mankind interested him, and the
art of living with the utmost simplicity. Diogenes's upbraidings,
as well as his claims as a reformer, made Crates laugh. He
considered himself far above such vulgar preoccupations. Mod-
ifying the maxim inscribed above the entrance of the temple
at Delphi, he would say: "Live thyself." The idea that any
knowledge at all might exist seemed to him absurd. His only

*last works: he had behind him, at the age of twenty-nine, a
literary career that had begun almost with his birth (in Nantes,
where his father edited a liberal journal). Trilingual at the age
of three, an almost monstrously precocious adolescent, a young
man of feverish, self-destructive brilliance, a mature writer
whose character and gifts captivated friends as different as Paul
Valéry, Colette, and Jules Renard, Schwob died young, in Paris,
after some ten years of painful invalidism against which scholarship and travel were his chief opiates.*

OTHER WORKS: *Stories:* Cœur double (*1891*), Le Roi au
masque d'or (*1892*), La Lampe de Psyche (*1902*). *Essays:*
Spicilège (*1896*). *Unclassifiable:* Le Livre de Monelle (*1894*).
Historical reconstruction: La Croisade des enfants (*1896*).
Scholarship: Étude sur l'argot français (*1889*). *Translations:*
Catullus, Hamlet, Macbeth, *Defoe's* Moll Flanders.

study was the relation between his body and its necessities, and he strove to reduce them as far as possible. Diogenes would bite like a dog, but Crates lived like one.

He had a disciple whose name was Metrocles. He was a rich young man from Maronea. His sister, Hipparchia, a beautiful, highborn young woman, fell in love with Crates. It is an established fact that she loved him and went to live with him. Such a thing seems impossible, but it is true. Nothing discouraged her, neither the dirtiness of the cynic, nor his complete poverty, nor the horror of his public life. He warned her that he lived like a dog in the streets and that he looked for bones in heaps of refuse. He also warned her that there would be nothing secret about their life together, and that when he felt like it, he would copulate with her in public as dogs do. Hipparchia was prepared for all this. Her parents tried to restrain her; she threatened to kill herself, and they took pity on her. And so she left the town of Maronea, naked, with her hair hanging loose and a piece of sackcloth as her only covering, and she lived with Crates and dressed like him. It is said that she had a child by him, called Pasicles; but this is not certain.

It appears that Hipparchia was kind to the poor, and compassionate. She would stroke the ailing with her hands; displaying no sign of disgust, she would lick the bloody wounds of the suffering, being convinced that she and they were as ewe lamb to ewe lamb or dog to dog. When the weather was cold, Crates and Hipparchia slept with poor people, holding them close to give them a share of the warmth of their bodies. They extended to the poor the silent help that animals give to one another. They had no favorites among the people who came to them. Anyone was welcome as a human being.

That is all the information that has come down to us about Crates's wife; we know neither when she died nor how. Her brother, Metrocles, admired Crates and copied him. But Metrocles was not at peace. His health was disturbed by continual flatulence, over which he had no control. He lost heart and decided to die. Crates, hearing of his unhappiness, resolved to console him. He ate a chœnix of lupin seeds and went to see Metrocles. He asked him if it was the shame of his infirmity which had brought him to such a pass. Metrocles confessed that he could no longer bear so distressing an affliction. There-

upon Crates, full of lupin seeds, broke wind in front of his
disciple and assured him that nature subjects all men to the
same misfortunes. He then reproached him with having felt
ashamed for other people and invited him to follow his example.
Crates then broke wind again, took Metrocles by the hand, and
led him away.

They remained together for a long time in the streets of
Athens, doubtless with Hipparchia. They spoke very little to
each other and were ashamed of nothing. Although they rummaged in the same heaps of refuse as the dogs, the dogs seemed
to respect them. It might have been thought that, under stress of
hunger, men and dogs would snap at each other. But Crates's
biographers relate no such incident. We know that he lived to
be an old man, and that toward the end he remained always
lying in the same place, under the sloping roof of a warehouse
in the Piræus where the seamen stacked their bales on landing.
He would no longer wander about to find bones to gnaw; he
even refused to stretch out his hand; at last, one day, they
found him withered away with hunger.

Translated by J. G. Weightman

PAOLO UCCELLO

by Marcel Schwob

His real name was Paolo di Dono; but the Florentines called
him Paolo Uccello, or Paul the Bird Man, on account of the
many drawings and paintings of birds and beasts which filled
his house; for he was too poor to keep any animals or to pro-
cure specimens of those with which he was not acquainted. It
is even said that when he painted a fresco representing the four
elements, at Padua, he used a chameleon to symbolize air and,
never having seen one, pictured it as a potbellied camel with a
gaping mouth. (Whereas, as Vasari explains, the chameleon is
like a little wizened lizard, and the camel is a big, gawky animal.) For Uccello did not care about the reality of things, but
about their multiplicity and the infinite number of their lines;
consequently, he painted blue fields and red cities, and horse-
men in black armor on ebony horses with flaming mouths, and
lances pointing like rays of light to all the quarters of the
heavens. And he was in the habit of drawing *mazocchi*—that is,
circles of wood covered with cloth, which are placed on the
head in such a way that the folds of the cloth, when thrown
back, completely surround the face. Uccello painted square
ones, pointed ones, others with facets or built up into pyramids
or cones according to all the vistas of perspective, and so discovered a whole world of relationships in the folds of the
mazocchio. And Donatello, the sculptor, used to say to him:
"Ah, Paolo, thou leavest the substance for the shadow."
But the Bird Man continued his patient work; he assembled
circles, he divided angles, he examined every creature from
every point of view, and he would ask his friend, the mathema-
tician Giovanni Manetti, to tell him the answers to the problems
of Euclid; then he would shut himself up and cover his parch-
ments and his wood with points and curves. With the help of
Filippo Brunelleschi, he applied himself constantly to the study
of architecture; but with no intention of building. He confined
himself to noting how the lines ran from the foundations to the

cornices, and the way the straight lines met at their points of intersection, and the way the arches turned about their keystones, and the foreshortening of ceiling beams, fanlike, as they seemed to come together at the ends of long rooms. He also drew, in addition to human gestures, all the beasts and their movements, in order to reduce them to simple lines.

Then, like the alchemist poring over his mixtures of metals and agents and watching for their fusion into gold in his furnace, Uccello poured all these forms into the crucible of form. He united them, combined them, and melted them down, in order to transmute them into that simple form on which all others depend. That is why Paolo Uccello lived like an alchemist, shut up in his little house. He believed that he could blend all lines into a single, ideal form. He wished to grasp the created Universe as it was reflected in the eye of God, who sees all shapes springing from one complex center. Around him lived Ghiberti, Della Robbia, Brunelleschi, and Donatello, all of them proud and masters of their art and contemptuous of poor Uccello and his mania for perspective, deploring his spider-filled, poverty-stricken house; but Uccello was prouder still. With every new combination of lines, he hoped to discover the method of creation. His aim was not to imitate, but to achieve the power of giving masterly development to everything, and his strange series of folded headgear was to him more revealing than the great Donatello's magnificent marble figures.

Thus did the Bird Man live, his pensive head wrapped in his hood; and he heeded neither his food nor his drink, but was completely like a hermit. And so, one day, in a meadow near a ring of old stones half buried in the grass, he saw a young girl with a garland bound about her head, laughing. She was wearing a long, pale dress, caught up at the hips with a pale ribbon, and her movements were as supple as the grasses she was bending. Her name was Selvaggia, and she smiled at Uccello. He noted the curve of her smile. And when she looked at him, he saw all the little lines of her eyelashes and the circles of her pupils and the curves of her eyelids and the subtle interweaving of her hair, and he imagined the garland about her brow in innumerable other positions. But Selvaggia knew nothing of all this, because she was only thirteen years old. She took Uccello by the hand and loved him. She was the daughter of a Florentine dyer, and her mother was dead. Another woman had come into the house and had beaten Selvaggia. Uccello took Selvaggia home with him.

All day long Selvaggia sat crouching in front of the wall on which Uccello drew his universal forms. She never understood why he preferred looking at lines, straight and curved, rather than at the tender face upturned toward him. At night, when Brunelleschi and Manetti came to study with Uccello, she would fall asleep after midnight below the nexus of intersecting lines, in the circle of shadow which lay wide beneath the lamp. In the morning she awoke before Uccello, delighted to find herself surrounded by painted birds and colored animals. Uccello drew her lips and her eyes, her hair and her hands, and recorded all the attitudes of her body; but he did not, like other painters when they loved a woman, make a portrait of her. For the Bird Man did not know the joy of limiting himself to the individual; he could not rest in one particular place; he wished to soar above all places. And the forms of Selvaggia's attitudes were cast into the crucible of form, with all the movements of animals, and the lines of plants, stones, and rays of light, and the undulation of terrestrial vapors and waves of the sea. And, forgetting Selvaggia, Uccello seemed to be forever poring over the crucible of form.

However, there was nothing to eat in Uccello's house. Selvaggia did not dare tell Donatello or the others. She held her peace and died. Uccello drew the stiffening of her body, and the linking of her thin little hands, and the line of her poor, closed eyes. He did not know that she had died, just as he had never known that she was alive. He only added these new forms to all the others he had collected.

The Bird Man grew old, and no one could understand his pictures any longer. They appeared to be nothing but a chaos of curves. Neither earth nor plants nor animals nor men were recognizable in them any more. For many years he had been busy on his supreme work, which he kept hidden from everyone. It was to embody the results of all his researches. The subject—Doubting Thomas feeling Christ's wound—symbolized these researches. Uccello completed his picture at the age of eighty. He sent for Donatello and uncovered it reverently before him. And Donatello cried: "Ah, Paolo, cover up thy picture again." The Bird Man questioned the great sculptor, but could not get him to say more. And so Uccello knew that he had accomplished the miracle. But Donatello had seen nothing save a confused mass of lines.

And a few years later Paolo Uccello was found lying dead from exhaustion on his pallet. His face was a rapture of wrinkles. His eyes were fixed on mystery revealed. In his sternly clasped hand was a small round piece of parchment covered with interlocked lines, beginning at the center and leading to the circumference and then returning from the circumference to the center.

Translated by J. G. Weightman

THESEUS

by André Gide (1869–1951)

I wanted to tell the story of my life as a lesson for my son
Hippolytus; but he is no more, and I am telling it all the same.
For his sake I should not have dared to include, as I shall now
do, certain passages of love; he was extraordinarily prudish,
and in his company I never dared to speak of my attachments.
Besides, these only mattered to me during the first part of my
life; but at least they taught me to know myself, as did also the
various monsters whom I subdued. For "the first thing is to
know exactly who one is," I used to say to Hippolytus; "later
comes the time to assess and adopt one's inheritance. Whether
you wish it or not, you are, as I was myself, a king's son. Nothing to be done about it; it's a fact; it pins you down." But
Hippolytus never took much notice; even less than I had taken
at his age; and like myself at that time, he got on very nicely
without it. Oh, early years, all innocently passed! Oh, careless

---

*"All Monsieur Gide does," a hotel-keeper is said to have
lamented when someone asked where M. Gide could be found,
"is go in and out." A more recent anecdote has the Catholic
writer François Mauriac, who supposed that the question of
where M. Gide could be found had been settled by his death,
receiving after the funeral a cablegram:*
    "HELL DOES NOT EXIST. GIDE."
*Elusiveness, raised to the dignity of a severe private discipline
and a subversive public show, was perhaps his chief contribu-
tion to modern intellectual life. Not to be where it would be a
comfort to oneself and others to find oneself snugly installed
became for him at an early age a first principle: one of the few
lifelong constants in a career given over—with the puritanical
strictness and fervor that sometimes characterizes French Prot-
estantism—to inconstancy. But to be inconstant on Gide's terms
is of course not quite the same thing as to be capricious or a
male coquette; though he did not mind seeming to be both*

growth of body and mind! I was wind; I was wave. I grew with the plant; I flew with the bird. My self knew no boundaries; every contact with an outer world did not so much teach me my own limits as awaken within me some new power of enjoyment. Fruit I caressed, and the bark of young trees, and smooth stones on the shore, and the coats of horses and dogs, before ever my hands were laid on a woman. Toward all the charming things that Pan, Zeus, or Thetis could offer, I rose.

One day my father said to me that things couldn't go on as they were. "Why not?" Because, good heavens, I was his son and must show myself worthy of the throne to which I should succeed. . . . Just when I was feeling so happy, sprawled naked among cool grasses or on some scorching beach. Still, I can't say that he was wrong. Certainly he was right in teaching me to rebel against myself. To this I owe all that I have achieved since that day; no longer to live at random—agreeable as such license might have been. He taught me that nothing great, nothing of value, and nothing that will last can be got without effort.

My first effort was made at his invitation. It was to overturn boulders in the hope of finding the weapons which Poseidon (so he told me) had hidden beneath one of them. He laughed to see how quickly my strength grew through this training.

---

when it would serve his purposes, just as he did not mind being mistaken for a discoverer of deep and final truths.

In Theseus, *a work of his old age (1946) which might be read as a partial symbolic autobiography, the acts of eluding, of leaving behind, of passing beyond, are represented—with Gide's customary ironic detachment from matters that are to him of the most intimate concern—as having something like the paradoxical senses that they had for him: the sense of naked and direct confrontations with the oddly human monsters that society keeps hidden in its labyrinths; the sense of cunning and arduous disciplines by which the spirit affirms (or, rather, invents, and even trickily fabricates) its "gloire"; the sense, more paradoxical still, of acts of creation. "Behind me," says Theseus grown old, "I leave the city of Athens. It has been dearer to me even than my wife and son. My city stands. . . . I have lived."*

Gide's own "city" of the imagination, like the dangerous one

With the toughening of my body there came also a toughening of the will. After I had dislodged the heaviest rocks of the neighborhood and was about to continue my unfruitful search by attacking the flagstones of the palace gateway, my father stopped me. "Weapons," said he, "count for less than the arm that wields them, and the arm in its turn for less than the thinking will that directs it. Here are the weapons. Before giving them to you, I was waiting to see you deserve them. I can sense in you now the ambition to use them, and that longing for fame which will allow you to take up arms only in defense of noble causes and for the weal of all mankind. Your childhood is over. Be a man. Show your fellow men what one of their kind can be and what he means to become. There are great things to be done. Claim yourself."

II

Ægeus, my father, was an excellent person; all that could be wished. In point of fact, I suspect that I was his son only in name. That's what I've been told, and that great Poseidon begat me. In which case it's from this god that I inherit my inconstancy of temper. Where women are concerned, I have never known how to settle down. Ægeus sometimes stood rather in

---

described here by the fabulous artificer Dœdalus, is full of secret passages and staircases (not to mention trapdoors) to which no abridged Baedeker can do a semblance of justice. The following fragmentary list of his works may suggest several ways in.

Personal writings: Journal, 1889–1949, Si le grain ne meurt . . . (*1926*), Et nunc manet in te (*1952*). *Lyrical meditation:* Les Nourritures terrestres (*1897*). Soties, *or narratives of an ironic and "preposterous" nature:* Paludes (*1895*), Le Prométhée mal enchaîné (*1899*), Les Caves du Vatican (*1914*). Récits, *or straightforward, sometimes tragic narratives with ironic overtones:* L'Immoraliste (*1902*), La Porte étroite (*1909*), La Symphonie pastorale (*1919*). *Novel:* Les Faux-Monnayeurs (*1926*). *Social and political "reporting":* Voyage au Congo (*1927*), Retour de l'U.R.S.S. (*1936*). *Drama:* Le Roi Candaule (*1901*), Saül (*1903*). *Criticism:* Prétextes (*1903*). Nouveaux Prétextes (*1911*), Dostoïevsky (*1923*).

my way; but I am grateful to him for his guardianship, and
for having restored the cult of Aphrodite to honor in Attica.
I am sorry for the fateful slip by which I brought about his
death—when I forgot, I mean, to run up white sails in place of
black on the ship that carried me home from Crete. It had been
agreed that I should do this if I were to return in triumph from
my rash venture. One can't think of everything. But to tell the
truth, and if I cross-question myself (a thing I never much care
to do), I can't swear that it was really forgetfulness. Ægeus
was in my way, as I told you, and particularly when, through
the potions of the witch Medea, who found him (as, indeed, he
found himself) a rather elderly bedfellow, he formed the ex-
asperating idea that a second meridian of enjoyment was his for
the asking—thus blocking my career, whereas, after all, it's
every man in his turn. Anyway, when he saw those black sails
. . . I learned, on returning to Athens, that he had thrown
himself into the sea.

No one can deny it. I think I have performed some notable
services; I've purged the earth once and for all of a host of
tyrants, bandits, and monsters; I've cleaned up certain dangerous byroads on which even the bravest could not venture without a shiver; and I've cleared up the skies in such a way
that man, his head less bowed, may be less fearful of their
surprises.

One must own that in those days the look of the country was
hardly reassuring. Between the scattered townships there were
huge stretches of uncultivated waste, crossed only by unreliable
tracks. There were the dense forests, the mountainous ravines.
At the most dangerous points robber gangs had taken up their
positions; these pillaged, killed, or at best held for ransom the
traveler, and there were no police to stop them. These incidents
combined with the purposeful ferocity of wild beasts and the
evil power of the deceitful elements until one could hardly tell,
when some foolhardy person came to grief, whether the malig-
nity of the gods had struck him down or merely that of his fellow men. Nor, in the case of such monsters as the Sphinx or the
Gorgon who fell to Œdipus or to Bellerophon, could one be
sure whether the human strain or the divine was preponderant.
Whatever was inexplicable was put on to the gods. Terror and
religion were so nearly one that heroism often seemed an im-

piety. The first and principal victories that man had to win were over the gods.

In a fight, whether with man or with god, it is only by seizing one's adversary's own weapon and turning it against him (as I did with the club of Periphetes, the dark giant of Epidaurus) that one can be sure of final victory.

And as for the thunderbolts of Zeus, I can tell you that the day will come when man will possess himself of them, as Prometheus possessed himself of fire. Yes, those are decisive victories. But with women, at once my strength and my weakness, I was always having to begin again. I escaped from one, only to fall into the lap of some other; nor did I ever conquer a woman who had not first conquered me. Pirithoüs was right when he told me (ah, how well we used to get on!) that the important thing was never to be unmanned by a woman, as was Hercules in the arms of Omphale. And since I have never been able or wished to live without women, he would say to me, as I darted off on each amorous chase: "Go ahead, but don't get stuck." There was one woman who, ostensibly to safeguard my life, would have bound me to herself by a cord—a thin one, it is true, but a fixed rein none the less. This same woman—but of that, more in due time.

Of them all, Antiope came nearest to catching me. She was queen of the Amazons, and like all her subjects had only one breast; but this in no way impaired her beauty. An accomplished runner and wrestler, she had muscles as firm and sturdy as those of our athletes. I took her on in single combat. In my arms she struggled like a leopard. Disarmed, she brought her teeth and nails into play; enraged by my laughter (for I, too, had no weapons) and because she could not stop herself from loving me. I have never possessed anyone more virginal. And little did it matter to me that later she could only suckle my Hippolytus, her son, with one breast. It was this chaste and savage being whom I wished to make my heir. I shall speak, during the course of my story, of what has been the greatest grief of my life. For it is not enough to exist, and then to have existed: one must make one's legacy and act in such a way that one is not extinguished with oneself, so my grandfather had often told me. Pittheus and Ægeus were much more intelligent than I; so is Pirithoüs. But people give me credit for good sense; the rest is added with the determination to do well that has never left me. Mine, too, is the kind of courage that incites me to desperate enterprises. On top of all this I was ambitious. The great deeds of my cousin Hercules, which they used to report to me, exasperated my young blood, and when it was time to leave Troezen, where I had lived till then, and rejoin my so-called father in Athens, I refused altogether to accept the advice, sound though it was, to go by sea because that route was the safer. Well I knew it; but it was the very hazards of the overland route, with its immense detour, that tempted me; a chance to prove my worth. Thieves of every sort were beginning once again to infest the country, and did so with impunity now that Hercules was squandering his manhood at the feet of Omphale. I was sixteen. All the cards were in my hand. My turn had come. In great leaps my heart was bounding toward the extremity of my happiness. "What have I to do with safety," I cried, "and a route that's set in order!" I despised comfort and idleness and unlaureled ease. So it was on the road to Athens by way of the isthmus of the Peloponnesus that I first put myself to the test, and my heart and my arm together taught me their full strength, when I cut down some well-known and well-hated robbers: Sinis, Periphetes, Procrustes, Geryon (no, that was Hercules; I meant to say Cercyon). By the way, I made a slight mistake at that time, where Sciron was concerned, for he turned out afterwards to have been a very worthy man, good-natured and most helpful to passing travelers. But as I had just done away with him, it was soon agreed that he had been a rascal.

Also on the road to Athens, in a thicket of asparagus, there smiled upon me the first of my conquests in love. Perigone was tall and supple. I had just killed her father, and by way of amends I got her a very handsome son: Menalippes. I have lost track of both of them—breaking free, as usual, and anxious never to lose any time. I have never allowed the past to involve or detain me; rather have I been drawn forward by what was still to be achieved; and the most important things seemed to me always to lie ahead.

So much so that I won't waste more time with these preliminary trifles, which, after all, meant only too little to me.

Here I was on the threshold of an admirable adventure. Hercules himself never had one like it. I must tell it at length.

III

It's very complicated, this story. I must say first that the island of Crete was a power in those days. Minos reigned there. He held Attica responsible for the death of his son Androgeus; and by way of reprisal he had exacted from us an annual tribute: seven young men and seven young girls had to be handed over to satisfy, it was said, the appetites of the Minotaur, the monstrous child that Pasiphaë, the wife of Minos, had brought forth after intercourse with a bull. These victims were chosen by lot.

But in the year in question, I had just returned to Greece. Though the lot would normally have spared me (princes readily escape these things), I insisted that I should figure in the list, notwithstanding the opposition of the king, my father. I care nothing for privilege, and claim that merit alone distinguishes me from the herd. My plan was, in point of fact, to vanquish the Minotaur and thus at a blow to free Greece from this abominable exaction. Also I was most anxious to visit Crete, whence beautiful, costly, and unusual objects were constantly arriving in Attica. Therefore I set sail for the island; among my thirteen companions was my friend Pirithoüs.

We landed, one morning in March, at Amnisos, a little township that served as harbor to its neighbor Knossos, the capital of the island, where Minos resided and had had his palace built. We should have arrived the previous evening, but a violent storm had delayed us. As we stepped ashore we were surrounded by armed guards, who took away my sword and that of Pirithoüs. When they had searched us for other weapons, they led us off to appear before the king, who had come from Knossos, with his court, to meet us. A large crowd of the common people pressed round to have a look at us. All the men were naked to the waist except Minos, who, seated beneath a dais, wore a long robe made from a single piece of dark-red cloth; this fell in majestic folds from his shoulders to his ankles. His chest, broad as that of Zeus himself, bore three tiers of necklaces. Many Cretans wear these, but of a trumpery sort. Minos had necklaces of rare stones, and plaques of wrought gold in the shape of fleurs-de-lis. The double-headed ax hung above his throne, and with his right hand he stretched before him a golden scepter, as tall as himself. In the other hand was a three-leaved flower, like those on his necklaces, and also in gold, but larger. Above his golden crown was a gigantic panache, in which were mingled the feathers of peacock, ostrich, and halcyon. He looked us over for some time and then bade us welcome to the island, with a smile that may well have been ironical, since we had come there, after all, under sentence of death. By his side were standing the queen and the two princesses, her daughters. I saw at once that the elder daughter had taken a fancy to me. As our guards were making ready to take us away, I saw her lean toward her father and say to him in Greek (she whispered, but my ears are sharp) : "Not that one, I beg you," and she pointed toward me with her finger. Minos smiled once again and gave orders that I should not be taken away with my companions. I was no sooner alone before him than he began to question me.

Although I had promised myself to act with all possible prudence and to let slip no hint either of my noble birth or of my audacious project, it suddenly occurred to me that it would be better to put my cards on the table, now that I had attracted the attention of the princess. Nothing would be more likely to heighten her feeling for me, or to win me the favor of the king, than to hear me say frankly that I was the grandson of Pittheus. I even hinted that the current rumor in Attica was that the great Poseidon had begot me. To this Minos replied gravely that he would presently clear up that point by submitting me to trial by water. In return I replied complacently that I had no doubt I should survive triumphantly any test that he cared to impose. The ladies of the court, if not Minos himself, were favorably affected by my self-confidence.

"And now," said Minos, "you must go and have something to eat. Your companions are already at table and will be waiting for you. After such a disturbed night you must be quite peckish, as they say here. Have a good rest. I shall expect you to be present toward the end of the day at the ceremonial games in honor of your visit. Then, Prince Theseus, we shall take you with us to Knossos. You will sleep at the palace, and tomorrow

evening you will dine with us—a simple family meal, where
you will feel quite at home, and these ladies will be delighted
to hear you tell of your first exploits. And now they are going
to prepare themselves for the festivities. We shall meet again
at the games, where you will sit, with your companions, immediately beneath the royal box. This courtesy we owe to your
princely rank; and as I do not wish to distinguish you openly
from your companions they shall, by contagion, rank with
you."

The games were held in a vast semicircular arena, opening on
the sea. Huge crowds, both of men and of women, had come to
see them, from Knossos, from Lyttos, and even from Gortyna (a
matter of two hundred stadia distant, I was told), from other
towns and their neighboring villages, and from the thickly pop-
ulated open country. All my senses were taken by surprise, and
I cannot describe how foreign the Cretans appeared to me to
be. As there was not room for them all on the tiers of the
amphitheater, they pushed and jostled their way up the staircases and along the aisles. The women, no less numerous than
the men, were for the most part naked to the waist. A very few
wore a light bodice, but even this was generously cut away, in a
fashion that I could not help thinking rather immodest, and
exposed both breasts to the air. Men and women alike were
tightly, even absurdly laced around the hips with belts and
corselets, which gave to each the figure of an hourglass. The
men were nearly all brown-skinned, and at their fingers, wrists,
and throats wore almost as many rings, bracelets, and necklaces
as the women, who, for their part, were perfectly white. All the
men were clean-shaven, except for the king, Rhadamanthus, his
brother, and his friend Dædalus. The ladies of the court sat on
a platform just above our own, which dominated the arena
from a considerable height. They had indulged a prodigious extravagance of dress and ornament. Each wore a flounced skirt;
billowing out oddly below the hips, this fell in embroidered fur-
belows to their feet, which were shod in little boots of white
leather. The sumptuousness of the queen, who sat in the center
of the dais, made her most conspicuous of all. Her arms and the
front of her person were bare. Upon her magnificent breasts,
pearls, emeralds, and precious stones were embanked. Long
black curls fell on either side of her face, and smaller ringlets

streaked her forehead. She had the lips of a glutton, an upturned nose, and huge empty eyes, whose expression one might
have called bovine. A sort of golden diadem served her as a
crown. It sat, not directly on her hair, but on a ridiculous hat of
some dark material, which came up through the diadem and
tapered into a sharp point, like a horn, which jutted far out in
front of her forehead. Her corsage uncovered her to the waist in
front, but rose high at the back and ended in an enormous cut-
away collar. Her skirt was spread wide around her, and one
could admire, upon their creamy ground, three rows of embroidery, one above the other—purple irises at the top, saffrons
in the center, and below them violets with their leaves. As I was
sitting immediately below, I had only to turn round to have all
this, as one might say, under my very nose. I marveled as much
at the sense of color and the beauty of the design as at the delicate perfection of the work.

Ariadne, the elder daughter, sat at her mother's right hand
and presided over the corrida. She was less sumptuously
dressed than the queen, and she wore different colors. Her skirt,
like that of her sister, had only two circles of embroidery: on
the upper one, dogs and hinds; on the lower, dogs and par-
tridges. Phædra, perceptibly a much younger girl, sat on Pasiphaë's left. Her dress had a frieze of children running after
hoops, and another of younger children squatting on their behinds and playing marbles. She took a childish pleasure in the
spectacle. As for me, I could hardly follow what was going on,
it was all so disconcertingly new; but I could not help being
amazed by the suppleness, speed, and agility of the acrobats
who took their chance in the arena after the singers, the danc-
ers, and then the wrestlers had had their turn. Myself about to
encounter the Minotaur, I learned a good deal from watching
the feints and passes that might help me to baffle and tire the
bull.

IV

After Ariadne had rewarded the last champion with the last
prize, Minos declared the games closed. Escorted by his courtiers, he bade me come to him separately.

"I am going to take you now, Prince Theseus," he said to me,
"to a place by the sea where I shall put you to the test, and

we shall see if you are the true son of the god Poseidon, as you claimed to be just now."

He took me to a small promontory with waves beating at its foot. "I shall now," said the king, "throw my crown into the sea, as a mark of my confidence that you will be able to retrieve it from the bottom."

The queen and the two princesses were there to see what would come of the test; and so, emboldened by their presence, I protested:

"Am I a dog, to fetch and carry for my master, even if it be a crown? Let me dive in without bait and I shall bring back to you something or other that will attest and prove my case."

In my audacity I went still farther. A stiff breeze had sprung up, and it happened that a long scarf was dislodged from Ariadne's shoulders. A gust blew it toward me. I caught it with a smile, as if the princess or one of the gods had offered it to me. Then, stripping off my close-fitted corselet, I wrapped the scarf round my loins in its place, twisted it up between my thighs, and made it fast. It looked as if I did this from modesty, lest I should expose my manhood before these ladies; but in fact it allowed me to hide the leather belt that I was still wearing, to which was attached a small purse. In this I had, not metal coins, but some valuable stones that I had brought with me from Greece, knowing that they would keep their full value, no matter where I went.

Then I took a deep breath and dived.

A practiced swimmer, I dived deep, and did not come up to the surface until I had removed from my purse an onyx and two chrysoprases. Once back on dry land I offered, with my most chivalrous bow, the onyx to the queen and a chrysoprase to each of her daughters. I pretended to have gathered them on the bottom, or rather (since it was hardly plausible that the stones, so rare upon dry land, should have lain promiscuously at the bottom of the sea, or that I should have had time to pick them out) that Poseidon himself had handed them to me, in order that I could offer them to the ladies. Here was proof, better than any test, of my divine origin and my good standing with the god.

After this, Minos gave me back my sword.

Soon afterwards chariots bore us off on the road to Knossos.

V

I was so overwhelmed by fatigue that I could hardly feel due astonishment at the great courtyard of the palace, or at a monumental balustraded staircase and the winding corridors through which attentive servants, torch in hand, guided me to the second floor, where a room had been set apart for me. All but one of its many lamps were snuffed out after I arrived. The bed was scented and soft; when they left me, I fell at once into a heavy sleep, which lasted until the evening of the following day, although I had already slept during our long journey; for only at dawn, after traveling all night, had we arrived at Knossos.

I am by no means a cosmopolitan. At the court of Minos I realized for the first time that I was Greek, and I felt very far from home. All unfamiliar things took me by surprise—dress, customs, ways of behaving, furniture (in my father's house we were short of furniture), household objects, and the manner of their use. Among so much that was exquisite, I felt like a savage, and my awkwardness was redoubled when people began smiling at my conduct. I had been used to biting my way through my food, lifting it to my mouth in my fingers, and these delicate forks of metal or wrought gold, these knives they used for cutting meat, gave me more trouble than the heaviest weapons of war. People couldn't take their eyes off me; and when I had to talk, I appeared a still greater oaf. God! How out of place I felt! Only on my own have I ever been good for anything; now for the first time I was in society. It was no longer a question of fighting, or carrying a thing through by main force, but rather of giving pleasure; and of this I had strangely little experience.

I sat, at table, between the two princesses. A simple family meal, without formality, I was told. And in fact, apart from Minos and the queen, Rhadamanthus, the king's brother, the two princesses, and their young brother Glaucus, there was nobody except the tutor to the young prince, a Greek from Corinth, who was not even presented to me.

They asked me to describe in my own tongue (which everybody at the court understood very well and spoke fluently, though with a slight accent) what they were pleased to call my exploits. I was delighted to see that the young Phædra and

Glaucus were seized with uncontrollable laughter at the story of
the treatment that Procrustes imposed upon passers-by, which I
made him endure in his turn—chopping off all those parts of
him which exceeded his statutory measure. But they tactfully
avoided any allusion to the cause of my visit to Crete, and
affected to see me as merely a traveler.

Throughout the meal Ariadne pressed her knee against mine
under the table; but it was the warmth of the young Phædra
that really stirred me. Meanwhile, Pasiphaë, the queen, who
sat opposite me, was fairly eating me with her enormous eyes,
and Minos, by her side, wore an unvarying smile. Only Rhadamanthus, with his long, fair beard, seemed rather out of humor.
Both he and the king left the room after the fourth course—"to
sit on their thrones," they said. Only later did I realize what
this meant.

I still felt some traces of my seasickness. I ate a great deal,
and drank still more. I was so liberally plied with wines and
liqueurs of every sort that before long I didn't know where I
was. I was used to drinking only water or diluted wine. With
everything reeling before me, but still just able to stand, I
begged permission to leave the room. The queen at once led me
into a small closet that adjoined her private apartments. After
I had been thoroughly sick, I rejoined her on a sofa in her
room, and it was then that she began to tackle me.

"My young friend—if I may call you so," she began, "we
must make the most of these few moments alone together. I am
not what you suppose, and have no designs upon your person,
attractive as that may be." And, protesting the while that she
was addressing herself only to my spirit, or to some undefined
but interior zone of my being, she continually stroked my forehead; later she slipped her hands under my leather jerkin and
fondled my pectorals, as if to convince herself that I was really
there.

"I know what brings you here, and I want to warn you of a
mistake. Your intentions are murderous. You are here to fight
my son. I don't know what you may have heard about him, and
I don't want to know. Ah, listen to the pleas of my heart! He
whom they call the Minotaur may or may not be the monster of
whom you have no doubt heard, but he is my son."

At this point I thought it only decent to interject that I had nothing against monsters in themselves; but she went on without listening.

"Please try to understand me. By temperament I am a mystic. Heavenly things alone excite my love. The difficulty, you see, is that one never can tell exactly where the god begins and where he ends. I have seen a good deal of my cousin Leda. For her the god hid himself in the guise of a swan. Now, Minos always knew that I wanted to give him a Dioscuros for his heir. But how can one distinguish the animal residue that may remain even in the seed of the gods? If I have since then deplored my mistake—and I realize that to talk of it in this way robs the affair of all grandeur—yet I assure you, Theseus, that it was a celestial moment. For you must understand that my bull was no ordinary beast. Poseidon had sent him. He should have been offered to him as a sacrifice, but he was so beautiful that Minos could not bring himself to do it. That is how I have been able ever since to pass off my desires as an instrument of the god's revenge. And you no doubt know that my mother-in-law, Europa, was carried off by a bull. Zeus was hiding inside him. Minos himself was the fruit of their union. That is why bulls have always been held in great honor in his family. And, if ever, after the birth of the Minotaur, I noticed the king knitting his brows, I had only to say: 'What about your mother?' He could only admit that it was a natural mistake. He is very wise. He believes that Zeus has nominated him judge, along with Rhadamanthus, his brother. He takes the view that one must have understood before one can pass judgment, and he thinks that he will not be a good judge until he has experienced everything, either in his own person or through his family. This is a great encouragement for us all. His children, and I myself, in our several ways, are working, by our individual errors of conduct, for the advancement of his career. The Minotaur too, though he doesn't know it. That is why I am begging you here and now, Theseus, not to try to do him any sort of injury, but rather to become intimate with him, and so to end a misunderstanding that has made Crete the enemy of Greece and done great harm to our two countries."

So saying, she became even more attentive, and a point was reached at which I was seriously incommoded, while the exhalations of wine heightened and mingled with the pungent odor which, in company with her breasts, was escaping from her corsage.

"Let us return to celestial things," she went on, "as return we always must. You yourself, Theseus—surely you must feel that you are inhabited by one of the gods?"

What put the final touch to my embarrassment was that Ariadne, the elder daughter (and an exceptional beauty, though less attractive to me personally than Phædra), had made it quite plain to me, before I began to feel so sick—had made it quite plain, as I say, as much by signs as by a whisper, that as soon as I felt better I was to join her on the terrace.

VI

What a terrace! And what a palace! Trance-like under the moon, the gardens seemed to be suspended in readiness for one knew not what. It was the month of March, but I could sense already the delicious half-warmth of spring. Once in the open air, I began to feel quite well. Never an indoor man, I need to fill my lungs with fresh air. Ariadne came running toward me, and without a word clamped her warm lips to mine—so violently that we were both sent staggering.

"Follow me," she said. "Not that I mind if anyone sees us; but we can talk more freely under the terebinths." She led me down a few steps toward a more leafy part of the gardens, where huge trees obscured the moon, though not its reflection upon the sea. She had changed her clothes, and now wore, in place of her hooped skirt and tight surcoat, a sort of loose dress, beneath which she was palpably naked.

"I can guess what my mother's been telling you," she began. "She's mad, raving mad, and you can disregard everything she says. First of all, I must tell this: you are in great danger here. You came here, as I well know, to fight my half-brother, the Minotaur. I'm telling you all this for your own good, so listen carefully. You will win—I'm sure of it. To see you is to banish doubt. (Don't you think that's rather a good line of poetry? But perhaps you have no ear.) But nobody to this day has ever managed to get out of the maze in which the monster lives; and you won't succeed either unless your sweetheart (that I am, or shall presently be) comes to your rescue. You can't begin to conceive how complicated it is, that maze. Tomorrow I shall introduce you to Dædalus, who will tell you about it. It was he who built it; but even he has already forgotten how to get out of it. You'll hear from him how his son Icarus, who once ventured inside, could only get out on wings, through the upper air. That I don't dare recommend to you; it's too risky. You'd better get it into your head at once that your only hope is to stick close to me. We shall be together, you and I—we *must* be together, from now on, in life and in death. Only thanks to me, by me, and in me will you be able to recapture yourself. You must take it or leave it. If you leave me, so much the worse for you. So begin by taking me." Whereupon she abandoned all restraint, gave herself freely to my embrace, and kept me in her arms till morning.

The hours passed slowly for me, I must admit. I have never been good at staying in one place, be it even in the very bosom of delight. I always aim to break free as soon as the novelty has worn off. Afterward Ariadne used to say: "You promised." I never gave a promise of any kind. Liberty above all things! My duty is to myself.

Although my powers of observation were still to some extent clouded by drink, Ariadne appeared to me to yield her last reserves with such readiness that I could hardly suppose myself to have done the work of a pioneer. This disposed of any scruples that I might later have had about leaving her. Besides, her sentimentality soon became unendurable. Unendurable her protestations of eternal devotion, and the tender diminutives with which she ornamented me. I was alternately her only treasure, her canary, her puppy, her tercelet, her guinea fowl. I loathe pet names. And then she had read too much. "Little heart," she would say, "the irises will wither fast and die." (In point of fact, they'd hardly begun to flower.) I know quite well that nothing lasts forever; but the present is all that matters to me. And then she would say: "I couldn't exist without you." This made me think all the time of how to get rid of her.

"What will the king, your father, say to that?" I had asked her. And her reply: "Minos, sweet chuck, puts up with everything. He thinks it's wisest to allow what cannot be prevented. He didn't complain of my mother's adventure with the bull, but according to my mother, after she had given him her explanation, he simply remarked: 'Here I have some difficulty in following you.' 'What's done is done, and nothing can undo it,' he added. When it comes to us, he'll do the same. At the most, he'll banish you from the court—and a lot of difference that'll make! Wherever you go, I shall follow."

That remains to be seen, I thought.

After we had taken a light breakfast, I asked her to be kind enough to lead me to Dædalus, and added that I wished to speak to him privately and alone. She agreed to this only after I had sworn by Poseidon that immediately our talk was over, I would rejoin her at the palace.

VII

Dædalus rose to welcome me. I had found him in a dim-lit room, bending over the tablets and working drawings that were spread before him, and surrounded by a great many peculiar instruments. He was very tall, and perfectly erect in spite of his great age. His beard was silvery in color, and even longer than that of Minos, which was still quite black, or the fairer one of Rhadamanthus. His vast forehead was marked by deep wrinkles across the whole of its width. When he looked downward, his eyes were half hidden by his bushy eyebrows. He spoke slowly, and in a deep voice. His silences had the quality of thought.

He began by congratulating me on my prowess. The echo of this, he said, had penetrated even to him, who lived in retirement, remote from the tumult of the world. He added that I looked to him to be something of a booby; that he took little account of feats of arms, and did not consider that physical strength was the godhead of man.

"At one time I saw quite a lot of your predecessor Hercules. He was a stupid man, and I could never get anything out of him except heroics. But what I did appreciate in him, and what I appreciate in you, is a sort of absorption in the task in hand, an unrecoiling audacity, a temerity even, which thrusts you forward and destroys your opponent, after first having destroyed the coward whom each of us carries within himself. Hercules took greater pains than you do; was more anxious, also, to do well; rather melancholy, especially when he had just completed an adventure. But what I like in you is your enjoyment; that is where you differ from Hercules. I shall commend you for never letting your mind interfere. You can leave that to others who are not men of action, but are clever at inventing sound and good motives for those who are.

"Do you realize that we are cousins? I too (but don't repeat this to Minos, who knows nothing about it)—I too am Greek. I was forced regretfully to leave Attica after certain differences had arisen between myself and my nephew Talos, a sculptor like myself, and my rival. He became a popular favorite, and claimed to uphold the dignity of the gods by representing them with their lower limbs set fast in a hieratic posture, and thus incapable of movement; whereas I was for setting free their limbs and bringing the gods nearer to ourselves. Olympus, thanks to me, became once again a neighbor of the earth. By way of complement, I aspired, with the aid of science, to mold mankind in the likeness of the gods.

"At your age I longed above all to acquire knowledge. I soon decided that man's personal strength can effect little or nothing without instruments, and that the old saying 'Better a good tool than a strong forearm' was true. Assuredly you could never have subdued the bandits of Attica and the Peloponnese without the weapons your father had given you. So I thought I could not employ myself more usefully than by bringing these auxiliaries nearer to perfection, and that I could not do this without first mastering mathematics, mechanics, and geometry to the degree, at any rate, in which they were known in Egypt, where such things are put to great use; also that I must then pass from theory to practice by learning all that was known about the properties and qualities of every kind of material, even of those for which no immediate use was apparent, for in these (as happens also in the human sphere) one sometimes discovers extraordinary qualities one had never expected to find. And so I widened and entrenched my knowledge.

"To familiarize myself with other trades, other crafts and skills, other climates, and other living things, I set myself to visit distant countries, put myself to school with eminent foreigners, and remained with them until they had nothing more to teach me. But no matter where I went or how long I stayed, I remained a Greek. And it is because I know and feel that you are a son of Greece that I am interested in you, my cousin.

"Once back in Crete, I told Minos all about my studies and my travels, and went on to tell him of a project I had cherished.

This was to build and equip, not far from his palace (if he approved the plan and would provide the means to carry it out), a labyrinth like the one which I had admired in Egypt, on the shore of Lake Moeris; but mine would be different in plan. At the very moment Minos was in an awkward position. His queen had whelped a monster; not knowing how best to look after it, but judging it prudent to isolate it and keep it well away from the public gaze, he asked me to devise a building and a set of communicating gardens which, without precisely imprisoning the monster, would at least contain him and make it impossible for him to get loose. I lavished all my scholarship, all my best thoughts, on the task.

"But, believing that no prison can withstand a really obstinate intention to escape, and that there is no barrier, no ditch, that daring and resolution will not overcome, I thought that the best way of containing a prisoner in the labyrinth was to make it of such a kind, not that he couldn't get out (try to grasp my meaning here), but that he wouldn't want to get out. I therefore assembled in this one place the means to satisfy every kind of appetite. The Minotaur's tastes were neither many nor various; but we had to plan for everybody, whomsoever it might be, who would enter the labyrinth. Another and indeed the prime necessity was to fine down the visitor's will-power to the point of extinction. To this end I made up some electuaries and had them mixed with the wines that were served. But that was not enough; I found a better way. I had noticed that certain plants, when thrown into the fire, gave off, as they burned, semi-narcotic vapors. These seemed admirably suited to my purpose, and indeed they played exactly the part for which I needed them. Accordingly I had them fed to the stoves, which are kept alight night and day. The heavy gases thus distributed not only act upon the will and put it to sleep; they induce a delicious intoxication, rich in flattering delusions, and provoke the mind, filled as this is with voluptuous mirages, to a certain pointless activity; 'pointless,' I say, because it has merely an imaginary outcome, in visions and speculations without order, logic, or substance. The effect of these gases is not the same for all of those who breathe them; each is led on by the complexities implicit in his own mind to lose himself, if I may so put it, in a labyrinth of his own devising. For my son Icarus, the complexities were metaphysical.

For me, they take the form of enormous edifices, palatial buildings heaped upon one another with an elaboration of corridors
and staircases in which (as with my son's speculations) everything leads to a blank wall, a mysterious KEEP OUT. But the
most surprising thing about these perfumes is that when one has
inhaled them for a certain time, they are already indispensable;
body and mind have formed a taste for this malicious insobri-
ety; outside of it reality seems charmless and one no longer has
any wish to return to it. And that—that above all—is what
keeps one inside the labyrinth. Knowing that you want to enter
it in order to fight the Minotaur, I give you fair warning; and
if I have told you at length of this danger, it was to put you on
your guard. You will never bring it off alone; Ariadne must go
with you. But she must remain on the threshold and not so
much as sniff the vapors. It is important that she should keep a
clear head while you are being overcome by drunkenness. But
even when drunk, you must keep control of yourself: everything
depends on that. Your will alone may not suffice (for, as I told
you, these emanations will weaken it), and so I have thought of
this plan: to link you and Ariadne by a thread, the tangible
symbol of duty. This thread will allow, indeed will compel you
to rejoin her after you have been some time away. Be always
determined not to break it, no matter what may be the charms
of the labyrinth, the seduction of the unknown, or the headlong
urging of your own courage. Go back to her, or all the rest, and
the best with it, will be lost. This thread will be your link with
the past. Go back to it. Go back to yourself. For nothing can begin from nothing, and it is from your past, and from what you
are at this moment, that what you are going to be must spring.

"I should have spoken more briefly if I had not been so interested in you. But before you go out to meet your destiny, I
want you to hear my son. You will realize more vividly, while
listening to him, what danger you will presently run. Although
he was able, thanks to me, to escape the witchcraft of the maze,
his mind is still most pitiably a slave to its maleficence."

He walked over to a small door, lifted the arras that covered
it, and said very loudly:

"Icarus, my dear son, come and tell us of your distress. Or,
rather, go on thinking aloud, as if you were alone. Pay no attention to me or to my guest. Behave as if neither of us were here."

VIII

I saw coming in a young man of about my own age who seemed in the half-light to be of great beauty. His fair hair was worn very long and fell in ringlets to his shoulders. He stared fixedly, but seemed not to focus his gaze on anything in particular. Naked to the waist, he wore a tight metal belt and a loin-cloth, as it seemed to me, of leather and dark cloth; this swathed the top of his thighs, and was held in place by a curious and prominent knot. His white leather boots caught my eye, and seemed to suggest that he was making ready to go out; but his mind alone was on the move. Himself seemed not to see us. Proceeding no doubt with some unbroken chain of argument, he was saying:

"Who came first: man or woman? Can the Eternal One be female? From the womb of what great Mother have you come, all you myriad species? And by what engendering cause can that womb have been made great? Duality is inadmissible. In that case the god himself would be the son. My mind refuses to divide God. If once I allow division, strife begins. Where there are gods, there are wars. There are not gods, but a God. The kingdom of God is peace. All is absorbed, all is reconciled in the Unique Being."

He was silent for a moment and then went on:

"If man is to give a form to the gods, he must localize and reduce. God spreads where he will. The gods are divided. His extension is immense; theirs merely local."

He was silent again, before going on in a voice panting with anguish:

"But what is the reason for all this, O God who art lucidity itself? For so much trouble, so many struggles? And toward what? What is our purpose here? Why do we seek reasons for everything? Where are we to turn, if not toward God? How are we to direct our steps? Where are we to stop? When can we say: so be it; nothing more to be done? How can we reach God, after starting from man? And if I start from God, how can I reach across to myself? Yet if man is the creation of God, is not God the creation of man? It is the exact crossing-place of those roads, at the very heart of that cross, that my mind would fix itself."

As he spoke, the veins swelled on his forehead, and the sweat ran down his temples. At least, so it seemed to me, for I could not see him clearly in the half-light; but I heard him gasping, like a man putting forth an immense effort.

He was quiet for a moment, then went on:

"I don't know where God begins, and still less where He ends. I shall even express myself more exactly if I say that His beginning never ends. Ah, how sick I am of 'therefore,' and 'since,' and 'because'! Sick of inference, sick of deduction. I never learn anything from the finest of syllogisms that I haven't first put into it myself. If I put God in at the beginning, He comes out at the end. I don't find Him unless I do put Him in. I have tramped all the roads of logic. On their horizontal plane I have wandered all too often. I crawl, and I would rather take wings; to lose my shadow, to lose the filth of my body, to throw off the weight of the past! The infinite calls me! I have the sensation of being drawn upward from a great height. O mind of man, I shall climb to your topmost point. My father, with his great knowledge of mechanics, will provide me with the means to go. I shall travel alone. I'm not afraid. I can pay my way. It's my only chance to escape. O noble mind, too long entangled in the confusion of my problems, an uncharted road is waiting for you now. I cannot define what it is that summons me; but I know that my journey can have only one end: in God."

Then he backed away from us as far as the arras, which he raised and afterward let drop behind him.

"Poor dear boy," said Dædalus. "As he thought he could never escape from the labyrinth and did not understand that the labyrinth was within himself, at his request I made him a set of wings, with which he was able to fly away. He thought that he could only escape by way of the heavens, all terrestrial routes being blocked. I knew him to be of a mystical turn, so that his longing did not surprise me. A longing that has not been fulfilled, as you will have been able to judge for yourself while listening to him. In spite of my warnings, he tried to fly too high and overtaxed his strength. He fell into the sea. He is dead."

"How can that be?" I burst out. "I saw him alive only a moment ago."

"Yes," he answered, "you did see him, and he seemed to be

alive. But he is dead. At this point, Theseus, I am afraid that
your intelligence, although Greek, and as such subtle and open
to all aspects of the truth, cannot follow me; for I myself, I
must confess, was slow to grasp and concede this fact: those of
us whose souls, when weighed in the supreme scale, are not
judged of too little account, do not just live an ordinary life. In
time, as we mortals measure it, we grow up, accomplish our
destiny, and die. But there is another, truer, eternal plane on
which time does not exist; on this plane the representative gestures of our race are inscribed, each according to its particular
significance. Icarus was, before his birth, and remains after his
death, the image of man's disquiet, of the impulse to discovery,
the soaring flight of poetry—the things of which, during his
short life, he was the incarnation. He played out his hand, as he
owed it to himself to do; but he didn't end there. What happens,
in the case of a hero, is this: his mark endures. Poetry and the
arts reanimate it, and it becomes an enduring symbol. That is
how it is that Orion, the hunter, is riding still, across Elysian
fields of asphodel, in search of the prey that he has already
killed during his life; and meanwhile the night sky bears the
eternal, constellated image of him and his baldric. That is how
Tantalus' throat is parched to all eternity, and how Sisyphus
still rolls upward toward an unattainable summit the heavy and
ever rebounding weight of care that tormented him in the days
when he was king of Corinth. For you must realize that in hell
the only punishment is to begin over and over again the actions
which, in life, one failed to complete.

"In the same way, in the animal kingdom, the death of each
creature in no way impoverishes its species, for this retains its
habitual shape and behavior; there are no individuals among
the beasts. Whereas among men it is the individual alone who
counts. That is why Minos is already leading at Knossos the life
which will fit him for his career as a judge in hell. That is why
Pasiphaë and Ariadne are yielding to their destiny in such exemplary fashion. And you yourself, Theseus, may appear care-
free, and you may feel it, but you will not escape the destiny
that is shaping you, any more than did Hercules, or Jason, or
Perseus. But know this (because my eyes have learned the art of
discerning the future through the present)—there remain great
things for you to do, and in a sphere quite different from that of

your previous exploits; things beside which these exploits will seem, in the future, to have been the amusements of a child. It remains for you to found the city of Athens, and there to situate the supremacy of the human mind.

"Do not linger, therefore, in the labyrinth, or in the embrace of Ariadne, after the hideous combat from which you will emerge triumphant. Keep on the move. Regard indolence as treachery. Seek no rest until, with your destiny completed, it is time to die. It is only thus that, on the farther side of what seems to be death, you will live, forever re-created by the gratitude of mankind. Keep on the move, keep well ahead, keep on your own road, O valiant gatherer of cities.

"And now listen carefully, Theseus, and remember what I say. No doubt you will have an easy victory over the Minotaur. Taken in the right way, he is not so redoubtable as people suppose. (They used to say that he lived on carrion; but since when has a bull eaten anything but grass?) Nothing is easier than to get into the labyrinth, nothing less easy than to get out. Nobody finds his way in there without first he lose it. And for your return journey (for footsteps leave no trace in the labyrinth) you must attach yourself to Ariadne by a thread. I have prepared several reels of this, and you will take them away with you. Unwind them as you make your way inside, and when the reel is exhausted, tie the end of the thread to the beginning of the next, so as never to have a break in the chain. Then on your way back you must rewind the thread until you come to the end, which Ariadne will have in her hand. I don't know why I insist so much, when all that part is as easy as good-morning. The real difficulty is to preserve unbroken, to the last inch of the thread, the will to come back; for the perfumes will make you forgetful, as will also your natural curiosity, which will conspire to make you weaken. I have told you this already and have nothing to add. Here are the reels. Good-by."

I left Dædalus and made off to rejoin Ariadne.

IX

Those reels of thread were the occasion of the first dispute between Ariadne and myself. She wanted me to hand over to her, for safe keeping in her corsage, those same reels which Dædalus had entrusted to me, claiming that to wind and unwind such things was a woman's job (one, in fact, in which she was particularly expert) and that she wanted to spare me the bother of attending to it. But in reality she hoped in this way to remain the mistress of my fate, a thing to which I would not consent at any price. Moreover, I had another suspicion: Ariadne would be reluctant to unwind, where every turn of the reel allowed me to stray farther from herself; she might hold back the thread, or pull it toward her; in such a case I should be prevented from going in as far as I wanted. I therefore stood my ground, in the face even of that last argument of women, a flood of tears— knowing well that if one once begins to yield one's little finger, they are quick to snap up the whole arm, and the rest with it.

This thread was neither of linen nor of wool. Dædalus had made it from some unknown material, which even my sword, when I experimented with a little piece, was powerless to cut. I left the sword in Ariadne's care, being determined (after what Dædalus had said to me about the superiority that man owes wholly to his instruments, and the decisive role of these in my victories over the monsters)—being determined, as I say, to subdue the Minotaur with the strength of my bare hands. When, after all this, we arrived before the entrance to the labyrinth, a portal embellished with that double ax which one saw everywhere in Crete, I entreated Ariadne on no account to stir from the spot. She insisted that she should herself tie the end of the thread to my wrist, with a knot that she was pleased to call a lover's; she then glued her lips to my own and held them there for what seemed to me an interminable time. I was longing to get on.

My thirteen companions, both male and female, had gone on ahead, Pirithoüs among them; I found them in the first big room, already quite fuddled by the vapors. I should have mentioned that, together with the thread, Dædalus had given me a piece of rag drenched with a powerful specific against the gases, and had pressed me most particularly to employ it as a gag. (This also Ariadne had taken in hand, as we stood before the entrance to the labyrinth.) Thanks to it, and though hardly able to breathe, I was able in the midst of these intoxicating vapors to keep my head clear and my will taut. I was rather suffocated, all the same, because, as I've said before, I never feel really well when I'm not in the open air, and the artificial atmosphere of that place was oppressive to me.

Unreeling the thread, I penetrated into a second room, darker than the first; then into another, still darker; then into a fourth, where I could only grope my way. My hand, brushing along the wall, fell upon the handle of a door. I opened it, and stepped into brilliant sunshine. I was in a garden. Facing me, and stretched at length upon a flowery bed of buttercups, pansies, jonquils, tulips, and carnations, lay the Minotaur. As luck would have it, he was asleep. I ought to have hurried forward and taken advantage of this, but something held me back, arrested my arm: the monster was beautiful. As happens with centaurs also, there was in his person a harmonious blending of man and beast. On top of this, he was young, and his youthfulness gave an indefinable bloom to his good looks; and I am more vulnerable to such things than to any show of strength. When faced with them, I needed to call upon all my reserves of energy. For one never fights better than with the doubled strength of hatred; and I could not hate the Minotaur. I even stood still for some time and just looked at him. But he opened one eye. I saw then that he was completely witless, and that it was time for me to set about my task. . . .

What I did next, what happened, I cannot exactly recall. Tightly as I had been gagged, my mind had doubtless been benumbed by the gases in the first room; they affected my memory, and if in spite of this I vanquished the Minotaur, my recollection of the victory is confused, though on the whole somewhat voluptuous. That must be my last word, since I refuse to invent. I have also many dreamlike memories of the charms of that garden; it so went to my head that I thought I could never bear to leave it; and it was only reluctantly that, after settling with the Minotaur, I rewound my thread and went back to the first room, there to rejoin my companions.

They were seated at table. Before them a massive repast had been spread (how or by whom I cannot say). They were busy gormandizing, drinking heavily, making passes of love at one another, and braying like so many madmen or idiots. When I made as if to take them away, they replied that they were getting on very well and had no thought of leaving. I insisted, saying that I had come to deliver them. "Deliver us from what?" they shouted; and suddenly they all banded together and covered me with insults. I was very much distressed, because of Pirithoüs. He hardly recognized me, forswore virtue, made mock of his own good qualities, and told me roundly that not for all the glory in the world would he consent to give up his present enjoyments. All the same, I couldn't blame him for it, because I knew too well that, but for Dædalus' precautions, I should have foundered in the same way, and joined in the chorus with him and with the others. It was only by beating them up, it was only by punching them and kicking them hard on their behinds, that I got them to follow me; of course there was also the fact that they were so clogged by drink as to be incapable of resistance.

Once out of the labyrinth, how slowly and painfully they came back to their senses and reassumed their normal selves! This they did with great sadness. It appeared to them (so they told me afterward) as if they were climbing down from some high peak of happiness into a dark and narrow valley. Each rebuilt for himself the prison in which every man is his own jailor and from which he could never again escape. Pirithoüs, however, soon showed himself aghast at his momentary degradation, and he promised to redeem himself, in his own eyes and in mine, by an excess of zeal. An occasion was offered to him, not long afterward, to give me proof of his devotion.

X

I hid nothing from him; he knew my feelings for Ariadne, and their decline. I did not even hide from him that, child though she might still be, I was very much taken with Phædra. She used often at that time to play on a swing strung up between the trunks of two palm trees; and when I saw her at the top of her flight, with the wind lifting her short skirts, my heart would miss a beat. But when Ariadne appeared, I looked the other way and dissembled my feelings as best I could, for fear of arousing in her the jealousy of an elder sister. Still, thwarted desires are not healthy. But if I was to abduct her, and thus bring off the audacious project that was beginning to simmer in my heart, I should need to employ a ruse of some sort. Then it was that Pirithoüs was able to help me by devising a plan

stamped with all his fertile ingenuity. Meanwhile our stay in the
island was dragging on, though both Ariadne and myself were
obsessed with the idea of getting away. But what Ariadne didn't
know was that I was resolved not to leave without Phædra.
Pirithoüs knew it, and this is how he helped me.

He had more freedom than I—Ariadne stuck to me like a
ball-and-chain—and he passed his leisure in the study and observation of the customs of Crete. "I think," he said to me one
morning, "that I've got just what we want. You know that
Minos and Rhadamanthus, those two model legislators, have
drawn up a code of morals for the island, paying particular attention to pederasty. As you know, too, the Cretans are especially prone to this, as is evident from their culture. So much
so, in fact, that every adolescent who reaches manhood without
having been chosen by some older admirer becomes ashamed
and regards his neglect as dishonorable; for if he is good-
looking, people generally conclude that some vice of heart or
mind must be the cause. Young Glaucus, the son of Minos, who
is Phædra's absolute double, confided to me his anxiety in this
respect. His friendless state causes him much distress. I made
the vain suggestion that no doubt his princely rank has discouraged admirers; he replied that this, though possible, did not
make his position in any way less painful, and that people ought
to realize that it was also a grief to Minos; and that Minos as a
rule disregards all distinctions of rank and position. All the
same, he would certainly be flattered if an eminent prince like
yourself were to be kind enough to take an interest in his son.
It occurred to me that Ariadne, who shows herself so impor-
tunately jealous of her sister, would have no such feelings about
her brother. There is hardly a single instance of a woman taking
serious notice of the love of a man for a boy; in any case, she
would think it unbecoming to show resentment. You need have
no fear on that score."

"What!" I shouted. "Can you think that fear would ever
stop me? But though I am a Greek, I do not feel myself drawn
in any way toward people of my own sex, however young and
attractive they may be. In this I differ from Hercules, and would
gladly let him keep his Hylas. Your Glaucus may be like my
Phædra, but it is she whom I desire, not he."

"You haven't grasped what I mean," he resumed, "I'm not

suggesting you should take Glaucus in her place, but simply that you should pretend to take him, in order to deceive Ariadne and let her believe, and everybody else, that Phædra, whom you are carrying off, is Glaucus. Now listen and follow me carefully. One of the customs of the island, and one that Minos himself instituted, is that the lover assumes complete charge of the child whom he covets, and takes him to live with him, under his roof, for two months; after which period the child must announce publicly whether or not his lover has given him satisfaction and treated him properly. To take the supposed Glaucus under your roof, you must put him aboard the ship that brought us here from Greece. Once we are all assembled, with Phædra safe in our hands, we must up-anchor; Ariadne will have to be there, since she assumes that she will be going with you; then we shall put out with all speed to the open sea. The Cretans have a large fleet, but their ships are not so fast as ours, and if they give chase we can easily outdistance them. Tell Minos about this project. You may be sure that he'll smile on it, provided you let him believe that Glaucus, and not Phædra, is involved; for, as for Glaucus, he could hardly hope to secure a better master and lover than yourself. But tell me: is Phædra willing?"

"I don't know as yet. Ariadne takes good care never to leave me alone with her, so that I've had no chance to sound her. . . . But I don't doubt that she will be ready to follow me, when she realizes that I prefer her to her sister."

It was Ariadne who had to be approached first. I took her into my confidence, but deceitfully of course, and according to our agreed procedure.

"What a wonderful plan!" she cried. "And how I shall enjoy traveling with my small brother! You've no idea how charming he can be. I get on very well with him and in spite of the difference in our ages I am still his favorite playmate. Nothing could be better for broadening his mind than to visit a foreign country. At Athens he can perfect his Greek, which he already speaks passably, though with a bad accent; that will soon be put right. You will set him the best of examples, and I only hope he will grow to be like you."

I let her talk. The wretched girl could not foresee what fate was in store for her.

Glaucus had also to be warned, lest any hitch should occur.

Pirithoüs took charge of this, and told me later that the boy was at first bitterly disappointed. Only after an appeal to his better sentiments did he decide to join in the game; or rather, I should say, to drop out of it and yield up his place to his sister. Phædra had also to be informed. She might have started screaming if we had tried to abduct her by force or surprise. But Pirithoüs exploited with great skill the malicious pleasure that both children would not fail to take in gulling their elders— Glaucus his parents, and Phædra her sister.

Phædra duly rigged herself out in Glaucus' everyday clothes. The two were of exactly the same build, and when she had bound up her hair and muffled the lower part of her face, it was impossible for Ariadne not to mistake her identity.

It was certainly disagreeable for me to have to deceive Minos, who had lavished upon me every mark of his confidence, and had told me of the good influence that he expected me, as an older person, to have upon his son. And I was his guest, too. Of course I was abusing my position. But it was not, and indeed it is never, a part of my character to allow myself to be stopped by scruples. The voices of gratitude and decency were shouted down by the voice of desire. The end justifies the means. What must be must be.

Ariadne was first on board, in her anxiety to secure comfortable quarters. As soon as Phædra arrived, we could make off. Her abduction took place not at nightfall, as had at first been agreed, but after the family dinner, at which she had insisted on appearing. She pleaded that as she had formed the habit of going to her room immediately after dinner, her absence could not, she thought, be remarked before the morning of the next day. So everything went off without a hitch, and I was able to disembark with Phædra, a few days later, in Attica, having meanwhile dropped off her sister, the beautiful and tedious Ariadne, at Naxos.

I learned on arriving at our territory that when Ægeus, my father, had seen in the distance the black sails (those sails which I had omitted to change), he had hurled himself into the sea. I have already touched on this in a few words; I dislike returning to it. I shall add, however, that I had dreamed, that last night of our voyage, that I was already king of Attica. Be that as it may, or as it might have been, this was, for the whole

population and for myself, a day of rejoicing for our happy
return and my promotion to the throne, and a day of mourning
for the death of my father. I therefore gave orders that in the
rites for the day lamentations should alternate with songs of
joy; and in these songs and dances we took a prominent part—
my companions, now so implausibly restored to their homes,
and myself. Joy and desolation: it was fitting that the people
should be made to explore, at once and the same time, these
two extremes of feeling.

XI

People sometimes reproached me afterward for my conduct
toward Ariadne. They said I had behaved like a coward; that
I should not have abandoned her, or at any rate not on an island. Possibly; but I wanted to put the sea between us. She was
after me, hunting me down, marking me for the kill. When she
got wind of my ruse and detected her sister beneath her brother's clothes, she set up the devil's own noise, broke into a series
of rhythmical screams, upbraided me for my treachery; and
when, in my exasperation, I told her that I did not intend to
take her farther than the first island at which the wind, now
suddenly risen, would allow or compel us to make landfall, she
threatened me with a long poem she proposed to write on the
subject of this infamous desertion. I told her at once that she
could not do better; the poem promised to be very good, as far
as I could judge from her frenzied and lyrical tones; moreover, it would serve as a distraction, and she would undoubtedly
soon find in it the best solace for her grief. But all this only
vexed her the more. Such are women, when one tries to make
them see reason. For my part, I always allow myself to be
guided by an instinct in which, by reason of its greater simplicity, I have perfect confidence.

The island in question was Naxos. One story has it that, some
time after we had abandoned her, Dionysus went there to join
her, and indeed married her; all of which may be a way of
saying that she found consolation in drink. People say that on
their wedding day the god made her a present of a crown, the
work of Hephæstus, which now forms one of the constellations;
and that Zeus welcomed her on Olympus and made her immortal. She was even mistaken, they say, for Aphrodite. I let

people talk, and myself, in order to cut short hostile rumors, did my best to confirm her divine rank by founding a cult in her honor. I also went out of my way to be the first to dance my reverences at the temple of the new cult. May I be allowed to remark that, but for my desertion, she would have enjoyed none of these great advantages?

Certain imaginary incidents have enriched the mythology of my person: the abduction of Helen, the descent into hell with Pirithoüs, the rape of Proserpine. I took care never to deny these rumors, for they all enhanced my prestige. I even improved upon some of them, in order to confirm the people in beliefs that they are all too inclined, in Attica, to discard. Popular emancipation is a good thing; irreverence quite another.

The truth is that after my return to Athens I remained faithful to Phædra. I took both the woman and the city for my bride. I was a husband, and the son of a dead king: I was a king. My days of adventure are over, I used to repeat to myself; where I had sought to conquer, I now sought to rule.

This was not easy. Athens at that time really did not exist. In Attica a mass of petty townships disputed for predominance; whence continual brawling, besieging, and strife. The essential thing was to secure a strong central unit of government—a thing I obtained only with great difficulty. I brought both strength and cunning to the task.

Ægeus, my father, thought he could assure his own authority by perpetuating these quarrels. Considering, myself, that the well-being of the citizens is compromised by such discords, I traced the source of most of the evils to the general inequality of wealth and the desire to increase one's own fortune. Myself caring little for the acquisition of wealth, and preoccupied with the public good as much as, if not more than, with my own, I set an example of plain living. By an equal division of all properties, I abolished at one blow both the fact of supremacy and the rivalries it had provoked. This was a drastic measure, which no doubt pleased the poor (the great majority, that is to say) but antagonized the rich, whom I had thereby dispossessed. These, though few in number, were clever men. I summoned the most important among them, and said:

"Personal merit is the only thing to which I attach any importance; I recognize no other scale of values. You have made yourselves rich by ingenuity, practical knowledge, and perseverance; but also, and more often, by injustice and abuse. Your private rivalries are compromising the security of a state that I intend to be a great power, beyond the reach of your intrigues. Only thus will it be able to resist foreign invasion, and prosper. The accursed love of money that torments you does not bring you happiness, for one can truly call it insatiable. The more people have, the more they want. I shall therefore curtail your fortunes; and by force (I possess it) if you do not submit peaceably to the curtailment. For myself I shall keep only the preservation of the laws and the command of the army. I care very little for the rest. I mean to live, now that I am king, just as simply as I have lived hitherto, and in the same style as the humblest of my subjects. I shall see that the laws are respected, and that I myself am respected, if not feared. I mean to have it said among our neighbors that Attica is ruled, not by a tyrant, but by a government of the people; for each citizen of the state shall have an equal right to sit on the council, irrespective of his birth. If you do not side willingly with all this, I shall find ways, as I said, to compel you.

"I shall raze and destroy utterly your little courts of local justice and your regional council chambers, and I shall assemble, beneath the Acropolis, the capital city which already bears the name of Athens. And it is this name of Athens that for the races of the future—and this I promise to the gods who show me favor—will be a name of wonders. I dedicate my city to Pallas. Now go, all of you, and take my words as meant."

Then, suiting my example to my words, I stripped myself of all royal authority, stepped back into the ranks, and was not afraid to show myself to the public without escort, like a simple citizen; but I gave my attention unceasingly to public affairs, maintaining peace and watching over the good order of the state.

Pirithoüs, after hearing me address the men of wealth, said to me that he thought my speech sublime, but ridiculous. Because, he argued: "Equality is not natural among men; I would go farther and say that it is not desirable. It is a good thing that the superior men should rise above the vulgar mass to the full height of their eminence. Without emulation, rivalry, and jealousy, that mob will be forever a formless, stagnant, wallowing mass. There must be some leaven to make it rise; take care that it doesn't rise against yourself. Whether you like it or not, and though you may succeed in your wish and achieve an initial leveling by which each man starts on the same plane and with an equal chance, yet differences of talent will soon bring about differences of station; in other words, a downtrodden people and an aristocracy."

"Why, of course!" He'd set me off again. "I certainly expect that, and I hope it won't be long in coming. But in the first place I don't see why the people should be downtrodden if the new aristocracy, to which I shall give all the support in my power, is, as I would have it, an aristocracy not of wealth, but of intellect."

And then, in order to increase the power and importance of Athens, I made it known that there would be an impartial welcome for everyone, no matter whence he came, who might choose to come and settle there. And criers were sent throughout the neighboring countries to carry this message: "Peoples all, make haste to Athens!"

The news spread far and wide. And was it not through this that Œdipus, the fallen monarch, saddest and noblest of derelicts, made his way from Thebes to Attica, there to seek help and protection, there to die? Because of which I was able later to secure for Athens the blessing that the gods had conferred on his ashes. Of this I shall have more to say.

I promised to all newcomers indifferently the same rights as were enjoyed by those who were natives of Athens or who had settled there earlier; any necessary discrimination could await the proofs of experience. For good tools reveal their quality only after use, and I wished to judge nobody except according to his services.

So that if I was later obliged none the less to admit differences among the Athenians (and consequently to admit a hierarchy), I allowed this only in order to ensure that the state would in general function better. Thus it is that, thanks to me, the Athenians came to deserve, among all the other Greeks, the fine name of "people," which was commonly bestowed upon them and upon them only. Therein lies my greatness, far surpassing that of my earlier feats; a greatness to which neither Hercules attained, nor Jason, nor Bellerophon, nor Perseus.

Pirithoüs, alas! the companion of my youthful exuberances, later fell away from me. All those heroes whom I have named, and others too, like Meleager and Peleus, never prolonged their career beyond their first feats, or sometimes beyond a single one. For myself, I was not content with that. "There is a time for conquest," I used to say to Pirithoüs, "a time for cleansing the earth of its monsters, and then a time for husbandry and the harvesting of well-cherished land; a time to set men free from fear, and then a time in which to find employment for their liberty, in which to profit by the moment of ease and coax it into bloom." And that could not be achieved without discipline: I would not admit that, as with the Bœotians, man should make himself his own boundary, or aim merely at a mediocre happiness. I thought that man was not and would never be free, and that it would not be a good thing if he were. But I couldn't urge him forward without his consent; nor could I obtain that consent without leaving him (leaving the people, at any rate) the illusion of liberty. I wanted to educate him. I would not allow him to become in any degree content with his lot, or to resign himself to furrow his brow in perpetuity. Humanity (such was always the cast of my thought) can do more and deserves better. I remembered the teaching of Dædalus, who wanted to enrich mankind with all the spoils of the gods. My great strength was that I believed in progress.

So Pirithoüs and I parted company. In my youth he had been my constant companion, and often an invaluable aide. But I realized that constancy in friendship can prevent a man from advancing—can even pull him backward; after a certain point one can only go forward alone. As Pirithoüs was a man of sense, I still listened to what he said, but that was all. He himself was growing old, and whereas he had once been enterprise itself, he now allowed wisdom to degenerate into temperance. His advice was now always for restriction and restraint.

"Mankind isn't worth all this trouble," he would say. And I would reply: "Well, what else is there to think about, except mankind? Man has not yet said his last word."

"Don't get excited," he used to reply. "Haven't you done enough? Now that the prosperity of Athens is assured, it is time for you to rest on your laurels and savor the happiness of married life."

He urged me to pay more attention to Phædra and there for once he was right. For I must now tell of how the peace of my fireside was disturbed, and what a hideous price was expected by the gods in return for my successes and my self-conceit.

XII

I had unlimited confidence in Phædra. I had watched her grow more beautiful month by month. She was the very breath of virtue. I had withdrawn her at so early an age from the pernicious influence of her family that I never conceived she might carry within her a full dose of inherited poison. She obviously took after her mother, and when she later tried to excuse herself by saying that she was not responsible, or that she was foredoomed, I had to own that there was something in it. But that was not all: I also believe that she had too great a disdain for Aphrodite. The gods avenge themselves, and it was in vain that Phædra later strove to appease the goddess with an added abundance of offerings and supplications. For Phædra was pious, in spite of everything. In my wife's family everyone was pious. But it was no doubt regrettable that not everyone addressed his devotions to the same god. With Pasiphaë, it was Zeus; with Ariadne, Dionysus. For my own part, I reverenced above all Pallas Athene, and next Poseidon, to whom I was bound by a secret tie, and who, unfortunately for me, had similarly bound himself always to answer my prayers, so that I should never beseech him in vain. My son whose mother had been the Amazon, and whom I set above all the others, devoted himself to Artemis the huntress. He was as chaste as she—as chaste as I, at his age, had been dissolute. He used to run naked through moonlit woods and thickets; detested the court, formal parties, and, above all, the society of women, and was only happy when, with his bearhounds, he could go hunting for wild beasts and follow them to the topmost mountain or the last recesses of a valley. Often, too, he broke in wild horses, tamed them on the seashore, or rode them at a full gallop into the sea. How I loved him then! Proud, handsome, unruly; not to me, whom he held in veneration, nor to the laws: but he despised the conventions that prevent a man from asserting himself and wear out his merits in futility. He it was whom I wanted for my heir. I could have slept quietly, once the reins of state were in his unsullied hands; for I knew that he would be as inaccessible to threats as to flatteries.

That Phædra might fall in love with him I realized only too late. I should have foreseen it, for he was very like me. (I mean, like what I had been at his age.) But I was already growing old, and Phædra was still astonishingly young. She may still have loved me, but it was as a young girl loves her father. It is not good, as I have learned to my cost, that there should be such a difference of age between husband and wife. Yet what I could not forgive her was not her passion (natural enough, after all, though half-incestuous), but that, when she realized she could not satisfy her desire, she should have accused my Hippolytus and imputed to him the impure longings that were consuming her. I was a blind father, and a too trustful husband; I believed her. For once in my life I took a woman at her word! I called down the vengeance of the gods upon my innocent son. And my prayer was heard. Men do not realize, when they address themselves to the gods, that if their prayers are answered, it is most often for their misfortune. By a sudden, passionate, mindless impulse I had killed my son. And I am still inconsolable. That Phædra, awakened to her guilt, should at once afterward have wrought justice upon herself, well and good. But now that I cannot count even upon the friendship of Pirithoüs, I feel lonely; and I am old.

Œdipus, when I welcomed him at Colonus, had been driven from Thebes, his fatherland; without eyes, dishonored, and wretched as he was, he at least had his two daughters with him, and in their constant tenderness he found relief from his sufferings. He had failed in every part of what he had undertaken. I have succeeded. Even the enduring blessing that his ashes are to confer upon the country where they are laid—even this will rest, not upon his ungrateful Thebes, but upon Athens.

I am surprised that so little should have been said about this meeting of our destinies at Colonus, this moment at the crossroads when our two careers confronted each other. I take it to have been the summit and the crown of my glory. Till then I had forced all life to do obeisance to me, and had seen all my fellow men bow in their turn (excepting only Dædalus, but he was my senior by many years; besides, even Dædalus yielded first place to me in the end). In Œdipus alone did I recognize

a nobility equal to my own. His misfortunes could only enhance his grandeur in my eyes. No doubt I had triumphed everywhere and always; but on a level which, in comparison with
Œdipus, seemed to me merely human—inferior, I might say. He
had held his own with the Sphinx; had stood Man upright before the riddle of life, and dared to oppose him to the gods.
How then, and why, had he accepted defeat? By putting out his
eyes, had he not even contributed to it? There was something,
in this dreadful act of violence against himself, that I could not
contrive to understand. I told him of my bewilderment. But his
explanation, I must admit, hardly satisfied me—or else I did not
fully understand it.

"True," he said, "I yielded to an impulse of rage—one that
could only be directed against myself; against whom else could
I have turned? In face of the immeasurable horror of the accusations I had just discovered, I felt an overwhelming desire to
make a protest. And besides, what I wanted to destroy was not
so much my eyes themselves as the canvas they held before me;
the scenery before which I was struggling, the falsehood in
which I no longer believed; and this so as to break through to
reality.

"And yet, no! I was not really thinking of anything very
clearly; I acted rather by instinct. I put out my eyes to punish
them for having failed to see the evidence that had, as people
say, been staring me in the face. But, to speak the truth—ah,
how can I put it to you? . . . Nobody understood me when I
suddenly cried out: 'O darkness, my light!' And you also, you
don't understand it—I feel that distinctly. People heard it as a
cry of grief; it was a statement of fact. It meant that in my darkness I had found a source of supernatural light, illuminating the
world of the spirit. I meant: 'Darkness, thou art henceforth my
light.' And at the moment when the blue of the sky went black
before me, my inward firmament became bright with stars."

He was silent and for some moments remained deep in meditation. Then he went on:

"As a young man, I passed for one who could see the future.
I believed it myself, too. Was I not the first, the only man, to
solve the riddle of the Sphinx? Only since my eyes of flesh were
torn with my own hand from the world of appearances have I
begun, it seems to me, to see truly. Yes; at the moment when

the outer world was hidden forever from the eyes of my body, a kind of new eyesight opened out within myself upon the infinite perspectives of an inner world, which the world of appearances (the only one which had existed for me until that time) had led me to disdain. And this imperceptible world (inaccessible, I mean, to our senses) is, I now know, the only true one. All the rest is an illusion, a deception, moreover, that disturbs our contemplation of what is divine. Tiresias, the blind sage, once said to me: 'Who wishes to see God must first cease to see the world'; and I didn't understand him then: just as you, yourself, O Theseus, do not understand me now."

"I shall not attempt to deny," I replied, "the importance of this world beyond temporal things of which your blindness has made you aware; but what I still cannot understand is why you oppose it to the outer world in which we live and act."

"Because," said Œdipus, "for the first time, when with my inward eye I perceived what was formerly hidden from me, I suddenly became aware of this fact: that I had based my earthly sovereignty upon a crime, and that everything which followed from this was in consequence tainted; not merely all my personal decisions, but even those of the two sons to whom I had abandoned my crown—for I at once stepped down from the slippery eminence to which my crime had raised me. You must know already to what new villainies my sons have allowed themselves to stoop, and what an ignominious doom hangs over all that our sinful humanity may engender; of this my unhappy sons are no more than a signal example. For, as the fruits of an incestuous union, they are no doubt doubly branded; but I believe that an original stain of some sort afflicts the whole human race, in such a way that even the best bear its stripe, and are vowed to evil and perdition; from all this man can never break free without divine aid of some sort, for that alone can wash away his original sin and grant him amnesty."

He was silent again for a few moments, as if preparing to plunge still deeper, and then went on:

"You are astonished that I should have put out my eyes. I am astonished myself. But in this gesture, inconsidered and cruel as it was, there may yet be something else: an indefinable secret longing to follow my fortunes to their farthest limit, to give the final turn of the screw to my anguish, and to bring to a close the destiny of a hero. Perhaps I dimly foresaw the grandeur of suffering and its power to redeem; that is why the true hero is ashamed to turn away from it. I think that it is in fact the crowning proof of his greatness, and that he is never worthier than when he falls a victim; then does he exact the gratitude of heaven, and disarm the vengeance of the gods. Be that as it may, and however deplorable my mistakes may have been, the state of unearthly beatitude that I have been able to reach is an ample reward for all the ills that I have had to suffer—but for them, indeed, I should doubtless never have achieved it."

"Dear Œdipus," I said, when it was plain that he had finished speaking, "I can only congratulate you on the kind of super-human wisdom you profess. But my thoughts can never march with yours along that road. I remain a child of this world, and I believe that man, be he what he may, and with whatever blemishes you judge him to be stained, is in duty bound to play out his hand to the end. No doubt you have learned to make good use even of your misfortunes, and through them have drawn nearer to what you call the divine world. I can well be-lieve, too, that a sort of benediction now attaches to your per-son, and that it will presently be laid, as the oracles have said, upon the land in which you will take your everlasting rest."

I did not add that what mattered to me was that this blessing should be laid upon Attica, and I congratulated myself that the god had made Thebes abut upon my country.

If I compare my lot with that of Œdipus, I am content: I have fulfilled my destiny. Behind me I leave the city of Athens. It has been dearer to me even than my wife and my son. My city stands. After I am gone, my thoughts will live on there for-ever. Lonely and consenting, I draw near to death. I have en-joyed the good things of the earth, and I am happy to think that after me, and thanks to me, men will recognize themselves as being happier, better, and more free. I have worked always for the good of those who are to come. I have lived.

Translated by John Russell

This book was set on the Linotype in *Bodoni Book,* a printing-type so called after Giambattista Bodoni, a celebrated printer and type designer of Rome and Parma (1740–1813). Bodoni Book as produced by the Linotype company is not a copy of any one of Bodoni's fonts, but is a composite, modern version of the Bodoni manner. Bodoni's innovations in printing-type style were a greater degree of contrast in the "thick and thin" elements of the letters, and a sharper and more angular finish of details.

The book was composed, printed, and bound by Kingsport Press, Inc., Kingsport, Tenn.

The typography and binding were designed by Herbert Bayer.